# NO TURNING BACK

SHANE LAING

ISBN: 978-1-80517-676-3

For both my grandfathers. Both of you were amazing.
I will forever cherish the memories I had with you.

# Table Of Contents

# Prologue

Without accurate information, how can you be certain of someone's innocence before deciding to end their life?

Logan Winters pulled the trigger back slowly in a controlled manner, but not enough so the bullet would be propelled out of the barrel. With a deep breath, Logan gingerly released his finger from the weapon, his hand trembling slightly.

Like a warning from his body not to go ahead with his mission. He had his shot lined up, the target in clear view, and he could feel the tension in the air as he steadied his aim. Although he had every intention of killing his target, something held him back from doing so.

He had a sense of unease throughout the day, as if something was off. The soon to be victim was an older individual, estimated to be in their fifties, and was larger than expected. He had a head of thinning, medium-long hair that had been diligently combed over. His scalp glistened in the light, visible to all. On his plump face, a pencil thin goatee was carefully groomed.

"Target in sight." He said.

Logan lay still on the crane, two hundred and fifty feet in the air, the metal beneath him cold and unforgiving. He'd been at the spot for almost four hours, the air around him still and oppressive as he waited for the target to return home from his suspicious meeting. Despite the job's significance, further information was conspicuously absent. The assassin was usually briefed about everything to do with the person they were paid to eliminate.

Logan loathed the lack of knowledge he had about Anthony Draiden. Apart from being the owner of a well-known medicine manufacturer, who was cheating on his wife. He looked harmless, and there were no signs that he could be a potential threat.

Being an intelligent and sympathetic killer, he was prone to over-thinking; the feeling of anxiety was tangible as he questioned himself. His rules stated that the person of interest must pose some kind of threat to society and he always asked for evidence of this. Information about the future victim's activities, people, and connections.

Yet, there was a dearth of information. They gave him a name, the business he owns, the location he would be and an approximate time, which was off by four hours. Also, that he had a rendezvous with individuals deemed potentially dangerous, with connections to terrorism. Those people were only known by the shadows of their silhouettes, their nameless figures remaining a mystery.

Anthony, serenely sitting in his armchair in his penthouse suite, exuded a peaceful aura that belied his true character. He held a glass of whisky on the rocks in one hand, the cold condensation forming against his skin, and the television remote in the other. His friendly face and warm demeanour gave no indication that he posed any harm. He seemed to be lost in his thoughts, unaware of his surroundings, and a sense of sorrow washed over him.

Despite being married and having two children, his face was void of any joy. His wife and kids were nowhere to be seen, so Logan assumed they lived in the house that he had purchased for them. Until she stumbled upon evidence of his recent infidelity. The penthouse had an austere feeling, only containing the bare necessities for when work required nearby accommodation.

Logan watched with pity as the miserable man chugged his drink, then stumbled out of his chair to get a refill. Instead of refilling the glass, he grabbed the bottle and chugged it down faster than Logan could have imagined.

A voice came through Logan's ear-piece. The man's voice came through the crackling, with a slightly tinny sound.

"So you still mean for this to be your final operation?" Evan asked.

"Doubt they will allow it, but yeah, that's the intention."

Logan answered with conviction.

"You really think they won't let you retire from the job, don't you?"

No contemplation was necessary. He expected them to be less than pleased at the prospect of one of their most highly rated operatives leaving. He was well-informed of the missions they had embarked on. And had a wealth of knowledge regarding the staff and the confidential information the organisation kept from the public. Logan had been working with them for so long that he had witnessed the desolation of those wanting to leave. The company had a motto behind their nice facade, 'Leave no loose ends'. Once Logan revealed his intention to go, he'd be a dangling thread.

"You are very aware of the fact that they don't like loose ends. You don't think that's what I become the second I want out of this job?" He uttered intensely.

Time seemed to stand still in the pause that stretched on endlessly. Evan mulled over his reply, weighing his words carefully. His colleague's argument made sense—the company wouldn't want to risk losing an asset who had insider knowledge of their operations.

"There is a possibility that they won't be thrilled about your decision. But you signed an non disclosure agreement anyway and I know you wouldn't reveal any details to anyone."

Peering through the scope of his silenced Barret M82, imported from the United States, he focused his gaze on the target. The semi-automatic, recoil operated rifle, while not typically favoured for personnel, was always Logan's go-to for these type of missions. The reassuring weight of it in his hands made him feel secure.

When it came to his tasks, he found himself more comfortable using his close, quarter combat abilities than a rifle or any other gun. Mainly so he could ensure that the death looked like an accident, such as one job. Where he made it appear as those his victim had drank too much and slipped in the bathroom and ended up impaled on a metal standing toilet roll holder. But this assignment, it was requested that he remain at a distance and use his chosen long-range weapon to take out the mark.

"Whatever the case. No matter what they say, I'm out."

Placing his finger back against the trigger, he prepared his shot once again. He felt a strange mix of curiosity and urgency, as he hesitated to find out more about this man he was about to erase from existence. Logan watched with anticipation as the man pushed himself up from the chair, the fabric of his clothing rustling. The trigger was pulled. Within a second, the bullet pierced the window and hit the left side of the sofa chair that Anthony was sitting on.

A warning shot.

A quick browse through the government database, mixed with internet searches. He tapped his finger on the screen, and the penthouse suite's phone number filled the display. With a heavy sigh, he pressed dial, feeling a sense of relief wash over him. The persistent ringing of the phone echoed through the room, yet the man remained motionless in his seat. He was so petrified that he couldn't move an inch.

Well aware that someone just took a shot at him; he knew

he was not fast enough to rush to any kind of cover. He was fifteen feet away from the nearest cover, the kitchen island. The phone was only two. The ringing ceased abruptly, leaving a silence in its wake.

So, Logan tried again. Anthony's gaze was glued to the phone, his eyes wide and unblinking. With unsteady steps, he rose from his seat and moved towards the ringing device, feeling a chill in the air.

"He…hello." His voice barely coming out.

The target's frightened expression clarified that he posed no danger. The man had either incriminating evidence against someone, or had unknowingly ruffled the feathers of an adversary.

"Anthony, I have given you a warning shot. They sent here me to eliminate you, but something tells me that you do not deserve to die. So, I'm giving you a second chance. I know you have a lot of money, so use that to disappear. Get out of the country, somewhere they wouldn't look for you. Don't make me regret my decision, or I will find you and I will finish the job they tasked me with. Understood?"

"Y…yes. Understood. Thank you."

Logan ended the call abruptly, the dial tone ringing in his ears. He felt the weight of the decision on his shoulders as he considered whether he'd made the right choice. If the man was smart, he would disappear and never be heard from again.

His target was still on the list, and the choice he made would not make his bosses happy. Anthony's gaze radiated innocence, and Logan felt a deep conviction that he could never take an innocent life.

“Target absconded before I could take the shot.” He said over the radio.

He received no response.

# 1

Death crept towards her, and she could feel its icy presence inching closer. Tears streamed relentlessly from her eyes, and there was nothing he could do to save her.

"Help me." She cried.

Those words cut through the silence of the room, rousing Logan from his brief sleep. Every night, Lilly called out for help, her voice trembling with fear. He gasped for air, struggling with terror as haunting memories filled his mind.

He felt the weight of his memories like an anvil on his chest, wishing he could be released from the burden of remembering everything. While having a photographic memory was advantageous in many ways, it also had its downsides, such as the burden of never being able to forget even the most painful memories.

The only thing that could be heard in the house was the low, ambient hum of his fridge.

His sheets were damp with sweat as he lay in bed, rarely sleeping more than four hours at a time. Eight hours of uninterrupted sleep was something he only dreamed of getting again.

As he got up from his bed, he felt his muscles release with a satisfying stretch and a loud yawn. The sun was slowly beginning to peek over the horizon, signalling the start of a new day. As the first rays of sunlight peeked into the room, his mind was consumed with his first thought of the day.

Logan wouldn’t consider his morning begun until he had a full mug of steaming black coffee, the warmth of the mug in his hands.

He was determined to make sure his stomach wouldn't grumble further by eating a hearty breakfast. He struggled to get his white t-shirt over his head, as it was a very tight fit. His stomach was slowly growing, although he wasn’t obese by any means. Though he was still perceived as being physically fit, he had lost some of the muscle definition and energy that he used to possess.

His hair was medium in length, thick and growing fast. Often brushed back, to make him look a tad more presentable. A scruffier beard was what brought his look down, he would comb through it, but not often enough.

It all needed a trim, but in his mind he saw no need to look neat and tidy. He used to be clean shaven, with short brushed to the side hair. His new look would make even those who sought him out, to do a double take.

He slid his trousers up his legs, the smooth fabric making a slight shushing sound as he looked at his reflection in the mirror next to his bed.

*You've let yourself go.*

The voice in his head began his verbal abuse earlier than usual.

"Really? I do my best to remain healthy." His voice, deep and melodic, had a soothing quality that put others at ease. The one in his head was similar, but more aggressive and instead put Logan on edge constantly and would have the same effect on other people, if it had the chance.

*You go for a thirty minute run now and then. If they found us now, your cardio is so bad that you'd be huffing and puffing your way through your enemies.*

Nine years of being alone had made an impact on his mental well-being, and he was frequently heard muttering to himself. His own thoughts and feelings were familiar to him, and he grew accustomed to the feeling of loneliness. He could often be seen with a distracted expression, as if having a silent conversation with someone in their head. Which in his case, he often was. Only it wasn't silent by any means.

Without anyone to hear him, sometimes it helped to just let out a few rants about his day, to feel better. Some considered it normal to have an inner voice, they just didn't tell people about it. Others called it insanity. Logan did not see enough people for them to see him communicating with himself. Sometimes on his ventures in land, people would catch him talking to himself. They would never say anything, just give a confused and concerned look before continuing with their day.

He lived on a small island off the coast of Penzance, Cornwall. He used his boat a couple times a month to journey to land, heading to the shops for food and essentials.

Descending the stairs, his footsteps echoed through the kitchen as he clicked the kettle to boil. He left the kettle full every night, so that the next morning he could quickly boil it and be greeted with the sound of the bubbling water. Ready to make his steaming hot coffee. The sun shone brightly through the dozen windows of the house, warming the interior with its golden glow.

After stepping into his dimly lit office, Logan slid into his comfortable leather chair and clicked open his sleek silver laptop. The soft hum of the computer filled the silent room as he delicately tapped his fingers on the keyboard, entering the pass-code. The faint scent of freshly brewed coffee lingered in the air. Upon completion, it produced an image of a woman, young girl and boy. Lilly, Leah and Ethan, his wife, daughter and son. His left eye brimmed with a tear at the thought of them, but the recollection of their happy times brought a grin to his lips.

The kettle switch pinged up to signal the water had reached the required temperature, and the room was filled with the sound of its whistling before it eventually died out. Above the kettle, a variety of mugs could be found, each with its own unique shape and weight. It was a mystery why one man needed such a large stockpile.

*All those mugs, yet you are the only fucker here to use them. Seems a tad excessive Logy.*

He ran his fingers across the colours, feeling the slight differences in shade as they shifted in perfect order. When things weren't in his set order, it created a stress filled itch inside him, that he had to scratch. Yet, Logan lived alone, so if that was to happen. He'd be at fault. Nobody else.

He added two spoonful's of the fragrant coffee into the cup, followed by a third for a stronger flavour. Today, he felt an intense desire for caffeine, the taste of it lingering on his tongue. His instinct told him that if he stayed more alert, he'd have an advantage for the day. He poured the boiling water into his magenta coloured mug, and the steam rose to warm his face. Most people would have flinched and moved backwards, not him. He welcomed the heat, feeling the intense warmth on his skin.

For some people, the sight of the sunrise on a dreary morning was nothing special. As he gazed out of his kitchen window, he felt peaceful watching the sun ascend into the sky. Over the course of a few minutes, he felt an unfamiliar sense of serenity.

The images of his past haunted him once again. He attempted to close his mind off from the memories of the past, yet they would still resurface. Until he could confront the darkness of his past, it would linger like a shadow, constantly plaguing him.

He stepped out onto his porch and breathed in the crisp morning air. Refreshing. Cornwall was a beautiful place, with its vibrant colours and calming atmosphere, and he knew it was the perfect place to hide. The serenity of the place made it the last area they would consider searching for someone.

His cottage was perched on a rocky outcrop on a small island off the Cornish county, and he could hear the crashing of waves against the shore. He had to re-fuel the generator every few days, the smell of gasoline wafting through the air, depending on how much electricity his appliances and electrical equipment had used. He stocked up on enough fuel to last him for at least a month at a time.

He knew it was best to stay close, instead of taking the chance to venture further inland, where he could be noticed by a possible foe. He was certain they wouldn't bother looking for him here, of all places, despite his doubts. In a couple of days, he'd have to go and stock up on food, fuel, and other necessities. He usually lingered on the island, but he was determined to feel the wind on his face and escape for a few hours.

The sky was a bright blue, signalling that it was going to be a beautiful day. He felt the slight chill of the wind as the early morning sun illuminated the glistening water and lush grass. He smiled as he looked into his mug, savouring the aroma of his coffee. As he stirred the liquid, it reminded him of days full of bliss and contentment.

The warmth of her smile filled the room as she entered the home they were eager to buy. Her round tummy was a reminder that the baby boy she was expecting was soon to arrive.

"It's perfect." She said.

Logan inspected the house, and the contentment in his voice suggested he thought it was ideal. As they stepped inside, they felt a sense of warmth and comfort, knowing it was exactly what they wanted for their family.

"It is indeed, and it will be ours."

When she opened the conservatory door, she was amazed by the intricate details of the design before her. There was enough space in the office for a desk, and he could also fit in his diverse collection of literature, both classic and modern. More than enough room to fit a comfy sofa and a big screen television.

The walls were built of bricks with a layer of concrete on the outer section, providing a cosy insulation from the winter chill. Sunlight streamed in through the two windows in the room, creating a cosy atmosphere. The side of the building had a long window that let in the sun's warmth. He felt a creative energy in the space and knew it would be a great place to write his novels.

"Well, hopefully it will be. They could turn down our offer." She said in a concerned manner.

Logan's hearty laughter bubbled up from his belly.

"They won't turn it down. Trust me. It's an offer no one would refuse."

He heard the sound of the young girl's laughter as she rushed up to him; her face aglow with a bright smile.

"Daddy, can we go play toys?"

Leah was a bubbly six-year-old who was always humming a tune. In the sun, her long brunette hair lit up with a brilliant shine. His heart would always beat faster at the sight of her beaming smile. She was a kid who was captivated by the simplest of things. She'd read books for hours. After finishing one book, she felt a rush of excitement as she began another.

When he looked down at her, his eyes sparkled with joy.

Ethan was eleven and a very curious child, he wanted to know every detail about literally every little thing. His inquisitive nature would serve him well as he grew older. Like his father, he had a place for things and could not handle people touching or moving them, he'd had dozens of out bursts because Leah had moved his books or toys. But he was a loving brother, often helping his sister however he could. He loved to build things and taught her how to build Lego and blocks.

Logan would often watch as the kids built their own little towns and would play tiny figures in. Informing him that they have built a civilisation. He envisioned his son becoming a phenomenal structural engineer in the future. But always said that whatever his children wanted to do, he would do his best to support it.

The memories began to fade, like a distant echo. He knew that one day he would hear their laughter again.

Looking out at the ocean, the salty breeze blowing against his face. He could see the distant outline of a large ship, but he couldn't determine if it was a cruise ship or a cargo ship. He glanced at the clock and realised it was time to go back and make another cup of coffee, so he could make progress on writing his new book.

"Such lovely weather." He remarked to himself.

*I prefer the rain.*

# 2

As he turned the key, the boat's engine sprang to life, its powerful vibrations resonating throughout the vessel. He completed his ensemble with a pair of dark blue jeans, a simple white t-shirt, a grey hoodie, and a cap with the word "captain" embroidered on it. He felt perfectly attired for a leisurely stroll through the town. He couldn't wait to get to Seaview Fish and Chip Shop, where he knew he could indulge in a mouthwatering plate of cod and chips.

As he sailed away from the island he called home, the wind whipped against his face, feeling like a barrage of tiny needles. On his way to Penzance harbour, he anticipated a travel time of approximately twenty-five to forty minutes, depending on the pace he set. In the afternoon, the sun's rays created a dazzling display of light on the ocean. The boat's hull violently collided with every wave, jolting Logan's grip on the steering wheel. Despite his initial doubts, he grew to love his boat and cherished every moment spent on it. The salty smell of the sea mixed with the earthy scent of the fishermen's bait as they set off in their boats. Passing Logan on their way out, some gave a wave, others did not.

While securing the boat at the harbour, he could smell the aroma of freshly brewed coffee from nearby cafes, a sign that the day was already in full swing. He observed the surroundings, but there was no one who caught his attention as suspicious or out of place. A wave of relief washed over him as he realised that everything was in order. He was famished, his stomach growling loudly, and hoped to avoid any potential trouble. Wherever he went, trouble seemed to follow closely behind, like a shadow. He was open to encountering challenges, as long as they weren't the exact kind he had been avoiding for years. His main goal was to remain inconspicuous, avoiding drawing any attention towards himself.

"Good afternoon." A voice said.

Turning to see on a nearby bench, a couple of elderly people were savouring their lunch, exchanging contented smiles. A pasty in each of their hands. The scent emanating from it was simply mouthwatering. They gave a wave.

"Good afternoon to you." Logan replied.

*You don't have to be so bloody friendly you know.*

Everywhere he went, he couldn't escape the feeling of being under constant surveillance. Even when people weren't looking in his direction, he could sense the piercing gaze of an unseen presence. His training emphasised the importance of being vigilant, always aware of his surroundings for any possible threats. Whenever he was out in public, that part of him was always on alert, making it difficult for him to trust people. No matter what, he was on edge, making it nearly impossible to venture off the island and find relaxation. A cloud of anxiety hung over him, as if he was always bracing himself for the worst. It was probably the catalyst for the confrontation he experienced several months ago. Logan's boat became the target of a group of inebriated young men who thought it would be wise to urinate on it and spray paint different sections.

He had spent the day in town, immersing himself in the vibrant atmosphere and diverse cultures. As the evening descended, he returned to his boat only to discover a group of vandals defacing it, which filled him with immense anger. Though it would have been effortless to eliminate them, he recognised their state of inebriation and idiocy, which tempered his desire for vengeance. He approached them, making sure to maintain a respectful distance, choosing the polite approach.

"Excuse me, can you all please step away from the boat?" He asked.

*Fucking little bastards. Break their arms, they won't be spray painting anything then.*

A chorus of disrespectful snickering and laughter broke out. One of them stepped forward, his biceps bulging and his imposing stature making it clear that he was the muscle of the group. Sporting a wide, self-satisfied grin, it was clear that they had no respect for anyone else's possessions.

"What are you gonna do if we don't? You're outnumbered."

The man's intoxication had him feeling sure of himself in a fight, not accounting for the fact that alcohol would impair his reactions. Not only did they have no idea who the man ahead of them was, but they were also completely in the dark about his background. He questioned whether they had the same level of combat prowess and experience as him. Given the circumstances, these men were at a severe disadvantage. He knew he'd have to control himself, or there would be a missing person report in the morning for five men who inexplicably vanished.

"Your confidence betrays you." Logan exclaimed.

*Nah, that's just the alcohol effect.*

He remembered back when Cornwall was filled with peaceful people, a trait that still held true for the most part. However, as younger people started to settle down in this picturesque location in the United Kingdom, there was a noticeable increase in troublemakers who seemed out of place. Laughter erupted from the drunk group as they giggled and whispered to one another. It was apparent that they didn't take the man's request to leave seriously, judging by their nonchalant demeanour.

"Oh really. Well, I think that you need to walk away before you get hurt, old man."

Logan shook his head in disappointment, offended by being referred to as old. He made an effort to be friendly, but it didn't have the intended effect. Faced with unexpected circumstances, it was time to switch to Plan B. As he offered them the chance, they should have recognised the danger and walked away.

"Old." He uttered. "You should have walked away when you had the chance to."

*They fucked up big time. You hate that word. Not that you are young. Maybe you should accept that you aren't exactly a spring chicken.*

The need to maintain secrecy clashed with his aversion to being treated disrespectfully. Their level of intoxication was such that his face and the boat would slip from their memory.

"I'm gonna fuck you up!" the big one yelled.

*Wow, drinking really does make people feel brave.*

With a burst of speed, the muscular one charged at him, his fist swinging. A powerful right hook came and missed its mark. Time seemed to crawl for him, giving him a split-second advantage as he saw the punch coming before it was launched. With a swift motion, he wrapped his arm around his attackers, feeling their surprise and resistance. He used his hand to push from the man's elbow, exerting pressure in an outward motion. With a sickening crack, the man's arm was shattered. In the midst of his screams, Logan delivered a forceful right hook, putting his entire weight behind it, and the impact against the man's cheekbone echoed through the air as it fractured. The impact of the hit was so strong that it immediately rendered the man unconscious.

*He is gonna feel that in the morning.*

Most of the remaining intoxicated individuals charged at him, their slurred shouts filling the air. With a swift kick to one of their legs, he caused them to topple over and collide with the floor. The final one, despite being intoxicated, seemed to anticipate the impending danger. His face contorted with fear as he watched the punch hurtling towards him. Lights out.

A passerby's sudden sneeze snapped him out of his memory. The sneeze startled everyone nearby, its volume comparable to that of an air horn. The noise was almost deafening to Logan. The taste of fish and chips lingered on his tongue, filling his thoughts with anticipation of their mouthwatering flavour. The promise of a delicious meal beckoned, just a minute or two away. Penzance bustled with activity, as people hurriedly manoeuvred past one another. Logan skilfully weaved through the crowds, drawn by the enticing aroma of freshly baked goods. That's when he saw it, warren's bakery. In the shop, a small queue had formed, consisting of six people patiently waiting. The wait wouldn't be too long. The moment he walked in, the delicious scent of pasties, cakes, steak pies, and various other foods overwhelmed his senses, tempting him like a hungry dog.

He didn't have to wait long before he was served, and he wasted no time in ordering two beef pasties. Lunch sorted. If he stayed in Penzance long enough, he could look forward to having fish and chips for dinner later. It didn't take the server long to bag up the delicious food, turning to see that Logan was no longer paying attention. His gaze became fixed on the window, his eyes filled with a mix of fear and disbelief, as if he had encountered a ghost.

"Sir, are you okay?"

As Logan glanced around, he thought he'd noticed someone walking past, their figure disappearing into the shadows. Doubt filled his mind as he questioned whether he was hallucinating. The person couldn't have walked past, though. Dead people can't walk. His eyes deceived him. Reversing, he retrieved his meal.

"Yeah, fine. Sorry. Thank you."

His survival for the past nine years can be attributed to paranoia, with his mind always perceiving everyone as a potential threat until proven otherwise. After leaving the shop, he sought out an empty bench to rest on. One hundred and twenty yards away, he caught sight of one up the hill. While getting closer, he remained observant of everyone nearby. Sitting down, he pulled out one of his pasties, biting into it, steam released from the inside. The taste was exquisite, a perfect blend of flavours dancing on his palate.

"Now that is a good pasty." He said.

"I've had better." His other personality broke through.

*Oh god. Not now.*

"Fuck off." He muttered.

An elderly man stopped beside him, confused.

"Excuse me?" The old man said.

"Oh god. Sorry, I wasn't swearing at you," Logan replied.

The older man looked behind him and around, puzzled by the absence of any potential verbal assailants in close proximity.

"Erm. So, who was you swearing at them?"

*If only you knew.*

Logan preferred not to delve into the specifics of his

madness. He would find himself locked away in a psychiatric hospital. Now, he grappled with the challenge of articulating that he was engaged in self-dialogue, without sounding utterly mad. The majority of his answers suggested the same notion. Then, his mind raced and he quickly formulated the right response.

"I served for years. And if I'm honest, I still get haunted by the things that happened."

The elderly man's wrinkled face broke into a knowing expression of acknowledgement. His face bore the unmistakable signs of a veteran haunted by the ghosts of his fallen comrades. Logan and Lincoln's shared commitment to serving for several years shaped their perspectives and values. The weight of their lost friends in war never left them, as they carried the memories of their fallen friends and the details of how they perished.

"It fades over time. But never truly leaves you. I served in the army during World War two. Saw some horrible things. I may not remember it all, but I remember a lot of the bad parts."

It felt surreal to engage in conversation with someone who had firsthand experience in that brutal war. Logan stood up, extending his hand for a handshake.

"Although the horrible things stay with you, just remember that it's because of what people like you sacrificed, that we are still here today. You are a hero and I'd love to buy you a coffee or tea. The names Lance."

A smile of genuine surprise and gratitude appeared on the older man's face, as if he hadn't experienced such respect in a very long time. Based on today's youth, it appeared that only a minority of them had a tendency to honour and respect their elders.

"Tea would be lovely. It's nice to meet you, Logan. My names Alexander. Most people call me Alec."

Their hands met, Alec's hand trembling in the grip. Logan was amazed to see someone in their nineties still walking with such agility. He hoped that he would still possess the same vitality and vigour at that age, but he harboured doubts about ever reaching such a milestone. Typically, he'd avoid engaging in conversations, opting to swiftly collect supplies and head back home. Being outside for an extended period heightened the possibility of being noticed by the wrong individuals. Something he hoped to avoid. However, on this particular day, he forcefully dismissed the thought from his mind. With a desire to talk to Alex and delve into his army stories.

"My grandfather was called Alexander."

As they walked to the cafe, he extended his hand to offer support to the older man. Alex had a walking stick, but appreciated the assistance. They wandered to the cafe a few minutes up the road, going over memories of their times in the war.

# 3

Looking out at the ocean from her bedroom window was the perfect way to start the morning, Madison Jones didn't have that, she got to look at the loft extension of her neighbours house. A horribly grumpy man, who didn't need to add on to his home. He had no children, his bungalow was big enough. He also couldn't walk very well, often seen using a wheelchair, walking stick or crutches. He did it to spite her because she could see the beautiful blue sea before from her window and didn't realise that in conversation, she bragged about it. Or that's how he saw it. He didn't have such a luxury anymore. Many years ago in the seventies, he could see it perfectly. Then more homes were built and his view was blocked. So he turned bitter about it and decided Abi didn't deserve the view either. Money wasn't an issue for him, he was a very wealthy man. Retired banker, who also inherited millions from family.

Most people would kick off about someone doing such a thing. Not Madison, she was sweet and caring. Believing that Jedidiah only needed someone to talk to, possibly a new loving female companion. Many times she has thought about making him a dating profile, but she figured he'd somehow take offence to her helping him find love again. His wife passed away fifteen years ago and he has clearly struggled to move on. Which as she knows very well, it is hard to move on, but sometimes after taking that first step, it gradually gets easier. Her husband didn't die, she left him, taking her daughter Bethany to Cornwall to live. Even after everything he done, she struggled to move on from him. Always wondering what if.

She'd cheer the elderly man up somehow. Eventually. It was almost half past seven and Bethany wasn't even awake for school, she was the typical teenager, never wanted to get up for school. Then usually once she was up, she complained about having to actually go. Approaching her daughters bedroom, she tapped on the door to see if Beth would answer. Nothing. Definitely still snoozing. Most likely turned off her alarm and passed back out. That was typically what she done.

When she opened the door, the unexpected sight of an empty bed where Bethany should have been astonished her. Terror filled her, she was not the type of person who rose before the sun. Had she snuck out in the night? Where would she have gone? Her mind was abuzz with numerous questions. Then she heard the chain flush in the bathroom. Every part of her had been ready to go out searching for her daughter, she'd seen too many true crime documentaries and they'd made her an extremely paranoid mother. There are thousands of monsters out there in the world and for all she knew, one lived nearby. As seen on the television, you can't always tell with the predators. It's why she trained in kick boxing and got Beth into it too. This way, they are much more capable of protecting themselves if they are ever attacked.

Her daughter would have fought off an attacker or screamed to signal her mum to help. Therefore, the only plausible explanation was that she left stealthily during the night. It dawned on her that her daughter had been pretty secretive recently, a boy had to be the answer. The thing that plagued her, was the fact that Bethany snuck out, rather than ask her own mother, who does her best to be understandable and supportive.

Pulling her phone from her pyjama shorts pocket, she scrolled to her daughters name in the contacts list and pressed to ring. It rang and continued to do so for a while, no answer. Then the sound of the front door opening alerted her. Nearly stumbling, she rapidly descended the stairs. She caught Beth walking through the door, looking shocked at her mum stood there, angered.

"Urmm…"

"Yeah, that's right urmm. Where have you been?" Madison asked.

Beth reached into her over the shoulder bag, pulling out several pieces of paper, each one filled with words.

"I had left my homework at Michael's. So got up earlier and went over to grab it, I hoped I could get it and get back before you got up. Sorry if I scared you."

It sounded like a believable story, but she knew her daughter better than anyone. Maybe she had left her homework, maybe it was actually that he had done it for her. Or there was a third option.

"You forgot your homework? I've seen your attempt at getting up early. You don't. When was you last at Michael's to leave it there? As you hadn't told me that you had been there."

Bethany stood in silence for moments, not thinking through what she'd say if she got caught. She wasn't known for planning ahead.

"Last week. Wednesday… I think."

"You think? You'd have a pretty good idea! I mean, I know you like this boy. You're sixteen and preferably I'd rather you focused on school."

Madison was a pretty strict parent, but tried not to be over the top. She wanted her daughter to have her freedom, but to a limit. Not believing it to be a bad thing to want your child to succeed in school and everything after, get a good career.

"Mum, he is a friend!! Trust me! He will never be anything more than a friend. I can promise you that. You are acting like I never do my homework. I always do, I do my best to get the best grades and you still aren't happy."

Madison didn't intend to give off the impression she did, and was unaware of the effect it had on her daughter. It was the last thing she wanted.

"I'm sorry, I don't mean to be so hard on you. It's just that I want you to be able to reach your full potential. I am very happy with how well you do and apologise that I don't say that enough. I will try to pull back a bit. As I know what you are capable of, so I believe that you will achieve what you aim for. I'm sorry baby girl."

Reaching out, they both embraced one another in a hug. A clearly needed one. It dawned on her that Beth would need some breakfast, it wouldn't be long and she'd be due at school.

"Want me to make you some pancakes for breakfast?" She asked.

"Yes please! I love your pancakes. Haven't had them in a while."

Both of them headed for the kitchen, which was glistening white, the cupboard were so bright, it was blinding entering. It had nice marble work tops. Madison had longed to be able to add in an island in the middle of the kitchen, as the room was huge. But cost held her back. She began pulling out eggs and butter from the fridge, self-rising flour from the cupboard and brought the sugar container closer to the other ingredients. Grabbing a frying pan from the draw containing several different sized pans. She began the pancake making process.

"So, did you actually get up early to go and get your homework? Or had you snuck out last night to go and get it and then fell asleep there?" She knew the answer, but it was always funnier to hear it.

"Well… I snuck out last night, you had passed out. So, I

thought I'd run there, grab it and get home, then get some sleep. But I got there, he handed me it and then we was chatting about drama at school and next thing I know, I was waking up on his floor. He'd put a blanket over me. He said he'd messaged you to say that I'd fallen asleep there."

Madison went to react and point out that he'd not left her a message. But she hadn't properly checked her phone that morning, she pulled it out and checked the messages and her daughter was correct. Michael had left a text to say that Bethany had come over to grab her homework and then after chatting for a while. She'd fell asleep and he was too afraid to wake a sleeping woman. Reading that made Madison laugh. Never wake a girl, unless it was an emergency. Especially Beth.

"Okay, I apologise. He did message. I just hadn't seen it. You could have gone over earlier to get your homework, at least I would have known."

Beth looked at her mother, knowing that even taking that approach would have caused an argument.

"I feel like even if I had done that. You would have reacted badly. I promise I won't just sneak out again. I will let you know. Now can we have pancakes?"

Both smile at one another, typically an event like this would have turned into a huge row. Beth knew that her mum had been through a lot over the last few years, she didn't know everything. But it was evident that it took a toll on her. Her over protectiveness was irritating, but not without reason. Madison pulled out the frying pan from the cupboard, along with a jug to mix all the ingredients together.

Only to venture to another cupboard and realise that there was no flour at all. Looked like no pancakes.

"I don't think we can have pancakes this morning. There's no flour. I thought I still had some. But apparently not. Want some cereal?"

Disappointment plagued Beth's face, she didn't attempt to cover it. The pancakes would have made that morning so much better, but it wasn't to be. She wasn't a big breakfast person, but that was always the one thing that would get her excited for the morning.

"It's okay."

Madison looked through the rest of the cupboards frantically searching for some flour. Or anything that would lift her daughter's mood back up.

"There's got to be some somewhere. I'm sure of it."

Beth wandered off into the living room, turning the news on. Reports of a member of parliament committing suicide. His wife found him hanging from the ceiling beam. Beth watched and wondered how much had driven the man to do something like that. Madison wandered in, after hearing what had happened.

"That's sad. He must have been under a lot of pressure to do such a thing. There's been quite a few suicides of government officials over the last few years. Then again, they are under so much pressure to fix the country. Has to be hard. Hopefully they can get others help, to stop this happening again. Poor man and his family." Madison said.

"Well, most of them are the reason the country is broken. Like covid coming along didn't help. But they had messed up this country before hand." Beth moaned. Politics wasn't something she followed, but she knew enough to know that a change was needed.

"That's true. It's still sad though, that all of the stress is causing some of them to take their own lives. I for one know that I couldn't ever comprehend trying to run a country. Anyway, we need to get ready to leave. You've got school and I've got to get to work."

The thought of having to go to the place she called work was exhausting. When she first started, she had the aim of it being temporary until she found a better paid job and one that suited her. But that had proved difficult, her past often causing issues with companies. So it seemed as though she was stuck where she was. In a little shop in st ives, the customers were mainly lovely. But her manager was horrible, always claiming the staff weren't doing enough and that some were stealing stock. Although she knew that it was him who was taking stuff. She went above and beyond for her customers, but never got any recognition for any of it. Apart from the people she serves. They often told her that she was the reason they came into the shop.

"Okay, although I don't think either of us want to go to where we are supposed to be." Beth laughed.

Both of them had a giggle together, neither was ready for the day ahead. But had to embrace it.

"What if, once I finish. I grab us a Chinese on the way home?"

Beth nodded in excitement.

"Yeah! You sure you can afford it?" She asked. Knowing

that they didn't have much money.

"Yeah. I got extra money from the over time I done last month. So, there's enough for takeaway."

Madison gave a big smile, seeing how happy the thought of getting Chinese made her daughter. It was rare that they got a takeaway. So, it was more exciting when they actually did.

"Come on then. We have ten minutes to get ready and leave."

# 4

Logan walked out of the cafe and felt the warm rays of the sun on his face. He turned and waved goodbye to Alexander, his hand lingering in the air for a moment. Alec remained in the cafe, now sat with another older gentleman, one of his friends. Who had made an appearance at the perfect time. With a sense of urgency, Logan had wanted to complete his task of gathering supplies and head home. However, he didn't want to be impolite and make an abrupt exit. Alec's friend showing up at that precise moment provided a convenient excuse to leave without causing offence.

*I thought you guys would never shut up.*

It felt as if a thousand pairs of eyes were boring into his skin, thoroughly examining every inch of him. The creeping sensation of paranoia took hold of him once more. He scanned the bustling crowds of people, but no one caught his attention. Nevertheless, he was fully cognisant of the fact that a hunter, in pursuit of its prey, would adopt a camouflage technique to blend in with its surroundings. Having dedicated countless years to his craft, he had become a master, confident in his ability to discern anyone who posed a threat. Even if they were attempting to blend in perfectly. Every fibre of his being had grown weary of concealment, as he meticulously devised a plan to deliver his own form of retribution upon those accountable for the tragic loss of his wife, son, and daughter. In the span of nine years, he had primarily retreated from the world and found solace on his island.

His books were filled with intricate clues and encrypted messages, holding vital information to dismantle his adversaries. His coded messages had proven to be an unsolvable mystery thus far. The securely safeguarded phone, which had the ability to bounce signals globally, had not received any incoming communication. If anyone managed to crack his messages, they would discover the phone number, alerting him that his intricate code had been successfully deciphered.

The coded messages within the books were a secret language, decipherable only by those who shared his unique mindset. The truth would not remain hidden for long; someone would uncover it. He knew it would just take time, like the gradual fading of colours at sunset. He pondered the possibility that people had cracked the code but hesitated to reach out due to the sensitive information concealed within the books. The act of helping could potentially jeopardise the safety and well-being of the individual and their loved ones.

In Penzance, he strolled through the narrow streets, taking in the aroma of freshly brewed coffee and pastries wafting from the local bakeries. As he walked, the bag on his shoulder weighed him down with its contents of packs of batteries, paracetamol, and important belongings. Another bag containing milk and orange squash. A shop caught his eye as it sat perched atop the hill, its presence unfamiliar to him. Pondering, he questioned whether the structure was freshly built or if they had simply revamped the outside to make it stand out. He approached the building and noticed the colourful display of clothes in the window. He usually purchased simple attire from places like Tesco, specifically from their F&F section. The clothes in this shop looked good from the window, lacking any words that would only make sense to someone obsessed with social media.

As he entered, it wasn't the scent of new clothing that overwhelmed him, but rather the unmistakable aroma of freshly brewed coffee. A drink sat untouched on the staff side of the counter, and he couldn't spot a single person inside the store. Emerging from the back of the shop, she seemed to materialise before his eyes, leaving him uncertain of what he was seeing. A flicker of hope crossed his mind as he thought he could see Lilly's familiar figure approaching. He was out of luck.

However, her beauty was unlike any other; she exuded a radiance that surpassed the conventional standards of an underwear model. Her body was that of a normal every day woman, with curves that accentuated her figure in all the right places. His gaze lingered for a moment before he snapped out of it, realising he had been staring. Being careful not to come across as creepy. Since Lilly's death, he found it impossible to see another woman in the same light, always feeling like they fell short in comparison to her. But this lady was different, there was an irresistible magnetism about her that immediately captivated him. Entering the shop turned out to be the right decision.

"Hello, how may I help you?" She asked.

*I can think of a way you could help.*

He took a moment to observe the variety of clothes on the racks, unsure if any would meet his taste.

"I wanna say I'm just browsing. But looking at some of the clothes, I'm wondering if I could even pull off wearing any of it."

Her eyes scanned him from head to toe, assessing his appearance and contemplating the most suitable attire for him. They were a mesmerising shade of bright green, held him spellbound.

"Well, I have a few ideas, if you don't mind me picking out a few items of clothing for you?"

No hesitation needed.

"Yeah. You probably have much better taste than me. Maybe you can improve my look."

She couldn't help but giggle, torn between agreeing that his taste in clothes was bland or keeping her opinion to herself. He typically wore blue or black jeans, paired with a white or grey t-shirt, and always donned one of his many brown leather jackets. Except today, he'd gone with a grey hoodie instead.

"Well, I wouldn't say you have bad taste. Just selective."

*She's just being nice.*

She carefully selected her words to ensure that no one's feelings were hurt, as it was her responsibility to maintain customer satisfaction. The job held no importance to her anymore; she harboured a deepening resentment towards the place and the owner. He frequently left her alone to manage the shop, while he gallivanted around on supposed business trips. It was clear to her that he had ulterior motives - to be with his mistress. Once his wife finds out about that affair, she doubted he'd be sticking around. The trust shattered like a broken mirror.

Logan's eyes scanned the shop worker, but there was no name badge in sight. It seemed out of the ordinary, given that most employees would wear one. He made a conscious effort to avert his gaze from her breasts, directing his attention to the absent name badge.

"What's your name? You don't have a badge." He asked.

"Madison. Sorry, I lost my badge. The boss was supposed to get me a replacement, but he is more interested in going off on his travels with his mistress." She realised that she just ranted about her boss in front of a customer.

"Sorry, I wasn't supposed to say that. Shouldn't be bad mouthing him. Some times I can't keep my mouth shut."

Logan empathised with the aggravation of a superior who disregarded their responsibilities and pursued extramarital relationships. He had experience dealing with people of that nature.

"No need to apologise. I've worked with a few people like that. You have every right to let out your frustration."

Her face lit up with a smile, revealing her relief at finding someone who understood that some bosses were indifferent to the business. Money had a way of disappearing as soon as it arrived, as they eagerly splurged on their desires. While the shop wasn't bringing in much money, Jeremy, the owner, had taken over after his father's passing. He was allowing the place to die off. His father Frank had a generous life insurance policy, evident in the way his son was now indulging in his newfound wealth.

"Honestly, I may as well take over the company. But don't want to, would be so much hassle and he wouldn't just give it up. I'm a supervisor doing a manager's job. If I ring him with an issue, his reply is always 'Well, sort it. Not my problem.' I'd love to hand my resignation in, but can't afford to, and I'd struggle to get a job elsewhere. He wouldn't give me a good reference. Jeremy would definitely do the opposite. He'd do everything he could to ruin my life. He is spiteful like that, he wouldn't do it because he cares about this place. Sorry, I'm doing it again. Told you I can't keep my mouth shut." She laughed.

"I can tell that it clearly needed to come out. I'm guessing you've just let it build up because you've not had anyone to get it out to?"

"Exactly! I am sorry if I do just rant away. I know you're a stranger and all."

"Names Lance. See. No longer a stranger. Typically, you

wouldn't know a stranger's name." He exclaimed.

Madison couldn't help but burst into laughter, her melodic giggles echoing through the air. In a sense, what he said held some truth. They knew each other's names now, but there was still so much they didn't know about each other. But they wasn't complete strangers to each other anymore.

"Well, nice to meet you, Lance. Never met anyone with that name before and I feel like I've met a lot of people. Met a man whose literal name was Sparky. He was named after his dads dog that died. Crazy right?!"

Their eyes were locked for several moments, and he couldn't tear his gaze away. Besides Lilly, he had never witnessed such beauty.

*I'd be looking further south if I was in control.*

"He was actually called that? I could imagine that poor fella got bullied in school."

They found themselves laughing together for a while. Before something caught Logan's attention, he noticed a shadowy figure peering into the window. He moved on quickly, but there was a lingering unease in the air. Or was it just a man gazing longingly at the stylish clothes inside? Window shopping. Paranoia consumed him once more, but he carefully concealed his suspicion from Madison. After much contemplation, he resolved that the time had come to accomplish his purpose in the shop.

"So what clothes do you think would suit me best? Whatever you do though, don't make me too colourful. I don't want to stand out too much."

Her eyes scanned the room, taking in the array of clothes

hanging neatly on the racks.

"Not too colourful. She mumbled "hmmm" as she sifted through the clothes, feeling the fabrics between her fingertips.

"What about these? We have a changing room at the back. Try them on. I'll be happy to help judge if they suit you or not. If that is okay with you?"

He looked at the pile of clothes in her arms, noticing that most of them were in his preferred colours. A coat, with hues of red, grey, and brown, stood out amidst the few blue tops and jackets.

"That is perfectly fine with me. Be good to have another pair of eyes to help me not look so boring. I wonder if you got my size, right?"

"Well, judging by the width of your shoulders and overall build. I assumed an extra large, so it fits comfortably, but isn't too tight and restricts movement. As I see that, you clearly work out." She gave a smile.

*She should have seen you all those years ago. You are a slob compared to then.*

She astounded Logan by getting his size spot on. Despite being able to wear large clothing, it sometimes constrained him, depending on the tasks at hand. He swiftly carried the clothes into the changing room and emerged in a new outfit in less than a minute. But his face did not match the expression Madison had anticipated. He tugged at his collar, his discomfort evident in his actions. The top was bright blue, with black jeans and a brown bomber jacket.

"You don't like it?" She asked

He glanced at the mirror beside him and critically

examined his appearance. Contemplating if he seemed ridiculous or if it strangely suited him, he couldn't help but question.

*You look like a fool.*

The other side of him hounded him all the time in his head. It was a constant presence, always lingering. As he continued to study himself, he gradually grew accustomed to the fashionable look. Compared to his usual appearance, there was a slight increase in brightness.

"If I'm honest. When I first put it on, I wasn't fond of it. But looking at myself, it's growing on me." He said, the grin on his face growing with each second.

"I must say, you look good in that outfit."

"Are you saying I didn't before?" He joked.

"Well… no. But if I say so from my perspective. This makes you look more approachable. No offence to the grey hoodie, blue jeans and white t-shirt."

Their eyes were fixed on the heap of his clothes sitting in the changing room. Laughter bubbled up from within him, confirming the truth in her statement. He was more accustomed to the less approachable look, which usually resulted in people keeping their distance. His face alone held the power to accomplish that task. Normally, he would be unyielding and inclined to maintain his customary appearance. But it was clear that the woman had a good flair for what suits someone and what doesn't.

"I guess the beard would look better trimmed, maybe a Hollywood style?"

She studied the bushy beard, along with his long brushed

back hair. Unsure whether his current look was on purpose, his scruffy beard gave him a rugged charm. But a gentle brush and attentive care would work wonders for it.

"I wouldn't say Hollywood style might make you look like one of those stuck up rich ass-holes. Trimmed slightly and a good brush, straighten it a little. "

*Who is this bitch? Telling us what to do. Don't be so fucking friendly all the time.* His other side was fighting to come out. He subdued the voice in his head as best as he could.

"So I don't already look like a rich ass-hole? Damn. I really thought I gave off that look." He laughed.

"I didn't want to say anything. That smugness is written all over you. You even intimidated me as you entered. I quivered in fear of being verbally abused by another rich prick. Then you spoke." She giggled.

*Hahaha, bloody hilarious.*

This had been the first time in a long time that he genuinely enjoyed talking to someone; their laughter echoed in harmony, a shared sense of humour that was a breath of fresh air. He and Lilly had a light-hearted banter that never crossed the line of offence.

"Do I not talk like a stuck up rich prick? I always thought I did. Maybe I need to sound more posh and demanding."

"Yeah, that would do it."

Laughter erupted from both of them, filling the air with their infectious mirth. The laughter abruptly ceased as he caught sight of the man at the window once more. They stared at Logan with a haunting gaze, as if he were a valuable prize waiting to be claimed.

"That man has appeared at that window multiple times now. He keeps just staring at us both." He said.

Motionless, the creep maintained unbroken eye contact with Logan, his piercing stare unsettling. A shiver ran down Madison's spine, causing her to tense up. Not recognising the man, her concern heightened as she wondered if he intended to harm either of them, or maybe even both. A sense of unease lingered in the atmosphere.

"I've never seen him before. Something is up. Why is he just staring like that? Like we are pieces of meat that he hopes to eat." She uttered.

Logan hastily entered the changing room, taking a mere thirty seconds to switch back into his initial attire. He was intending to inquire, to ascertain if the man would be interested in engaging in conversation.

"I'll see what his problem is. Maybe he has a reason for just staring at us. Could be someone with a mental illness or something."

As her worry intensified, Madison instinctively reached for his hand, finding solace in the connection. Her fingers brushed against his, causing him to freeze in his steps. He turned towards her, captivated by the concern in her beautiful eyes. He had the sensation of Lilly's presence, but it wasn't her at all.

"Be careful. He could be dangerous."

A warm smile spread across his face. It felt comforting to have someone genuinely concerned about his well-being once more. Strangely, he couldn't help but feel a sense of longing for that. Especially after so many years.

"Careful is my middle name. I'll be back."

*No it's not, it's Johnathan.*

As he opened the door, the man began walking away at a brisk pace. Suddenly not wanting to play the staring game, or talk. Logan was not in the mood for games. In the midst of his day, this man intruded. That was something that no person should ever do. He took a guess that the man worked for them, confident that they had located him after all of these years.

Why would they send just one man?

# 5

Moving through the bustling crowds of people, Logan's patience was dwindling. For close to ten minutes, he had been tracking the man from the shop. Frustration grew within him as the cat and mouse game continued, fuelling his determination to catch his target. As he tried to predict the man's path, he swiftly turned into a hidden alleyway, hoping to intercept him.

The man fought the temptation to glance back, focusing instead on the steady rhythm of his steps. However, his curiosity got the better of him, and he couldn't help but turn around. As he turned back, he was taken aback to discover that Logan had completely vanished from sight. Had his pursuer given up? He wondered. It was hard to believe that a man like that would give up so easily. He started to think that perhaps all the writing, sitting on his ass, had made him too unhealthy to maintain the pursuit. Choosing to press on towards his destination, he was startled to unexpectedly collide with the person who had been hunting him.

"If you make a sound or attempt anything, you'll die painfully. Understood?" Logan said, his face determined.

*Just kill him anyway.*

As he nodded, a wave of weakness washed over the smaller man, making his legs feel like jelly. Standing at six foot two, Logan was an imposing figure. This man had to be around five foot six, give or take a few inches. The fear of death consumed him, as he imagined the man before him as a walking encyclopaedia of lethal techniques.

"Why were you watching us?" Logan asked.

Fear gripped the man, rendering him motionless and silent. Logan wondered if the terrified act was truly authentic. Was this man a threat? Or just a confused civilian?

"I'd answer if I was you. I can give you a long and agonising death, and I'd enjoy every moment." His other side was coming out and was not the most patient version of him.

"Sorry, I'm Simon. I just… I saw you and recognised you. You're Lance Shephard, right? The author. I remembered seeing your picture in your book."

For several moments, Logan said nothing, his thoughts holding him captive.

*Lies!*

His books were popular, having sold an impressive half a million copies. However, his gut feeling told him not to trust this man. Questioning was needed, and Simon would regret ruining Logan's day.

"Oh, you're a fan? Well we can chat, I know a place. Chat about the books. Give you some clues on the next book."

He knew of a place indeed, a derelict one, where interrogation could commence, undisturbed. Whether through aggression or his ability to sway others with his words, he was determined to uncover the truth. Simon was caught off guard by the surprising response and found himself at a loss, grappling with the decision to accept or refuse.

"Erm… Well, I do need to get home." He said shakily.

"I have about ten or twenty minutes to spare. Come on. My treat. I'll buy you a coffee and cake, for this entire misunderstanding."

Simon pondered if he should accompany the man for a drink. His right hand trembled uncontrollably, a visible manifestation of the threat he had just faced moments earlier.

"I guess I can go for a coffee. You aren't going to kill me, are you?" He asked bluntly.

"Sorry about all of the seriousness before. I'm just a very private man. So when I saw you at the window staring, I made assumptions and I was wrong to do that. Honestly, I forget that people like me because of my books. I do apologise. Let me get you a coffee."

*Should just kill him right now and get it over with. He has to be with them.*

The voice was always there, nattering away. Wanting to do everything in the darkest way. It became more difficult each day to suppress his other side. It wanted out.

"Yeah, I get that. Coffee sounds good."

Logan gestured for Simon to follow him, leading him through a dimly lit alley, with the sound of distant traffic echoing in the background. They took a left, then a right, before arriving at the back of a building that appeared to be an abandoned cafe, its windows covered in dust and its paint peeling. As Simon looked it over, a sense of suspicion began to creep in. Noticing, Logan was quick thinking. He reached out and placed his hand on the man's shoulder, guiding him in with a reassuring touch.

"I know the owner, so he always lets me come in through the back. I can introduce you to him. Maybe he will start by giving you coffee on the house. If he likes you."

Opening the back door, they entered cautiously, the creaking hinges echoing in the silence. It didn't take long for Simon to deduce that the place had once been a cafe, now left deserted. The front of the building was sealed off with wooden boards, making it impossible to see what was inside. As he attempted to retreat, Logan's strong grip locked onto his arm, preventing his escape. Logan cornered Simon, forcefully driving his palm into his elbow, prepared to shatter it without warning.

"Now you're going to tell me who you really are. My books don't have an author image. There is nowhere online that even knows what Lance Shephard looks like. Did you really think I wouldn't see through your lie?"

Simon grimaced in agony, feeling his arm being pushed to its breaking point. With tears streaming down his face, he let out a pained cry that seemed to pierce the silence.

"I swear, there's a picture. Please. I'm not lying. I swear." He cried.

"If you were trained by them, then you aren't going to admit why you're here easily. Tell me the truth!" Logan demanded.

With a firm push, he moved his palm up the man's arm, eliciting a bone-cracking sound. The man's arm fell with a lifeless motion, devoid of any resistance. His attempt to scream was abruptly halted by a swift punch to his face, leaving him unconscious. With the handcuffs he had concealed in the air vent, he was prepared for moments like this. Logan went to work, making sure to securely fasten the man to the radiator in what would have been the bustling main eating room of the cafe. Logan began pacing up and down, his restless energy filling the space with a sense of unease. How had they found him? Had they known for a while where he had been hiding?

"They know exactly where we are." His voice was alien, like a completely different person. The sound was lower and had an anger to it. Magnus was no longer caged.

"It's possible. But it's also possible that this man is telling the truth. Maybe somehow there is an image. Maybe they discovered who Lance Shephard really is, so put my picture on the book. Makes it easier for their agents to locate me. But then they'd already have some kind of images of me in their system. So they wouldn't need to use a book. Unless they did it, to attract fans into finding me. Luring me out." He replied to himself.

"You always have to complicate stuff. Let's just kill this prick and move on. Plenty of places in the world that we could go to."

The tranquillity is shattered by an unexpected sound, causing him to turn his head. The sound of footsteps echoed through the building, indicating that someone had entered. Back up? As Logan hid behind the door, he could hear his own breathing, slow and controlled. Time seemed to stretch as he anxiously awaited the arrival of his adversary. He listened intently to the sound of their footsteps, gauging the perfect moment to strike. However, as he peered through the small crack in the door, he recognised the familiar sight of long, flowing hair.

"Lance. Are you in here?" Madison called.

She noticed the man from earlier, his eyes closed and his hands securely handcuffed to the radiator. In shock, she instinctively covered her mouth with her hands. Logan's sudden appearance from behind the door sent a shiver down her spine.

"Madison. What are you doing here? I didn't want you to see this."

She looked at the man she had spoken to in the shop, someone she wouldn't have thought capable of causing such harm. Her attention was drawn to the man's broken arm, which hung limply by his side. But she reminded herself that she had only met Logan thirty minutes ago, a mere blink in time to understand a person.

"What have you done to him?" She asked.

"When I asked him why he was watching us. He said he

was a fan of mine. He'd seen a picture of me in my book. I don't have any picture of me on any of my books. I think someone sent him."

When she looked over at the man attached to the radiator, he seemed rather harmless. But maybe that was the idea. Send someone who seemed unsuspecting and non-threatening. However, they posed a significant threat.

"You broke his arm?"

"Well, he wouldn't tell the truth."

"And did he after breaking his arm?"

*He would have, if you didn't show up.*

"No. He went to scream. So I knocked him out."

In a panic, she began pacing back and forth, regretting her decision to leave the shop and fearing her life was on the verge of unravelling.

"I should have stayed in the bloody shop." She moaned.

"How did you find me?" Logan asked. Puzzled, to how she located him.

"Well, once you left, I quickly closed the shop. I saw the direction you'd gone in. So followed that direction. Eventually, I found you and the man. Both chatting before he began following you. So I tailed you, doing my best to not be seen. I was unsure if he would harm you. But looking at him now. I should have been more worried about what you would do to him."

Logan's gaze shifted to Simon, who was starting to regain his senses. Waves of pain pulsed through his head, evidence of the brutal punch he had endured. Questions hung in the air, demanding resolution, and the suspicious man would eventually be compelled to provide answers.

"I've got it under control. Trust me, he is going to give me the truth."

Simon's eyes widened in horror as he registered his location, the intense pain in his arm confirming his worst fears. Logan rushed over before a scream was released, clamping his hand over the man's mouth.

"Shhhh. Now, I can put your arm back into place and splint it. But only if you promise not to scream or do anything stupid. Understand?"

Agonised, the man nodded, a tear escaping and tracing a path down his face. Madison saw the man as someone who couldn't possibly be involved in anything wrong, completely innocent. But she did not see people, how Logan did. He may have been rusty from being out of the business, but his skills were still sharp. He removed his hand from Simon's mouth and walked over to the vent, retrieving a collection of medical supplies - bandages, an arm brace, and a sling.

"Please, I don't know anything. I came here looking for Lance Shephard, I love his books and some people online said that he resided in the Cornwall area. So I came here, asked a lot of people. Some had no idea who I was talking about. But a couple people said about a man who lives on an island, comes over for supplies now and then. A man who keeps to himself, isn't big on conversation. I thought, well that sounds like an author to me. They typically love to write, but are usually pretty shy people, who want to be left alone. That's the truth, honest." He cried in fear.

*The bastard will make her believe his lies. Look at him and his fake tears. Pathetic. Blow his brains out, he will only use it to convince her.*

"I believe him. Why would he lie?" Madison asked.

With care, Logan tended to the man's arm, providing him with a rudimentary splint made of a small piece of wood and tightly wound rope. Along with a piece to bite down on, while he moved the bone back into place.

"Bite on that."

Crack! Simon's teeth were on the verge of breaking as he chomped down with all his might on the wooden piece. As he spat out the piece of wood, a sharp pain immediately radiated through his jaw. The arm was back in place. The brace consisted of two planks of wood, roughly three inches wide and five inches long, that were carefully positioned on both sides of his arm, giving it the necessary support. Taking the bandage, he gently wrapped it around, providing support and stability.

"The thing is. He could be telling us what we want to hear. If you don't want someone finding out something, you reveal the things that they want to hear." Logan revealed.

"But maybe that's not the case here. Does he look like a man who poses a threat to you? I mean look at him, he is a scrawny little guy. I just don't think he is as dangerous as you think."

She doesn't know anything. Don't listen to her. That man is with them, you know it. You let him go and you will regret it.

"I'm just a really big fan of your books. Honestly, I wouldn't and couldn't hurt a fly. Have you not had any other fans seek you out? Surely there have been some?"

*Remove his tongue. He is only going to change your mind, if you allow him to keep talking. Let me take over.*

"He is not going to cause any harm." Madison said.

*Shut up bitch!*

"Please, I meant no harm." Simon cried.

*Really? That's a bloody lie.*

The voice in his head, Madison, Simon. The sensation of his head about to burst overwhelmed him, accentuating his longing for the peacefulness of the island. Only having to deal with one voice, instead of three. As the three voices spoke, his anxiety tightened its grip on him, growing more and more unbearable. His heart raced as the cacophony of sound overwhelmed him, causing his fists to clench. Until he felt a hand touch his. Madison sensed a growing unease, as if something was slowly unravelling inside him. When her fingertips lightly brushed against his skin, he instantly felt a wave of serenity wash over him. Something that no one, other than his wife or kids, could do.

"Lance, sit down. You look ready to explode. I know that look, because my daughter suffers with anxiety."

He obeyed her without hesitation, finding solace in her soothing aura. Instead of questioning everything about her, he simply accepted her, despite barely knowing her.

"Thanks. I don't know what to do. We release him and it could literally come back to bite us in the ass. But if he does speak the truth, then it would be wrong to do what I would do."

She didn't even consider asking him about his intentions towards the man. Despite her fear of the man in front of her, she couldn't help but feel a magnetic pull towards him.

"Madison, I know we literally met earlier. But I'm telling you now. It's probably best that you return to your shop. You don't want to be involved in this." Logan knew that either way, she would most likely stay. But he wanted to give her the option to leave and hope that nothing came back to her.

"I'm staying. He has seen me anyway. So if you let him go, he knows what we both look like, so if he was some kind of bad guy. Then we are both pretty much fucked. But I truly don't think he is."

She knelt down to meet the man, positioning herself at eye level with him.

"Can you look me in my eyes and promise that you are not a bad man, that what you have said is the truth?"

Looking into her eyes, he didn't blink at all. The main thing she could see in him was the way his eyes were filled with destabilising fear.

"I promise, I am just fan. I have a family, 3 kids and a beautiful wife. My wife could vouch for my reason for coming here. She thought I was mad coming to Cornwall in search of my favourite author. Please, I'm telling the truth. I can give you her number and you can call her and ask."

*Who would believe that? Not bloody me.*

Logan felt his theory about the man slipping away, as each word uttered only deepened his doubts. Had his once-sharp ability to read people dulled? Had the years alone messed with his head that much? Living every day with paranoia of an imminent attack had become unbearable, surpassing the limits of what a typical person could endure. With each passing day, the loneliness gnawed at his sanity, pulling him deeper into madness. His instincts rarely led him astray, and this time was no exception. His gut feeling told him that Simon was undoubtedly working for them. Posing as a fan. However, a difficult decision loomed, and Madison's presence only made it more challenging.

"No need. Maybe you are who you say you are. Maybe my mind has played tricks on me."

With each careful step, he made his way towards the apprehended man, his mind consumed by the uncertainty of whether his choice would have negative repercussions. As he reached down to his trousers, his fingers brushed against the cold metal of his pistol hidden beneath his t-shirt. Moving down, he fumbled in his pocket and finally found the key for the cuffs.

"Be glad this lovely lady showed up. I'm sorry about your arm. To make amends, I'd be happy to give you money for your troubles and a copy of my new book."

After being released, the man stood up and his expression conveyed a deep sense of relief and gratitude.

"Honestly, it's okay. To be honest, the way I went about everything was wrong. I should have known that the way I sometimes stare may freak some people out. I apologise for ruining your day."

*You fucking idiot! I'm telling you, this is gonna end badly. He is lying!*

"You get off, get the arm looked at. It should heal fine. But get it checked."

Every fibre of Logan's being screamed at him to warn the

man, but he couldn't risk scaring Madison. She must already think that he is a dangerous man because of his actions. Simon gave a brisk nod and hurried out the door.

"Hopefully, I won't end up regretting letting him go." He mumbled.

"You really thought he was some kind of bad person?"

She sensed his determination, knowing that deep down, he was already contemplating pursuing the man. His face bore the unmistakable signs of what he was feeling. Her gaze fixed on him, she felt a deep appreciation for his willingness to believe in her and hear her out. Not something her ex ever did.

"We will have to wait and see. Hopefully, I was wrong."

Despite the need to return to the shop, she couldn't resist the allure of the mysterious man known as Lance. Torn between logic and emotion, her head advised caution while her heart craved deeper connection. His bushy beard did not detract from his attractiveness in her eyes. One could even say that he was her type. Although she wasn't seeking a romantic connection, she was hopeful to establish a fulfilling friendship. With few friends in Cornwall, she often felt lonely.

"Bad timing and all. But would you like to get a coffee? With me, obviously." She asked.

As he turned to her, his face lit up with a radiant smile. After dealing with someone he suspected to be a potential threat, he finally let go of the tense look on his face.

"Well… Yeah, coffee sounds good to me. I don't mind coffee alone. You sound like you're unsure if you will be a part of getting coffee." He joked.

Both giggled. She cherished the presence of someone who could bring a smile to her face through laughter. The thought of the unknown part of him, which she hadn't witnessed yet, sent shivers down her spine. But maybe he had a reason to possess the skill to easily shatter a man's arm. Former military? The police force had a reputation for being ruthless when necessary.

"Oh, I would never say no to coffee. I mean, I need it to literally be able to process existing. I know a great cafe. Their food and coffee are outstanding."

"Oh, we're getting food too? Sounds a bit like a date." Logan laughed.

Her face changed. She was unsure on what to say.

"A date? Well, kind of get to know each other date. Not in the romantic sense. Also, feel free to shut me up, otherwise I will just blab on."

Her cheeks turned a rosy shade, and he couldn't suppress his smile.

"Come on, let's go and get that coffee. And maybe some food. I'm feeling peckish."

# 6

Stepping into the cosy little cafe, they were greeted by the sound of soft jazz music playing in the background. She and Logan found a seat by the window, where they could marvel at the sight of the ocean, waves crashing with a soothing rhythm. As a waitress approached, the aroma of freshly brewed coffee wafted through the air.

"Hello, are you ready to order?" She asked.

Logan knew what drink he was getting, always the same one - a steaming cup of black coffee. He hadn't been given enough time to thoroughly examine the array of food options. Aware of the ticking clock, he swiftly perused the menu, pinpointing a dish he was certain he'd find delight in.

"I'll have a black coffee, two sugars. With a large all day breakfast, could you add in an extra egg and two more slices of bacon please? I'm starving."

After carefully jotting down his order, she gave him an affirming nod. She turned to Madison, who was deep in thought, her finger tracing the options on the menu. With lunchtime fast approaching, she felt indecisive about what to satisfy her hunger with.

"I'll have a white coffee, no sugar. Can I get..." She moved her finger over the menu. Found it.

"Scampi and chips, please."

The disappointment in Logan's eyes was palpable as he expected her to order a proper piece of fish with chips. It seemed peculiar to him that someone would opt for scampi and chips, and he couldn't grasp the rationale.

"Scampi. Interesting choice."

She couldn't grasp his lack of appreciation for her chosen dish; she thought it was a delicious meal.

"You don't like scampi?"

"Never have. It is basically the chicken nuggets of fish based meals. I can't stand chicken nuggets either."

Madison found it odd, but she looked at him with an open mind, refraining from passing judgement.

"You're more of a steak man, right? Or in this case, a nice bit of cod."

It was that obvious. However, he knew that a considerable number, approximately forty to fifty percent, of men had a fondness for a mouthwatering steak. It would always bring about a joyful expression on a man's face. It may not elicit as big a smile as sex does. Or seeing the love of your life every morning when you wake up or the joy on your child's face as you walk through the door after a long day. But it definitely put a big smile on many men's faces.

"I would never say no to a good steak."

As the waitress approached their table with their drinks, they thanked her simultaneously, their gratitude echoing in perfect unison. He took a sip of his black coffee, savouring the rich, bold flavour that awakened his taste buds.

"So what made you move to Cornwall?" Logan asked. Deciding to get in first with the questions.

For several moments, she didn't answer, her eyes locked on the swirling patterns in her coffee. Her mind churned with possibilities as she carefully contemplated her response.

"Simple answer. To start a new life. I had a rough break up, didn't want to be around that area or those people anymore. So decided to move here. I always came here with my parents as a child. Dad would take me out on his boat. I fell off it multiple times, because I'm just stupidly clumsy."

"I get that. A fresh start tends to help. I know that very well. I wouldn't have pegged you as a clumsy person. But then we've not known each other very long." Both of them came to the same place to start new, it was as if they were destined to meet.

"You had a bad break up to?" She asked.

*He wishes. It's so much worse. Prepare for happiness to fall down the hill.*

"Not exactly. My wife and two children died in a house fire. I came here because staying where I was, everything reminded me of them. I have good memories of them. But I just… I struggled to get over the fact that they were gone."

The mood suddenly shifted, causing a palpable shift in the atmosphere. Her eyes met his face, and she saw a solitary tear escaping from his eye. The urge to hug the man overwhelmed her, but she resisted, aware of the context. It was the first time since it happened that he found the courage to talk about it with someone.

"I'm so sorry to hear that. It's hard enough to lose a loved one, but something like that... I can't imagine how that affected you."

"I locked myself away from the world. It was my way of dealing with it all. But anyway, we don't want to be sat her moping about the sad things in our lives. Do you have any kids?" He asked, attempting to move away from talking about his family.

As she took a couple of sips of her coffee, the rich flavour of roasted coffee beans danced on her tongue, leaving her craving for more.

"I do indeed. I have a daughter. Bethany. She can be a right pain in the ass, but I love her. She has helped me get through a lot."

"It's good that you have that. Even when they frustrate you with the things they do. The love for them never falters. The father not around? If you don't mind me asking." He didn't always like asking that question, just in case it turned out that the dad had died recently or there was some really long story. But he wanted to know more about Madison and her life. She intrigued him.

"Not anymore. He disappeared a couple of years ago, probably went off with another woman or something. He hadn't shown much care towards me or Beth. So, in a way, it was a good thing."

Logan despised men like that, who would disappear without any explanation. Show some courage and communicate honestly with the person you no longer love, letting them know your intentions to leave.

"I never understand why people do that. Just leave. If I fell out of love with someone, or was just extremely unhappy in the relationship. I'd sit them down and tell them. But we may never understand the minds of others, right?"

As he took the last sip of his coffee, the waiter arrived with his food, filling the air with delicious scents. As they caught a whiff of the appetising food, their mouths couldn't help but water. Logan's eyes lit up with excitement as he eagerly grabbed his fork and prepared to indulge. Although he fancied another drink. The waitress was showered with thanks, as each of them beamed with appreciation.

"Could I have another coffee, please? That one was probably one of the best coffees I've ever had."

The waitress gave a nod, and her wide grin stretched from ear to ear. Her gaze remained fixated on him, clearly drawn to his irresistible allure. She took his smile as a positive indication and promptly made a note on her pad. Ripped it off and folded it, awkwardly leaving it on the table, as she picked up his empty mug.

"I can indeed. It is a very nice coffee, made by my uncle. He never tells us how he makes it so good."

"Well, I will just have to come here more often for the coffee. It is amazing."

Giggling, she shuffled off to the kitchen, her footsteps creating a soft patter on the floor.

"I think you have an admirer." Madison exclaimed, pointing to the paper on the table.

He picked it up and carefully unfolded the note, revealing the woman's phone number scrawled in elegant handwriting. It surprised him, as he hadn't been flirtatious and didn't think he was looking particularly attractive.

"Apparently so. Has she looked at me properly? I mean, I'm not exactly looking my best or anything. Plus, I'm sitting here with a woman. It seems a little insensitive, doesn't it?"

He had to admit; the lady serving them was very pretty, with her youthful charm, but she seemed too young for him. She had to be in her mid twenties. He was forty-one and wasn't looking for someone who was significantly younger than him. Not that he was looking at all.

"Well, we aren't dating. We are potential new friends, right? I mean, you seem nice and it's good to just chat to someone, have a normal conversation. Guessing she isn't your type? If you have a type."

"I don't know about that. I don't know you. Well, I know a bit more about you now, your name, why you moved to Cornwall, some little bits. So yeah, I guess we could be friends. Maybe." He gave her a wink.

"Everyone has a type, don't they? She is just too young for me. I have to be at least sixteen or seventeen years older than her."

Madison couldn't help but be entertained by his amusing and light-hearted responses. As they chatted away, the memory of the broken arm momentarily slipped from her mind. But where most people wouldn't want to be involved with someone like that, she felt different. Her desire to know more about him was insatiable - she wanted to delve into his past and learn everything. It was refreshing for her to engage in light-hearted banter with someone, and she cherished their shared sense of humour. Her customers, for the most part, were not in the mood for joking around.

"Well, I can just take my friendship elsewhere then." She laughed. "What is your type?"

He thought hard about his answer. His wife was his type, her beautiful long brunette hair and perfectly proportioned curves making her irresistible to him. Her body was perfect and after giving birth to their children, he loved her body more. The moment his son was born, he was in awe of the flawless being they had brought into the world. Ethan was their first, followed by Leah. When he thought of his type, the only image that came into his mind was that Lilly. Her smile. He could recall the memory of their first holiday as a couple, her dancing on the bitch as the sun went down behind her. A perfect moment, which made him grin from ear to ear.

"Lilly. My wife. She was my type. Long brown hair and perfect in every way." He paused in thought for a moment.

"Her hair was similar to yours, I loved it when the sun would shine down on it and for that time, her hair would be brighter, a tint of ginger would appear."

While he spoke, the sun's rays flooded through the window, illuminating Madison's hair in a similar fashion. He surmised that it was a characteristic frequently found in people with that particular hair colour. While he possessed a wealth of knowledge, the intricacies of hair and how the sun could affect it remained a mystery to him. Madison looked at his face, noticing the nostalgic expression that clearly indicated he was reminiscing about those cherished moments. She wanted to know more about his wife, her curiosity always driving her to uncover every detail about people.

"What was she like? If you don't mind me asking."

He rarely shared his past with acquaintances, but something about her made him believe she was trustworthy and genuinely interested.

"She was amazing, kind and always willing to help others. She was extremely selfless, always put others before herself. We met at a government fund-raiser. She was the daughter of the host. Jack Renley, brilliant, but sometimes scary man. But he knew how to throw a party. I was there working security. I saw her sitting in the corner, looking fed up, like she didn't want to be there. It sounds silly, but something drew me to her that night. Nothing would have stopped me from going over to her. So I radioed for someone to cover my post and then approached, asked her if she was okay. Turns out, she just wanted to be involved, but her father had refused because he believed that somehow she would mess everything up. He may have been brilliant and rich, but as I learnt, he was not a good father. He had little to no belief in his daughter's capabilities, but just by sitting and talking with her that night. I knew she was capable of many great things. We ditched the place, went and got a hot drink and donuts, then sat on a bench at Hyde Park, watching the stars and eventually the sunrise."

Never before had anyone done something like that for Madison. While she wouldn't deny that her ex-husband Damien had his nice moments, their relationship was still complicated. Her recollection was primarily filled with the unpleasant moments. It was during her lowest moments, when she was craving emotional support, that she encountered him. In the park, he stumbled upon her, tears streaming down her face, and he took a seat beside her, offering words of comfort. Within the hour, they found themselves in his house, their naked bodies pressed against each other, basking in the sheer joy of the moment. Whenever her friend Jess asked, she never failed to rave about the mind-blowing sex she had. Other than that, they had nothing in common; he could be extremely mean, with his words cutting like shards of glass.

"Wow! That is beautiful. I've never really had that. Mine is pretty dull. I was down and sad. Damien came along and found me upset. He cheered me up. We went back, had sex, and nine months later Bethany was born. But I'd decided shortly after getting pregnant that it probably wouldn't work. We had nothing in common and honestly, he could be very mean. But I stuck it out because we were going to have a baby. But it only got worse. That's why I left. I needed a new start. Cornwall is beautiful, and I thought, well, if I don't find a good man. At least I get to grow old with good views."

Logan was shocked. He thought getting Lilly pregnant after almost two years was quite early. But within the first month. He knew, though, that if you were feeling unwanted and down, you would cling to anyone who gave you attention, like a lifeline.

"It sounds like you are definitely better off without him. Must have been hard bringing a child up alone?" He said.

"Luckily for me, when I mentioned to my mum that I was going to move to Cornwall. She gave me enough money to get a deposit down on a place and pay for six months' rent. So that helped. I was lucky and managed to get a job within a couple of days. I had to bring Bethany with me to work for the first couple of weeks. Luckily, she was a perfect baby. Didn't cry constantly and the customers would often entertain her with funny faces."

As she continued talking about having a baby at work and finding a suitable baby sitter. As Logan glanced around, a familiar face caught his attention, walking confidently towards the cafe. Simon. He wasn't alone either.

*I fucking told you. Should have killed the bastard.*

# 7

The men behind Simon all held AK47's, their fingers tightening around the triggers as they raised their weapons and aimed at the cafe. The man Logan had interrogated was unmistakably the leader of this group, his confidence and demeanour giving him away. His transformation was remarkable - gone was the petrified person from earlier, replaced by the fierce gaze of a killer in his eyes. He raised his hand into the air, gesturing for his men to hold position. With a menacing grin, Simon stared directly into Logan's eyes. His hand dropped down, a silent cue for the onslaught to commence.

"End them."

With instinct, Logan swiftly turned the table onto its side, creating a makeshift barrier between them and the danger.

"Everybody get down now!" Logan yelled.

In a swift motion, others followed suit, flipping their tables with more of a struggle and seeking refuge behind them. Fear gripped the others, their hearts pounding as they stared down the barrels of the guns. Chaos erupted as the gunmen opened fire, the sound of breaking glass mixing with the screams of those caught in the crossfire. A deafening sound of bullets echoed throughout the cafe, they relentlessly struck the five-inch thick wooden tables, some managing to break through the sturdy barriers. The room was now a macabre sight, with the walls and floors splattered in a deep shade of crimson and pools of blood dotting the tiled surface. The deafening sound of gunfire came to an abrupt halt.

"Logan, your smart move would be to come out now. Before anyone else is killed."

Madison's gaze wandered, her mind filled with curiosity as she tried to figure out who Simon was addressing.

"Who the hell is Logan?" She whispered.

*Is she that stupid? You are looking at him.*

He grappled with the decision of whether to answer or not, ultimately deciding to remain silent. The kitchen beckoned to him, a mere ten feet away, as he thought up a strategy to escape. He knew he could make that distance without being shot, but the smell of fear mingled with Madison's scent made him hesitate. The other option was to attempt to kill the men, but at that moment, he could sense the futility of such a reckless act. He needed to find a place where he could manipulate the situation to his advantage. He locked eyes with Madison, and the fear in her gaze was unmistakable.

She needed to be there for her daughter. He was prepared to go to great lengths to reunite her with Bethany.

"Listen. We are going to run for the kitchen, stay low. From the kitchen, we can get out the back and onto the street. We stay here and we die. I'll get you to your daughter. We stay here, we die. Are you with me?" He asked.

A confirming nod escaped her lips, the gesture saying more than words ever could. With each passing second, time slipped away. Simon's impatience grew, and the threat of his men opening fire loomed closer. He cautiously peeked through the bullet hole in the table, trying to catch a glimpse of what lay beyond. There were a total of five men, with Simon among them. The key was speed; if they were fast enough, they could slip into the back without any shots being exchanged. He reached for Madison's hand, intertwining their fingers and holding on with a grip that made her knuckles ache.

"Now."

They raced towards the kitchen, their hearts pounding in their chests, trying to stay as inconspicuous as possible. Madison's journey to the kitchen counter was abruptly interrupted when she stumbled, her head meeting the hard wooden frame. She winced as the sharp edge grazed her skin, leaving a tiny cut above her right eye. The fall slowed their progress. Ducking behind the counter, the bullets began colliding with the walls again. The sound of a woman's anguished cries echoed through the air as a bullet found its mark in her leg, followed by a second hitting her shoulder. In a split second, Logan took hold of her arm and swiftly pulled her to safety. In the kitchen, they discovered a group of staff members hiding behind the ovens, their terrified expressions evident. They hurried towards the back door, bursting out into an alleyway that sloped uphill.

Logan's lack of exercise made it challenging for them to maintain their speed while running as fast as they could. But fear of death fuelled them both. Running had never been Madison's cup of tea. She much preferred the smooth ride and convenience of driving. The worst part was the flat surface of the path, with its bricked texture and noticeable gaps between each brick. The uphill terrain posed an additional challenge, making it even more arduous to reach the top.

With every step, Madison's muscles throbbed, her breaths came in ragged gasps, and she yearned for a break. Yet, she acknowledged that stopping would almost certainly result in death. With sheer determination, she pushed herself to keep moving forward. Logan felt the same, his breathing laboured and his leg muscles screaming with pain. Their hands were locked together, refusing to be separated.

Their attackers wasted no time and quickly started chasing them up the hill, their determined strides gaining momentum. Logan looked back and felt a surge of adrenaline as he realised he needed to level the playing field. Taking in his surroundings, he noticed a turn off approaching, offering a potential detour. He glanced over at Madison, his eyes lingering on her for a moment and giving a nod in the direction of the turning.

"That way. I've got an idea."

She nodded in acknowledgement. Wondering what his plan was. As she turned down the street, the sight of cars parked on both sides and houses with neatly manicured lawns greeted them. Logan's gaze shifted to a house further down the street, its red door standing out against the surrounding buildings. The sight of a car parked in the driveway suggested that the occupants were present.

"House with the red door. Get inside it. Hopefully, they will let you in." He exclaimed.

"What are you going to do?" She asked.

*Ask them to nicely not shoot us.*

"Even the odds."

She raced to the house, her heart pounding in her chest as she knocked on the door. As the door swung open, a man with a bald head and a big brown beard came into view. He looked to be in his mid forties. His facial hair was starting to show signs of greying, with a few scattered silver strands. A perplexed expression crossed his face as he gazed at the woman in front of him.

"Hi, would it be okay to hide in your house for a few minutes? I know it's random. But there are some bad men coming and I don't want to die. Please. I am sorry for the intrusion."

The weight of indecision settled on his shoulders, leaving him feeling stuck. He looked out the door, didn't see anything. Yet, he believed that she must be in danger, as evidenced by her decision to knock on his door.

"Erm… Okay. Come in. I can call the police for you."

As quickly as she possibly could, she darted into the house, her feet barely touching the floor.

"Yes please. Thank you."

The man shut the door. As Logan dived underneath a nearby range rover, the sound of a car engine roared past him. He hoped that Simon and his men would assume that the people in that car were him and Madison, driving away into the distance. Give chase, and they could escape beyond reach before their assailants returned. Nevertheless, he remained sceptical about the likelihood of that occurring. Simon's impeccable training was evident as he successfully deceived both him and Madison.

*Let me take care of these idiots. They won't know what hit them.*

Was it time to unleash his darker side? The personality called Magnus. He had complete confidence in his ability to eliminate the men, especially knowing that Madison was out of harm's way. The approaching footsteps echoed in his ears, and he could see the men's boots coming into view. Military boots. It was the attackers, their malevolent intent palpable in the air.

"They are around here somewhere. Find them. He'd be happy that we found her. Capture her alive. Kill Logan. He poses too much of a threat to be left alive." Simon demanded.

Who would be happy that she had been found? A perplexed expression crossed Logan's face. They had multiple targets, he was just one of them. Why would someone want Madison? He watched, his senses heightened, as he patiently waited for the perfect moment to strike. Two men stood perfectly aligned, their feet side by side, as they paused and surveyed their surroundings. Logan swiftly drew his gun from his waistband. With precision, the attacker aimed low and unleashed a shot towards the ankles. With the force of a bullet, the bone shattered as easily as butter being sliced by a knife. Another shot was fired to ensure the other man's downfall.

"Arghh!!!!" They screamed in agony, clutching at their legs.

He took aim and fired another shot, abruptly silencing them. The sickening smell of gunpowder filled the air as a bullet pierced through the side of one attacker's head, and then met its mark in another. Two down. Three to go. Rolling out from the other side of the car, Logan remained hidden from their view. Simon was unsure which direction the bullet had originated from. His men fanned out, scouring the area for any sign of the shooter. However, he had covertly ventured down the road, carefully concealing himself behind another car. In the middle of the road, two soldiers walked, diligently searching under cars for any signs of danger. With precision, he aimed his weapon and fired off two rounds. A well-aimed shot landed in the middle of the left man's spine, instantly immobilising him. Like a puppet with its strings cut, he fell to the ground in a heap. The other turned to take a shot of his own, but was too late. The bullet entered through his left eye, exploding out of the back of his head.

Simon stood in awe, astonished at how rapidly his men had been dispatched. His broken arm made it a struggle to pull his gun from his holster. As he readied himself for a shootout, he positioned himself in the centre of the road, mirroring the iconic scenes from western movies.

"You're good Logan. If I'm going to die anyway, duel me. Like a western."

Unbeknownst to him, Logan had already stealthily advanced and was now just a mere nine feet away from the man he should have eliminated earlier in the day. As he got to his feet, he discharged a single round into the man's arm, causing him to drop the weapon, before firing two more shots into his legs. His defences were completely stripped away, leaving him helpless.

"Arghhh. Shit. That was good. I didn't expect that." He mumbled in pain.

"What did you mean when you said He'd be happy that you'd found her?"

Logan moved in closer, applying pressure to the bullet wound in Simon's leg, causing him to grimace in pain.

"I'd answer quicker if I were you."

*Chop, chop.*

"Okay… okay."

As he released the pressure, he could hear his own heartbeat pounding in his ears while he awaited his answer.

"There is more to that woman than you know. I don't know much. But I know the man who works with my boss will be very pleased to learn of her whereabouts. I don't know why he wants her, but he does. That's all I know. Ask her why someone would be after her."

Logan began walking towards the house, a sense of determination filling his every step. He needed answers and his patience was at an all time low.

"Wait. You can't just leave me here. At least call an

ambulance or…"

The sudden impact of a bullet to the head rendered him mute. He had reached his limit with that insufferable bastard and had no intention of putting up with him any further. Was Madison involved with them? Was she playing him this entire time?

He was going to find out.

*I knew she was hiding something.*

# 8

As Madison cautiously looked out of the door, her nostrils were assaulted by the metallic scent of blood and she saw Logan, or Lance as she recognised him, standing over the lifeless body of Simon. He was more than a writer; every event that unfolded solidified that fact. Who was he? As he gazed up at her, he wrestled with the decision of whether or not to probe her about Simon's words. A small part of him questioned if the man's intention was to sow seeds of doubt about his companions.

"It's clear. We need to get moving now. Get you to your daughter."

Prioritising finding Bethany, what was said remained unspoken for the time being. He prayed fervently, hoping that the enemies hadn't already reached her. She nodded in confirmation, satisfied that there were no potential killers in sight, except for the one who had taken on the role of protecting her. Turning to the man who owned the house, she flashed him a warm, genuine smile.

"Thank you for letting me in when you didn't have to. I will repay you somehow one day. I promise."

He shook his head. His unwavering moral compass wouldn't allow him to stand idly by as someone was gunned down.

"No need. There was no chance that I was going to just leave you out there, not with gun men trying to hurt you. Thankfully, your friend took care of them. Stay safe." He said, looking to Logan in the background.

Fear and confusion flashed across the owner's face as they tried to make sense of the situation, ultimately opting to let it go unquestioned. Outside of his house, five lifeless bodies lay sprawled on the street, a sight he had managed to avoid until that unfortunate moment. Logan approached the house, noticing the car parked outside it. A stunning dark blue BMW X5 shimmered under the warm sunlight.

"How much for the car?" Logan asked.

Looking at his car, the owner couldn't help but find it amusing and let out a laugh.

"It's not for sale. Even if it was, I doubt you could afford it." He wore a self-satisfied smirk, seemingly underestimating Logan's wealth by a significant margin. Logan had a way of silencing doubters, proving that he should never be underestimated.

"I'll give you thirty-six thousand for it."

The smugness on his face disappeared as though it had been abruptly severed by a sharp blade.

"No way you could afford that. You don't look like a man with a lot of money to spare."

In the distance, the wailing sirens pierced the air and caught their attention. Sensing the urgency, Logan knew he had to accelerate the process. He moved closer to the man, pulling his phone from his pocket. The universal application he launched looked like a banking app at first glance, but its features went well beyond financial transactions, incorporating maps and various data filters.

"What's your bank details? Be fast about it. We are short on time. I will give you fifty thousand right now, if you are quick, and let me buy your car. We need to get to this woman's daughter, and fast."

He'd paid a fraction of that price for the car, practically nothing, as it was a hand-me-down from a disinterested family member. Their desire was for a model that was both better and more modern. He reached into his pocket, pulling out his phone and opened up his banking app. The account details were given to Logan, and in less than a minute, the entire amount was deposited into his bank account. He was left in awe, as he had never witnessed such a substantial amount of money in his account before.

"Wow! Thank you."

In a rush, he darted over to a sideboard in his hallway, his fingers fumbling as he grabbed the keys and handed them over to the new owner of the car. Logan took the keys swiftly out of the man's hand.

"Pleasure doing business. Thank you."

With a click of a button on the key, he unlocked the car and briskly walked over to the driver's side, sliding into the seat. Turning around, he saw Madison standing completely still, as if frozen in time. She was in shock at everything that had occurred, her senses overwhelmed by the sight, smell, and presence of so many dead bodies. From an ordinary day, chaos erupted as she found herself in a thrilling chase, dodging bullets, and witnessing the swift demise of her attackers by the mysterious man she had only encountered that morning in her shop.

"You coming?" Logan asked.

Coming back to reality from her state of complete awe, she looked at him and saw the faintest smile on his face. Giving him a nod.

"Yes! Sorry."

She darted over and hastily climbed into the passenger seat, securing the seat belt tightly around her. Logan done his too, safety first. With precision, he skilfully reversed the car out of its tight parking space, narrowly avoiding the neighbouring cars. Careful to avoid driving over the lifeless bodies of his victims, he accelerated down the road. He took a left turn, his heart pounding as he anticipated the approaching police.

"Where did you learn to kill people?" Madison asked bluntly.

"Served in the army for six years, before being moved into special ops. Killing is the easy part, it's how you deal with the taking of a life that is hard." He replied.

As he drove down several unfamiliar streets, he felt a growing sense of uncertainty about his destination. Completely engrossed in learning more about him, Madison neglected to mention the specific school her daughter needed to be picked up from.

"What school is your daughter in? So I know where I'm going."

"Humphry davy school. It's not far, should be able to get there in five minutes. I'll call and let them know I'm coming to get her."

She furrowed her brows as she searched for the school's number on her phone, but before she could find it, Logan handed her his mobile.

"Use that instead. It's encrypted. So they won't be able to trace the call."

A puzzled expression crossed her face as she obediently typed the number on the phone and dialled, after copying it from her own phone. The phone rang incessantly, each ring growing more desperate as the seconds ticked by without a response. When a voice came through.

"Hi, this is Madison Jones, I'm ringing to inform you that I will be taking Bethany out of school earlier than expected. A family member has fallen extremely ill, so we are going to go and see them, just in case it's the last time we get a chance to." She said, sounding incredibly believable.

"Sorry, but Bethany left earlier. She informed us that she had been sick multiple times. She told us that you were picking her up. Did you not?" The receptionist asked.

Her mind went blank, and she struggled to find the right

words in her stunned state. Bethany seemed perfectly fine in the morning, exhibiting no symptoms of sickness.

"I will ring her now and check. Sometimes she gets our neighbour to pick her up. May I ask why no one rang me to inform me that my daughter had left school early due to sickness?"

The school receptionist paused, the weight of responsibility settling heavily on their shoulders as they realised they had neglected to inform the parent about their child's illness.

"Ermm… the teacher who dealt with the situation assumed that you had been notified. We are truly sorry that you hadn't. I can check with the teacher to see who it was who collected her?"

It was evident that their response was a hastily concocted falsehood, a desperate attempt to protect themselves. Once again, they resorted to the familiar excuse of miscommunication.

"If I'm correct in thinking, it would have been my neighbour. Bethany has contacted her before because I've been at work. I'll give her a ring. Bye."

Before another word could escape the receptionist's lips, she was abruptly cut off. Madison could feel anger building up inside her, frustrated that her daughter had chosen today of all days to go home sick. As she turned to face Logan, a sense of clarity washed over her, and she instantly knew her daughter's destination.

"Can you head to Heamoor. She has most likely either gone home or to Michael's. Who luckily lives pretty close to us." She said as she typed in the post code on the cars navigation system.

"Does she often leave early?" He asked.

"A few times, but she usually avoids doing so, because it means having to either get a lift with someone who isn't me or getting a bus. Michael's mother has picked her up several times. Michael is home schooled, since deciding that the teachers were too slow in teaching him the right things. He is smart and knows it. He does some online teaching course, but usually finishes the work so fast, that he has nothing else to do. So he asks for Bethany to go over and she is head over heels with him, but hates to admit that to me. She has used the excuse that he is doesn't like woman, but I've seen him checking out plenty of woman. Sometimes not even attempting to be subtle about it. Sorry, I'm droning on. Surprised I've not put you to sleep."

Logan laughed. Her passionate ranting didn't bother him; he found it oddly comforting to just listen. He yearned for Lilly's animated complaints about the teachers neglecting their duties and the unsightly mess left by the neighbour's cats in the garden.

"Actually, it has the opposite effect. Wow, gotta be subtle with doing something like that, or come across creepy. So she is most likely there then. Use my phone to call her."

Madison began pressing on the phone aggressively as she typed in Beth's nu's number. Tapping the green button to call, he was amazed that her finger didn't go through the phone. It rang, continued ringing, no answer. She tried again. Same outcome and again.

"She probably won't answer because she wouldn't know the number or I'm guessing it comes up as private. I may have to use my phone instead."

"Send her a text, telling her it's you and can she answer the phone, it's incredibly important. Might work."

Worrisome thoughts invaded her mind, causing a knot to form in the pit of her stomach. What if someone else had taken her? Her heart started throbbing with an unbearable ache. Had the attackers had dispatched additional individuals to search for Bethany? As she wrote out the text, her fingers moved with such rapidity that Logan couldn't believe his eyes. He wished he had the ability to text quickly, but his fingers simply couldn't keep up with the pace. While he was skilled at working on a computer, he felt out of his element when it came to using a phone.

"What if those people sent others after her? I can't have him find..." Her voice trailed off, leaving an unfinished sentence hanging in the air, concealing the remaining words. Confirmation of what Simon spoke of?

"What do you mean by him? Him who?" He queried.

She attempted to ring the phone again, desperately avoiding the question asked at that moment. She questioned whether he would be willing to help once he discovered the truth. Her mind was constantly haunted by the mystery surrounding Logan's identity. He was clearly in that cozy cafe, but she couldn't help wondering if he was the same man in the car with her. As the phone rang incessantly, she tried to unravel the intricate puzzle. Yet, she was lacking crucial information to fully grasp the whole picture. Just as she was about to speak, Bethany answered the phone.

"Hello." She said, unsure if it was truly her mother on the other end.

"Beth, thank god. Where are you?"

"I didn't feel great, so asked Michael's mum if she could pick me. You were at work and I didn't want you to have to leave and lose money because of me."

It was touching how she considered her mother's well-being, not wanting her to suffer any more financial burdens.

"The receptionist said that you was sick? How are you feeling now? I'm on my way to get you."

A momentary silence hung in the air, indicating that Beth was carefully considering her mother's statement and trying to avoid any unwanted encounters.

"I'm okay here at Michael's. You don't have to get me. I'm fine, mum. I was sick a couple times, but i feel a bit better now."

Madison had a knack for detecting when her daughter was lying. It was clear from the panic in Bethany's voice that she had unintentionally disturbed something. She desperately hoped it wasn't the disturbing idea that had initially crossed her mind. Part of her wanted to tell her daughter off for being at Michael's once again, but she didn't want to start an argument on the phone.

"Well, I'm coming to get you, anyway. I'll explain more soon, but we need to get somewhere safe. I will be there in about ten minutes, okay?"

Beth was left bewildered by her mum's words, unable to comprehend the urgency of finding a safe place. Was she not safe at Michael's?

"What? What's going on?"

"I'll explain soon. Can you go home and pack some clothes into a couple of bags? Take Michael with you, to be safe."

"Ermm... yeah okay. I don't get what's going on. But okay."

"Love you and see you shortly."

Beth cut the phone off. As Logan shifted gear, the car's engine growled, responding to the pressure he applied on the accelerator. He could sense the urgency in the woman next to him by the way she tapped her foot anxiously. Despite his limited acquaintance with them, he felt a strong urge to safeguard them in any possible way. First, he wanted a few answers and was prepared to give some of his own.

"My name is Logan, Logan Winters. Those men, I assumed, were solely after me, and I thought I'd managed to get you dragged into it. But Simon spoke of a man who would be very happy to know where you are. Who? Have you worked for them before?"

One piece of the puzzle slotted into place for her. But his question confused her, especially the part about a man who would be happy to see her. She could only think of one man, a very dangerous man. She had a past, tangled with memories she preferred to keep hidden, and she wasn't ready to divulge it all to a man she barely knew. With the revelation of his real name. What else was he keeping from her?

"That's why he said that name back at the cafe. Well, my name is my real name. The person he spoke off, was probably Damien, my ex. The them you ask about, I have no idea what you are talking about. I've not worked anywhere, other than in shops."

The name instantly set off warning signals in Logan's mind. The man was a familiar face, as he had crossed paths with him on numerous occasions. With a complete absence of compassion, he was a merciless killer. He had no qualms about killing anyone, regardless of their age. Amongst all the hired assassins, he held the reputation of being the most insane and merciless.

"Your ex is Damien? Damien Jones?!" He asked more aggressively.

The way he asked sent a wave of concern through Madison. He knew her ex-husband, the man she hadn't officially divorced yet. Filing for divorce meant risking her and Beth's safety, so she couldn't do it without giving away their whereabouts.

"You know him? How?"

He was aware that if he shared the entire truth, she would probably want to run in the opposite direction and avoid him. Faced with the urgency of the situation, a decision had to be made swiftly.

"I worked with him, running a couple of special ops missions. He was hot headed and if I'm honest, one of the most brutal people I've ever met. Never cared for much or anyone. He often went off mission, killing several people without reason. We had a bust up, I refused to work with him, who if I remember right, I said, had no heart."

Trying to comprehend it all was no easy feat. She knew Damien had a military background, but when she met him, he skilfully concealed his true profession and made her believe he worked as a security detail for a businessman.

"After the military, though, he worked as security for some business man, I can't remember his name. He never mentioned any special ops missions."

As they approached Madison's home, the navigation screen in the car displayed that they were just three minutes away from their destination. He knew that for him to disclose his past, the air would become thick with the heavy burden of their intertwined fates. Most likely, she would want to take her daughter and escape from him and Damien, as far away as possible. Which he'd understand. Keeping them close was the optimal way to ensure their safety at that time.

"The thing with those missions, was they were classified. So he couldn't discuss them with you even if he wanted to, let alone tell you that he was doing it. Probably thought it was safer for you not to know. I had to do the same with my wife, sometimes it's so they aren't filled with worry for every second you are gone."

Just as she was about to speak further, they came to a stop outside her house. Logan looked about and noticed the pleasant, peaceful ambience of the neighbourhood. Her house was a nice size, with a combination of brick and wooden panelling. As Bethany exited the front door, she took in the sight of the car and the man occupying the driver's seat. Her mother's arrival with a strange man left her feeling perplexed.

"Nice house." He said.

Madison dove out of the car and rushed over to her daughter, her heart pounding with relief. After the day she'd had, hugging her felt like a warm embrace of solace.

"Who's that man, mum?" Bethany asked.

"His name is Logan. Did you pack a couple of bags?"

Bethany remained silent, her attention drawn to the man in the car behind her mother. Despite his burning desire to yell for a quicker reaction, he maintained a facade of patience. With every passing second, his anticipation grew, fearing that enemies could appear at any minute.

"Yeah, they are in the house by the front door. What's his deal? Have you been having sex with him?"

Her daughter's inquiry left Madison dumbfounded and speechless. The audacity of that question hung in the air, creating an uncomfortable tension.

"He is going to help us. No. I am not having sex with him. Why would you ask such a thing?"

Her daughter raised an eyebrow, a look of doubtfulness crossing her face. The disbelief in her eyes was evident as she shrugged off her mother's words.

"Help us, what's going on? Also, he is literally your type. You've definitely been getting some of that."

"I can't explain right now. But there are dangerous men after us and he can help us. He is not my… okay, he may be my type. But no, I have not been getting any of that and even if I did, that's none of your business."

Bethany never held back and always spoke her mind with her mum. Never afraid to ask her about anything. Always intrigued by sometimes the smallest things, when she started learning sex education at school. Upon returning home, she would interrogate her mother about every minuscule aspect.

Madison hadn't anticipated such a thing, and the shock of it had caught her completely off guard. Like a detective, her daughter questioned everything, a naturally curious teenager. Almost sixteen years old.

"So we literally need to leave like right now? Are we coming back?" She asked. Her face filtered with concern.

*I feel like these two are going to get us killed.*

"Yeah, we need to get going. I don't know right now."

Beth stood in awe. She had begun to adjust to life in Cornwall, cherishing the friendships she had made, knowing that she might never see them again. She raced off, feeling the pavement beneath her feet as she sprinted down the street. There was a loud banging on the door of a sleek, modern home, with large white pillars supporting the porch roof. The walls were a striking combination of black and white. The house had a clean, minimalist style that evoked a surgical atmosphere. The door opened and Michael stood and before he could speak. Bethany couldn't resist the temptation and pulled him outside, their lips colliding in a passionate kiss as they wrapped their arms around each other. Madison watched on, a bittersweet feeling settling in her chest as she realised this might be their last time here. Bethany will hold her mother responsible for destroying her relationship and depriving her of the chance to see her friends once more.

As Beth moved off Michael, his eyes widened, and he could feel his face turning red as he realised that her mum had witnessed the whole thing. He was smart, but his anxious demeanour overshadowed his intelligence. Especially around Madison, he found her to be intimidating.

"Your… Your mum is there." He mumbled.

"It's fine. I don't care right now. I have to go with mum and I don't know when I'll be back. I'm going to miss you. I'll see you again. I…" She'd never said the words before, the beautiful three words.

"I love you." She cried.

Every part of her wanted to stay, but if her mother thought they were in danger. She knew she couldn't, and that broke her heart. Michael leaned in and kissed her, gently cupping her cheeks with his hands.

"I love you too!"

Their faces were adorned with the biggest smile, yet tears of sadness streamed down their cheeks. Their hearts sank, filled with uncertainty about the next time they would lay eyes on each other. They embraced once more, their bodies melting into each other's warmth. Madison sprinted into the house, hastily grabbed the bag, and now stood by the car, anxiously waiting.

"Beth, we have to go." She said, not wanting to ruin a special moment for her daughter.

As she moved away from Michael, their hands remained tightly intertwined, reluctant to let go. The tears poured down her face, as if a river had burst its banks. Michael watched intently as she gracefully climbed into the car, a longing building up inside him, urging him to join her. Despite his desire to leave, he felt a strong obligation to stay with his parents. He waved goodbye.

"I love you Bethany Jones!!!" He shouted.

Leaning out of the window, she felt the rush of wind

against her face from the backseat of the car as they set off.

"I love you too!!!"

They drove down the street, feeling the slight incline pulling them forward. The distant ocean shimmered as the sun's rays bounced off its surface. Madison turned her gaze towards Logan, taking in his confident posture.

"So where we headed?" She asked.

*I don't like her. She is irritating me already.*

"I have an island. I need to get some supplies." He answered.

# 9

Walking through the hall of an office building, he marvelled at the pristine white walls, gleaming under the bright fluorescent lights. Striding elegantly, a man in a tailored suit held a file tightly in his left hand. With shaved sides and a brushed-back top, his hair had a sleek and polished appearance. His attempts to appear youthful were undermined by the visible greying hairs that stood out amidst his hairstyle. His face had a chiselled appearance, highlighted by a meticulously styled goatee, and his suit jacket struggled to contain his bulging muscles. He resembled a heavily built man in his forties, futilely striving to appear half his age. Ultimately failing. The way he walked, coupled with his intense gaze, conveyed a strong message: he was all business. He walked briskly, the urgency of his delivery evident in his determined strides.

Opening one of the heavy-duty double doors, he was met by an older man whose short, grey hair added to his distinguished appearance. The lines etched on his face hinted at a life well-lived, placing him in his late fifties or early sixties. His face bore the mark of a prominent scar, reaching from his right ear to the edge of his mouth. Even at his age, it was clear that Kane Hunt was no stranger to the gym, as his toned muscles suggested. Sat down, he had an intimidating presence, but once on his feet, he was downright terrifying. With his imposing stature of six foot four inches, he could intimidate even the bravest of souls. He was seated behind a massive desk, its grey surface adorned with swirling patterns of black and white. Positioned ahead of him, his two sons sat comfortably in the welcoming embrace of two brown leather sofa chairs, just like his own cherished seat. Evan, though slim in build, emulated his father's style and was always seen wearing a suit. Among the sea of muted suits, his wardrobe choice always stood out - today, it was a bright orange suit.

In contrast, Marcus had the same fierce and menacing appearance as his father. It was obvious who had seen more combat by the way they carried themselves, with a hardened and vigilant posture. The sight of his bald head, marked with burn scars on the top, left side, and back, hinted at a horrifying past. His face told a similar story, with a rugged eye patch concealing his left eye, while scars from a vicious stab wound peeked out from its edges. His black suit was accentuated by delicate shades of crimson, adding a touch of sophistication. Marcus had a greying bushy beard. The fear he evoked was so intense that even the boogeyman would think twice before crossing his path. As the door opened, each of them turned their heads in unison, their curious eyes locked on the man who stood there, pausing for a moment. He couldn't help but wonder if he had interrupted an important meeting, considering the irritation on their faces. With a flick of his wrist, Kane signalled for him to proceed.

"Come. What news do you bring?"

Every part of him debated handing the file over, fearing that if it angered them, they could take out their frustration on him, as he was the messenger. The tension in the room was palpable. Another colleague had fallen victim to their violent tendencies before, enduring a merciless beating that left him paralysed. Evan, unlike others, was the composed one who consistently advocated for peaceful resolutions in any given situation. Kane and Marcus, however, had a reputation for being two of the most savage men alive. Their path was paved with bloodshed, as they would not hesitate to kill anyone who crossed their path. With a careless gesture, he let the file fall onto the desk.

"I'm afraid it's not good news I bring."

Kane's gaze was drawn to the disturbing images within the file, revealing the tragic fate of men who had recently caused havoc in a nearby cafe. They were all victims of precise marksmanship, leaving no room for doubt that it was him.

"I'm afraid all of them were killed. Simon had reported in that he'd located the target, been interrogated and then released after convincing him that he was just a fan of his books. The interesting thing is who was with him."

In a stroke of serendipity, Kane discovered a captivating image of Logan and Madison, their faces illuminated by the soft cafe lights.

"So, after all this time. We've found him. Better yet, we've found her. He will be very happy. We get two birds with one stone."

While perusing the pictures, Marcus's countenance underwent a noticeable change upon encountering the photograph of the two of them.

"There he is, that bastard! Now we can kill him for good. He won't get away this time."

Kane rose from his seat and turned his attention to the panoramic view outside the expansive window. The distance spanned roughly twenty-five, maybe thirty feet.

"Send a team, more men this time. I can imagine that now his location is compromised. He'd want to get out of the area. Have people tracking the woman's phone and her daughters. Find them. Call Damien, let him take care of this."

Marcus looked disgusted, a wave of disappointment washing over him as he realised he had been overlooked for the hunt. His eyes narrowed with irritation. Considering his turbulent past with Logan, his thirst for the man's death surpassed that of anyone else. Marcus was left for dead by the man, who callously plunged a blade into his eye, leaving him to burn.

"Are you serious?! I'm going, let me kill this man. I will not fail this time, that bastard will die and painfully."

The absence of Kane's response hung heavily in the air, creating an awkward tension. Silence hung in the room, creating an eerie atmosphere. As Evan sat, the weight of uncertainty settled upon them, prompting the consideration of a detailed plan. Being aware of his brother's impulsive nature, he was cautious in his approach.

"So what's your plan, Marcus? You need one. No point going there filled with rage. He'd beat you again. They didn't call him The Contingency man for no reason. The man seemed to have a back-up plan, on top of another and another."

In a sudden burst of anger, Marcus leaped out of his chair, his fist clenched tightly, ready to deliver a blow to his brother's face. With a burst of speed, Kane leaped over the table, his hand snatching his son's arm in mid-air. Considering his age, it was surprising to see him move at such a rapid pace.

"Stop now! Your brother is correct, if you go there without a good enough plan. Logan will beat you again."

Disappointment washed over Marcus as he looked down, realising they didn't have faith in his capabilities. Ever since they last fought, he'd been honing his skills, training relentlessly to ensure he would be ready when the opportunity for revenge presented itself.

"I'm sorry, father. You're right. Give me this chance to take him down. I will plan and I will not fail. I promise."

Kane's hand rested gently on his son's shoulder, while the glint of fear in his eye was hard to miss. It was the fear he found within himself that had become his greatest protection from death.

"I see a fear in you, fear of failure."

Marcus opened his mouth to speak, but his words were abruptly silenced.

"That same fear has always been in me. It's what has kept

me alive. If you have no fear of failure or death, then there isn't that part of you striving to survive. Keep that in you and I'm sure you will bring me Logan Winters' head."

Stepping backward, he motioned for his sons to make their exit. They approached the door, their anticipation building, only to halt abruptly at the sound of their father's voice resonating from the other side.

"Evan, go with your brother. Take the jet. Work together for once. Two minds are better than one. When you see that son of a bitch, make it as painful as possible."

Evan's expression shifted to one of complete surprise. The thought of working with Marcus filled him with unease, recalling the mission where he had been shot in the leg because of his brother's eagerness to engage in battle. However, out of sheer terror, he couldn't bring himself to reject his father's demand. Unlike the rest of his family, he had no desire to partake in their murderous endeavours, always feeling like the odd one out. He was inclined towards non-violence in his approach to everything.

"Yes, father." He moaned.

"Oh, he will wish that he'd made sure I was dead." Marcus exclaimed.

# 10

The humidity hung in the air like a heavy blanket, weighing down on everything. Francis Kingsley despised the stifling heat, even in the most pleasant moments. In the corner of his office, he sank into his plush reading chair, ready to escape into a world of words. It resembled a library rather than an office, with rows of bookshelves and cosy reading nooks. The walls of the room were adorned with oak bookcases, their shelves filled with a vast collection of books. Only by looking above the neatly arranged wooden frames could you catch a glimpse of the dark yellow walls. The walls were painted that colour to make the room feel brighter as he worked on cases that should have been left at work. Yet he would often obsess over solving each one, his sleep disrupted by the relentless pursuit of answers. Whenever he saw the yellow walls, a sense of joy washed over him.

The light blue chair, with its inviting cosiness, was the ideal spot for him to curl up with a good book. With its slight curve at the lower section, the chair provided excellent support for the spine, thanks to its cushioning of memory foam and wool. The top had a cushion attached, which could be folded over the back or, as it was then, used as a soft headrest. With each page turn of the third book in The Contingency series by Lance Shephard, he could feel himself being drawn deeper into the captivating story line. The action-packed story had Francis on the edge of his seat, his heart racing as he neared the shocking conclusion filled with surprising twists. In the first book, the narrative unfolded around a covert operative who found himself betrayed by the very individuals he had once held in high regard, leaving him with no choice but to flee for his life. With his family held captive, they devised a plan to lure him into a trap, unaware of the strength and intelligence he possessed. It was a story that could continue with various threats lurking around every corner, ready to pounce on the world and its main character, Jason Knight. However, the author decided to create a trilogy instead of prolonging the story.

While reading each book, he picked up on something that would easily go unnoticed by most readers. Nevertheless, his sharp eye for detail allowed him to see what others missed. Throughout, there were intricately woven messages, each one requiring careful deciphering. In book one, he encountered the first hidden message on page three. The words were carefully chosen and arranged in a zigzag pattern, requiring readers to read them downwards to notice their significance. The clever twist was that they did not follow a chronological sequence. Once all the words were discovered, they had to be connected to form a coherent whole. The first sentence he deciphered caught his attention immediately.

*'Never believe the lies fed to you by the government.'*

Plenty of people had a reason to despise them for their constant deceit, a fact he had witnessed countless times. But then he continued finding an abundance of messages, one after another. With each new clue, he felt closer to piecing them together and solving the mystery.

*'Do you really believe so many powerful people die by accident?' One sentence asked.*

*'Anyone who poses even the smallest threat becomes collateral. They are always watching, always listening.'* Another read.

Each message sinking Francis further into the depths of a truth that had always eluded him. The government's reach extends to every corner of society. They have become masters of manipulating the world, employing a range of strategies, deceit, and even deadly assassins. Those who dared to defy their authority were promptly eliminated. If you were not part of their plan, then you were swiftly deemed dispensable to their cause. The outcome would be extermination. The painstaking process of decoding and mapping out each message divulged a disturbing revelation - a vast horde of deadly assassins stood prepared for any given moment. It seemed that they were methodically eliminating people who didn't align with their vision for a new world, gradually reducing the global population.

The reading of one message deeply disturbed him.

*'Have you noticed government officials dying every couple of months, in a pattern? An organisation is doing this. They are*

*working with certain people in the government to take full control of it. There are those within who have fought to stop the senseless killings and have been taken out and replaced because of it. Soon they will have complete control, no resistance to slow their progress.'*

Francis diligently recorded each message, pinning them in chronological order on his board, which had once been dedicated to solving crimes. But to him, this was a crime that went against the very fabric of humanity itself. The third book contained cryptic messages with numbers interspersed, suggesting the formation of a phone number. With only one missing, he speculated that it must be located towards the end of the novel. As he read, the soothing melodies of orchestral music played softly in the background. Looking over at his board, he saw a kaleidoscope of words and ideas. Out of the selection, four were emphasised as potentially vital.

*'I need help in stopping what they have planned.'*

*'Decipher the codes, contact me. When I answer, use the phrase hidden in one of these messages, Which I will not detail here, because you never know who is reading. Maybe the devil. Find the phrase.'*

After meticulously reviewing each sentence multiple times, he finally pinpointed its location and began isolating specific words. Piecing them together.

*'Using the clue within that message. Decode the message, and once you obtain the number, contact me and use the phrase. Without it, I will not speak with you.'*

The phrase was, The devil is in the detail. The final

highlighted message on the board, was one was the one he thought most about.

*'If you choose this path. I cannot promise that we will succeed or survive. But we will die trying.'*

Being sixty-one years old, he had left the police force seven years ago to enjoy his retirement. His cases were his lifeline, providing him with a sense of fulfilment and drive. He deeply yearned for his wife Pamela, feeling her absence greatly. A few days earlier, the air was heavy with the weight of the one-year anniversary of her passing. At the age of sixty-seven, she succumbed to lung cancer, a consequence of her past smoking habits. Despite frequently acknowledging that smoking would be her downfall, she persisted in taking drags from the cigarettes. She had successfully fought against breast cancer, opting for a mastectomy to remove her breasts. Then, for years, she was all clear. Yet, it reappeared with even greater intensity. A picture of her, captured in a moment of joy, sat on the small brown table beside his chair.

Pam always said he had the keen instincts of a detective. As he started his career in law enforcement, their paths intertwined when she assumed the role of his commanding officer for several years. She was amazed by his ability to think on his feet and analyse a crime scene, even though he hadn't become a detective yet. He could vividly recount the sequence of events. She'd first suggested that he would excel as a crime scene investigator, and he pondered the idea before eventually sitting with her one evening after successfully solving a murder case. She reached into her hidden compartment and retrieved her private stock of whisky, and they joyously toasted to their victory. A much needed one. It was during that night that they formed a strong bond, the sound of their laughter filling the air as they shared stories about work and their personal lives. At that moment, he felt a deep connection with her, knowing she was the one he wanted to be with. Had she thought the same? No, not on that night. But she had seen a potential for romance to blossom, like a delicate bud waiting to bloom.

His eyes moved swiftly across the text, eagerly seeking the elusive message that might reveal the author's true identity and contact information, which he doubted was Lance. Someone providing such perilous details about a company would be deemed foolish to reveal their true identity in the book. The man clearly wasn't your average individual; he had devised an unconventional plan to thwart dangerous individuals. There must have been a strong justification for him to initiate such a crusade. They must have completely shattered his life in some manner. It was evident that he had been involved with these individuals; perhaps he had experienced a sense of betrayal. Francis contemplated the countless conceivable motives. The author's enigmatic nature piqued his interest, driving him to unravel the mysteries of his past, his origins, and everything in between. But first he had to find that last number.

Weeks earlier, he had cracked a code that revealed a secured website, accessible only with a pass-code. Fortunately, the code was located in a different section, but it was jumbled into a chaotic arrangement. But after nearly two days of relentless effort, he finally broke through. When he accessed the website, he discovered a multitude of files, each labelled with unique code names. First one he clicked on was under the name operation storm cloud. The attached information outlined a meticulously planned operation to dismantle a politician, revealing the intricate details of the mission. He strongly resisted becoming involved in the new world order, recognising it as a tragic massacre of innocent souls. He had taken a holiday to the Maldives, a place he frequently visited, and as per the records, he always sailed on his yacht.

The mission brief included detailed blueprints, ensuring they had a comprehensive understanding of the floating vessel's layout and strategic points to plant explosives. As he scanned through the folder, his eyes landed on the incident report. Severe storm sinks yacht, none survived. Although no specific details were given about the state of the boat, he surmised that it had likely disappeared without a trace. A haunting final transmission echoed from the captain's voice, revealing the grim truth that the ship was going under and the lifeboats had vanished. He had said something else, but it was redacted. This could have been a sign that he harboured suspicions of sabotage.

Checking how many pages remained in the book, he was surprised to find sixty-four still to go. He was going to finish it, finally have all the messages. Then it will be time to reach out to the author of the book, excited to engage in a conversation about his work and the hidden details within it.

# 11

Logan pulled into the car park closest to the boating docks and found a spot right in the middle. In case the entrance was obstructed by enemies, he had a contingency plan - he would navigate the car through the fence on the left. He turned to Madison, uncertain whether to have her and Bethany wait with the car, the engine humming softly in the background. Leaving both of them alone could expose them to even greater danger in the absence of his protection.

"I can get my stuff and you could wait with the car if you like. But you'd have to remain in the car."

*Yes. Please stay in the car.*

Her displeasure was evident in her narrowed eyes and pursed lips. The thought of her and Beth remaining there, with hunters on their trail, was absurd to her. Without him, she knew they would be vulnerable and unprotected.

"There is no way that we are staying here. If they come, how are me and Beth exactly supposed to defend ourselves? We are coming with you."

Logan had guessed that would be her answer. He'd only suggested it as an option, just in case they had not wanted to join him. He could almost hear the disappointment in her tone. Logan was glad that the weather had remained bright, as he could feel the warmth of the sun on his skin, reminding him to grab his sunglasses.

"That's fine with me. I just thought I'd suggest it as an option. I didn't know whether you wanted to go on the boat. Are you both okay on boats?"

A hesitant expression crossed Beth's face as she looked around. The look on her face made it clear that she was both unfamiliar with and unenthusiastic about the idea. Her mother beat her to the punch and answered for them both, leaving her silent.

"Yeah. Boats are fine." Madison said, her voice became high pitched near the end.

*No, you hate them. Stay with the car.*

"Okay. That's fine then. The journey to the island is usually about twenty-five to forty minutes. Come on, then."

As Logan climbed out of the car, he could smell the scent of exhaust fumes mingling with the faint aroma of freshly brewed coffee from a nearby cafe. He made his way to the ticket machine, carefully selecting a four-hour ticket. He hoped they'd only be there for an hour, maybe less. Aware that more men would be searching the area, he scanned his surroundings, listening for any signs of movement. Looking out for enemy drones in the air, using high-resolution cameras to capture and transmit images to surveillance systems. Each one would have been programmed using vivid images of Logan, Madison, and Bethany, bringing them to life in a way that surpassed the capabilities of any publicly available technology. They were consistently adept at quickly identifying and finding their targets. The choice of drone determined its capabilities; some were armed with weaponry, allowing for efficient target elimination. The skies were clear. His eyes swiftly swept across his surroundings, confirming that there were no potential threats to worry about.

As the girls emerged from the car, he couldn't help but wonder if Madison's secretive behaviour indicated she was hiding something important from him. His paranoia whispered that she was colluding with them, but his heart vehemently disagreed. Little did she know that he would unexpectedly walk into her workplace that day.

*Leave them. We don't need them. They are a liability and will get us killed.*

The relentless voice in his head persisted, a constant reminder of the darker side that lurked within. Each day, he struggled to prevent its dominance, exerting every bit of his willpower. Walking past cars, he caught a quick glimpse of himself in a window, but his reflection seemed distorted and unfamiliar. He saw his alter ego Magnus waving at him, a mischievous smile on their face. Despite his doubts and shaking his head, the sight persisted, making him question his sanity. With each passing second, Magnus' grin grew wider, spreading from ear to ear. With every window he passed, it inched closer. He turned around to face Madison and Bethany, and there it was, lurking in the reflection behind them.

*You won't be able to resist forever. Let me out. I will solve all of your problems.*

"No, you won't." He mumbled quietly to himself.

Bethany tilted her head to the side, her curiosity piqued as she observed him muttering to himself. His failed attempt at hiding it was evident.

"Did you just speak to yourself?" She asked.

He couldn't deny it, but also didn't feel the need for them to know the full extent of his mental anguish. In his loneliest days, Magnus became a voice that embodied both love and hate, creating a complex dynamic between them. But Magnus proved time and time again that he only saw killing as the answer to each scenario, leaving no room for negotiation or peaceful resolution. Logan fought a daily battle to keep him at bay, but it wasn't always successful. The nine years of solitude had acted as a catalyst to awaken Magnus. In silence and loneliness, he was born. Or had he always been there?

"Yeah, happens sometimes. Sometimes when I am thinking of a plan or working something out. I mumble to myself. Don't worry, I'm sure I'm not crazy." He laughed.

"You don't sound it. Mum, seriously? Who is this man? I've never heard you mention him before and suddenly he is helping us. I'd also like to know what the fuck is going on? Why are people after us?" She demanded.

"We need to get to the boat." Logan interjected. Not

wanting to stand around, waiting to be picked off.

As they started descending the slope and steps, they could hear the distant sound of water lapping against the boating dock. Beth stomped her way down, her face flushed with anger at the inadequate responses she had received. Reluctantly, Madison divulged some of the information to her.

"He worked with your father for a short time. So you know that your father wasn't the nicest of people, which is why we left. Well, he found us. Now he has sent men after us and they don't seem very friendly. If it wasn't for Logan, I'd probably be dead."

As Logan paced forward, he kept a vigilant eye out for any potential threats near the boating docks. He had a nagging intuition that something was wrong, causing unease to wash over him.

"Really? So what are we going to do? We can't just run. If he found us in Cornwall, he will find us anywhere. He'd always proved resourceful before mum. Don't underestimate him again. I don't get how he isn't…"

Bethany's heart raced as she stopped abruptly, her eyes fixated on the sight of an armed man emerging in front of them. She stood frozen, unable to move a muscle, paralysed by fear. With his hand firmly on his gun, Logan was prepared to discharge and fire the moment he deemed it necessary upon seeing the man. Madison instinctively threw herself in front of her daughter, protecting her from any potential harm. Oblivious to her surroundings, she failed to notice the man approaching from behind, trailed by another. They could hear the clicking of weapons as armed personnel encircled them. Logan contemplated the situation, realising that eliminating the closest man would be effortless, but neutralising the remaining two without endangering the girls would present a challenge. He needed to devise a plan swiftly, with no time to waste. Each man discharged their weapon, their eyes focused on their intended targets, determination etched on their faces.

"Do not make a move, or we will shoot." From the group, it was the man nearer to Madison who spoke up, his words laced with authority.

*Let me out. I can deal with them. They'd be dead in seconds.*

He hesitated, briefly entertaining the idea of setting Magnus loose. He was unsure who Magnus was referring to, and his uncertainty gnawed at him. Would his darker side's violence be directed solely towards men, or would it put everyone in the vicinity at risk? With a vigilant gaze, he scanned the area, seeking out any objects that could potentially aid him in his mission to stop the men. Nothing. Faced with the failure of plan A, he had no choice but to proceed with plan B.

"Take me. Leave them be." He said.

But the man closest to her vehemently shook his head in disagreement.

"Can't do that. Under strict orders. Kill you, capture them."

Filled with anticipation, Logan moved sideways a little, edging himself closer to the water. Madison realised his intentions and smoothly coordinated her movements with his, ensuring Bethany stayed close by. Being within jumping distance, he needed to come up with a distraction to divert the men's focus.

"I'm taking a guess. That order came from Kane. Did he not want to kill me himself? I mean, I am the man who took his son from him."

They exchanged a knowing look, silently acknowledging that he lacked crucial knowledge about Marcus.

"Jump." Logan mumbled, trying to not let the men hear.

Bethany and Madison flung themselves off the edge, plunging into the cool water just as the sound of his weapon being fired pierced the silence. It wasn't a great distance down, but enough that their pursuers would not follow. Logan shot two of the men, one bullet piercing through the left eye of its target, and the other forcefully drilling into the forehead. As they fell, the sound of their bodies hitting the ground echoed through the air, while a pool of crimson slowly formed beneath them. Within seconds, a bullet found its mark in Logan's shoulder, causing him to lose his balance and plummet into the chilling embrace of the ocean below. Glancing over to confirm his fate, the shooter only saw a macabre scene of blood mixing with the water. Taking everything into account, it was a reasonable assumption that Logan would not have lived. Putting his finger to his earpiece.

"Winters is down. Repeat Winters is down."

The voice crackled through the equipment, filled with annoyance.

"You killed him? He was my kill. Mine! Where are the

other two? The mother and daughter." Marcus moaned.

The man stood frozen, his mind racing with fear for his own life, unsure of how to respond. He should have known that attempting to eliminate the target personally would have made him vulnerable to Marcus' fury.

"They jumped into the water. He… he pulled a gun on me. I had no choice."

"Should have let him shoot you. If he is dead, I'll kill you myself. That was my kill. Mine! Find them now!"

Stood in awe, he was unsure whether to respond, not wanting to anger his boss further.

"Sorry sir. I'll find them." He muttered.

Looking back at the water again, searching for any signs of his target's survival. He doubted it, but the uncertainty of where his bullet struck lingered in his mind. He'd reacted quickly, his reflexes kicking in without hesitation. Had it been a fatal shot? Self-doubt slowly seeped into his thoughts, casting a shadow over his confidence. Setting off in search of Madison and Bethany, he could feel the adrenaline coursing through his veins. They'd have to resurface somewhere, and he'd be relentless in his pursuit to catch them.

# 12

Small waves crashed against the boats, creating a rhythmic sound that filled the air. Madison ascended from the ocean, caught between two boats, and her heart raced as she realised the potential catastrophe if they moved towards each other. Gasping for breath, Bethany finally reached the surface, her lungs burning from the effort. Neither of them were the type to actually go swimming in the sea, despite living near the beach. The view was breathtakingly beautiful and that was enough for them.

"We need to get onto one of these boats before we are crushed between them both. Quickly."

Beth gave a quick nod, signalling their readiness, and together they climbed onto the boat to their right, their eyes scanning the surroundings for any signs of unwanted company. Madison rose onto the deck of the boat, her heart pounding in her ears as she cautiously peeked to see if the coast was clear. With determination, one of the men strolled purposefully along the docks, his footsteps echoing against the wooden planks. Her memory was hazy, but she had a nagging feeling that it could have been one of the armed men. Everything happened in a blur, like a whirlwind of events. Where was Logan? The moment she hit the water, the sharp sound of gunshots pierced the air. Had they killed him? She hoped not. Their lack of defence would make her and Beth easy targets for their determined pursuers. The man moved further away, causing her to suspect that he had already scanned the area they had emerged from and failed to spot them.

"I think we are clear." She said.

As she lifted Bethany onto the boat, her muscles screamed with exhaustion. They collapsed onto the ground, panting heavily, and rolled onto their backs to catch their breath. In that moment, Madison's mind was filled with thoughts of Logan. Where was he? Looking over the side, she felt a cool breeze brush against her face, but there was no sign of anything on the water. He was nowhere in sight.

"Where is he?" She mumbled to herself, worried for his safety.

"Well, there were gun shots. So most likely dead. What do you care? You barely knew him."

Her daughter's observation was accurate - she hadn't had much time to get to know the man. No matter the duration of their relationship, her caring nature remained unwavering.

No matter the circumstances, she would always lend a helping hand to those in need, whether they were injured or in peril. She had a strong desire to help him however she could. Worry began to set in, and she couldn't help but bite her lip in concern.

"He saved me! When we were attacked, he could have left me there to get captured. But he didn't. It is only right that I help him. Don't ever tell me if I should or shouldn't care about someone!"

Noticing Bethany's shocked face, she couldn't help but wonder if her own reaction had startled her. But Beth's gaze was drawn to something else.

"I don't mean to yell Beth. Sorry. It's just everything that has happened..."

Beth pointed behind her mother, her finger trembling slightly. The sound of a click made Madison turn her head, only to be met with the chilling sight of the armed man, his glock 17 aimed directly at her. Without hesitation, she raised her hands in surrender, and her daughter quickly followed suit. The thought of death was equally unwelcome to both of them.

"Please don't hurt us." She cried.

He reached into his pocket, pulling out two cable ties.

"Her first, then she can do you. Now!"

Bethany wondered to herself. The absence of police was conspicuous and raised questions. Her mother had mentioned the harrowing experience of being targeted by gunshots earlier in the day. They had been chased and going by what Madison heard, more shots were fired. Strangely, not a single police officer had made an appearance. The cops would be quick to investigate a situation like this, particularly in a place such as Cornwall. Big shootings are not a common occurrence in this place. It plagued her mind. There was no doubt that these people had some kind of influence over the authorities.

"Why are you doing this?" Beth asked, her voice shaky.

Their wrists were firmly connected as they fastened the cable ties around them. They exchanged worried glances, determined not to exacerbate the man's emotions. Each of them pondering the question. Where did the other two go? Had Logan taken two down with him?

"You two are going to make him very happy. Well the kid will. You on the other hand, you might not survive the night if he has his way."

As memories of her traumatic past with Damien resurfaced, fear washed over Madison once again, causing her to relive the uncertainty and dread she had endured. Would he be in a good mood when he got home that night? Or a bad one? She would spend each day filled with unease, constantly on edge, waiting for his return from work. His occupation as a security guard was something she had accepted without question until recently. However, deep down, she always had a lingering suspicion that he was hiding a secret life.

"Mum. What does he mean?" Bethany was puzzled by the man's remarks about her father's hatred of her mother.

The truth was a painful prospect, yet she couldn't resist contemplating how much longer it could remain undisclosed.

Within twenty-four hours, she could find herself on the verge of death, uncertain of how events would unfold.

"He is probably still angry about us leaving. He was never good at letting things go."

Beth's intelligence was a defining trait that set her apart from others. There had always been a lingering suspicion in her mind that there was a deeper reason behind their sudden departure from London, something her mother never fully explained. Something had happened. In her youth, she was unable to fully grasp the significance of the situation. Nevertheless, she no longer considered herself a child and had a deep aversion to being lied to. Even though she'd lied about her relationship with Michael.

"Why have you never told me the full truth about why we had to leave? I've known you lied for a while. I just want the truth."

As they spoke, the sound of a thud caught their attention. They turned to see an armed man, fallen to the ground with a knife protruding from his back. In the distance, Logan stood, a solitary figure against the backdrop of the horizon. The sight of his left arm covered in crimson red caught their attention. Madison's eyes widened as she noticed him, causing her to instinctively rise to her feet.

"Logan!"

With a burst of energy, she sprinted towards him and embraced him tightly. She held him close, cherishing the feeling of his presence after fearing she would never see him again.

"I knew you weren't dead. Oh God, your arm." She was

concerned by the blood covering his clothing and arm.

"I'm not that easy to kill. Don't worry, it's fine. Got supplies at mine, so will get it patched up." He laughed.

Beth was as motionless as a statue, not making a single move. The sight of the dead body sent a wave of shock through her. The sight of the blade jutting out of the man's spine held her captive, unable to look away. It wasn't fear that consumed her, but rather a morbid curiosity about the way he was slain. Rising to her feet, she approached her mother and Logan, the warmth of their presence filling her heart.

"You did good, old man. Even I thought you were dead."

"Are you both okay? Not harmed at all?"

They shook their heads in relief, and he smiled, reassured that neither of them had been harmed. He looked to his boat, its sleek white exterior gleaming in the sunlight.

"Come on. Let's get on the boat. Our time frame for getting supplies is now a lot shorter."

He approached his boat. He pulled the key from his back pocket, feeling its cold metal against his fingertips. Logan skilfully untied the boat from the sturdy post it was securely fastened to while Madison and Beth eagerly climbed aboard. After finishing, he climbed onto the driver's spot, feeling the discomfort of its seat-less design. He had the option to install one, but ultimately chose not to. Now he regretted that decision. As the key slid into the ignition, the engine came alive with a sudden roar, accompanied by a subtle stutter. Pushing the accelerator up, they headed off towards his island.

"Thank you." Madison said.

"For what?"

*Well, obviously for saving them. Idiot. At least I'd know that.*

"Saving us and just being here. Can I ask you something?"

The mere thought of someone potentially asking more about their past sends most people into panic mode, their minds racing with anxiety. Uncertain, he wondered if she would press for more details about his ties to their attackers or if her curiosity would lead her elsewhere. Either way, he was prepared. He knew that he had to stay prepared for anything that might happen, no matter what. Make sure you have a detailed plan, a contingency plan, and multiple alternatives. He had learned through experience that being highly knowledgeable and prepared for all eventualities was the key to success. Unexpected events had taken him by surprise at times in his life. He felt prepared for whatever she was bound to ask.

"Sure."

"Before, you'd mentioned them, when asking about Damien being glad to find me. Who did you mean by them?"

"Damien works for some horrible people. Ones whose main goal is to take over the government and build their version of a new world. I worked for them for many years, doing odd jobs. Gathering intel on people, typical recon. Sometimes I'd have to keep watch of one person for a week or a month. Damien was one of the right-hand men to the boss and he was always willing to do whatever was necessary for the cause." He exclaimed.

Aware of Bethany's presence, he chose not to disclose

certain details as she sat and listened. The fear of his children's reaction haunted him as he confronted the reality of his job: eliminating those considered dangerous to the government. As he looked at Beth, he noticed the same sparkle in her eyes that his daughter Leah had, but with a touch of wisdom that only time could bring. He longed for the chance to rewrite his past and create a better future. Be there for his children. His work had always been top priority.

"Who are the people he works for?"

"An organisation lead by a man called Kane Hunt. Used to be both of his sons by his side. But one of them was killed. The other Evan, he was always different. Looking for peaceful solutions to everything. Out of everyone I worked for in my life, when I worked with Evan for a time. It made me realise that not everyone is bad." He revealed.

"So these people are the type of villains you see in movies?" Bethany asked.

"That's actually a pretty good description for them."

As she looked out at the sea stretching endlessly around them, she couldn't help but ponder the multitude of questions she had about her father. He was a distant memory to her, always away and perpetually discontent when he was around.

"Was my dad a killer? Don't lie to me. I'll know."

"Is. He is a killer. I'll be honest, he has a dark side that I'd never seen in anyone else. I've seen him do things that made my stomach churn and I thought nothing could really do that."

She couldn't bring herself to believe him, with every inch

of her being opposing it. Her father, a brutal, unforgiving killer. She was reluctant to accept it. She wondered her father would say differently. Make it clear that Logan was the cold-blooded killer instead. Not him. It would be hard for any child to come to terms with the fact that their parent's job was to end lives.

"Would he say differently, though? Maybe he will say that you are that man."

Logan hadn't expecting that, he guessed there would be resistance in believing that the girls dad was a 's dad was a murderer. But not that it would be turned on him. He had no plan to argue with her. He sympathised with her lack of trust in a man's word given their limited acquaintance.

"He may do. I'm not that man, though. But if you do encounter him, you can ask him yourself."

He turned to see Madison, her eyes filled with disappointment, silently conveying her disapproval.

*She looks ready to kill you. Guess you shouldn't have said that.*

"Although I don't know if your mother wants him near you. It's not up to me."

*Quick thinking. Smart.*

As she looked at Madison, her expression revealed her unwavering resolve.

"If I see my father. I am going to ask him and no one is going to stop me. I know you have reasons to keep me away from him. But you aren't the most forthcoming with information and either is your new friend. So I will ask my dad myself if I get the chance."

Suddenly, a hush fell upon the boat, broken only by the

relentless crashing of waves.

# 13

Through Penzance's bustling streets, a sleek Range Rover glided past, its tinted windows shielding the occupants from prying eyes. Peering through the window, Marcus scanned the environment, his senses heightened as he looked for the man who had haunted his thoughts for years. One of their agents claimed they had successfully killed him, or at least believed they had accomplished the task. But he doubted a regular agent had the skills necessary to defeat the formidable Logan Winters. Logan's unparalleled skill and intelligence were undeniable. Even Marcus had to admit it. Though they were adversaries, he couldn't help but admire his enemy's skills as both a fighter and a killer. The man callously left him behind, a blade embedded in his left eye, as if it were a trophy. Despite the odds stacked against him,

Marcus cheated death and survived the burning building, where he was abandoned and unconscious. The taste of revenge consumed him, driving his every action.

Not focused on finding an enemy, Evan leisurely observed the stunning scenery from the back seat of the car. Cornwall was uncharted territory for him, but now he was enticed by the idea of vacationing there. Looking at the ocean, his eyes widened with delight, his love for the vastness of the big blue sea evident in his expression. Damien's steady hands firmly grasped the wheel as he sat in the driver's seat. The back and sides of his hair were cropped short, but the top boasted a well-maintained length. With a left-parted top, he displayed a fresh, clean-shaven look. His face bore the evidence of battles fought, with two scars tracing over his right eye and a unique serrated scar on his lip. The large circular scar on his cheek revealed the aftermath of being shot in the side of the mouth. The mere thought of Damien sent shivers down Evan's spine, knowing the evil he was capable of.

"Don't you think if he was still alive, he'd have fled by now?" Evan said.

"He's alive. I know it. He isn't that easy to kill. Logan would need supplies, which he'd have stored somewhere. We find where the supplied are. We find him." Marcus replied adamantly.

Damien, who typically had a lot to say, was uncharacteristically quiet on this day. With unwavering determination, he kept his mind focused on finding Madison and Bethany, his eyes filled with a fiery rage. Evan often pondered the idea that Damien, with his apparent lack of soul, was actually a devil imprisoned within a man's physical vessel. Marcus had deployed his network of agents worldwide, leaving no stone unturned in the search for Logan. He doubted that Logan would risk staying in the country after the events that transpired. But then he knew that Logan would expect him to think that, and most likely do the opposite, just to keep things unpredictable.

"When we find him, I will kill him. No matter what, he is my kill."

"As long as no one harms Maddie or Beth, I don't care what you do. I will say though, what makes you think you will best this man in combat this time around." Damien spoke with conviction, his voice deep and authoritative.

"I have something he doesn't this time."

"What's that?" Damien and Evan asked, almost in sync.

"Surprise. He believes I am dead. He isn't going to be expecting me to make an appearance. Being a dead man and all." He rubbed his fingers over the burns on the side of his face and his neck.

"He's gonna pay for what he done to me."

The sight of a boat in the distance immediately caught Evan's attention, while the others remained oblivious. Its destination was unmistakable - a small island on the horizon. He wondered if that secluded spot was Logan's secret refuge from the chaos of the world. Utilising his intelligence, he had successfully hacked into the systems when Logan initially vanished. After some investigation, he managed to discover that the man's money had been transferred to multiple accounts, all registered under different names. However, the money remained untouched and unused. With each passing month, it continued to sit idly in the accounts. Evan's regular check-ins were fuelled by his determination to demonstrate his capabilities as a soldier. He was resolute in his mission to find the contingency man and deliver him to his family. Prove himself to them once and for all. After a year, he had grown weary and decided to quit. But one day, curiosity got the better of Evan, and he decided to investigate. To his dismay, he found that all the money had disappeared.

Determined and focused, he tirelessly worked to trace the path of the missing money, discovering that it had been transferred. But the money was untraceable, a challenge that required exceptional skill and resourcefulness. He spent weeks infiltrating various government programs, using any means necessary. His father's lack of trust meant that he had few resources at his disposal. Despite having limited resources, six months after the money vanished, he stumbled upon a clue that shed light on its whereabouts. A fraction of the money was donated to a cancer charity, with the majority of it being invested in the purchase of an island. He had never been successful in pinpointing the specific coordinates of said island. It was clear that Logan was intelligent, evident in his flawless skill at covering his tracks. The company had a strong reason for not wanting to let him go - he was their greatest asset, and no business wants to lose such valuable talent.

As he sat there, he observed the boat in the distance drawing nearer to the island. In his thoughts, he contemplated how to inform the two killers in the front that it could potentially be Logan's residence. Marcus was a piece of work, and the satisfaction that surged through Evan when he believed Marcus was dead was indescribable. In comparison to Marcus, he didn't possess the same strength, leaving him constantly perceived as inferior. Despite his lack of power, he compensated with his sharp intellect. With a watchful eye, he managed the business's funds, meticulously ensuring that everything was done according to regulations. Still, he was never given the proper recognition by his family, despite his deserving of it. Now he questioned whether divulging his discovery to his brother could bring him the admiration he longed for.

"How has Logan managed to evade you for all these years?" Evan asked.

With a swift motion, Marcus turned in his seat, his fists poised to collide with his brother's face as a result of his audacious question.

"Evade. He hasn't evaded me for all these years. He thinks I'm dead."

"Well, I meant the company in general. All those agents that have searched for him for the past what eight and a half years. I found information that might be of use to you, though." He said, his voice getting higher near the end.

Whether it was a short temper or an inability to wait, patience was never his brother's virtue. He was a volcano of fury, constantly on the brink of eruption.

"Spit it out then. What fucking information?!" He shouted.

"So, a while back, I hacked the systems, checking for where Logan's money had gone. We knew he'd spread it between different accounts and dad had informed us not to freeze the money, as it's one thing that could lead us to him. So I kept an eye on it. Months went by and that money didn't move at all. I gave up and then, after about six months, I thought I'd check it again. It was all gone, but somehow he'd made it appear on the systems that it was all still there, even when it wasn't. But I had noticed…"

As his brother continued the story, Marcus grew increasingly restless, leading him to interrupt.

"Are you going to get to the information part, or read us a fucking book?"

"He bought an island. I could never pinpoint where, though, but there is a small island off the coast of Penzance. I'm thinking that is his hideout."

As the two men in the front pondered, they exchanged knowing glances, aware of their adversary's cleverness. Damien swiftly dismissed it, not even bothering to entertain the idea. Knowing Logan's thought process, Marcus could easily envision him buying an island to live in seclusion and evade detection.

"The last place our guys saw him, before apparently being killed, was at the boating docks. So your theory makes sense, brother."

Marcus tapped his hand on his brother's leg, recognising his brilliance for once.

"See, you can be useful."

It wasn't the ideal form of respect he longed for, but he was willing to tolerate it for now. If only his brother understood that their father's vision of them working as a team was the key to their success in capturing Logan. Combining his cleverness with his brothers' tactical expertise and raw strength, they would be an unstoppable force.

"We're gonna need a boat." Marcus exclaimed.

# 14

Arriving at the island, Madison and Bethany were taken aback by the sight of a picturesque dock waiting for them at the rear. Positioned in the middle of the island, his home offered a strategic advantage for escaping, if necessary. He had multiple directions to go in, each offering a different path to escape. Being a prepared man, he already had various escape routes meticulously planned, accounting for every possible scenario. Concealed beneath the surface, his bunker sat undetectable from the ground. The house contained a hidden hatch, creating a clandestine passage leading directly into it. The side of the house boasted a reinforced shed, its exterior showing the signs of multiple storms it had braved. Inside both the bunker and shed, there was an array of weapons, beverages, sustenance, and crucial provisions needed to survive during emergencies.

As Bethany surveyed her surroundings, she marvelled at the diverse assortment of grasses and trees that enveloped the house. It astonished her to see signs of human habitation in such a remote location.

"Do you get wifi?" She asked.

*Bloody teenagers, all they care about is the internet. Do something useful!*

He chuckled at the irony that, of all things, the Internet held the highest significance in her mind. Logan was baffled by the constant need for online connectivity among the youth in the current generation.

"There is internet yes. But trust me, we won't be staying here long enough to be using it."

Her expression of disappointment resembled that of a child who had just been told they couldn't have ice cream or sweets. Bethany studied his appearance, hoping to gain some insight into his true nature.

"Are you rich?" She asked.

"Beth!" Madison lightly slapped the back of her daughter's shoulder.

"What? The man owns a freaking island. He has to have money."

Bethany turned her attention back to Logan, her curiosity piqued.

"Also, why do you live on an island alone? Do you hate people that much? Or is it that you want to keep yourself away from others because you are secretly a serial killer?" She questioned him bluntly.

*Or maybe it's that people hate you. Did she not think that?*

It must have been odd for them to comprehend why a man would choose to live alone on an island, distancing himself from society. It didn't give any indications of a nice man, instead, it emanated the feeling of him safeguarding others from his own presence. The island was shrouded in mystery, leaving Bethany to wonder if it was the site of his deadly deeds. It brought a light heartedness to his mood as he saw the humour in it.

"I am definitely a serial killer, bringing my victims here by boat and then killing them, cutting them up and eating them. Do I give off serial killer vibes, then? I hope I don't. I thought I had more of a hobo look than that of a killer." He laughed.

"I live on the island for the peace and to stay away from people. My old job was one that made a bunch of people want to kill or torture me. So I chose a life off the grid. Also, no, I wouldn't say I'm rich. I have money."

*Why are you so modest? The work you did brought in a lot of money, we basically live off the interest.*

Madison and Beth followed him up the hill, feeling the burn in their legs with each step as they made their way towards his house. Meanwhile, her daughter seemed more concerned with checking her phone and discussing Logan's wealth. Madison's heart raced as she fretted over Logan's wound, also dreading the possibility of more armed men showing up. And hoping that fate would be kind enough to spare her from encountering the one person she had purposely kept her distance from for years.

Damien had been absent from Bethany's life for several years; the last time she saw her father, she was only five years old. He had informed her before leaving that he wouldn't be back for a couple of weeks due to work commitments. With her mother's support, Madison had been actively involved in the process of acquiring a house in a distant location. She had to escape from a sadistic man, who had repeatedly come dangerously close to ending his own wife's life. The overwhelming sense of fear that Damien emitted caused her legs to tremble uncontrollably. She collapsed, the world spinning around her in a dizzying blur. With swift reflexes, Bethany and Logan immediately reached out to assist her in standing up.

"Are you okay?" He asked.

"Yeah, just tripped over my own feet. See clumsy, like I said." Brushing it off quickly.

She had a sense of her own mortality, knowing that she might not survive the week, but she didn't want them to fret over her. Damien had made her a promise before. If she had the audacity to snatch his daughter away, he promised to find her and subject her to a protracted, excruciating end. Their love, once a blazing fire, dwindled to mere embers within their relationship. She remained with him out of fear, trapped in a cycle of uncertainty and dread. She hoped that he'd never discover their whereabouts. Now she had Logan by her side, which gave her a newfound sense of security for herself and Bethany. Still, she kept the truth hidden from him. Revealing that truth would undoubtedly erode his trust in her, and the possibility of her daughter leaving with her dad loomed over Madison's thoughts.

As they approached his house, Logan reached the front door and welcomed them inside with a sweeping gesture. They both followed him in, their curious eyes scanning the area. The mix of grey and dark blue walls, combined with the minimalist layout of the two-bedroom house, gave it a distinctly masculine feel. Madison felt like a needed a female touch.

"What did you do for work before you became a recluse?" Bethany asked.

"I was a soldier for many years, then I worked as security."

Logan hesitated, contemplating whether to ask a few questions himself. She pondered his response, her attention shifting between the perfectly maintained living room, office, and kitchen. The cleanliness of the place left both her and Madison in awe.

"Did your wife clean before we got here?" Beth didn't know any better. She hadn't been informed of the man's history.

Madison went to stop her daughter from prying for more information. Yet Logan intervened, understanding that while he couldn't disclose everything, he could still share some pertinent information.

"My wife died nine years ago. It is me who keeps it clean, I don't like mess. Never have. My father always got me to clean up, so it was drilled into me at a young age that a home should always be spotlessly clean. Plus, I live alone, not like I'd make much mess."

The absence of noise created a stillness that permeated every corner of the house. Suddenly, the young girl found herself at a loss for words. Worried about saying the incorrect thing and unsettling him.

*Why would you let strangers into your home? Stop being so*

*fucking nice! Eliminate them. No loose ends. Then find those fuckers who killed Lilly, torture them, and then remove their fucking heads from their bodies. Burn that fucking company to the ground. Better yet, let me do it!*

Fighting against the force within him, he felt a sharp pain radiating in his head. He felt weaker than usual, his strength waning as the mental battle raged on. The last time it happened, Magnus made an unexpected appearance, and everything descended into mayhem. Logan engaged in a daily struggle to keep him from breaking free once more. Bad things always seemed to follow in Magnus's wake, like a dark cloud of misfortune. 'No. Stop being so aggressive.' He thought to himself, attempting to fight back.

"I'm sorry about your wife. That's really sad. You shouldn't be alone, though. Company is good, stops you from losing your mind." Bethany said.

If only she knew. Years ago, his mind fractured under the weight of the things he had seen and done, and the loss of his wife and children shattered it completely. Living alone, he tried to fortify his mind, constantly reminding himself to stay focused, like a captain steering a ship through rough waters. On the island, his routine included engaging in activities like reading, writing, and going for refreshing runs multiple times throughout the day. The burden of his fractured mind compelled him to seek solace in companionship, and as fate would have it, Magnus was there, patiently waiting for him. Born from the realm of insanity, Magnus found his true calling within its turbulent grasp.

"No need to apologise, you didn't know. I've always been

a bit of a lone wolf."

Stepping into his kitchen, Logan's hand instinctively reached for the cupboard on his far left, the smooth surface cool to the touch. Inside, there was a green box adorned with a vibrant red plus symbol. He carefully pulled it out and opened it, revealing a stash of medical supplies that he reached in and grabbed. He pulled open the cutlery drawer and quickly selected a knife, passing it to Madison as she entered the kitchen. A quizzical expression crossed her face as she glanced at him.

"Erm… what am I doing with this?" She asked.

"I need you to heat it up on the stove. I'm gonna get the bullet out and clean the wound. I need you to quarterize it."

She began shaking her head vigorously, her hair flying in all directions. It was an unfamiliar task that she had never encountered and had no desire to undertake. What if she did it wrong? Panic began to set in, and she could feel her palms becoming sweaty.

"Don't worry. You can't really do it wrong. If that's what you're thinking. I can see the panic on your face."

Removing his top, he revealed a body that had the strong, solid build of a father figure. He was far from being fat; instead, he had a fairly trim figure. His beer consumption had caused his stomach to become slightly distended. Nonetheless, her eyes wandered aimlessly, uncertain of where to settle. Flustered by the man's body, she couldn't help but blush. From the green box, he retrieved a pair of tweezers, their stainless steel glinting in the light. Reaching into a lower cupboard, he felt the cool glass of the vodka bottle in his hand. He poured some over the little metal utensil, the liquid making a soft hissing sound as it hit the surface. Taking several gulps of the alcoholic beverage, he set the glass down with a heavy thud and focused on the task at hand - getting the bullet out. By narrowly missing any veins or arteries, the injury proved to be non-life-threatening and caused no significant damage. With precision, he dug into the wound and recovered the bullet in no time, as Madison heated up the blade.

"I think it's hot enough, it's glowing."

With the knife held firmly in her hand, she locked eyes with him, silently seeking confirmation. As their eyes met, he offered her a reassuring nod.

"That's perfect. Now press it against the wound. I may pass out, I may not. But just be ready for that. I'll be fine though. Hold it there for at least nine seconds."

She approached. He prepared with a grimace, his face contorting in anticipation of the impending searing pain. The intense heat of the metal on his skin made him grit his teeth, fighting back the urge to cry out. It felt like being stabbed with a hot iron. He hastily reached for the vodka once more, the strong scent hitting his nostrils, and drank until she moved the knife off his skin.

"Fuck that hurt."

Being in close proximity to him, she observed the numerous scars that marred his torso. Stab wounds, bullet wounds. From his scars and wounds, it was clear that he had endured his fair share of pain, or perhaps he found pleasure in being shot and stabbed. Madison swiftly wrapped the wound, making sure to cushion it with padding and secure it with a bandage.

"So, you've been shot before?" She asked, looking at the scars on his back. His body was riddled with them.

"A few times, yeah. It came with the job."

She gently ran her finger over a few of them, feeling the rough texture and wondering about the stories they held. As she looked at the man in front of her, she couldn't help but feel a combination of intrigue and unease. It wasn't that he would hurt her, but rather what he was capable of doing to others. Her thoughts were consumed by the temptation to remove his remaining clothing. As she continued to brush her hands over his scarred body, she could feel the warmth radiating from his skin. In that instant, he felt a rush of emotions and pulled her closer, their lips almost brushing against each other.

Holding nun chucks, Bethany entered the room and clumsily swung them, accidentally hitting herself.

"Ow. Shit!"

Both adults turned towards her, their eyes wide with surprise, as if she had interrupted something unexpected.

"Don't play with that, Beth. It's not a toy." Madison said.

"Sorry. It looked cool."

Noticing that Logan was not impressed, she let the weapon fall to her side with a disappointed sigh.

"I'll put it back." She rushed off.

Madison left, feeling awkward, and cautiously began to explore the house. She was taken aback when she realised that the living room was devoid of a television. Instead, the walls were lined with bookcases, filled to the brim with books, and when she entered his office, it was no different. The laptop stood out as the primary electronic device amidst the other items. In the corner of the room, a table displayed a Black Olivetti typewriter from the 1930s, its glass moulding protecting it from dust and time's wear. She couldn't help but wonder if he had ever put it to use, or if it was merely a valued possession. Before she could utter a word, Logan dashed outside and vanished into his shed, the creak of the door closing behind him was the first indication that he'd disappeared.

While searching through his shed, he quickly retrieved a conveniently packed bag containing canned food, an ample supply of water, multiple changes of clothing, and, of course, a couple of weapons. He carefully inspected the contents of the bag, making sure that everything he had placed inside was still present. Magnus was known for his tendency to prioritise weapons over everything else, resulting in an imbalanced inventory. It appeared that everything was there, except for his M4 Carbine and its stockpile of five, five, six bullets. The gun used a gas operated, magazine fed carbine. The weapon was his trusted ally, a reliable companion that had seen him through years of combat. Magnus had a strong preference for the AK-12, a Russian assault rifle known for its 5.45×39mm cartridges, while Logan insisted the weapon perfectly embodied his psychotic alter ego.

With a sigh, he withdrew the unwanted gun and began his quest for his desired weapon. It was evident that it had been cleverly concealed.

*Oh, I wonder where it could be? I don't get why you like that pile of garbage. Use a proper gun.*

"It's a good weapon. I like using it!" He yelled.

Madison emerged, peeking her head through the shed door.

"Are you okay? I heard you yell..."

Her eyes were drawn to the weapon on the ground beside him, as well as the assortment of weapons hanging on the walls. She had never witnessed such an arsenal of weapons before, and this man appeared ready to engage in warfare. Admittedly, she had only witnessed one gun in her life, and it was during a traumatic encounter where it was held to her head and then inserted into her mouth. But she preferred to bury that memory deep within her mind.

"That is a lot of guns. Who are you planning on going to war with?" She mumbled.

Logan did not want her seeing all of his weapons, knowing that they were not all confined to his shed. He had plenty hidden in discreet places, carefully tucked away from prying eyes. The sight of countless firearms would have sent most people into a state of terror, but Madison showed no signs of fear. Her gaze shifted to a look of intrigue, as she leaned in closer to get a better view.

"I've collected these over the years. Some have never been used. But I believe in being over prepared for every situation, than under prepared." He said.

Thorough investigation and over-preparation were his firm beliefs. Having multiple backup plans is crucial when you already have a plan, as it helps mitigate the impact of unexpected events and provides a safety net. The reason behind his code-name, The Contingency Man, was his knack for handling unforeseen circumstances. His unique trait among assassins was his ability to have an intricate web of plans, far beyond the typical plan A and B. Despite occasionally testing the patience of his bosses by requesting additional time for missions, he stood alone as the hired assassin with an impeccable track record of success. He chose not to complete his final assignment because he couldn't bear to kill a man who wasn't considered a significant threat. Logan's conscience was a constant source of frustration for the company. Most of their contractors were ruthless assassins, motivated solely by money. They were ruthless killers, showing no mercy to anyone, regardless of age. No questions asked. Not Logan. His curiosity compelled him to delve into the specifics and grasp every detail.

"Why do these people want you dead so bad? I get you killed someone. But there's got to be more to it."

Logan hesitated to reveal the full truth, despite sensing a level of trust between them. He was keenly aware that she was harbouring a major undisclosed matter, Unbeknownst to Bethany.

"A job went bad, someone died. They never forgave me for it. What is it that you are hiding, though? I know how dangerous Damien is, but it sounds like he wants his daughter and you are collateral. Something really bad happened between you for him to want you dead. I'd heard of him having a partner. He spoke of you highly and what you'd done for him."

She was caught off guard by his kind words, which stirred up a whirlwind of confusion, fear, and anger within her. Throughout their time together, she observed that he seldom showed appreciation for her, except in the initial stages of their romance. If it weren't for her pregnancy, she would have left him earlier than she did. However, the desire for love consumed her upon meeting him, his embrace providing solace during a time of darkness and hopelessness. He saved her, if he'd have walked through that park ten minutes later, she'd have not been there. Instead, she had intended to be at the train station, getting ready to throw herself in front of a moving train. Despite hitting rock bottom, she found solace in Damien's presence and the gift of their beautiful daughter. She was smitten with him in no time, charmed by his tendency to wine and dine her when he wasn't busy with work. Taking her home to indulge in passion in the bedroom, their intimate moments were the most fulfilling aspect of their relationship, as she had confided in her former best friend on numerous occasions. He had an innate ability to navigate a woman's body with ease. Reflecting on the happy memories they had together, doubt started to creep into her mind. Was her decision to run wrong?

"I mean, it's difficult. I barely know you and in my head, I feel like over sharing won't get me anywhere. He was nice for a time. He made me feel happy at a time when I no longer wanted to live. But things changed and let's just say the real him made many appearances and that scared me. I feared for my own life and my daughters."

Knowing the man she spoke of, he couldn't help but feel a

mixture of fear and relief that she had survived being with someone who he considered heartless. Unaffected by the loss of innocent lives, the man showed no emotion as he carried out the brutal killings in a village in Africa. Instead, he found amusement in the cacophony of their screams as they burned. Logan contemplated the notion that Damien's relationship with Madison was supposed to be short-lived, only to have his plans shattered when she became pregnant. He couldn't just abandon her. He was a disturbing man, emitting an unsettling aura, but one thing Logan learnt about him was his unwavering loyalty to family, willing to defend them at any cost.

"I get that and honestly, I feel the same. We barely know each other, but we are now stuck together in this mess and I feel guilty, because if they hadn't have found me, they wouldn't have found you. It was them looking for me, that dragged you into this because unfortunately, you have a history with Damien. I know we don't know each other very well. But I can promise you now, I will do everything in my power to protect you and your daughter."

Beth's face was etched with concern as she hurried towards her mother.

"There's a boat coming! Three men are on it." She yelled panicky.

Logan's gaze fixed upon the living room window, where he could make out the vehicle drawing nearer, its engine rumbling in the distance. The limited time available left little room for thorough preparation. But he was a man with nefarious plans for such an event, ensuring they would deeply regret stepping foot in his domain. As Logan caught sight of the man he thought was no more, a jarring shock coursed through him, hitting him like a tonne of bricks. Marcus Hunt was alive. The last time he saw him, he had plunged a knife into his eye, after beating him senseless. Abandoned in the burning building, there was no indication that the man could escape. But it was clear that he had somehow slipped through death's fingers.

"Impossible."

As he turned to Madison, his hand instinctively found its place on her shoulder.

"Can you drive a boat?" He asked.

"I drove my dad's once." She replied.

Satisfied, he deemed it to be sufficient.

"That's okay then. I need you and Bethany to get to the boat, I will lure those men to me. If I'm not at the boat within six minutes, I need you to go okay?"

Reluctantly, she turned away from him, her heart heavy with the thought of leaving him behind. She could sense it in his touch. It felt like he was saying goodbye, his fingertips lingering for a moment longer than usual.

"I can't leave you here."

"You may have no choice. Think about you and Bethany, okay. If I don't make it there, I need you to leave. Trust me, I've got this. Now go, quickly."

# 15

Marcus, Evan and Damien grew ever closer to Logan's island. The sight of the two men, with their Glocks holstered and mac 17 machine guns strapped to their bandoliers. Their target was on the brink of experiencing the repercussions for his deeds. From his seat at the rear of the boat, Evan marvelled at the endless blue of the ocean surrounding them. His comrades had fierce gazes, but his was soft and understanding. He sat serenely, watching the rhythmic dance of the waves. Like Logan, he was a man who enjoyed meticulous planning and having a contingency plan. On the other hand, his brother believed that they could tackle their target on the island with little need for extensive planning.

"I'm unsure about this." Evan uttered.

Spinning around abruptly, Marcus's displeasure at his

brother's doubt was palpable. Damien remained focused on driving the boat.

"About what? You seem to be unsure of everything. Stop being an anxious idiot and be the man our father wants you to be."

"Do you really think that he isn't going to have a plan for unwanted visitors?"

Paying no mind to his brother's words, Marcus returned his attention to the captivating sights of the island. Only thirty seconds remained until they reached their destination, and his burning desire to annihilate the man who robbed him of his eye and left him to die intensified.

"He is going to die. I will make sure of that. Have faith, little brother. Have faith."

With a swift motion, he withdrew a walkie talkie from his pocket, which was hidden within his cargo trousers. By pressing the button on the side of the device, he brought it close to his mouth to initiate communication.

"Red one, are you in position?" He asked.

After a brief pause, a voice reverberated and filled the silence.

"You should be seeing us any second."

The sound of the helicopter's propellers spinning rapidly filled the air, foreshadowing its imminent arrival before it came into view. Coming in from behind the island, their arrival would surely catch Logan's attention, whether he was prepared or not. Inside the chopper, the pilot and co-pilot were focused on the controls while three armed soldiers sat in the back. Equipped with a L115A3 Long range sniper rifle, one of the soldiers had the advantage of being able to target and eliminate enemies from the comfort of the air vehicle. Marcus shot a smug grin at his brother as he quickly looked back.

"Did you think I didn't have a plan. They are trapped, any attempt to escape and they'll be killed."

He couldn't help but smile with satisfaction, knowing that Logan Winters was trapped and revenge was within his grasp. Evan was still uncertain, but amazed by his sibling's rare display of foresight. The helicopter reached the sky above the island, its rotors slicing through the air with a steady hum. As the sniper surveyed the ground, he focused on detecting any potential threats.

"Two females are approaching the boat to the rear of the island."

Before Marcus could reply, Damien swiftly snatched the walkie talkie from his hand.

"Take out the boat's engine. Do not harm either of them."

"Copy." He replied.

The sharp sound of a shot pierced the air, accompanied by the unmistakable sound of more bullets being fired. A sharp crack rang out from the island, hitting the target with deadly precision. The bullet pierced through the sniper's eye, causing a violent explosion of blood and brain matter as it exited through the back of his head, tearing through his helmet before ricocheting off the metal inside the chopper.

"Sniper down! I repeat, sniper down. We are under…" The pilot's words were abruptly halted.

With a deafening bang, a bullet tore through the window,

finding its way into his neck and leaving a gruesome splatter of blood on his seat. The weight of his body crashing onto the controls sent the helicopter into a wild, uncontrollable spin. The co-pilot's attempts to regain control were in vain, as the fast-approaching demise of him and his comrades became undeniable.

"Jump!!" He yelled, diving out of the door and into the waters below.

As the chopper soared through the air, the two soldiers leaped out of the side, one of them mistiming their jump. The propellers tore through his flesh, reducing his body to a gruesome pulp, while blood sprayed across the water like a torrential downpour. Upon reaching the water safely, the other man dove in and felt the refreshing embrace of the cool waves, propelling himself away from the descending helicopter. CRASH! The moment it made contact with the water, a massive wave engulfed him, leaving him gasping for air. Fortunately, the chopper missed him, avoiding the terrifying prospect of being dragged down into the depths or just killed on impact.

Marcus, Evan, and Damien stood frozen, their hearts pounding in their chests as they witnessed the horrifying scene before them. That unexpected turn of events was not part of his plan. A fury grew within him, fierce and untamed, just like the raging flames that had left him scarred.

"I'm gonna kill that bastard!" He screamed.

With a smug expression, Evan sat back confidently, as if he had been waiting for this moment to prove his point. Upon reaching land, his brother and Damien hastily disembarked from the boat, their footsteps echoing on the solid ground. He, on the other hand, lingered, apprehensive of what awaited him. He decided to take a step back and oversee the situation from a distance, adopting a supervisory approach. It surprised him that his brother and fellow colleague chose to go their separate ways. Their approach was a daring and captivating mix of intrigue and recklessness. As they exited the water, droplets cascaded off the co-pilot of the chopper and the soldier, who then trailed behind Marcus towards the house. Logan appeared at the front door, unaffected by the enemies approaching, his expression calm and composed. A trap? Reaching for his phone, he put his finger to his ear.

"Marcus turn back now!, It's a trap!"

A deafening silence followed his words, leaving him feeling uneasy. Uncertain if Marcus had received his transmission through the earpiece, he waited in suspense. He was torn between his own desire to live and his fear of witnessing his brother's demise. Despite their contrasting personalities, they were united by their familial ties. Despite being a member of the family, he often felt like the odd one out, the black sheep. Memories of his mother were hazy and distant, like a faded photograph. Had she been like him? Was that where he got more of the brains that the brawn from? Questions gnawed at him incessantly, day in and day out. But his father never provided answers, leaving a void of information about her. A haunting memory etched into his young mind, Evan was forever marked by the car crash that took his mother's life when he was only nine years old. Her face eluded his memory, always slipping away like mist in the morning, leaving him with a sense of longing and frustration. Not a single photograph of her could be found, as if she had never been captured on film. Something that he never understood. What had she done to be erased from existence?

Racing up the grass hill towards Logan's house, he could feel the adrenaline pumping through his veins after diving off the boat. With a sense of urgency, he pushed himself to reach his brother before it was too late. An unsettling feeling settled in the pit of his stomach, alerting him that something was extremely wrong. Logan was a man with many plans. Logan would have long anticipated the moves his enemies would make and had developed countermeasures to thwart their every attempt.

Marcus and his two men crept closer to the house, the silence so thick it felt suffocating. Crouching down behind a bush, he pointed two fingers forward, silently directing his men to advance. He was determined to take his target down, but anticipated a minefield of traps. His men would be regrettable but indispensable casualties in service of the cause. As the sound of footsteps grew nearer, he swiftly pivoted on his back foot and fired a shot, momentarily hesitating when he saw that it was Evan. The bullet grazed his brother's right arm, a chilling reminder of how close it came to ending his life. Evan clutched at his arm, feeling the searing pain shoot through his body.

"Ow! What the fuck was that for?!" He yelled.

"Don't come up behind me! Are you trying to die?" Marcus responded.

"I came to warn you. He has set a trap."

Marcus shook his head in disappointment, feeling hurt by his younger brother's lack of faith in him.

"Do you really think I hadn't thought of that. It's why I let them go first."

Suddenly, a deafening shot echoed through the air, causing the co-pilot to crumple to the ground, blood spilling from his chest. The soldier swiftly retrieved his AK-47 from his back and unleashed a barrage of bullets into the building. Within a short period, he found himself in need of reloading his weapon. Swiftly ejecting the magazine and seamlessly inserting a fresh one. Then continuing his onslaught. Something reached Marcus's nostrils, and he desperately hoped it wasn't the smell he thought it was.

"Do you smell gas?" He asked.

Evan did not have the chance to give a response. In a violent explosion, the house erupted into flames, extinguishing the soldier's life instantly. The impact of the blast was enough to force them to the ground, both hitting their heads and being rendered unconscious, their bodies motionless on the floor.

# 16

Madison and Bethany raced towards the boat, their hearts pounding in their chests. They both stopped abruptly when they heard the unmistakable sound of a helicopter closing in. Noticing the presence of several armed men inside the flying vehicle, their chances of escape dwindled. Madison's grip tightened around Beth's arm as the approaching danger grew nearer, and she quickly yanked her behind a tree for cover. It wasn't the most concealed spot, but it was preferable to being out in the open.

"What do we do now?" Bethany asked.

"We might be able to still make it to the boat. But I don't know." Her mother said, her voice filled with uncertainty as she debated with herself.

"We need to get to that boat." Madison exclaimed.

Realising that it was their only shot at getting out, she insisted they move forward. The deafening sound of gunshots filled the air as the chopper unleashed its attack, leaving the mother and daughter frozen in fear. Each one crashing into the sea vehicle's engine, creating a loud and jarring noise.

"They are taking out the engine. Shit!" She yelled.

"What now?" Panic began to consume Bethany as she asked the question.

She was stumped by her daughter's question, as she had no clue how to proceed. As the weight of their impending doom bore down on her, she felt her breath become shallow with terror. As she was in the midst of contemplating a solution to their problem, her concentration was shattered by a sound that came from behind. As she turned to see what or who approached, her legs weakened instantly at the sight of Damien. The look on his face mirrored the same expression she had seen the last time they were together, a chilling reminder of the threat he had made to her life. The face was familiar to Bethany, and it lacked the fear-stricken expression her mother had.

"Dad?"

Madison's body became rigid with fear, rendering her immobile. Was her death fast approaching? There was no noticeable change in his appearance, except for the addition of several new scars on his face. He reached out his arms towards his daughter, his eyes filled with longing, and she didn't hesitate to rush over and embrace him tightly.

"Hello baby girl. Long time no see." He smiled.

They wrapped their arms around each other in a tight embrace, squeezing so tightly that it was a wonder they could still breathe.

"I've missed you."

With a smile that reached his eyes, he leaned down and planted a tender kiss on his daughter's forehead. With a daring and murderous stare, Damien locked eyes with Madison, sending chills down her spine.

"Madison." He said bluntly, his voice deep.

Madison stood petrified, her breath caught in her throat, unsure of what to say. What was she to do? His fingers twitched near his holster, a dangerous glint in his eyes as he contemplated drawing his gun and ending her existence. She was aware that he usually suppressed his violent nature whenever he was in Bethany's presence.

"I've been looking for you for a long time. Both of you." He said, his tone more softer.

He had always been a man of words, using his silver tongue to navigate his way out of most predicaments. She was aware that his response to potential defeat in an argument or disagreement was to cause harm to those involved. His ability to wield words and violence made him a force to be reckoned with. She knew he had the power to sway Bethany against her, and if he exposed the real reason they left, persuading their daughter to side with him would be effortless. Trembling legs, shaky hands, and a racing heart were all signs of her overwhelming anxiety.

"Who are the men you came with? They don't look like security. Funny that. Maybe Logan was telling the truth and confirmed what I thought for years. You are a murderer." She said, her voice laced with suspicion, hoping to catch him off guard and expose his true identity as the man Logan had described.

After speaking, her mind became a whirlwind of thoughts, each one racing through possible scenarios that could unfold. Her words, sharp as daggers, could cost her dearly in the end.

"They are my colleagues. I haven't worked as security for a while. Who are you to judge me for the company I keep? Oh, so you trust a man who literally killed people for a living and was considered one of the greatest killers in the world. You fucking him to?"

There it was, exactly what she expected him to say, his words hitting her with the deserved blow. She couldn't help but feel that she had provoked such a response, especially as she watched her daughter's confused expression.

"What does he mean, mum?" Beth asked, puzzled.

With a snarky smirk, he strode forward and deliberately placed himself between both women. His head swivelled to look at his wife.

"So, would you like to inform her? Or I could do the honours."

With determination, she stepped closer to him, her knuckles tightening, even though she was fully aware that her punch would have no impact. A previous attempt, many years ago, ended in utter failure, and it seemed highly likely that history would repeat itself, if not with even more disastrous consequences. In that moment, she weighed her options, trying to determine her course of action. In a cataclysmic blast, Logan's house erupted into a fiery inferno, flinging them forcefully onto the rugged ground below.

"Logan!!" She yelled concernedly, as she rose to her feet.

With her attention elsewhere, she failed to notice her daughter's unconscious form lying near a boulder up ahead. With lightning speed, Damien rose from the ground and sprinted to his daughter's side.

"I see another man is clearly more important than your daughter and husband again." He shook his head disapprovingly, tutting under his breath.

Realising that Bethany had been hurt, she rushed over, forcefully pushing Damien aside and cradling her daughter tightly in her arms. As her husband grabbed her left arm tightly, she could feel his strength and determination.

"I told you that if you tried to take her, I'd kill you. I keep my promises."

Focused solely on his anger towards her, he remained oblivious to the presence of someone approaching from behind. In a split second, his head was met with the impact of a foot, catching him completely off guard. The force of his face meeting the boulder left him in a state of complete unconsciousness. Looking up, Madison's heart skipped a beat as she saw the man, feeling a mix of shock and immense relief. Logan.

"I guessed you were done talking."

He noticed that Beth had been injured. There was a deep gash on the top of her head, blood slowly trickling down her unconscious face. However, they couldn't linger in their current location; their priority was to escape the island. With a gentle motion, he knelt down and effortlessly lifted Bethany up, holding her close.

"We need to go." He said.

"But they destroyed the engine of the boat." She informed him.

He gave a smile.

"That's not the only boat. They brought one for us."

Steal the enemy boat, cutting off their only means of transportation and leaving them isolated. Smart. A small laugh escaped him as he reflected on how Marcus, yet again, had neglected to think through his plan. Prioritise destroying the getaway vehicle and avoid abandoning your own means of transportation. Instead, consider trapping the targets on the island, ensuring they have no way to escape.

*Kill him now. Stop being considerate. She'd prefer him dead anyway and the daughter is out cold. So won't know.*

'Leave me alone!' He thought.

He carried Bethany through the dense forest area of the island, the sound of rustling leaves accompanying each step. Madison trailed behind, her heart pounding in her chest as she struggled to keep pace with the man carrying her daughter. She marvelled at his quickness, realising it would have been impossible for her to move that rapidly while cradling her daughter. Far from being heavy, Bethany had a slim physique. Madison lacked the physical strength and endurance required for such a demanding task. After she thought he had died, yet somehow didn't, a question arose in her mind that she couldn't ignore, and now she had to ask him.

"How did you survive that explosion?" She asked.

"When I bought the island, I knew one day that something like this could happen. So planned ahead, dug out a tunnel, lined it with lead and copper, planting wooden stilts every ten feet, so it wouldn't collapse. Made an escape hatch in the house. Which I'd planted several explosives within the walls of, for an event like this. I knew they'd find me, eventually. It took them a long time."

Madison was taken aback, impressed, and slightly worried as she realised that the man had meticulously planned for this precise moment for years. He must have had countless hours at his disposal to achieve something as impressive as what he did. He had predicted that his enemy would most likely sabotage his getaway vehicle, but knew they had made the mistake of travelling by boat and leaving it unguarded.

"Wow. So you've had a lot of time to plan for this?" She said.

"You could say so, yeah."

Upon reaching the other side of the island, they could see the enemy boat in plain sight, a target ready for the taking. It was apparent that Marcus and Evan were either incapacitated or painstakingly scouring the wreckage, hoping to find any remnants of Logan. The roles had reversed, and they would be finding themselves stranded and without any means of escape.

Should have done what I had said. Planted bombs all over the island, so as we drive off. You detonate and boom. Enemies perish. But no. You chose this path, where they will get off that island and they will find you guys again. You are going to need me then. You know it and so do I.

He considered it as an option, but ultimately dismissed it due to the potential catastrophic consequences if something went awry. Magnus was known for his tendency to take a more savage and merciless approach to everything. Like a shadow of Logan, he possessed equal intelligence, yet lacked the tendency to analyse every detail or anticipate the consequences of his actions.

Madison took the lead and climbed onto the boat, feeling the warmth of the sun on her face as she looked back to see Logan assisting Bethany. Lifting himself up, he brushed off the dirt and made a beeline for the driver's seat. Laughing as he noticed the key was still in the ignition. Could they have made it any easier? With a twist of the key, the engine shuddered and emitted a series of grating noises, but failed to start. Another attempt, the same thing happened. It rattled the entire boat. Maybe third times the charm? With a sudden jolt, the engine burst into action, its vibrations coursing through the vehicle. With his hand on the accelerator, he was startled by the unexpected noise of a gun being fired. The bullet struck the window above the steering wheel, narrowly missing him by six inches.

With a quick push of the throttle, the boat surged forward, sending Madison teetering towards the back. He turned his head back and caught a glimpse of Marcus, his finger tightly gripping the Glock 17, unleashing a barrage of shots. The piercing sound of bullets filled the air, and one of them found its way to the left side of the steering wheel. Logan was impressed by the noticeable improvement in his aim since they last crossed paths.

Still can't hit a target that is going in a straight line. Pathetic. Also, why are you going in a straight bloody line? One of those terrible shots could still hit us.

Despite their movement into the ocean, his enemy refused to cease shooting, the piercing sound of gunfire filling the air. The veins bulged on his forehead, his face a canvas of rage. Logan deftly guided the boat to the left, feeling the subtle shift in the water's current, before swiftly veering to the right. Ensuring none of those bullets hit any of them. Madison's grip on the boat tightened, her fingers trembling, as she held onto her daughter for dear life. As Bethany began to regain consciousness, confusion washed over her like a tidal wave. The events were a blur in her mind, but she vividly remembered the sight of her father.

"What happened?" She mumbled, rubbing her head.

"There was an explosion. We had to get off the island quickly. You hit your head." Madison said.

Madison hugged her daughter tightly, feeling the warmth of relief flood over her. But she was at a loss for words when it came to describing what happened with her father. Hoping she wouldn't ask. Nevertheless, she was aware that if she could recall seeing her dad, she would most certainly inquire about it.

"Where's dad? He was there. Is he okay?"

Did she reveal that he was prepared to kill her? It was a close call for her, but Logan's timely arrival saved her from certain death. Bethany wouldn't believe that what her mother's new friend done, was to save her. Should she uncover the truth of his actions towards her father, he would be forever branded as the villain in her perception.

"He's okay. He… he remained with his colleagues. Said he needed to help them."

The image of her father with someone other than her mother was completely foreign to Bethany. Her memory was fragmented, holding onto fleeting images of their encounter and the sensation of his arms around her.

"He was with people? I don't remember that." She exclaimed.

Logan glanced over his shoulder and caught sight of Madison's perplexed face. He had encountered individuals who had been rendered unconscious and experienced memory gaps upon regaining consciousness.

"He had a few people with him. You'll remember most of it in time. You took one hell of a knock to the head. So for now, get some rest. We will keep an eye on you." He said in a fatherly manner.

In a rare moment, Bethany's intense stare softened, revealing a glimmer of acceptance rather than offence. Instead, she nodded and nestled her head into her mother's lap, feeling the warmth and comfort. Madison's gaze shifted to Beth's head, where a crimson stain contrasted against her pale skin. Luckily, it was just a small cut, but the impact left her with a visible bump on her head, even beneath her hair. Her mind was overwhelmed with worry about her daughter's pain. Even though Logan was also being targeted, she couldn't help but feel responsible for the chaotic turn of events.

"Do you think she will be okay? She has a bump on her head."

Despite understanding that the body would release fluid to shield the area from additional harm, her worry persisted due to its location on the head.

"I'm not going to stand here and say yeah, she will be fine. We will have to monitor her, make sure she doesn't get worse."

*Possibly fucked, why not just say that? Some people have died from such wounds. You lie for the sake of this women that you barely know. I don't trust her, she is hiding something big, maybe not from us so much. But it's clear that something happened that she does not want that young girl to know about. I'd work on finding out what that is, if I were you.*

Magnus had a point; Madison's guarded behaviour hinted that she was withholding information, but he trusted she wasn't an enemy. It was obvious that she hid something and knowing what that was, could help him to protect her from Damien. He wanted to understand if she had done something more than just take his daughter from him. Despite his sick and twisted nature, he displayed unwavering loyalty towards those he loved. It made him question if the man had ever genuinely cared for her. Maybe he cheated? Or vice versa.

"Can I ask you something?" He said.

"Yeah sure."

"What did you do to make Damien want to hurt you so bad? I know that he is pretty messed up and I haven't always seen eye to eye with him. But the man was always loyal to those that he loved."

Her face dropped. It was obvious that she hesitated to speak the truth, fearful of her daughter overhearing. She needed to confide in someone about the terrifying incident that had unfolded, and what had driven the man she loved to become so enraged.

"When I met him, he was lovely and I think I fell for him very quickly. But I was also at the lowest point in my life. He helped pick me up when I was down. Showed me affection that I hadn't received in years. So I thought he was perfect. I was wrong."

She gently moved Bethany aside and settled her onto the plush cushions of the boat's rear seat. She approached Logan, standing next to him and hearing the boat collide with the waves as it chased after the shore.

"He seemed to work a lot, often not coming back for days, sometimes weeks at a time. I'm not going to lie. I often wondered whether he had another woman somewhere. I got jealous. It wasn't long after we first met, that I got pregnant. We moved in together, but he was never really there. So one day I questioned him on his whereabouts. He broke my wrist that night, along with my nose and I had a fractured cheekbone." Her tears fell uncontrollably as she cast her gaze downwards, consumed by a wave of shame.

Logan furrowed his brow, pondering the possibility of someone like Damien committing such an act, unable to ignore the fact that the man had ruthlessly taken the lives of men, women, and children. It struck him like a bolt of lightning - he could have prevented Damien from ever hurting Madison. While on a mission in Moscow, a heated confrontation between him and Damien escalated to the point where he came dangerously close to taking Damien's life. But he refrained from snuffing out the man's existence. The realisation weighed heavily on his mind that the man he allowed to go free could potentially harm the woman, who was both kind and caring, with a beauty that captured hearts.

"Shit. I'm taking a guess that it got worse than that? Fuck."

"Yeah, I began enjoying when he was away for work. It would give my body time to heal before he came back." She wept.

"I would say why didn't you leave. But I know that if you love someone, you do everything to stay with them. Even when you know what they are doing to you is wrong. For you to survive as long as you did makes you a strong woman."

*Should have got away much sooner, or killed the bastard. She could have poisoned him easily. Only a fool would stay with that bastard.*

Despite his inner voice urging otherwise, Logan dismissed Magnus' words and rolled his eyes. Magnus was nearly as chaotic as the man he was evaluating. Madison didn't resonate with the idea of being a strong woman because his relentless beatings left her feeling powerless. She'd often tell herself that it was the intoxicating intimacy that kept her with him. Because he was often away, their chances for intimacy were few and far between. Jack Renley, her friend and coworker, would regularly implore her to leave everything behind and seek respite elsewhere.

"I never felt like a strong woman. Quite the opposite, actually."

With determination, she had sworn to herself that she would walk away from him. A month later, they exchanged vows and became husband and wife. He had just returned from a trip and treated her to a lavish dinner before whisking her away to a luxurious penthouse suite in a fancy hotel. As they stood on the balcony, the sound of distant traffic filled the air as he declared his desire for her to become his wife. No proposal. But she didn't refuse; an inexplicable yearning compelled her to accept. Saying yes was the biggest mistake, not only because he was an abuser, but also because of her own actions.

# 17

Marcus stood on the island, his gaze fixated on the rhythmic crashing of the waves against the shore. As fury built up inside, it felt as if smoke would billow out of his ears and nose, if humans were capable of such a thing. Well, his would be like fiery infernos. Logan had escaped, and he couldn't help but feel like his hasty plan had left loose ends. Marcus was aware that his failure would provide his father with another justification to seize the leadership position from him. Kane had carefully orchestrated a contingency plan, designating Damien as the leader of the company's militia, in case Marcus failed to capture his target. However, his son had given his word to show that he was deserving of his spot. He believed he was the catalyst collective's key to a successful transition of power, and his self-assuredness was palpable.

Despite their brotherly bond, he couldn't help but see Damien as his fiercest rival among their father's employees.

Evan had no interest in taking charge of a company that didn't align with his values. He found himself working there due to familial pressure, as his family had created the business. While he wasn't seen as a threat, he consistently voiced to his father that he felt underappreciated, yet it seemed as though his words fell on deaf ears. Whenever his younger brother spoke, Marcus would dismiss him without a second thought. They always considered him the black sheep of the family, so it became a regular occurrence for him to playfully tease Evan about being adopted. Laughing it off, he found himself pondering the validity of the claim - he saw himself as completely different from his father or brother.

"When I catch that bastard, I'm going to give him the slowest and most painful death. Winters is a dead man walking." Marcus promised.

The temptation to gloat and give his brother a smug "I told you so" was irresistible to Evan. However, taking that approach may trigger such a strong surge of anger that it could potentially lead to fatal consequences. He battled with himself, determined to hold back the cocky remark swirling in his mind. A small smirk crept across his face, impossible to suppress. Despite his warning about Logan's superiority, nobody paid attention and failed to plan accordingly. As per usual.

"We'd have to catch him first." He remarked.

Marcus's back foot pivoted as he spun, the force of his right hook landing squarely on his brother's face. The force of impact knocked him to the ground after it connected with his eye. Looking up, he felt a mix of regret and relief, understanding the potential repercussions of his unspoken thoughts.

"You are lucky I don't kill you. Always got something to fucking say. Haven't you?"

"All I said is we have to catch him." Grimacing, Evan gently touched the area where the fist had struck before regaining his footing.

Frustrated with constantly being underestimated, he contemplated standing up to his brother. Frustrated by their lack of attention, he knew that if they had listened to him, they might have already caught Logan. But every cell in his being stopped him from doing so, deeming it a fruitless confrontation. They'd dismiss him in a heartbeat, not bothering to listen to what he had to say.

"It's the way you say it. Being snarky towards me will get you killed. Trust me on that."

"Sorry." Evan muttered.

Pulling his phone from his pocket, Marcus dialled the headquarters' phone number. He pressed the call button, and the phone rang once, the sound reverberating in the air.

"Mr Hunt. How may I be of assistance?" A woman's voice said.

"We need picking up, send a chopper and be quick about it. I'll send our coordinates now."

In the absence of any noise, a stillness settled over the surroundings for several moments. It was clear that the woman was engaged in a conversation with someone else. As he spoke, he couldn't help but wonder if his father was silently present, absorbing every word. If so, his mood would sour like spoiled milk.

"May I ask what happened to the chopper that was sent before with personnel on board?"

"Really? You can't figure that out for yourself. They are dead and that chopper is sinking to the bottom of the ocean. Now send me a fucking chopper!" He shouted. Cutting the phone off in a rage.

Footsteps approached from behind, their rhythm growing louder with each passing second, and Marcus instinctively reached for a weapon. As he turned his head, a familiar figure caught his attention in the corner of his eye. Damien.

"What the fuck happened to you?" Marcus demanded.

"That fucker got me from behind. Gonna tear him a new one when I see him. Ruining my fucking reunion with my daughter."

A chuckle escaped Marcus as he found humour in the fact that they were all outmatched by one man. Their target had meticulously prepared for their anticipated arrival. He resented the fact that the man he desperately wanted to be rid of was, in truth, the more commendable individual at present.

"Well, he has won this battle. But this war is far from over. He will pray for death, just like his wife did."

"Madison will do the same. She will beg me to kill her. That bitch took my kid from me. She signed her death warrant the day she took Bethany. She will die just like I killed that pathetic piece of shit, Jack." Damien moaned.

Evan wanted no part in that conversation; his deep respect for human life outweighed any interest in taking someone's from them. The two men with him were sadistic killers, their callousness evident in every word they spoke. Both made him feel a chill run down his spine. Despite being presented with multiple occasions, he never disclosed their brutal acts to the authorities. It was no secret to Evan that Catalyst Collective had a strong hold on a number of authoritative figures. There would be no difficulty in determining who leaked the information. Otherwise, his brother and Damien would be stuck in a damp, dark prison cell. Despite his deep-seated hatred towards his brother, there was still a flicker of love within him that prevented him from betraying him. Which meant the killing would continue.

He was aware that even if they were taken down, replacements would emerge. The company had become a dominant and influential entity. They went to great lengths to enlist a diverse group of assassins and spies, ensuring they had a wide range of expertise. Any member who showed the slightest sign of betrayal was swiftly eliminated or coerced into remaining loyal, making them all dispensable. Typically by threatening to take out family members. Evan had a vision to steer the business towards a new path, utilising its resources and influence to make a positive impact on the world. Changing their mission to work on curing diseases, help the poor and establishing various community outposts. Give back to the world. Yet, the rest of the company saw it as a trivial and time-wasting endeavour.

Evan had made an unsuccessful attempt to leave in the past. In the hospital bed, he awoke to the realisation that his arms and legs were shattered, leaving him completely immobile. That was his warning. His father reminded him that, despite being his son, he possessed an extensive understanding of their work, making it impossible to abandon the business. They doubted his loyalty, fearing he would divulge perilous details to those plotting the company's demise. The mere idea of Logan leaving was enough to make them take drastic measures to keep him with them. Immersed in Lance Shephard's literary world, Evan skilfully decoded the messages concealed within the books. He knew that it was Logan writing the books, but he chose to stay silent, preserving the mystery behind the author's identity. With the coded information concealed within the books, his hope rested on the possibility that enough individuals with influence and power would decipher it, granting Logan the opportunity to exact vengeance on those accountable for his family's demise.

One day, with bated breath, he envisioned a future where Logan emerged victorious. It was clear to him that if he tried to take them down by himself, he would meet an early end. Evan stood no chance against them, but Logan did. Their opponent was equipped with the necessary abilities and cunning to complete the task. It triggered Evan's imagination, causing him to envision different scenarios playing out. In Evan's mind, he pictured Logan exacting justice on his family's killers and the company behind the order, finally putting an end to their reign of terror. Yet, in many cases, he fell short of accomplishing his mission and instead met his end in a fierce fight against Marcus and Damien.

"Where do you think he will go now?" Evan asked

inquisitively.

His brother took a moment to pause, as if trying to see the situation from his enemy's perspective. They were once like brothers, so he had many chances to observe how the man's mind worked, and from his analysis, he deduced that Logan would gravitate towards the one location where danger awaited him.

"Home. He would go to the place where everything began. He will die where he should have the first time around."

# 18

Docking the boat at the docks, Logan extended his hand to help Bethany step off the vehicle securely. The girl needed rest. The blow to her head had left her feeling queasy and disoriented, so she would require ample support. Madison followed her daughter and protector, feeling the slight bounce of the wooden platform beneath her feet. Up the steps, the car stood waiting, parked in the same spot where they had left it. He knew the journey would be a long one, and it was imperative to ensure that Beth received the necessary medical attention. He knew Cornwall was not the place to seek medical help. The constant fear of Marcus and his team finding them again loomed over their every move. The safer option was to wait until they reached their destination to seek help for Bethany. They planned to keep a close eye on her throughout the journey to ensure her well-being. They had a solid hour to take advantage of and put as much distance between them and their pursuers as possible.

Logan couldn't shake the thought that he had the opportunity to defeat Damien and Marcus effortlessly, but instead chose to temporarily disable them in order to make his escape.

*Should have got rid of the bastards once and for all. But no, apparently my approach is the wrong approach. Regretting that now, aren't you?*

He regretted the decision, but was torn between two choices. The thought of being responsible for Bethany's father's death haunted him or not being that man. Her lack of trust in him was palpable, and he was determined to prove himself worthy. Although they were practically strangers, he couldn't bring himself to deprive her of one of her parents. The circumstances would have to be dire for him to even consider taking Damien's life. He hoped that maybe he could reason with Damien, hoping to appeal to his sense of logic. Aware of the man's psychopathic tendencies, Logan was hesitant to believe that this approach would yield favourable results. Reasoning with him felt like trying to grasp smoke, slipping through your fingers no matter how tight your grip.

*Both men deserve to die for everything they have done. I don't get why you are constantly torn against taking the lives of those who destroyed yours.*

'Taking a life isn't always the answer. There are other ways sometimes.' Logan thought to himself

Upon reaching the top of the stairs, they were greeted by

the sight of a bustling car park filled to capacity. With a furrowed brow, he mentally sifted through his memories, attempting to pinpoint the spot where he had parked the car. Sometimes, his mind would deceive him, causing time to slip away unnoticed. He couldn't recall where he had parked the car. Often, these memory lapses were attributed to Magnus taking control. To the best of his knowledge, he hadn't. Magnus had been itching to be set free on several occasions, but Logan had always managed to keep him under control. Or had he?

"I can't remember where I left the car. My memory is usually good, but it seems really foggy right now. I can't see it anywhere." He mumbled.

Thankfully, Madison's memory didn't fail her as she remembered the spot where they had parked the vehicle. Amidst a multitude of cars, her eyes landed on the distinct dark blue BMW X5. As he held Bethany in his arms, passersby cast judgemental glances his way, but for the most part, they just walked past. A handful of spectators stood still, their eyes locked on Logan, pondering what had taken place.

"There it is." She said.

The fact that people were watching them, as if they had committed a misdeed, was a source of irritation for her.

"Why is everyone staring at us? Have they not seen an injured person before?"

"They are deducing what happened to her. Coming up with their own silly theories, probably involving one of us harming her. Which, in a way, my house explosion was the cause of her injury." He said, his voice filled with remorse.

Although she knew that he was correct, she couldn't help but feel a pang of guilt that her daughter got hurt. Aware of the potential danger of capture or death, he took decisive action to ensure their escape. Madison had never considered the possibility of dying that day, or at any point in the near future. The looming possibility of her demise played on a loop in her mind. What would happen to Bethany? Her thoughts were consumed by concern for her daughter's well-being, overshadowing any personal worries.

"Don't put that on yourself. It's not your fault. If you hadn't had done that, we might not have escaped."

Pressing the button on the car key, she heard a beep and saw the lights flash, indicating the vehicle was unlocked. As Madison opened the rear passenger door, she felt the cool breeze brush against her face as her and Logan helped Beth into the car. She was coming around again, feeling a dull ache spreading through her body.

"Hey. How are you feeling?" He asked.

She rubbed the back and top of her head, trying to ease the lingering ache, but her eyes were now wide open and attentive. Logan hoped that meant the feeling of being lightheaded and the queasiness had improved slightly.

"My head hurts and I've got one pounding headache. But other than that, a bit better. Are we in London?"

"Unfortunately not. We are just getting ready to leave, though. It's going to be a long journey. So be best to get some rest."

She gave him a nod, her eyes conveying a silent

understanding, before she let her head fall back against the plush headrest. He reached for the seat-belt, carefully securing it around her and hearing the satisfying click as he locked it into place. Safety first. Climbing into the passenger seat, Madison could hear the soft creak of the leather as she settled in. Logan closed the rear door and exhaled deeply, releasing the tension built up inside. Unsure fully, he grappled with conflicting emotions - relief that Beth and Madison were safe and a looming fear of what awaited them. They were faced with a formidable battle. The task before him seemed insurmountable, leaving him uncertain of his chances of success.

As he stood there, lost in his thoughts about the endless possibilities awaiting him in London, a realisation dawned on him. The weight of grief consumed him after the loss of his wife and children, leaving him without any hope. While the coded messages in his books were a viable option, it would have been a lengthy process to recruit enough people to help him dismantle the catalyst collective. But now he had a reason, stronger than ever, to fight. Their presence alone was enough to ignite a flicker of hope within him. Saving them would provide a chance to atone for the guilt of not being able to protect his family.

Suddenly, a knock on the driver's side window jolted him out of his thoughts.

"You coming?" Madison asked. Wondering why he just stood outside the vehicle.

He wasted no time and flung open the door, feeling the weight of himself settle into the driver's seat as he turned the key in the ignition. The engine roared to life, its vibrations pulsating through the steering wheel. He inspected the fuel gauge. The fuel gauge showed three quarters full, indicating they could potentially make it just over halfway before needing to fill up. He turned to Madison and even after everything they'd been through. Her hair was dishevelled, a testament to the chaos she had endured. Despite the black marks and scratches on her face, there was an undeniable allure about the woman beside him. Despite the imminent danger, he managed to flash her a smile, cherishing the thought of getting to know her better once their ordeal was over.

But would her opinion of Logan change once she learned the truth?

# 19

Salah Abdulla had not left the compound in almost six hours since entering, leaving everyone curious about his intentions. The world narrowed down to a single point as Logan focused through the MK-13 sniper rifle. The sideways and height-adjustable cheek-piece design of the weapon ensures a more comfortable and convenient experience when using the telescopic scope and night vision equipment. Under the veil of the night sky, he remained still, his eyes fixed on the suspected operations base of Al Akbuh, the notorious terrorist leader. Situated in a small town in Samarra, Iraq, the place was on the outskirts of the Skherh zone, surrounded by barren landscapes. With thirty-seven hours of over watch under his belt, he understood the importance of patience in such a task.

In contrast to his restless comrade, Marcus Hunt, he decided to adopt a more inconspicuous approach. With his voluminous beard and turban, he effortlessly merged into the crowd of Iraqi militants, camouflaged by the soldier's uniform he had acquired, possibly through deadly means. Despite his aversion to wearing them, Marcus acknowledged the necessity of such attire for the mission. In order to get as close to the target as possible, he was assigned the task of posing as one of Al Akbuh's guards. Learning various languages was a crucial aspect of his job, enabling him to converse reasonably well in Arabic. Logan would often chuckle at Marcus' efforts to speak in their tongue, feeling a twinge of sympathy for his struggle. According to new intelligence, their target, who had ties to members of parliament, was plotting to carry out an attack on a summit arranged by the prime minister. He was a man of questionable character, suspected of being involved in dubious dealings with unsavoury individuals. The belief from headquarters was that his assistant, who tragically died of what seemed like natural causes, was actually murdered after stumbling upon the damning secrets of the United Kingdom's parliamentary leader.

With a nonchalant gesture, he inserted his finger into his ear, mimicking the act of cleaning it. Marcus watched the buildings around him for any suspicious movement.

"Anything Winters? Got nothing here. What the fuck is he doing in there?" He asked.

Before providing an answer, Logan thoroughly scanned the area using the magnified view of his rifle's scope.

"Nothing. I don't like this. There was supposed to be a delivery today, but not a single vehicle has even come by.

Something is wrong."

They were no strangers to such missions, so they had a clear vision of how it would all unfold. After entering the compound, the target seamlessly transitions into the back of the vehicle, smoothly continuing their journey to the next location undetected. Yet this time, the target entered the premises and never reappeared, and the long-awaited delivery remained undelivered. The sound of a voice echoed through their earpieces, much to Logan's dismay.

"I've got this, lads. I'll get him out of the building."

From behind the compound, Damien materialised, his attire mirroring that of the guards, making it difficult to distinguish him from the rest. The lingering presence of death filled the air, indicating his presence in the area all along. There was no trace of the two guards who had been stationed on the roof. Logan's attention was so focused elsewhere that he failed to notice Damien effortlessly dispatch the rooftop guards. No one could deny his undeniable skill. However, it was his disturbing penchant for murder that sent shivers down Logan's spine. Taking lives brought him a twisted satisfaction, akin to mastering a video game. They received clear instructions before undertaking the mission: prioritise minimising fatalities. Their goal was clear: take out the target efficiently and reach the exfiltration point as quickly as they could.

"Damien, what are you doing? We were told to keep deaths to a minimum." Logan exclaimed.

"I am. I've only killed six people. I wanted to kill fourteen of them." Damien replied sarcastically.

While Marcus shared Logan's opinion, he couldn't help but be impressed by his comrades' sharp wit and sarcastic remarks. He was the one person who got on well with the man who loved murder, sharing a twisted sense of humour that others couldn't comprehend. They'd often laughed about the countless lives they'd taken, joking about the effortless ease with which they accumulated the number. Not wanting to exacerbate his father's anger, which had already been ignited by his outburst during the previous mission resulting in the deaths of numerous innocent people. To cover up his actions, Kane Hunt had to put in a lot of effort, creating a narrative of agents stumbling upon a building that served as a bomb factory. They cautiously approached a suspected terrorist, unaware of the imminent danger that awaited them - several bombs that exploded in an instant. With the corpses strategically positioned inside, they proceeded to demolish the entire building, leaving no trace of their heinous act.

"Damien, stand down. At least for now." He said, throwing his authority around.

"Really? But I can get him out, prime and ready for Logan to take him out. Why the fuck was I brought here, if you just wanted me to sit patiently and wait until you were done?" Damien moaned.

Logan did not want him there at all and had vehemently opposed his presence, but Kane gave the order and was not known to yield easily.

"I didn't want you to come in the first place." Logan mumbled.

"You know what? Fuck you! You think you're better than

me, yet you're the one who Kane was unsure of sending on this mission. He doubts your abilities. With me, he knows I won't hesitate. You don't give him the same confidence."

Was he lying? It didn't seem like he did, but his ability to deceive was unparalleled. Damien had grown up in a rough neighbourhood, where he honed his skills at pilfering from shops, houses, and unsuspecting pedestrians. Deceiving his family about his methods of earning money was a common occurrence for him. He was a master at using his words to extricate himself from challenging circumstances. The mere thought of being forced into the army by his father filled him with anger and a stubborn resolve to defy it. But the only person who ever struck fear inside him, was his dad, whose footsteps echoed through the house like thunder. He found it difficult to adjust to being told what to do when he first joined up, frequently getting into altercations with his peers. But then he got to use the weapons and felt the weight of power in his grasp. Waiting for the moment that he got to use one. The act of taking a life confirmed his obsession with death, overshadowing all other desires. In the end, his expulsion from the forces became inevitable as a result of his violent conduct. Also, nine of his fellow soldiers were killed during what was supposed to be a straightforward mission. His colonel had suspicions that it was not the enemy who had decimated his team. He had a strong suspicion, but no concrete proof to substantiate it, as Damien had cunningly employed an enemy's weapon to massacre his team.

"You know what? I will handle this myself. Watch and learn Logy."

"Stand down Damien." Marcus demanded.

The only response to his demand was a deafening silence. No reply was expected from the man going rogue, as he had severed all communication. Damien lobbed a smoke grenade, causing a sudden burst of smoke to materialise between the two guards at the front of the compound. Gasping for air, they emerged from the smoke, only to meet their demise as he fired his silenced glock 17, hitting them both in the head. With a heavy impact, both bodies crashed onto the hard concrete. With each step, he drew closer to the entrance, his senses heightened, alert for any signs of potential adversaries. One caught sight of the billowing smoke from a nearby alleyway and immediately bolted towards it, but his momentum was abruptly halted by a bullet tearing through his throat. Courtesy of Marcus. From Logan's view, the mission appeared to be descending into chaos. His team could compromise them all completely.

"Marcus! You both realise that you are going to give our presence here away. All because Damien is an egotistical maniac." He said, with his finger pushed against his ear.

Glancing through his scope, he spotted a team of five men closing in on Marcus and Damien, their tense expressions indicating their preparedness for combat. They held their guns aloft, aiming them steadfastly towards the billowing smoke.

"You guys have got company." Logan said.

The thought of leaving his comrades to fend for themselves against the enemies crossed his mind, but his empathy wouldn't let him do it. As the armed personnel inched closer, he remained vigilant, searching for the ideal instant to take his shot. Marcus witnessed the men closing in and was confused by Logan's inaction. He was typically adept at handling such matters, neutralising threats before they could harm his team. What was with the hesitation?

"Logan? You got a shot or not?" Marcus said, concerned.

No answer.

"Logan?"

Peering through the scope, Logan finally had the perfect shot lined up, the sound of his own breath the only thing he could hear. Pulling the trigger, there was a moment of hesitation before getting two kills with one bullet.

"What's in that compound, Marcus? Don't tell me it's only the target, I'm not stupid, there's another objective, one I was not briefed on."

His enemies and colleagues often underestimated his intelligence, to their own detriment. As they were given the mission briefing, he couldn't shake the feeling that there was more to it. He sensed an ulterior motive, a hidden agenda. Deducing that they must have tried to buy something, but Al Akbuh turned down their proposal. The rumours spoke of a weapon, a dreadful invention capable of vaporising anyone unfortunate enough to be within a mile of its activation. If the classified intel, which was leaked online, proved to be accurate. Utilising uranium as its source, the machine emitted waves that resonated with a deafening echo, obliterating anything unfortunate enough to be within its lethal range.

"What? We have a target to take out and that's it. Do your job, Logan, and focus on the enemies."

With a swift pull of the trigger, the bullet soared out of the barrel of his MK-13 rifle, leaving a trail of smoke in its wake. The bullet tore through the side of one enemy's head, ricocheting into the next guy. Another shot rang out, and a third soldier crumpled to the ground. In a swift motion, Marcus and Damien aimed and fired, eliminating the last two with precision.

"You aren't telling me something. I know it. I'll find out, you know I will." Logan muttered.

"Why do you care? We come here, do our mission, and leave. End of. We have a target to take out and with you questioning everything, it's giving him more time to get away." Marcus shot back.

Recognising their reluctance to divulge the true motive, he chose not to respond. He made up his mind to remain in the same spot without any intention of changing his position. It was his responsibility to keep a watchful eye for any signs of approaching enemies and promptly relay the information to Marcus, a duty he was determined to carry out. Despite being the most prepared for the situation, they still denied him entry into the compound. They had been no match for him in training, as he consistently bested them both. Yet every time they embarked on joint missions, he found himself relegated to the position of over watch.

The thought of staying with Catalyst Collective any longer was unbearable to Logan. As he anticipated his departure from the company, he couldn't help but imagine the anger that would arise from losing their most valuable asset. He could no longer trust any of them, they were keeping him in the dark more often.

Kane had a secret agenda in the works.

# 20

As the trio arrived in London, they were greeted by the sounds of honking horns and bustling city life after their lengthy six-hour journey. The car was filled with the soft sound of the girls' steady breathing as they slept. He pulled up outside where his home once was. Before the fire and death. The new house, a sleek and contemporary structure, stood in stark contrast to the sturdy, century-old homes that surrounded it.

As he reminisced, he could vividly remember the day they bought their home. They walked through the front door into a grand hallway, with a door on the left that opened into a cosy living room, perfectly sized, not too large. He found it cosy, as he never had an affinity for massive houses. The door to the right opened to reveal the dining room, imagining the aroma of freshly cooked meals wafting from the kitchen beyond. The upstairs had two bedrooms, they were expecting their first child at the time of buying. A bathroom was conveniently located between the bedrooms, situated at opposite ends of the house. In the master bedroom, there was a stylish en-suite, complete with modern fixtures. It only took a few minutes of exploring the house for them to feel a sense of familiarity and comfort. Being on Polygon Road, the house was just a short distance away from St Pancras station, making it convenient for Logan's work trips. He relied on trains as his primary mode of transportation, especially during his early days at Catalyst Collective.

Looking at where his home had been, sadness overwhelmed him. A tear escaped from his eye, tracing a path down his face. Like a flurry of punches and a piercing stab, the memories overwhelmed him. Laughing with his wife Lilly, he could taste the spicy flavours of the Indian takeaway they enjoyed instead of his failed attempt at cooking. He fondly remembered the laughter of his children echoing through the back garden as he pretended to be a hungry tyrannosaurus rex. Attempting to imitate the beast, the sounds he made were outrageous, resembling a goat being choked. Ethan and Leah Winters, aged six and three, couldn't stop giggling at their father's antics. Whenever he was home, he made sure to give his undivided attention to his kids and wife. With them, he discovered the art of compartmentalising work and focusing on the present.

Lilly remained oblivious to her husband's true occupation, as he couldn't bring himself to disclose his real line of work to her. Falling into the same cliche as others in his line of work, he told his wife he was employed in security. Normally for some egotistical CEO. Easier when he had to go away for work. He was always able to relay the news that the boss would be jetting off to another country for a series of meetings. His assignments typically required a few days of work, but occasionally they would demand an entire week. The time needed was contingent upon the target. He always observed them for a couple of days, taking note of their daily routine and searching for advantageous opportunities to strike. He also took the opportunity to gauge whether they were truly a potential danger to the country and world. Employing clever disguises, he would infiltrate the areas where his targets worked or engaged in illicit activities, meticulously placing bugs to gather vital intelligence.

With Logan's reputation as a job success rate of one hundred percent, Kane and his superiors relied on him for the majority of tasks. He had a relentless drive to prove himself, so he eagerly took on and completed every mission that came his way. Then he noticed something peculiar about the targets - they were all high-ranking government officials or individuals closely connected to them. He came to the realisation that following the death of government individuals, new ones would step into their roles with astonishing speed. After completing one mission, the announcement of a replacement caught his attention as he recognised the person from somewhere. Margaret Lawton, a woman who had collaborated with Kane on numerous occasions and reported directly to him. Despite her long-standing role in his science division, she had never demonstrated any particular enthusiasm for a career in politics. It was at that very instant that Logan became aware of Kane's plans to overthrow the government, using his council of killers and loyalists. They were cautious, playing the long game to ensure that no suspicions were raised. Yet, Logan's innate curiosity kicked in, driving him to dig deeper and uncover the hidden secrets.

As he thought about it, the memory of when he broke into Kane's office played out in his mind like a movie. He'd learnt that his boss was going out for lunch with his sons, Marcus and Evan. So knew that they wouldn't be back for at least two hours. With ample time at his disposal, he dedicated himself to uncovering details about the assassinations of politicians and their connections. Security personnel were a constant presence on Kane's floor, even in his absence, protecting his room as if it contained valuable treasures. The secretary, Dorris, posed another problem - her nosiness and unwavering focus made her difficult to distract. But he knew of one way to get her away from her desk, which overlooked Kane's office. He needed a distraction for the guards and considered pulling the fire alarm, but knew that the moment it rang, an automated security measure would alert Kane. The system was designed to notify him promptly in case of a fire or if any of the building alarms were activated.

Riding the elevator up to the thirtieth floor, he could hear the soft hum of the machinery and the occasional ding of each passing floor. Security personnel closely monitored anyone who entered the floor, prepared to neutralise any potential danger. As the doors opened, Reginald Vorman, a towering figure at six foot nine, emerged with his glock 17 aimed directly at Logan. With a quick motion, Logan threw his arms in the air. Ronnie Kolchek, though shorter in height, boasted a muscular build, evident from the impressive size of his arms and shoulders, suggesting he frequented the gym and lifted heavy weights. Standing together, they bore such a striking resemblance that one could easily mistake them for brothers. Both men kept their weapons aimed and ready, their fingers hovering near the triggers. They knew the man exiting the elevator, but their training taught them to always be cautious.

"What are you doing up here, Logan? The boss is out." Reggie asked.

"Calm down, boys. Kane asked me to wait for him. Got mission intel to go through." Logan said informatively.

Puzzled, both men exchanged uncertain glances, unsure whether to lower their guns.

"We weren't informed of anyone due to come up here. Until later, he has a meeting with Damien." Ronnie revealed.

This new knowledge caught Logan off guard; he hadn't been briefed about any upcoming missions, if there were any. Why was Kane going to Damien first? Known for his tendency to deviate from the mission path and his inability to follow orders, the man was labelled as a complete psycho.

"Did he not? I have the meeting marked on my calendar on my phone. I can show you."

With a slight movement of his hand towards his pocket, Logan elicited a flinch from both guards and a swift repositioning of Ronnie's weapon, now aimed at his face. Knowing him well would have prevented them from making that choice. He paused his movement, his muscles tensing with the desire to disable them both, but the potential interrogation from Kane and the superiors deterred him.

"I'm reaching for my phone. Why are you treating me like I'm an enemy? If I was here to cause harm, I'd have killed both of you within the first thirty seconds of getting out of the lift. So calm down. I'm unarmed and am literally reaching for my phone."

As he reached into his pocket, his fingers brushed against the small bomb trigger next to his mobile, and he pressed it. In a matter of seconds, a sudden explosion outside jolted everyone's senses. With a surprised expression, he leaped backward.

"Oh shit!" He yelled.

Reggie and Ronnie hurried to the wide window beside the office, its bulletproof glass providing a sense of security against potential sniper threats on Kane. The two guards witnessed a staff member's car engulfed in flames, followed by another car exploding moments later. Logan watched on, perplexed as to why they hadn't immediately sprinted to the elevator and begun investigating the scene. Despite it being protocol, they observed the situation without any sense of haste. Both men kept their guns trained on Logan as they cautiously approached him. Their mistake, they were only three feet from him now.

"Are you not going down there to investigate?" Logan asked.

"We aren't allowed to leave this floor until the next shift starts." Reginald replied.

"Yeah, not allowed. Boss would kill us. He is one scary man." Ronnie uttered.

His plan failed, leaving him no choice but to resort to plan B. The situation he wished to avoid.

"I've met him."

Logan's mind wrestled with the decision, torn between following through with his next steps or finding an alternative way to gather the information. Kane was already seething with anger towards him for his failure to eliminate Anthony Draiden. So going through with this wasn't going to make it much worse, but the failure of that mission had already tarnished his success rate. Yet, he had ceased to feel any concern or interest. The intel within that office would put a target on his back, but the way he saw it, he already had a bullet waiting for him after informing his boss that he planned to leave the company. The office walls seemed to close in on him, suffocating him with their silence. That meeting turned tense as threats were exchanged, but he stood his ground and responded in kind. Logan was privileged to be the sole individual aware of one of Kane's greatest secrets, as he was a man who guarded his mysteries closely. He kept his foot on the tiger's neck and threatened to use it against him to exert control.

"Sorry lads." He said, forewarning them.

"For what? You haven't let one off have you?" Ronnie joked.

Without warning, he seized Reginald's wrist, exerting such

force that the bone snapped, causing the gun to slip from the man's grasp. Logan swiftly caught the weapon with his left hand, his grip tightening around it as he aimed towards Ronnie. The shot echoed through the air as the bullet tore through the man's left eyeball, piercing his brain and erupting out the back of his skull. With a swift motion, he put an end to Reggie's existence by delivering a bullet straight into his forehead. His eyes scanned the lifeless bodies, a wave of disappointment washing over him as he reflected on his actions. Despite knowing that neither of them had any children, he believed there were other more important aspects. They still had families, people who would forever long for their presence, and he had mercilessly robbed them of their lives. All for intel on Kane's wrong doings. As he glanced sideways, he detected a subtle movement in his peripheral vision. Margaret's hand extended towards the phone, her fingertips just barely grazing its surface. He aimed the glock towards her, his finger poised on the trigger.

"Don't do it. Please." He cried.

Her body tensed up, immobilised by fear. From the terrified yet determined look on her face, he could tell she was still contemplating calling Kane. He couldn't allow that to happen, but the thought of taking someone's life in their sixties was unbearable to him. The weight of killing two innocent men, who were simply employed by the wrong individual, burdened him.

He had a history of killing, but only those who had committed unforgivable deeds. Despite his strong stance against taking innocent lives, he couldn't escape the reality of the situation as he stood over the bodies of two innocent victims.

# 21

With no way out and the walls closing in, he was engulfed by an oppressive darkness that left him feeling utterly trapped and disoriented.

"Logan, are you okay?" Madison asked.

He snapped out of the trance, his heart racing and his palms sweaty. Glancing at the woman beside him, he seemed mortified, his face pale and his body visibly trembling.

"Yeah, fine. Just bad memories."

Madison's eyes locked onto the house Logan had been gazing at, and a shiver ran down her spine. She could tell, by the way his face contorted that it was a place filled with haunting memories.

"That's your home?" She asked.

As he turned back to it, he felt a deep sense of sorrow

welling up inside him. The image of Leah running around in the front garden, which had a decent enough size, remained vivid in his mind. The door stood at the end of a twenty-foot stretch of grass, separated by a pathway of pavement.

"It's where my home used to be. Before the fire."

As he spoke, she could sense a deep undercurrent of sadness and regret in him. She reached out and touched his shoulder, aware that revisiting the place where his family had met their tragic end would evoke a complex blend of memories and emotions. His sombre demeanour hinted at the fact that this was where their lives had tragically ended. The weight of her grandparents' absence hit her like a freight train as she returned to their home. She could empathise with his emotions and truly understand how he felt.

"It's gotta be hard for you. What happened there all those years back? If you don't mind me asking."

*She doesn't need to know.*

"Marcus Hunt and his father Kane happened." Logan uttered.

*Don't fucking tell her anything at all. It's our business. Not hers!*

A tear welled up in Logan's eye and slowly made its way down his cheek, finally finding its resting place on his leg, where it soaked into his blue jeans. That painful, heart-wrenching night from years ago still lingered in his memory, haunting Logan like a ghost. On that fateful day, his family were cruelly ripped away from him. His family was brutally murdered as a consequence of his decision to quit working as a contract killer for those plotting to overthrow the government.

*She doesn't need to know! I don't fucking trust her. She is working with them; I know it.*

"Shut up!" Logan yelled.

Madison's quick backward movement in response to the shock resulted in her inadvertently hitting the back of her head against the passenger side window. Suddenly, Bethany leaped up from the backseat, her body tense with fear. Logan recognised that he had inadvertently shouted aloud, rather than keeping it internal. How would he explain why he shouted? No one was yelling at him. So that excuse was out the window. The thought of confessing the constant voice in his head filled him with fear, worried that she would leave with her daughter. Though he pondered whether she would truly understand, she already knew about his island existence and his conscious choice to steer clear of people. This action was known to drive people insane. Loneliness can be both a soothing companion and a formidable adversary. Would she be understanding? Or consider him a mad man?

"Sorry. I wasn't…" He paused.

Madison was far from unintelligent. As she studied his puzzled face, she sensed his internal struggle to articulate his actions and find the right explanation. She had guessed that he wasn't yelling at her. This left two options: either he had an earpiece in, which she doubted because she would have spotted it. Which left the other option. Something she already had knowledge of.

"You hear voices Logan, don't you?" She asked.

He found himself speechless, his mind blank and unable to

form coherent sentences. How did she know?

"How… Well…." He couldn't finish what he was saying.

Verbalising the confirmation amplified his sense of vulnerability. He couldn't shake the feeling that the people he was trying to protect would doubt his ability to make sound judgement, a thought that lingered in the back of his mind. There were moments when he couldn't shake off the nagging feeling that Magnus had a greater influence on him than he realised, leaving him uncertain about his decision-making autonomy.

"My brother had Dissociative Identity Disorder, some times he came across as himself and you knew you were talking to Luke. But other times, it was obvious that it was one of his alters. Alter egos. He had one that he would argue with, so you'd often find him in his bedroom having a full-blown argument with himself. I'm not saying that's what you have, or trying to diagnose you with anything. But I know a troubled man when I see one."

*She doesn't know anything about us.*

Learning about her brother was a revelation that completely blindsided him. The thought of having a flaw or defect was unbearable to him, even though he knew deep down that the isolation on the island, after losing his family, had taken its toll. However, he couldn't deny the inner turmoil he experienced as he contemplated Magnus' impending resurgence, causing him to question whether he could ever regain his former dominance. He steeled himself for the fight, making a conscious effort to keep that darker side of him hidden within the recesses of his thoughts.

"You have a brother? Is he okay now?" He said, sidestepping any discussion about his own mental health issues.

"He is doing better. But has lived in a mental health hospital for twelve years. If he isn't there, he doesn't take his medication and then he loses it again. So our parents decided that it was safer for him to remain there, for his own health and for the safety of society."

Doubts began to fill his head as he questioned if a mental hospital was the more suitable place for him. Was she thinking similar? Overwhelmed by self-doubt, he hung his head low, ashamed of his own personal battles and paralysed by fear of seeking support. The thought of Magnus gaining control and causing harm to everyone in the mental institute filled him with dread, so he immediately dismissed the idea.

"So, are you basically nuts?" Bethany muttered from behind with a grin going across her face.

He turned back to face her, and a mischievous grin danced on her lips, hinting at an imminent burst of laughter.

"Unsure whether I'd use the term nuts." A forced laugh escaped from him, as he tried to make the situation seem less grave.

Beth giggled, a smile spreading across her face as she realised that her initial uncertainty about Logan was giving way to a growing fondness. Initially reluctant to engage with him, she had viewed him as a questionable character. However, upon learning about his mental struggles and tragic loss of family, she recognised his humanity, and the fact that he had rescued Madison and her only further solidified her change of heart.

"Well, I guess everyone is a little nuts in their own way, right?"

"I agree with you on that." He said with a smile.

Their laughter mingled together, creating a harmonious symphony of joy. Madison was relieved to see signs of progress as Bethany began to warm up to Logan, but she knew that it would still be a slow process. While gazing at each of them, her heart quickened, but it skipped a beat when she locked eyes with Logan. Despite the turmoil, a shared moment of laughter filled her with a soothing, cozy feeling. Her daughter and Logan shared playful banter, reflecting on the wild events that had unfolded and expressing relief that they were still alive. It felt refreshing to loosen up and embrace a light-hearted moment.

"You know what? You're not too bad, old man." Beth said.

"You aren't too bad either. Also I'm not that old."

Madison couldn't suppress her amusement and released a playful giggle.

"I mean, you aren't young either." She joked.

Logan was being verbally tag teamed by a mother and daughter. They were both mocking him for his age, and he reluctantly acknowledged that he wasn't as youthful as he once was - his body reminded him of it.

"Hey. I'll have you know that my body is more like that of a twenty-year-old. Just with a touch more aching." He laughed.

In the midst of his duty to protect, he found joy in sharing a laugh with the two individuals, reminiscent of the laughter-filled days with Lilly, Ethan, and Leah. As he ran after the kids in the garden, panting for a break, they would mockingly call him old, and Lilly would often nod and laugh in agreement. A flood of memories from those moments overwhelmed him, painting an even brighter smile on his face.

"It doesn't look it. I can see a few wrinkles." Bethany giggled.

As Logan looked in the mirror, he ran his fingers across his face, searching for those elusive wrinkles.

"Where? I can't see any."

Bethany couldn't contain her laughter at the fact that he actually checked, causing her to double over in amusement. Madison did the same, and they both found him hilarious, laughing uncontrollably.

"Look closer. They are definitely there." She said, barely able to stop giggling.

Logan squinted and strained his eyes, but still couldn't catch a glimpse of any. But he laughed, finding amusement in the taunts and jeers about his age. It was a beautiful family moment for him, and when he gazed at Beth, he saw Leah's joyful expression staring back at him.

"You must be seeing things. I don't see any wrinkles at all."

"Maybe you need to have your eyes tested. They do say your eyes get worse with age." She laughed.

"I feel like you two are just picking on me now."

Madison decided that although it had been entertaining to tease Logan for a brief moment and share a laugh, they needed to refocus on their destination.

"Do you have another place in London where we can stay? As I'm taking a big guess that it isn't there."

Bethany's gaze fell upon her mother, disappointment etched on her face.

"Way to kill the mood, mum."

"Yeah, I've got a place. It's off the radar, so they won't find us there." Logan said.

With a renewed focus on the road, he restarted the engine, the vibrations of the car beneath him reaffirming its readiness to go. He ensured the road was clear before pulling off. Taking a quick glance back, he could almost hear the echoes of laughter that once filled his home. As they got further down the road, he became more vigilant, his senses heightened as he searched for any signs of agents working for catalyst collective. As he looked around, noticing the absence of any potential dangers. The coast was clear, for the time being. A sudden interruption occurred when his pocket began to ring, diverting his attention.

Only those who deciphered his messages could ring that phone.

*Here comes the Calvary.*

# 22

Lilly Winters, a statuesque and slender woman, stood at an impressive height of six foot one inch. Many of the girls she knew looked up to her, both figuratively and literally, due to her height. Standing at the sink in the kitchen, she could feel the remnants of food on her hands as she scrubbed the messy bowls clean. The chicken breasts, diced into perfect cubes, sizzled in the pan as she added a generous sprinkle of paprika, mixed herbs, and garlic. She added it into the tagliatelle pasta she had just boiled and drained, mixing it all together. It was a hearty and satisfying meal for the kids.

In a rush, Leah entered the kitchen, her face flushed and her breath heavy. Her face, resembling her father's, displayed a determined demeanour at the tender age of six. Leah's maturity beyond her years and remarkable intelligence had always been praised by Logan. Among her peers, she was known as the brainiac in school because of her sharp mind. Her teachers often said that she would grow up to become a trailblazer in her chosen profession. Some kids relished the feeling of a cosy blanket wrapped around them as they delved into several pages of a book before bedtime. Leah was different, she'd read an entire book before the time to got to bed was upon her. Her love for reading surpassed her age, as she delved into books meant for older children with an insatiable curiosity. Reading scientific books brought her immense joy, as she imagined herself conducting experiments and making groundbreaking discoveries. It was astonishing to Lilly and Logan how rapidly their daughter grasped concepts and the intricate workings of her mind. At just five years old, she had already mastered five languages. French, English, German, Swedish and Spanish. By six, she had become proficient in a dozen more languages, effortlessly switching between them.

"Mummy! Ethan fell out of the tree! He has hurt his arm." She yelled in a panic.

With lightning speed, Lilly exited the house through the back door, which was located in the hallway to the left, adjacent to the kitchen. The office was arranged with a desk placed prominently in the middle, encircled by bookcases containing a diverse collection of books. Ranging from thriller, horror, fantasy to romance. At the corner of the room, a kids reading section featured a snug chair that seemed perfect for little ones. Leah was in there more than Ethan. Walking out into the garden, she was taken aback by the sight of Ethan sprawled on the ground beneath the grand tree, adorned with Logan's tree house. The tree house, expertly constructed, boasted two spacious rooms to prevent any squabbles among the kids over space and clutter. They still did, but thankfully, it wasn't as awful as it could have been. On either side of the bulking tree, there were ladders leading to separate rooms, inviting exploration.

"How did you fall, Ethan? You need to be careful." Lilly asked.

She noticed that he had cut his arm in the fall as she approached him, the wound still fresh and bleeding slightly. Although his arm didn't appear to be broken, the cut on it would require cleaning. Her nursing instincts kicked in, and she meticulously examined him for any fractures, drawing upon her past experience.

"I was trying to see if I could climb onto the roof of the tree house, and I did. But I slipped."

With his fearless nature, Ethan was often referred to as a little daredevil by his mother. Fear of heights was foreign to him, just like many other things. Being only eleven years old, his enthusiasm for sports was undeniable; he had always excelled in physical activities. His father funded his boxing initiation, and the coaches quickly recognised his immense potential. Logan had been to several sparring sessions and was amazed by his son's boxing prowess. Unlike his sister, Ethan didn't find much enjoyment in learning at school. However, he eagerly looked forward to Tuesdays and Thursdays, when physical education class allowed him to indulge in his favourite sports like football, rugby, rounders, and cricket.

"Why did you want to climb on the roof? One day you are going to do something like that and end up breaking a bone. I don't want you trying to climb up on the roof again. Okay young man?" She said firmly.

As her son looked up at her, she could sense the sincerity in his gaze, unable to tell her anything but the truth. He would, without a doubt, make another attempt at such a thing, convinced that he wouldn't fall off next time.

"Well, maybe one more time. I don't think I'd fall off next time." He laughed.

"No. No more climbing up there. Promise me. I don't want you getting badly hurt."

The thought of her children getting hurt was unbearable to her, and she couldn't help but worry that, like his father, Ethan would disregard her warnings and put himself in harm's way. Logan's refusal to listen to Lilly's advice often resulted in him hurting himself, showcasing his stubbornness.

"Okay. I'm sorry for climbing up there."

"Your father will be home later and I'm sure he doesn't want to get home to find that you've broken and arm or leg."

Little did Ethan and Leah know that Logan was scheduled to return that day, and anticipation started to grow in both of them. Having been away for work for six days, they assumed that he wouldn't return for another few days. Leah ran over in excitement at hearing of her dad's return.

"Dad's coming home!?" She asked.

"Yeah, he should be back tonight, ready for dinner."

"I can't wait to see him!" Ethan yelled in utter excitement.

Due to Logan's frequent work commitments, Lilly found herself shouldering the responsibility of raising the children on her own. His absence was noticeable, as it meant she was missing out on the feeling of safety he always brought. Since the robbery at their old house in Kent, she had been plagued by mental anguish. The people who robbed them had carefully observed Logan's schedule. As a corporal in the army, he had the privilege of being stationed at a base close to his home, allowing him to return most evenings. That evening, he was running behind schedule. The thieves had timed it perfectly, taking into account that the husband wouldn't be back for several hours, rendering it inconsequential. They quietly broke in through the back door, careful not to make a sound. During that period, Ethan was still a baby, unaware of the world around him. So he was asleep upstairs in his cot, for his afternoon nap. Upon entering, Lilly was immediately seized by one of them, who forcefully pressed a gun to the side of her head. The threat was constant - if she made a sound, he would not hesitate to take her life, leaving her brain scattered in a pool of blood. His accomplice ransacked the house, hurriedly stuffing jewellery and valuables into a bag.

She remembered that day vividly, the details replaying in her mind like a never-ending film reel. They stole a necklace and ring, both cherished heirlooms that had been passed down in her family for decades. Spotting an opportunity, the armed man's gaze fell upon Lilly. In the summertime, she chose to wear a white t-shirt and a brown skirt, finding comfort in the lightweight materials. Her body tensed as she caught him staring, his touch lingering on her breasts before slowly trailing downwards, stopping just short of where she expected. Once more, he cautioned her, his tone laced with urgency, emphasising the need for silence, this time invoking her baby's life as a consequence. Her body went rigid with fear as he violently pulled up her skirt, forcefully tearing off her underwear before bending her over the kitchen side. He had his way with her, leaving her feeling powerless. She found herself unable to do anything but weep. She felt a strong urge to fight back, but she found herself completely immobile. She felt her legs turn to jelly, trembling and unstable, as if they could give out at any second. It wasn't long before the man's comrade returned from looting, and she felt a surge of fear, worrying he would also try to take advantage of her. Instead, his friends' actions provoked anger within him. They argued, their heated words filling the air, until the one who looted abruptly departed, abandoning his accomplice.

After finishing what he was doing, she believed it was all over. With a sudden, violent motion, he ripped off her top, bra, and proceeded to strip her bare. Collapsing onto the floor, she was consumed by a torrent of tears, unable to regain her composure. She pleaded with him, her voice filled with desperation, begging him to just leave. He swiftly took several pictures of her before vanishing, abandoning her on the kitchen floor, naked and in tears. She remained there until Logan returned, finding her huddled on the ground. Ethan was upstairs crying. The memories of that day and their actions were permanently imprinted in her mind. Weeks after that fateful day, the stolen items were finally recovered, but the two men responsible had already met their demise. She was aware that Logan had a hand in the killing of the men, and though she couldn't support it, she couldn't ignore it either. With a mix of emotions, she found comfort in the thought that they wouldn't be able to victimise anyone else again.

After giving the cut a clean, she carefully applied a plaster to Ethan's arm. He was off again, his fingers grazing the petals of the flowers as he passed through the garden. He climbed up the ladder, this time with a different purpose in mind, not to reach the roof again. Inside his room in the tree house, he was surrounded by the colourful chaos of his toys, each one waiting to be picked up and brought to life. The kitchen welcomed Lilly back with the familiar clattering of pots and pans, as Leah hurriedly ascended the stairs, the thud of her footsteps echoing through the house. The stillness in the air hinted at a temporary restoration of peace. However, Lilly's tranquillity was short-lived as a knock at the door demanded her attention. Not anticipating any visitors, she reached under the drawer in the lower kitchen cupboard and retrieved a Glock 17, prepared for any surprises. Logan had trained her in its usage, wanting her to feel a sense of empowerment and safety when he wasn't present. She approached the door. Another knock. Nothing defined this person more than their unwavering persistence and impatience.

She peered through the peep hole and caught sight of a

bald man, his unruly beard giving him a rugged appearance. She knew that face. Opening the door, she greeted Marcus Hunt with a warm smile and a twinkle in her eyes. Only he didn't return a smile. Instead, his face was devoid of any trace of humour, his eyes fixed on her with unwavering intensity. The way he carried himself gave the impression that he had important tasks to accomplish.

"Marcus. We didn't know you were coming. Logan isn't back until later." She said.

"That's what I was hoping for."

# 23

Pulling into a parking spot outside a dilapidated house in Bethnal Green, she noticed the graffiti that covered its exterior walls. Madison and Bethany peered at the uninviting building from the warmth of the car, hesitant to enter its foul-smelling interior. It wasn't in a welcoming neighbourhood either, but that was precisely the intention. The enemies would hesitate to venture into an area ridden with violence and despair. The house, previously owned by Logan's second cousin Andrew, had been neglected since he relocated to Spain a year ago. Despite his efforts to rent it out, most people found the neighbourhood unbearable and would move out within a couple of months.

Logan purchased the property from Andrew, envisioning it as a secure sanctuary for future emergencies. He employed a network of offshore accounts, manoeuvring the purchase through multiple shell companies that he had ownership stakes in. As he surveyed the surroundings, he couldn't help but think that it was the ideal location for their circumstances. Although it lacked charm, the house would serve their needs adequately. The girls' faces fell with disappointment, mirroring the expression he knew Lilly and his children would have worn.

"It's not as bad as it looks. They won't think of searching here, not for a while." He said.

They all got out of the car, the sight of the hideous building looming before them. Bethany's eyes were drawn to a group of hooded men further down the road, their collective gaze filled with irritation at the sight of newcomers on their block. Logan anticipated encountering a few people in the area who would react negatively to their arrival. The area was infested with several gangs that were frequently tied to robberies, stabbings, and, on occasion, shootings as well. It troubled him, but not enough to discourage him from remaining.

He stared intently at his phone, fixated on the one missed call notification. The voice mail notification flashed on his phone, making him wary of a possible ploy by Marcus' henchmen to uncover his hiding spot. He'd soon find out, but for now, he wanted to get settled in.

"This area seems nice." Bethany's remark was accompanied by a sarcastic smirk on her face.

With a soft beep, Logan entered four numbers on a square dial device attached to his keys, the device emitting a faint glow with each press. A sudden bleep echoed through the house, immediately followed by the distinct sound of the door locks disengaging. Logan then proceeded to open the door and was met with a sight of cobwebs that hung from every corner, but despite the neglect, the interior appeared modern and significantly improved compared to the exterior. He punched in the same number sequence on his device, and the distinct bleep resounded, filling the air. The windows were equipped with sturdy metal framing and titanium metallic shutters, engineered to endure even the force of explosive blasts. The walls were fortified with a solid layer of concrete, almost four feet thick. From the outside, it appeared unimpressive, but within its walls, it stood as a formidable fortress. Breaking into this house would be an incredibly challenging task, requiring the strength and numbers of an entire army.

"In here, you are safe. No one can get in here. Even if they did, I have safety measures in place. We are safe here."

As Madison looked around, she couldn't believe the stark difference between the inside and outside of the house. Logan sparked even more curiosity in her. Observing the extensive preparations, it was evident that he had accounted for Marcus and his men inevitably tracking him down in Cornwall. The level of detail in the man's planning for these events piqued her curiosity. She comprehended that he was a soldier and worked security, but the more she reflected on it, the more she realised he was withholding a significant piece of information from them.

"How are you so prepared? It had to take some time to set up this place." Madison asked.

"I did it over a few years, in between work. I prefer to be over prepared than under prepared and dead."

"Did you think that because of your job, you'd make a lot of enemies?" She became puzzled by him.

She'd always been an inquisitive person, and it was evident that Bethany inherited that trait from her. Her desire to be in the know was strong, even if she chose to keep certain things hidden from others. Even though they were practically strangers, she had a gut feeling that being with him offered more protection for herself and her daughter. With Damien in pursuit, she had full confidence in Logan's ability to deal with her ex. Logan was undoubtedly the safest choice, yet the weight of his undisclosed information greatly concerned her. She hesitated, unsure if she should delve deeper into his past; he had already shared bits and pieces. But now, doubts crept in as she questioned whether his words were merely tailored to please her.

"In a military based line of work, you are bound to make enemies. Even when in a different country, taking out a target or those close to them. Can always have repercussions. Terrorist cells have their own way of discovering who gave the order and who fired the bullet. In any job, you can make enemies. Sometimes without realising you'd done something to offend or hurt them."

He made a good point, triggering memories of previous workplace experiences where certain individuals seemed to hold a grudge against her. Among the individuals who would often voice their grievances against Madison, Karen Martin stood out, passionately narrating the ways in which she felt she had been wronged. Madison would hear these stories and be completely clueless about what the woman was referring to. In no time at all, the crazy woman's actions escalated from eccentric to vindictive, resulting in the slashing of Madison's car tires. Hiding drugs in her locker. On one occasion, Madison found herself running behind schedule and had to rely on the facilities at work to shower and change. Little did she know, Karen took advantage of her absence and swiped her clothes and towel. The sight of Madison scrambling around in the nude to find her stuff brought a smile to her face. Filming the entire event ended up being her downfall and resulted in her being fired.

"I'll agree with you there. I had a woman consider me her enemy, where I used to work. The horrible things she did to me because I apparently offended her several times. I was surprised it took so long for her to actually get fired."

"What did she get fired for?" He asked.

"Stealing from the company, she'd been pocketing cash from the register. The owner had overlooked it at first, as it began as the odd tenner. Then it got to fifty and continued up to two hundred."

Logan couldn't believe someone would go to such lengths, acknowledging that desperation or a misguided sense of impunity can push individuals to do so. The outcome made it clear that she couldn't get away with it all.

"Sounds like she got her comeuppance, then."

"You two make yourself at home. I've just got to make a phone call." He continued.

Logan ventured into the back garden, where the

overgrown grass tickled his legs and created a jungle-like atmosphere in the thirty by forty-foot space. Neglected and forlorn, a large tree stood in the back left, serving as a stark reminder that no one had cared for the place in ages. Pulling out his mobile, he activated the encryption program he had installed, adding an extra layer of security to his call. With the number dialled, he pressed the call button. The persistent ringing of the phone seemed to go on forever until it finally switched to voice mail. Just as he was about to try again, the phone rang, breaking his concentration. He quickly glanced at the screen to verify that it was the same caller as earlier. It showed up as private. A debate raged inside him, urging him to ignore it. Despite his uncertainty, his inquisitive side won out, and he decided to investigate further.

"Hello." He said.

The lack of a response hung in the air, leaving a lingering sense of uncertainty for several moments. All that met his ear was a subtle, hushed breathing noise.

"Is this Lance Shephard?" The person on the other end asked.

"Who may I ask, is asking?"

"My name is Francis. Francis Kingsley. I read your books and uncovered the coded messages you left within each one. Is it all true?"

After deciphering his messages, the first person to contact him finally emerged. Logan was caught off guard, particularly by the man on the phone's polished and articulate manner of speaking. The way he spoke gave off an impression of having once held a position of authority. Logan could tell, his observations sharpened by countless interactions, enabling him to form a rough outline of someone's background. Some low lives, their speech peppered with mispronunciations and grammatical errors, revealing their lack of mastery in their native language. Instead, they opted for abbreviated words or a slang that no one had ever heard before. The super rich rubbed him the wrong way, as they often spoke condescendingly to people. It was as if they were on a completely different level, leaving everyone else feeling inferior. From the way Francis carried themselves, it was clear they had experience in the emergency services or a higher rank.

"You've deciphered them all?" Logan asked.

"Yes. It took some time, but I have a lot of that free. I am a retired detective. So I notice things that a normal person wouldn't, but being that you left the coded messages. You'd already deduced that people with experience in the force or military would decipher your messages easiest. So the catalyst collective. Everything you wrote about them, is it all true?" Francis said.

"Everything in those messages is true. All of it. It won't be long and they will control the entire country."

Logan paused for a moment. As the man spoke on the phone, his voice carried an air of authenticity, leaving room for the possibility that he was telling the truth. But it was also plausible that he was in the employ of Kane or Marcus, which would suggest he possessed the ability to deceive with ease. He needed more information about him.

"How long were you in the force? What made you leave?"

He asked.

"Thirty-four years. Every part of me wanted to stay, but I could do all the running, being a London detective. We'd often end up chasing criminals who were fit and healthy. As I began to feel my age, I made the decision to hand in my badge. I wanted to spend my remaining years with my wife Pam."

Based on his extensive detective career, Francis appeared to be in his late fifties or early sixties, if one were to make an educated guess.

"It's hard leaving a job like that after so long. Did your wife help you with the coded messages?" Logan questioned.

As the seconds ticked by, he realised that his question had evoked a strong emotional response, filling him with regret. He'd never knowingly cause distress or hurt anyone's feelings.

"She passed a few years back. Cancer got her." Francis croaked, his voice strained with the effort to suppress his emotions.

As Logan moved the phone away from his ear, a wave of melancholy washed over him, reminding him of the pain of losing someone dear. As he slowly brought the phone back to his ear, he felt a lump forming in his throat, holding back the tears.

*What a loser. Be a man! People die, move on.*

"I'm sorry to hear that." His voice breaking as a spoke.

"How did you learn of the catalyst collectives intentions? Did you work for them? If so, in what kind of role?" Francis asked.

Logan hesitated to answer the barrage of questions over the phone, fearing that Kane's hackers may have bypassed the encryption.

"They are questions that I'd prefer to answer in person. Even though the call is encrypted, they may still be able to break through it and listen in. Would you be free to meet tomorrow? Frankie's cafe at ten am?"

He spoke with an air of certainty, assuming the older man's knowledge of the cafe, but also confident in the former detective's ability to deduce its location if he had not previously encountered it.

"Nowadays, with the tools available to hackers. I wouldn't put it past them. I know the place. I'll be there."

Logan cut the phone off. He knew that tracing the call to determine his location would be a challenge for them. His encryption algorithm scrambled his location, making it appear as if he was in multiple cities around the world. He doubted that they'd successfully hacked through his encryption, as it was designed to be impenetrable. His phone was a digital fortress, safeguarding an arsenal of programs that were made to be impossible to crack. They would face a formidable obstacle in trying to make their way through it all. It seemed that he had finally found someone who could join him in his mission, a small but significant development. In addition, there was another person who needed some persuasion, but if he agreed, it would level the playing field.

As Madison walked outside, she felt the soft breeze brush against her face as she went to check on him. It was like a choreographed dance; she appeared from the house mere seconds after he put down the phone.

"Everything okay?" She asked.

"It looks like ours odds may be changing. I'll know for sure tomorrow." With a cryptic smile, he gave his reply.

His caring nature was evident as he approached her, his hand landing softly on her shoulder. He found himself drawn to Madison, unable to ignore the growing affection he felt. The lingering pain of his wife's death kept his heart and brain in constant conflict, preventing him from embracing any potential relationship with the new woman in his life. Torn between honouring his past and embracing his future, he grappled with the idea that finding happiness would somehow be betraying Lilly's memory. She would encourage him to open his heart to a new kind of happiness and release himself from the grip of everlasting sorrow.

"We should get some rest. I feel like we all need it." He exclaimed.

His hand on her shoulder radiated warmth, making her struggle to resist the urge to kiss him. The timing didn't feel right, especially with people out hunting for them. She couldn't help but wonder if he had developed feelings for her, and the urge to find out grew too strong to ignore. As she leaned in for a kiss, her cheeks flushed with colour, adding to the sweetness of the moment. He didn't make any effort to escape; instead, he took pleasure in the present.

"Ewww, gross. Get a room, you two," Bethany muttered from the door.

They were completely unaware that she had been in their midst, unnoticed. Both pulled back, their eyes sparkling and grins stretching across their faces. Despite feeling self-conscious, the sweetness of the kiss left an indelible mark on their day. As Beth looked at her mother, she couldn't help but be captivated by the immense grin that adorned her face, a sight that warmed her heart.

Damien and the devastating deaths in the family had already taken their toll on Madison.

# 24

Marcus stood on the highest point of the Catalyst Collective building, feeling the cool breeze brush against his face as he surveyed the vast expanse of London below. The bustling streets were alive with the sound of traffic, the horns blaring in a symphony of chaos. Peering down, he could barely discern the shapes of people moving and shuffling amongst one another. With the wind blowing fiercely, a cold breeze cut through the air. That would cause most to shiver. Not a single muscle moved as Marcus stood there, his black military-style jacket, though not the thickest, providing adequate warmth. When the weather turned cold, he remained stubbornly resistant to wearing additional layers of clothing. He believed that the layers would make it difficult for him to react quickly if he were attacked, giving his opponents an advantage in battle.

The roof became his sanctuary whenever he longed for solitude and a moment of introspection. As he thought, his mind became a carousel of scenarios, spinning faster and faster. It felt like he was in a dream as he conjured up the images of them. His thoughts were consumed by the persistent question of where Logan could be. They were stranded on the island for hours before managing to get off. In that time, his brother and Damien's never-ending provocations and irritations tested his patience, but he restrained himself from resorting to violence. Despite his reputation for impatience, he discovered a reservoir of patience while waiting on that island.

Kane expressed his disappointment with Marcus for failing to capture Logan, repeatedly berating him over the phone for being an utterly useless son. According to his father, failure seemed to be the only thing that defined him. When was he going to do something worthy to be proud of? A mixture of anger and longing consumed Marcus as he increasingly despised his father but yearned to earn his admiration.

While Kane utilised him for multiple purposes, Marcus understood that his father favoured Evan's approach, which involved analysing every conceivable scenario, similar to Logan Winters. Despite his modesty, Evan's capabilities in combat were unmatched, surpassing even the elite in the field. Nonetheless, he loathed the necessity of causing bodily harm, leading him to actively avoid confrontations and any type of combat. His brain was a powerhouse, capable of going head-to-head with the likes of Mr. Winters. But unless he could embrace his dark side, victory would always elude him.

Marcus was often labelled as the deranged brother,

characterised by his perceived stupidity and inclination towards murder. The assumption about him infuriated him, but even his father conceded, in the midst of a heated argument over Logan's miraculous survival and sudden departure from the company, that soldiers were listening to Marcus. He was a good leader and was willing to make the difficult decisions that his brother couldn't. Memories of his mother Maggie flooded his mind, and he could hear her voice echoing with the words she often told him.

"Never allow anyone to belittle you. No matter who they are."

Since he was a child, she taught him that he should never let anyone bully or disrespect him without consequences. This journey eventually brought him face to face with his ultimate tormentor, Shaun, the bully who had made his life miserable since they entered middle school. Shaun, a large and robust individual, was no match for Marcus, who had been taught by his parents how to swiftly incapacitate opponents. With a forceful kick to the side of his left knee, he swiftly brought the big guy down to the ground, where he writhed in pain. He'd broken the boy's leg, and without hesitation, he unleashed a merciless onslaught, inflicting the most severe beating the boy had ever experienced. He felt it was what the bully required. Having experienced many toilet dunks, Marcus found the sensation of payback to be bittersweet. It was only with the help of a teacher that he was finally restrained from fatally harming his victim. That day, he realised that there was a burning fury within him, a sinister force that he took pleasure in unleashing.

He became aware of movement behind him, causing him to turn around. When he turned around, he saw Oliver, who was fairly new to the company. With a mere five weeks under his belt at the company, he already harboured aspirations of ascending to the ranks of Kane's elite guards or, better yet, being entrusted with missions alongside the battle-hardened soldiers. However, for now, his duties were limited to being a personal assistant to Marcus and acting as a secretary. He was nice and suited the role he was put into, but Marcus saw no potential for him to rise above that level. Oliver's three years of military service weren't enough; he needed to exhibit greater courage to climb the ranks in the business.

"Boy, sneak up on me like that again and I'll put a bullet between your eyes." Marcus moaned.

"Sorry sir." Oliver uttered.

"There is news on Mr Winters."

Marcus was annoyed by his tendency to beat around the bush, which was another reason why he found him irritating.

"Well, spit it out then. Or are you waiting for me to rip the words out of your mouth?"

"They narrowed down his possible locations to three spots. It took some time because… of the software he has on his phone, it bounced his location… around the world to almost a hundred and fifty areas." He stuttered as he attempted to get the words out, as he handed over a piece of paper with the information on.

"Why are you explaining that to me? I know how it all works. You are lucky I don't throw you off this building."

Marcus began walking towards the door, feeling the coolness of the doorknob in his hand. But he paused, his gaze shifting towards his assistant, and a wicked grin crept onto his face.

"On second thought."

In a split second, Oliver was catapulted over the four-foot high ledge, leaving him no time to react. With each passing moment, his screams grew weaker until they ceased altogether. Marcus, devoid of any remorse, casually pulled out his phone from his jacket pocket and dialled Damien's number after clicking on his name. It rang with no answer. With determination, he tried again and this time; he was instantly connected.

"Oliver, get the information to you?" Damien asked.

"He did indeed. Get those locations sent over to me and get a team ready. We move out within the hour."

"Will do."

Before cutting off the call. The thought crossed his mind that finding a new assistant would be a top priority.

"Oh, and I'll be needing a new assistant. My one took a tumble." He laughed.

# 25

Logan awoke gasping for breath, another night of Lilly asking him to help her and him not being able to save her. He turned his head and on the other side of the bed, Madison lay fast asleep and naked, the cover only covering the lower half of her body. He remembered kissing her and Bethany catching them, but after that it was blank. As if his memory had been wiped. Had they? He could not recall the night before.

*Having problems remembering?*

No. Not him. The thought that Magnus had broke through his barrier and taken control of him, frightened Logan. He immediately checked Madison's neck for a pulse, feeling the steady beating. She was fine. It surprised him that she slept through him waking from a nightmare and checking her for a pulse. She had to be a very deep sleeper.

*You missed out big time. She was amazing, I want another night like that. Did you really think I'd kill her? I mean, I could have. But I saw an opportunity for sex and I took it.*

'Shut up! Why can't you just leave me alone?!' Logan thought to himself.

*Leave you alone? This body is mine, just as much as yours. Now I'd prefer it if it was just mine, I mean I am better than you at everything.*

Logan shook his head and laughed quietly.

'How can you be better than me at everything, we have the same brain and body. I will get rid of you some day. I promise you that.'

*I will always be here, you can never get rid of me!*

Magnus was the biggest fight for Logan, bigger than everything else. If he couldn't get rid of him, then it would cause issues in the future. He dreaded the thought of his alter ego taking full control on a permanent basis, he'd cause chaos and would relish within it. Sitting on the edge of the bed now, stuck in a battle for his own mind. The touch of a hand on his back made him jump, almost making him dive off the bed and onto the floor.

"Good morning." Madison said with a great big smile.

"Morning. Did you sleep okay?" Logan asked.

"After last night, how could I not. It was amazing."

He couldn't recall any of it, but couldn't confess that to her. Unbeknownst to her, it was his alter ego that she had a fantastic time with, which deeply unsettled him. Magnus could have harmed her and he would have been none the wiser to it, until he got back control of his own body.

"Yeah, it was." He exclaimed.

*How would you know? It was me who gave her the best night of her life. She will never forget last night. What can I say, I know my way around a women's body. Your wife knew all about my talent in the bedroom.*

Logan ignored him, attempting to shut off from that damn voice. Madison sat up and then leaned towards him, kissing him on the neck. Her bare breasts pressing against his back, although he had to head out to meet Francis. Excitement won over, he turned and kissed her on the lips, his hands moving to her breasts and within seconds they were laying down again. Him on top of her and they began making love to each other and a happiness overcame him that he had not felt in many, many years.

*Move your hands down, put them around her waist and lift her onto you instead. Do it rough. She likes it rough.*

Magnus would not give him any peace, it was becoming off putting. He was so absorbed in banishing his inner darkness that he was becoming disconnected from the present moment, and Madison could see it.

"Logan, look at me." She said.

He looked into her eyes, those big beautiful eyes.

"Are you okay? You seem preoccupied."

He attempted to continue the love making, giving her a nod and choosing to remain silent. He moved down her body, kissing her all over on his way down. Her skin was so smooth. Moving under the cover, he planned to make her morning the best one she'd ever had. That is until the bedroom door opened and an extremely shocked Bethany stood in awe.

"Oh my god!" She yelled, slamming the door shut behind her.

The moment was truly ruined and embarrassment was written over both of their faces. No one wants to be caught in such a moment, except some people. But neither of them wanted Bethany to catch them. Logan had hoped that he'd have heard her moving around the house and that she'd have the decency to knock on the door before opening it. Madison dove out of the bed, racing to put her clothes on. Her cheeks were as red a tomato from the embarrassment. It surprisingly did not take her very long at all to get changed, it had to be around the twenty five second mark. Logan debated following her, but decided against it. Bethany was old enough to understand what was happening and did not even think to knock. But then he wondered whether she thought that he was asleep downstairs, not sharing a bed with her mother.

*Well, well, look who missed out. All because of that little bitch. Should get rid of her, then it would be just us and Madison.*

"Wow. I should have guessed that would be what you say. Always violence with you, isn't it?" Logan said, forgetting that he was not completely alone and that the girls could have heard him.

*Hey, it's not that violence is always the answer. I make the hard choices, so you don't have to. If that's killing whoever is in our way, then so be it. They should just avoid being in our way in the first place.*

"Don't fuck this up Magnus. If you harm either of them, then trust me, I will get rid of you for good." He threatened.

*How the fuck would you do that? You've tried for all these years and oh look. I'm still here.*

"Do you really think I haven't thought of a different way to get rid of you? Without me, there can't be a you."

A silence filled the room and Logan took in the tranquillity, the peace. He laid down on the bed again, it was comfortable and he fought with himself to not fall back to sleep. He had a meeting with a potential ally to attend to and planned on getting to the location thirty minutes before the planned time to meet. Survey the environment for enemies, ensure that it was not a set up. He knew the area very well, so was well aware of every possible escape route, if the meeting did not go as planned. There would be various plans in place for if it turned out to be an enemy attempting to trap him.

Madison and Bethany wouldn't like it, but they would have strict instructions to not open the door to anyone. One because it it would set the alarm off and signal Logan that something was wrong. Two it could result in them being captured and killed. Only he would word it in the way of, staying within the house until he returned was their safest option.

Placing his thumb against a small marking on the wall to the left of the living room, he felt a subtle vibration. Which looked as those it just needed another layer of paint put on it. The room filled with a deep, resonating hum, and within seconds, a faint shimmer formed the outline of a door on the wall. Suddenly, it swung open, exposing a hidden room. The room was cluttered with guns, grenades, and a variety of explosive equipment. Among the contents inside was a rack, neatly organised with various black carry bags. With a sense of purpose, he gathered all the essential items needed for the day ahead, leaving no room for chance when meeting an unfamiliar person. It was time to find out if Francis was truly who he said he was or whether he was playing Logan for a fool.

Like some of the others who had called before.

# 26

As he watched Frankie's cafe from a distance, she remained vigilant, searching for any signs of potential threats. While most people would be on edge, Logan felt a surge of energy coursing through his veins, as if he had regained a long-lost vitality. The mere thought of dismantling the catalyst collective ignited a newfound sense of purpose within him, and he understood that enlisting the help of others would amplify his chances of triumph. His constant paranoia and deep-seated mistrust of others made finding people to help him an even greater challenge. The mere idea that Francis, the one who cracked Logan's coded messages in his books, could be a spy for Kane haunted Logan's every thought.

Throughout the years, Logan had become adept at ignoring the sounds that filled his surroundings. Despite the constant beeping of cars and people's chatter, he managed to block out all distractions and search with unwavering focus. Three Colts Lane was abuzz with activity that morning as people of all ages traversed the paths. The roads were practically paralysed due to a collision that occurred further down the road. If Francis was driving, there was a high possibility of him being delayed. Concealing his identity, Logan wore a cap and sunglasses while keeping a watchful eye from across the street. Although he hadn't observed anyone who seemed menacing, he understood that if trained adequately, they could seamlessly blend in with the general population. However, the majority unconsciously revealed themselves through subtle behaviours, remaining stationary for prolonged periods, scanning the surroundings as if in pursuit of someone or something. The worst one, though. Their finger touched their ear, their voice carrying on the wind, making it obvious to onlookers that their attempt to remain undercover had failed.

The minutes ticked away, and there was still no sign of Francis, despite their agreed meeting time. Despite having no visual reference of Francis, Logan was on the lookout for a man who would take a seat at the cafe, displaying a clear sense of anticipation. It would be easy enough to pinpoint him, as long as there weren't a whole bunch of men doing the same thing. The presence of a solitary man in the cafe intrigued him. His young appearance contradicted the notion of being a retired detective investigator. He was promptly dismissed as a potential candidate. Catching sight of an older gentleman approaching, he noticed the distinguished greying hair and wondered if this man was Francis. Dressed in black jeans, a white shirt, and a blue suit jacket, he exuded the air of a retired authority figure. Despite its short length, his hair exhibited no signs of receding; however, the grey patches on his black hair were noticeable even from afar. Logan would be surprised if this turned out to be someone other than him. He looked to be in his sixties, his stooped posture and wrinkled hands reflecting the wear of time, which would match the weathered sound of his voice on the phone.

The older man found a comfortable spot in the cafe, opting for a table by the window to soak in the natural light. He glanced around, his brows furrowed in concentration. There was no mistaking it; it had to be him. Logan quickly scanned his surroundings, taking in the familiar sights and sounds, reassuring himself that it was all clear. For now. The moment he began his approach, an unsettling sensation crept up on him. Despite being the one to arrange the meeting, he couldn't shake the feeling that something was amiss. He expected some kind of enemy presence, but nothing. It concerned him, but his curiosity pushed him forward. With his eyes fixed on Francis, he patiently watched for any additional clues of his involvement with the people on his trail, while the aged gentleman sat silently, waiting. There was no visible indication that he was receiving instructions through an earpiece. Before making his approach, he cast a lingering gaze over his surroundings, taking in every detail with his sharp, observant eyes.

*This is a trap. But you already know that don't you?*

While Francis was engrossed in his surroundings, he

suddenly became aware of a man making his way towards him, prompting him to redirect his complete attention to the stranger. It was as if his intuition was screaming at him that it had to be the man who called himself Lance. Seeing the man approach, he quickly got to his feet, preparing to greet him with a handshake. But Logan motioned him to sit back down, silently implying that they needed to remain cautious and low-key during their encounter. Instead, he wore a friendly smile, as if he were meeting a friend for a casual coffee. Sitting down across from the older man, Logan's senses prickled with discomfort, unsure about this unfamiliar encounter. The task, although familiar from past experiences, felt even more overwhelming due to his solitary lifestyle.

"Nice to finally put a face to the voice. You look younger than I expected." Francis exclaimed.

"You assumed I was in my sixties? Because of everything I know and my past? I'd have probably done the same in your shoes."

Francis had indeed deduced that with the intel collected, and the way Lance/Logan's eyes scanned the room with a trained precision, it seemed highly likely that he had spent several years in the military too. It made sense for him to be in his late fifties, early sixties. It was very apparent that his assumption was wrong; retirement had dulled his instincts.

"I had. I was very wrong. Clearly retiring has made me rusty." Francis laughed.

*I don't like him. He is old. What can this guy to do help us?*

Logan tried to keep Magnus out, but didn't want to exhaust himself. To ensure his safety, he had to anticipate and be prepared for any potential threats, in case this meeting was a trap.

"I know the feeling. I've lived off the grid for a long time and I can still do what I used to do, but not as well."

Carrying two menus, the waiter walked over and placed one in front of each of the men at the table.

"Can I get you both a drink?" He asked.

"Coffee please. Black." Logan said.

He had never been a fan of milk in coffee, convinced it diminished the distinct aroma and flavour. He craved the complete sensory experience of his hot beverage, from the first sip to the lingering aftertaste. While Francis was lost in his thoughts, the waiter studied him, waiting patiently for his decision.

"Erm… Can I have a cappuccino please?"

With a kind nod of acknowledgement, the man walked off to the kitchen, the aroma of freshly brewed coffee wafting through the air.

"So you worked for the catalyst collective right? What was your role in the company? To be able to obtain so much information." Francis questioned, getting straight into it.

"Straight to it. I like that. I did a lot of bad things for them, things that I'm not proud of and I know that if my family were still alive, they wouldn't be proud of the stuff I did either." He paused. Images of his wife and kids with disappointing looks on their faces, popped up.

"I'm not going to sit here and reveal every detail to a man that I don't fully know. I have trust issues, but then as a former detective, you'd know that I wouldn't be so trusting of someone. You have made every attempt to find out as much out about me as you possibly could." He continued.

Francis had indeed made attempts to uncover information about Lance Shephard, but apart from his profession as an author, there were only minor fragments about his past. He desperately looked for any details that could provide insight into the enigmatic man's background, but came up empty-handed.

"You got me there. Other than your books, you are pretty much a ghost. Which means you either have very powerful friends or the one I've gone with. Lance isn't your real name. I mean, being that you done bad things in the past and the catalyst collective want you dead. You would fabricate a name and a little history and remain hidden from the world. The trust thing goes both ways, I mean for all I know, you are planning to kill me. I doubt it, especially if your former job was as a killer. You'd have taken me out from a distance, avoiding being seen. Plus other than not knowing me very well, you have no reason to kill me. But I know that you are probably on edge, under a belief that I am probably not the man I say I am. So I brought some evidence of who I am and what I've done in my life."

Francis reached down and into a carrier bag that was sitting on the floor beside his leg, one that Logan had noticed when he waited for the man to arrive. Nevertheless, he brushed it off, thinking it was a snack or a beverage for later in case he couldn't eat during their meeting. As he reached into his bag, he carefully retrieved a thick dossier, containing a jumble of newspaper clippings, cherished family photos, and meticulously organised notes. The man had come prepared. He opened it and began going through the pages.

"These are newspaper clippings of me receiving a medal for saving my fellow officers and several civilians from a collapsing building. One which I was told to evacuate, but I wasn't willing to leave anyone behind. Even if it meant me dying trying to save people. That one is me, my wife, son and daughter on holiday in Cornwall."

As he went through the images and clippings, he didn't even break his concentration when their drinks arrived. The man's meticulous preparations made it clear to Logan that Francis had foreseen the possibility of being viewed as a spy for the enemy. Logan could feel the caffeine working its magic, giving him a much-needed buzz of energy. Something felt off as he listened to the man ahead of him, his instincts sending warning signals. Fixated on the distance, his eyes were startled by the sudden movement to his left. A postman, but there was no sign of any letters or packages in his hands. A cacophony of alarm bells echoed through his mind. A figure stepped out of a van, dressed as a delivery man, but conspicuously without a package.

With a quick glance, he covertly scanned the rooftops, taking in the details without attracting any notice. During his search for snipers, a tiny sparkle of light caught his eye, causing him to pause. Pretending not to notice, he continued his conversation while Francis opened up about his wife's deteriorating health and eventual demise. A sense of impending action hung in the air, but the man in front of him seemed completely oblivious to it, casting doubt on his affiliation with Kane. Francis detected a sense of unease in Logan/Lance's demeanour.

"Are you okay? I detect from the way your eyes keep looking elsewhere, that something is wrong?" Francis queried.

There was no immediate reply to his inquiry, leaving him in a state of uncertainty. Logan's mind raced with dozens of scenarios, each one playing out like a fast-paced movie. Each imaginary scenario brimmed with intricate details of potential means of attack, showcasing how Kane or Marcus would meticulously execute a capture or kill operation. Additionally, it would have been important to consider the various strategies that Logan might employ to run such an operation, in order to anticipate and prevent any potential escape attempts. Think like the man they planned to take down. The crowd grew with an influx of suspicious individuals, each failing miserably in their attempts to go unnoticed.

"Did you notice anyone suspicious tailing you on your way here?" Logan asked.

With that question lingering in his mind, Francis couldn't help but notice the dozens of military-trained personnel blending seamlessly into their various disguises - postmen, cafe workers, construction workers, business people engrossed in phone calls - their act flawless. If they were trying to deceive someone, their efforts were failing miserably, much to Francis's amazement. Logan's apprehensiveness made him notice much quicker than he would have otherwise. Logan's expertise in covert operations allowed him to effortlessly camouflage himself amidst crowds and his surroundings, making him an efficient target eliminator. Francis had a talent for uncovering individuals who possessed an uncanny ability to remain unseen by the average person, his perceptive nature making it difficult to deceive him. But both of them were a little rusty.

"I'm pretty certain no one followed me. I'm taking a guess these people are probably ordered to capture or kill you and anyone you are involved with? Even a man you've just met."

"I warned you that getting involved with me, puts your life at risk." Logan said bluntly.

"I didn't think the first time meeting you could result in me possibly getting shot."

Francis and the man in front of him paused, their eyes scanning the area, absorbing every detail. Despite the high likelihood of facing gunfire within minutes, Logan displayed an astonishing level of serenity.

"Do you have a plan? You seem very calm for a man who could be getting shot at soon."

As they conversed, Logan's eyes darted around, instinctively assessing the number of potential threats in their vicinity. He counted nine, but that didn't include the snipers that could have been positioned on the rooftops. If so, based on the angle and trajectory, there were two potential spots for a marksman, ensuring both positions were covered. If so, that made the total eleven. Logan tapped his finger rhythmically on the solid oak table, creating a gentle, echoing sound.

"The man dressed as a postman, will be the first to attack due to his position. He is closest to us, so has a better chance of hitting one or both of us. It would take him maybe two or three seconds to discharge his weapon, I'd give you a signal and that's when we flip this table, so it provides us with cover. I can take him down quickly, there's nine of them on the ground surrounding us and two possible snipers."

The mention of enemies with sniper rifles made Francis instinctively scan the rooftops, trying not to give away his intentions. He couldn't see any glimmers from the scope of a rifle. To his surprise, Logan swiftly provided a detailed account of the multitude of enemies encircling them. He had not even counted how many there were himself. His instincts, once sharp, were now showing signs of rustiness due to age.

"How do you know there are snipers?" Francis asked, puzzled because of not seeing any when he looked.

"Because that is what I would do." Logan uttered.

Francis was left feeling utterly bewildered by something. Why had the enemies not attacked? Instead, their feeble attempts to blend in only made it more obvious who they were, and they were well aware that Logan would catch on swiftly. Or was that the plan?

"I have a question. Why did they not attack us immediately? Take us by surprise."

"He wants us to be very aware that they are here and could attack at any moment. He'd hope that it would have us panicking that we are cornered with no way out. They want to think like me, but forget that I know them better than they know themselves."

"Who tries to think like you?" Francis pondered.

"Marcus Hunt."

A black range rover glided to a stop next to the cafe, its dark exterior reflecting the surrounding buildings. Only six feet from both men. Logan's hand rested on his baretta M9, concealed under the table, as he prepared to confront anyone emerging from the vehicle. Francis undone the clip on the holster, preparing to remove his pistol if the situation demanded it. Stepping out from the driver's side of the car, Marcus emerged. Seated in the passenger seat was Damien, his discontent evident as if he wished he could be elsewhere. He lingered inside the vehicle.

"I see you have made a new friend."

Marcus donned sunglasses, yet the remnants of scarring around his missing eye were evident, even through the shades. A wide grin spread across his face, as if he had emerged victorious from a game competition. With his hands raised in the air, he walked towards the table where the two men sat, their intense gazes fixated on him.

"I'm unarmed. Trust me, I would not be approaching if I was armed and going to kill you. I'd have just killed you immediately."

*You'd try and fail miserably. Fucking one eyed pirate wannabe.*

"Do you really think you'd have succeeded in that approach?" Logan queried.

"You know me. I'd have given it a damn good try. I'm a stubborn bastard."

"That you are."

"You must be wondering how we knew you'd be here?"

Logan was keenly conscious of the abundant resources available to Catalyst collectives, giving them the power to track almost anyone. Determined to evade their surveillance, he implemented foolproof measures. On the other hand, Francis was skilled at concealing his footsteps, but he underestimated the true might of the company and its capabilities.

"You should be dead."

There was no mistaking the intense loathing directed at Marcus. The man, whom Logan once held in high regard as a colleague and friend, forever tainted their relationship by committing the unthinkable act of taking the lives of his family on that dreadful night. Their friendship remained intact, despite the differences they had beforehand. The act of driving the knife into Marcus' eye that night was a visceral reminder of the complete dissolution of their once unbreakable bond.

"Death evades me. You could say I'm unable to be killed. You did a number on me last time. I'll admit, that night you bested me and I should have died. But clearly I'm not very good at the dying part."

Marcus moved closer to the two men sitting at the table, pulling a chair from another table and placing it at the end section. He settled himself into a chair and grinned at Logan, well aware that his very existence was irksome. Logan was like a volcano seethed with a fiery rage, poised to erupt at any moment. Yet to take a shot, would mean all three of them sat at that table would die. Fully aware, he understood that Logan had no intentions of dying anytime soon and would go to great lengths to protect their new friend.

"You don't mind if I sit right?" Marcus asked.

He received no answer from either of the men, only the silence echoing in the air. The absence of words indicated their reluctance to engage in conversation. Francis did not personally know the man ahead of him, but could sense an air of malevolence surrounding him.

"You were smart to remain hidden away on your island for all those years. I mean, if I was you, I'd run too. Who wants to feel the wrath of Kane? I wouldn't. He's my father, but he is one fucking scary fella. Even at his age, he could kill us all easily. I mean, he found Blake and took care of him. You remember Blake from the early days right?"

He was an old friend, and with his intelligence, it seemed impossible that he could be dead. It couldn't be. No one could deny that Blake Wilson was the epitome of excellence when it came to marksmanship. Like Logan, his combat skills were top-notch, making him a formidable force on the battlefield. They forged a strong friendship during their military days, bonding over shared experiences and camaraderie. Both then worked for Kane, but Blake left after a year, no longer able to bear the weight of taking lives. Logan's last known whereabouts suggested that he had adopted a reclusive lifestyle, keeping to himself. Their humble abode was nestled within a forest, where they sustained themselves by living off the land. He was completely unreachable, as he deliberately avoided all electronic gadgets and even refused to use old-fashioned means of communication.

"He wasn't an easy man to kill. So I doubt your father took him down easily, if he did actually find him." Logan said, doubting Marcus.

"I guessed you'd doubt it. I'd say I have proof, but nothing was left alive. We dropped a bomb on the bastard, then followed that up with a bombing run. There was no way he would have survived."

As his patience with Marcus dwindled, Logan's grip on his weapon tightened beneath the table. Aiming it in Marcus' direction. The temptation to pull the trigger was an irresistible urge, gnawing at him relentlessly.

*Shoot the fucker! Then kill the rest. It wouldn't be difficult.*

"If you are thinking of shooting me, maybe reconsider. We have two snipers and eleven men ready to take you out. So either way, I'd win. You'd die and we can continue to battle it out in hell. As you know that's where we are both heading. Especially after the things we've done."

Logan had missed two men. He was confident that he had detected every single one of them. It appeared he was wrong.

"What do you want Marcus?"

"I want to see you suffer. Before I just wanted you to die. Not anymore. You see, that night I did what I did because of you. You killed them, not me. I pulled the trigger and started the fire, but it was your fault. My father warned you that you couldn't just leave. Yet you still did. You killed your family!"

Francis looked at Logan, who was glaring at Marcus with a fierce, murderous expression.

"I don't know you very well. But trust me, don't react. That's what he wants. You not reacting will piss him off instead. You are clearly the better man here and I can see that every part of you wants to rid the world of this man. But not yet. He will get his comeuppance."

"Who the fuck do you think you are old man?! Don't get between us, I will not think twice about putting a bullet between your eyes." Marcus said, his anger building.

"Right now, I'm probably the one person that can maybe stop him from slaughtering you and your men. But you want that. Why do you want to die Marcus?" Francis asked, puzzled to the motives behind the mad man.

"Listen old man! If you don't stop talking, I'll have one of my men shut you up with a bullet. Okay?"

His hands shot up in recognition, a silent signal that he grasped the message. He had no intention of meeting his demise anytime soon. Marcus returned his attention to Logan.

"Now. I forgot to inform you of one detail. The house you left the girls in, we have had someone watching it for years. So imagine our surprise when you took them there."

Logan paused in thought. How did they know about the house? He took a wild guess that Evan had managed to determine that it was owned by Logan, marvelling at Evan's brilliant deduction. Usually, he chose to keep intel to himself, as he never received any appreciation or acknowledgement, even when he passed it on to his father. Unless he thought that behaving in that manner would gain him approval. Clearly it hadn't, otherwise he'd be sat with Marcus.

"Your men wouldn't be able to get in, not without being killed."

The look of realisation on his enemies' face revealed that he was aware of the house's alarm system and booby traps, designed to detect and eliminate anyone carrying a weapon. The place was fortified with layers of defences, making it a time-consuming task to penetrate its security.

"The thing is. You added all those security measures, fortified all the walls. But one thing you forgot about, the roof. It didn't take my men long to get through the roof, they used an EMP grenade to take down your security systems. If you had fortified the roof, then that place would have been impregnable, because you were smart enough to have the front and back door locked. Even an electro magnetic pulse couldn't unlock those bastards. So you see, you failed. You thought you could protect them and you failed. We beat you. They are in safe hands. For now."

With rage building inside, Logan carefully felt over the device in his pocket. It was only small, but with a clear indent which indicated the location of the button. He pressed it.

"Have you?" He uttered.

The sudden explosion on the roof of one of the adjacent buildings grabbed everyone's attention, and moments later, another blast echoed from a rooftop just twenty feet away. In a swift and aggressive motion, Logan lunged at Marcus, catching him off guard. The sound of a powerful right hook echoed through the room as he sent him flying off the chair and crashing onto the ground with a heavy thud. Francis was taken aback by the unfolding events, feeling a wave of disbelief wash over him.

"Now we run!" Logan yelled.

The older man reluctantly started running, but soon the rush of adrenaline propelled him forward, keeping pace with

Logan. Bringing his walkie talkie to his mouth, Marcus stood up, ready to transmit his message.

"Go after them. Capture them both." He grinned.

As Marcus approached the vehicle, he felt a wave of confusion emanating from Damien as the window slowly lowered.

"Why did you not kill him?" He asked.

"I have him rattled now. He won't be thinking as clearly. He will come to us."

"Unless our men capture them." Damien uttered.

"They won't. Do you really think they could capture him?"

"Why did you send them after him then?"

"Collateral."

# 27

Madison felt disoriented and out of place, surrounded by unfamiliar surroundings, with only her daughter by her side. Bethany's priority was trying to connect to the WIFI, so she paid little attention to everything around her. The man who had been their protector had left to rendezvous with a possible ally. Even though she was a novice in the world of espionage and military operations, an intuition warned her that Logan's next move was leading him straight into a trap. Recent experiences had taught her that he was a man who took precautions and wouldn't easily walk into an ambush - he would probably arrive earlier than expected. With vigilance, he'd meticulously examine the area, keeping a watchful eye out for potential threats, all in an effort to safeguard himself from capture or harm by the enemy. Still, there was a nagging sense of wrongness in the air.

Was the man he meeting reliable and trustworthy?

Unable to resist her inquisitive nature, she found herself

snooping around the house as she wandered aimlessly. Despite her curiosity, there wasn't much to learn about the man who had saved her in the sparsely decorated house. The rooms lacked any personal belongings or signs that he was the owner or had stayed there before. No pictures of his wife or kids.

Who was Logan Winters?

As she pondered the question that consumed her mind, she realised that she might have fallen for a man who could potentially leave once everything was resolved. Despite her growing affection for him, she pushed aside those feelings as desperation, unwilling to admit them to him or Bethany. Having someone who showed her attention and affection, she knew she couldn't resist acting on her desires. The image of her dad's face and his wise words filled her mind, bringing back a cherished memory.

"Never fall for a man. Unless you know he is a good man, be able to protect you, provide for you and above everything, truly love you. I never want to see my daughter with a broken heart. You deserve happiness and that is all I ever wish for you." Geoffrey said.

Bethany's face told a story of pure frustration as she made her way towards her mother. Not only were they in a house they had never visited before, they were forced to hide from relentless enemies, whose motives remained a mystery to her. As if things couldn't get any worse, the absence of WIFI was a cruel blow.

"I can't connect to any of the networks around here. All of them require pass-codes. This is stupid! What am I supposed to do? He might not come back for ages, there's no tv, which is ridiculous. Who doesn't watch tele?" She moaned.

It was hard to argue with her daughter's point. Madison was well aware that the house offered no sense of belonging for Logan; it merely functioned as a temporary sanctuary in times of danger. From what he said about the place, it was definitely safe. She hoped it was. The moment he departed for his meeting with the man who deciphered the code, she felt a sense of vulnerability, as if her main source of security had vanished. He instructed them to stay indoors, assuring them that it would keep them out of harm's way. So that was what they were going to do?

"Do you really need to be on the internet that bad? Trust me, that is the least of our problems. Read a book. He seems to have a bunch of them in the office."

Beth's disapproving gaze felt like a blade slicing through her.

"Are you for real? I haven't been on instagram, facebook or tik tok in literally ages, all because of these stupid people who want to kill your new boyfriend. Really? Like he would have any of the type of books that I'd read. Bloody hell mum."

The events that had transpired since their encounter with Logan were less than favourable. However, Madison was aware that it was only a matter of time before Damien discovered their whereabouts, with assistance from these dreadful individuals or independently. She had to admit, he was a man of resourcefulness, always finding creative ways to overcome challenges. She was surprised by her ability to keep herself and Bethany hidden from him for such a long time.

"I know the circumstances aren't ideal. I'd rather not have been shot at and hunted, but it's happening and Logan is probably the one person who can stop it. Also, he is not my boyfriend." She said, attempting to fool herself. Very aware of the feelings that she had begun to develop towards him in a short amount of time.

"Well, from what I saw, you two are definitely more than friends. I mean, you were literally naked in bed together. Don't try to treat me like I don't know what that means. I also know my mother. Sometimes I think I know you better than you know yourself. Like when you fancy someone, I'm not stupid mum. So don't treat me like a child anymore."

Her daughter's surprising comment left Madison speechless, a rare occurrence after all this time. She couldn't help but be amazed at the remarkable transformation of Beth into a strong-willed young woman, unafraid to challenge her own mother. As she watched her daughter fearlessly take charge, she couldn't help but stand in awe. It was clear to her that she couldn't continue with the charade; Beth deserved to hear the unfiltered truth. She needed to know everything.

"You know what? You're right. I do like him, but until I know more about him and actually spend proper time with the man, I won't be calling him a boyfriend or anything like that. I admit, yes, we did sleep together. But I think it was more that a man was showing me some attention, something I hadn't had in years. I'd need at least a couple dates with him, that don't involve being shot at, to truly get to know him. I would never consider you stupid. You have grown into such a beautiful and amazing young woman. I'm glad to call you my daughter, you make me proud everyday. Even when you are driving me nuts. That's why I can't lie to you anymore."

Choking back the tears, Madison paused, taking a deep breath to regain her composure. Her mind became a cinema screen as images of the years spent with Damien flickered through her thoughts. Whenever he was home, he subjected her to countless beatings, some of which left her injured to the point of requiring hospitalisation. He would coerce her into inventing tales, like tumbling down the staircase, being attacked, or once having to feign getting hit by a car. It was clear from her broken bones that she had experienced a forceful impact. Then happy memories flooded her mind, but none of them included Damien.

"About what, mum? Lie about what?" Beth asked.

"Your father and why we had to leave."

With a tear rolling down her cheek, she despised the necessity of recounting the horrors to her daughter, shattering her illusions about her father Damien. Behind his friendly facade, he concealed a terrifying, beastly nature.

"Damien, your dad. He wasn't a nice man, I mean when I first met him, he seemed perfect. But that wasn't him, not truly. I fell for him quickly, at a time when I was not in the best place in my life. I was at my lowest. He found me and I thought we connected really well, it didn't take long before I was engaged to him, then married. That was when he let his true self out, he'd kept the hideous monster at bay for long enough. Our wedding night should have been amazing and although the day was perfect, the party was outstanding. Once we got to our hotel room, it was like once that door shut. The devil came out. He broke two of my ribs, fractured my cheek bone and broken my wrist that night. I hadn't done anything wrong. His words were that I was his now and he could do whatever he wanted and if I tried to tell anyone, he'd kill me and very slowly."

Bethany struggled to find the right words to make sense of her mother's revelation. How had her dad successfully eluded punishment for his actions? Her core was left in a state of confusion and shock, completely disoriented by what she experienced. As she listened to her mother recount the story, she could see the distress in her eyes, a vivid reflection of the pain she had endured. As Madison spoke, her voice occasionally broke, revealing the pain and vulnerability behind her decision to leave Damien.

"Dad? I just... I can't believe it. I guessed he'd done something, but I thought that maybe he cheated and that's why we left. I'm so sorry that you had to endure that, mum." She cried, leaning in and giving her mother a hug.

"The thing is... it got worse after I fell pregnant. He... he didn't." With a heavy heart, Madison came to a halt, reluctant to disclose the next devastating revelation. However, she couldn't ignore the importance of revealing her daughter's true father. Ready to listen intently, Bethany took a step back, preparing herself for what was to come.

"He didn't want a baby. He told me several times to have an abortion, but I couldn't. I wanted to be a mother so bad. So while I was pregnant, the beatings stopped, although he would sometimes break a finger or two. Once you were born, he was adamant that we needed a nanny to help look after you. I didn't want one, because I wanted to bring you up. But he did it, so he could resume his torturous ways. The nanny was a friend of his and he'd paid her to look the other way, often telling her that if she told anyone what he did, he would kill her and her entire family. He was a brutal man. I was glad whenever he went away. It gave me time to rest."

"I get why we had to leave now. He'd have eventually beaten you to a point of no return and probably felt no remorse. I never thought I'd think of my dad as a monster, but shit. He is the fucking devil reincarnated." Absolutely gob smacked, Beth's mouth hung open as she learned the shocking truth about her father.

"He is a horrible man. But that wasn't the only reason we left. One of the times your father went away, I spent the night with another man. That's a lie, it was more than one night. I fell in love with another man, I said I wasn't going to lie and so here it is. That man was Jack Renley. One of our neighbours, who had supported me several times when I would need help. Either with you or if I was on crutches, he helped in various ways. We bonded and I realised he was the man I should have been with, he was the man I should have married. We planned to run away together, he had gone on holiday and then once he returned, we was going to leave and hope that your father never found us. Only Jack got stuck abroad and then my time line for leaving was getting shorter. So with the help of my mum, your nan. We left. I haven't heard from Jack since. I've been too afraid to try to contact him, just in case it led Damien to us. But he found us in the end anyway. I just can't seem to escape that evil bastard."

The revelation hit Beth like a ton of bricks, causing her jaw to hang limply. Her mother and Jack. He was widely recognised as the fittest man in the neighbourhood, making him the object of desire for many women. Despite being caught off guard, she couldn't help but feel a deep sense of pride for her mum. She grasped the fact that her mother, enduring the cruelty of a violent spouse, would have longed for love and attention from anyone other than him. Just like anyone else in that predicament, they yearned for someone who could love them and provide an escape from the perilous circumstances.

"You and Jack! Wow! Go mum! You hooked up with the hottest guy in the neighbourhood. I mean, I'd say that you shouldn't have cheated on dad, but fuck him. He was or is a wife beater. Who the fuck would want to stay with someone like that? I'm gutted because it turns out my father is literally a psychotic ass hole, but at the same time. You survived him, you got through all of it alive! Not many people get out of such a relationship alive. I hate that you had to endure all of that and wish you hadn't. But it proves how strong you are! If you survived him back then, then you will do it again. Plus now, you have me. I don't care if he is my dad, I'll kick his ass myself if I have to!"

In a heart wrenching moment, Bethany and Madison tightly embraced each other, their tearful cries reverberating off the walls.

"No matter what, mum, I'm always gonna be here for you. I won't let anyone hurt you ever again." Beth cried.

As they were cherishing their mother and daughter moment, their focus was abruptly shifted by the unmistakable sound of drilling coming from outside. Was someone trying to get in? Once again, fear wrapped its tendrils around Madison, its presence more palpable than ever, as she worried not only for herself, but most importantly for Beth. Logan assured her that the house was secure, but she couldn't shake the nagging feeling that the enemies might exploit a hidden vulnerability. Her concern grew as she contemplated the possibility of them gaining entry; she knew it could spell her doom. Damien wouldn't want to keep her alive; instead, he would manipulate his daughter into seeing Madison as the villain.

"What is that?" Beth asked, puzzled by the sound, trying to decipher its origin.

"No idea. But I don't like the sound of it." Her mother's response was filled with uncertainty, her voice wavering slightly.

Suddenly, a monitor in the office emitted a loud bleep, startling Madison and Bethany. They both hurried over to the screen, their hearts pounding with anticipation, only to be met with the sight they dreaded. The enemies had found them, and the frantic sounds of their attempts to break in filled the air. At the front of the house, a black transit van was parked, and a group of at least seven men were busy rummaging through it, pulling out various tools. They were trying each tool on the door, creating a symphony of scraping and banging noises. Madison wondered how long it would take them to breach the supposedly fortified house. Even for a team of experts, gaining entry would be a daunting challenge that could take several hours to accomplish. Beth couldn't help but question the security of the house.

"I don't think it will take them long to get in." She said, very concerned.

"Logan said the walls and doors are fortified. We should be okay." Madison's voice trembled slightly, betraying her true motive - to convince herself, rather than her daughter.

Their focus was interrupted by another noise from outside, drawing their attention away from their conversation.

"Is that a helicopter?" Bethany asked.

As the chopper's propellers spun, their whirring sound filled the air, creating an intense auditory experience. The sound seemed to be coming from directly above the house, creating an eerie sense of hovering. Just moments later, they heard a heavy thud on the roof, causing them both to startle, and then another one followed. Two people were on top of the house. As she listened, the relentless pounding of sledgehammers on the roof filled the room, growing louder with each strike.

"Shit. They are going to get in!" While he diligently fortified the walls, doors, and windows, he unintentionally neglected the importance of securing the roof.

"Fuck... fuck!" Panic coursed through Madison as she yelled, her legs trembling like jelly. With a heavy heart, she sank to the floor, her tears cascading uncontrollably.

As she stood there, a serene stillness settled upon Bethany.

Observing her mother's fear-induced breakdown, she recognised the necessity of remaining calm as the threat of certain death drew nearer. Madison's breathing became laboured, her chest heaving with each unsteady inhalation.

"Mum. Breath slowly, deep breaths. In... hold... out. I know we don't know Logan very well, but in the time we have known him. He has fought to protect us and take care of us. So I know that once he finds out that we have been taken, he will do everything in his power to find and rescue us. I've seen how he looks at you. He cares for you, mum, trust me. Logan will save us."

Looking into her daughter's eyes, Madison instantly felt a sense of tranquillity wash over her. Her breathing gradually returned to its regular rhythm. The sound of something crashing from upstairs filled the house, prompting her to wrap Bethany in the most intense embrace she had ever experienced.

"I love you so much, Bethany!"

Down the stairs, two men in cavalier armoured uniforms and masks swiftly made their way, armed and ready. With precision and focus, they directed their weapons towards their intended targets. A giant of a man, standing at least six foot four, was among the duo. In contrast, the other person was of a much more diminutive stature.

"Don't move! Move a muscle and we will shoot." The bigger man yelled.

He moved his finger to his ear.

"Got them boss. Targets located and secured."

# 28

With adrenaline coursing through their veins, Logan and Francis pushed themselves to keep running, desperate to escape their pursuers who had been chasing them for twenty minutes. Logan was taken aback by how the older man effortlessly matched his speed. Death was not a welcome visitor for either of the men, and they were far from ready to entertain its arrival. As they looked back, they could see the enemies gaining ground, their menacing figures growing larger with each passing moment. Both men were acutely aware that they had two choices: either evade their pursuers or confront them head-on. Glancing ahead, Logan's attention was drawn to a towering four-story car park, standing out amidst the urban landscape. It could be a place to gain an advantage, whether by evening the odds or acquiring a vehicle for a swift getaway.

"Head for the car park. Follow my lead." Logan said.

"Get a car and get out of here. Good idea." Figuring it was

a solid plan, Francis confidently uttered his approval.

With a shake of his head, Logan silently conveyed his disagreement. Their issue couldn't be solved by simply getting away; the relentless pursuit of the hunters would continue. Their determination knew no bounds; they would stop at nothing until Logan and anyone even remotely linked to him had met their demise.

"Or use the vehicles as cover and even the odds. We need to stop them, otherwise they won't stop. Looks like that gun is going to get some use."

Francis laughed, his eyes sparkling with excitement as he relished the opportunity to finally see some action and wield his weapon once more. Given his position at Scotland Yard, he seldom had the opportunity to employ the weapon. Refusing to let his skills with a gun deteriorate like everything else, he continued his target practice without pause. He forever longed for a final case, a conclusive endeavour. He often contemplated his fate, believing that his life would ultimately be claimed in the field, whether it be while serving in the army or the police force.

These criminals pushed the boundaries of brutality, shocking even the most seasoned law enforcement officers. With his arsenal of drugs and cunning methods, a single kingpin seized control of London's streets, leaving a trail of chaos and despair in his wake. Disobeying his orders came with dire consequences - a choice between being hurled from an overpass, risking collision with oncoming vehicles, or being forcefully ejected from a tall residential building. If they truly wronged him, then their punishment would be a prolonged and torturous demise, leaving them to suffer every moment until their last breath. The process began with the removal of the feet, followed by the precise detachment of the hands, and ultimately, the separation of the rest of each leg and arm. After being hacked off, each limb was immediately cauterised to prevent excessive blood loss. He was committed to keeping them alive, subjecting them to prolonged pain without mercy. Francis couldn't contain his joy when they finally took down that notorious criminal - it was an extraordinary drug bust, unparalleled in the annals of the United Kingdom. Refusing to surrender, he engaged in a battle that left several officers injured and a couple dead. The shot that dropped the vicious killer was fired by Francis, the deafening sound reverberating in the air.

"I agree there. Can I ask? Did you plant explosives in strategic spots, knowing that snipers were going to show up? Or was that coincidence that the explosions just so happened to go off at the perfect time?"

His questions hung in the air, unanswered and lingering. Survival took precedence over communication for Logan. That could come later. In a rush, they reached the car park and quickly ascended the stairs to the left of the entrance, their hurried breaths filling the air. They climbed higher and higher until they finally reached the third floor, feeling the burn in their legs with each step. The parking lot was filled with vehicles, providing ample hiding spots. Logan turned to Francis.

"Split up. I'll go right, you go left. At least then we can flank them. They will expect us to stick together. Don't hesitate to pull the trigger, trust me that won't."

Francis signalled his agreement with a nod. The thought of their lives hanging by a thread made most feel a knot in their stomachs, their nerves on edge. Not him. With a good and long life behind him, he faced death without trepidation.

"Oh, don't worry, I won't," Francis replied.

The hesitation of the police officers he was responsible for had tragic consequences, as their kind-hardheartedness often prevented them from using force when needed, resulting in numerous deaths. This vulnerability was exploited by certain criminals who would disable the officer, effectively ending their pursuit. He had adapted to dealing with such individuals and understood that hesitation was a dangerous luxury that could have deadly consequences. He recognised that there were instances when a moment of hesitation could serve as a lifesaving measure. In a harrowing incident, one of his colleagues found himself trapped inside a drug dealer's mansion following a disastrous drug bust that resulted in multiple fatalities. Overwhelmed by fear, she darted into a bedroom, her senses heightened as she anxiously listened for the sound of approaching footsteps. Upon hearing footsteps approaching, she swiftly aimed her weapon at the door, prepared to fire. However, she hesitated as the door swung open, and she breathed a sigh of relief when she saw that it was one of the housekeepers. If she hadn't hesitated, that person wouldn't be alive today.

Both men quickly sought cover behind vehicles positioned at opposite ends of the stairway exit. With their pistols in hand, Francis took a moment to ensure that his safety was disabled before they proceeded. He didn't want to risk being killed due to a rookie mistake; it would tarnish his reputation as a seasoned veteran. Their senses on high alert, they detected the faint, rhythmic sounds of footsteps steadily ascending the staircase. Using his acute hearing, Logan made an effort to tally the approaching men. The estimate settled at six, but the thought persisted that there had to be at least nine of them, casting a shadow of uncertainty. Marcus wouldn't have sent these men to their deaths unless it was solely for the purpose of showcasing his abundance of replacements. The movement halted abruptly as they reached the door, frozen in place. Were the men strategic enough to anticipate the ambush that awaited them?

Time seemed to stretch on endlessly as no one walked through the door for what felt like hours. Sensing their intention, Logan surmised that they were carefully plotting their approach, predicting that the first person to enter would execute a quick roll to minimise the risk of getting hit. It was expected that the next pair would divide, going in opposite directions, in an effort to disorient their target. The final batch posed the greatest threat as they possessed a vague understanding of the targets' locations, allowing them to provide covering fire for their comrades to take accurate shots and potentially hit their intended objective. The first three were sacrificial lambs, fully aware of their impending doom. This would provide an explanation for the extended amount of time it took them to get through the door.

As he suspected, the first one went into a barrel roll as he burst through the door. But before he could get a shot off,

Logan fired, the sharp crack of the gunshot shattering the silence. The bullet forcefully entered the man's temple, exiting with a violent explosion. A vivid splash of crimson adorned the open door and the adjacent wall. With swift precision, the second and third men entered the scene, unleashing a hail of bullets towards Logan, the noise reverberating around them. As he crouched behind the blue BMW M3, a bullet ricocheted off its roof, narrowly missing him by three inches. In an instant, he fired back, the recoil of the gun jolting through his arm. With a well-aimed shot, he managed to drop one of the attackers to the ground. Francis's bullet found its mark, striking the other man square in the chest, causing him to collapse instantly. Gasping for breath, he clutched his chest and within seconds, his life slipped away. The remaining men, concealed behind the walls next to the door, kept their presence unknown.

"You're outnumbered Logan. Why bother trying to fight? You are going to lose." One of the men called out.

"If we're outnumbered. Then why are you hiding?" Logan laughed.

There was complete silence as none of the men offered a response. Knowing the man's unparalleled expertise, they understood that a shootout would be futile, as he could swiftly neutralise them all, even if they had superior weaponry and stronger numbers. Logan Winters, known as the lethal guardian, had a multitude of stories dedicated to his legendary feats. They were all aware of the stories circulating about him - the times he had found himself completely surrounded by foes, with no one to rely on but himself. His superiors had given up hope, convinced he would never make it out alive. Yet he prevailed, his mind constantly churning with strategic plans. He had a strong aversion to the code-name the contingency man, but he had undeniably earned it.

*Let me take control! I'll kill these bastards. I'd get rid of that old fucker, too. We don't need a liability on the team. Come on, let me take care of this.*

'Francis could be useful. Your answer to everything is to just kill everyone.' Logan thought to himself, replying to Magnus.

*Really? That old fucker is going to be useful? At what, reading the newspaper? Hey! I'll have you know, I can be very diplomatic when I need to be. I just find a weapon helps when diplomacy fails.*

'You doubt him because of his age, yet he didn't hesitate to take one of those fuckers down did he? Why would I listen to you? You are literally the psychopath stuck in my head.'

*Correction, I'm not just in your head. I'm you, a better version. I mean, Madison seemed to love it when I took over.*

He could feel the anger bubbling up inside him, threatening to overflow. In his imagination, he yearned for Magnus to be a living being, allowing him to unleash his anger on the vile individual. He declined to provide any additional answers.

*Did I hit a nerve?*

The men stormed in, their guns firing recklessly, six foolhardy individuals hastening towards their own downfall. One by one, the lives of two men, then three, and finally four, were swiftly extinguished. Logan and Francis dodged the hail of bullets, their hearts pounding as they realised they had miraculously escaped unscathed. Not a single target was missed by either man, their aim was spot-on. Logan couldn't help but be impressed by the older gentleman, who seemed perfectly comfortable and in his element. With a final act of defeat, the last two men tossed their weapons aside and raised their hands in surrender.

"Don't shoot! Let's finish this like men, no weapons. Come on, Mr Winters, I've heard good things about you and would love to be the man to take you down in combat."

Was this man being serious?

Logan couldn't help but question the man's intelligence and determination to stay alive. Additionally, he observed his partner's silence, a clear indication of his reluctance to engage in hand-to-hand combat with a seasoned assassin.

"What's your name?" Logan asked.

"Jason."

"Well, Jason, you could have surrendered, and we'd have let you live. Because although your boss would say differently, I'd rather not have to kill any of you."

"Just because you are good at what you do, doesn't mean you are better than me. I have trained for a moment like this. Face the man that I'd heard so many stories about. Kill the man and be praised by Kane, maybe promoted." Jason said confidently.

*Gotta give it to him, he has the confidence. Shame we're gonna have to kill him. Wait… it's not a shame, this fucker brought it on himself.*

"You could have left alive, could have lived your life. But I like your confidence. It's good to be confident in your abilities." Logan said.

With a sense of urgency, Jason left no more time for talk and sprinted towards his target. His fists moved like lightning, unleashing a right hook, a left punch, and then another right hook, displaying his formidable fighting technique. Adding to his repertoire, he started incorporating kicks into his moves as well. His speed and strength were impressive, evident in the force behind each strike, but there was a distinct lack of conviction in his execution. Logan's swift reflexes allowed him to dodge each attack thrown at him, leaving his opponent surprised and vulnerable. Another punch was thrown, and in that split second, he spotted an opening. With his left hand, he firmly grasped Jason's arm, and then exerted an immense amount of pressure on Jason's elbow using the palm of his right hand. The bone snapped with a sickening crack, piercing through the flesh—a horrifying scene that elicited a piercing scream of pain from the man. As Logan stepped back, he assessed the situation, realising that dispatching the confident younger man would be a simple task. However, he ultimately opted against it. Jason's strength abandoned him, causing him to collapse to his knees, his tears pouring down like a river.

"You broke my fucking arm!" He screamed.

"One thing when fighting someone that you have never fought before. Never just go on a reckless attack. I could see every move you were going to make. You weren't anticipating any movements, just throwing punches and kicks aimlessly and hoping one or a few would it. Honestly, I could kill you right now. But I see potential in you. Once you are healed, work hard and improve on your abilities. Keep the confidence you have, but think ahead, fight with conviction. Like every fight could be your last. Which this could have been, but I have allowed you to live. Be better. I expect that I will see you again."

*What the fuck are you doing? Put a bullet between his eyes. No mercy! Never show mercy!*

The disbelief on Jason's face was evident as he processed the fact that he should have met his demise, yet here he was, being granted another opportunity.

"Why are you letting me live? You are a killer, a very good one, from what I've heard."

"That was my life before, when I worked for a man I wish that I never had to work with. Kane and his family took everything from me, all because I no longer wanted to work for them anymore. Being a good killer, doesn't mean you enjoy the act of killing. I never have, or ever will."

Francis watched intently, absorbing every word, even though they weren't directed at him. Despite their limited acquaintance, the man displayed an unexpected wisdom, as if he had lived many lifetimes. He considered that Logan was genuine, his previous doubts about ulterior motives fading away. Francis grasped that the individuals Logan sought to bring down had shattered his life beyond repair. In a situation where revenge often led to death, he couldn't help but question if the man in front of him had a more noble goal—to dismantle the company and ensure that those who had harmed him faced a lifetime behind bars. Though he was capable of killing without hesitation, he chose a less lethal strategy.

There was no response from Jason; his eyes cast downward, filled with a mixture of shame and defeat. He debated within his mind, questioning whether accepting a job working for Kane was the worst decision he had ever made. In an attempt to gauge the individual he would soon be working alongside, Francis's mind was filled with a pressing question. Logan urgently motioned for Jason's colleague to swiftly remove him from the scene, and without any hesitation, he promptly obeyed. They quickly fled the car park, the sound of their hurried footsteps fading into the distance.

"So once we get to this Kane fella. Are you killing him or would you prefer to see him rot in prison for the remainder of his life? It's clear that he wronged you greatly, same as that Marcus guy from earlier."

As Logan started his descent down the car park stairs, he could hear the distant hum of traffic. Francis reluctantly trailed behind, dreading the upcoming walk down. Stairs, in his eyes, were the epitome of inconvenience, and he despised their existence.

*They are dying slow and painful deaths. Bastards!*

"Honestly, I'd love to kill them all. But if there's a way to bring them down and have them rot away in prison, then I'd love to see them have to live with their decisions. But currently, my aim is taking the fuckers who killed my family down. I've waited long enough, losing my mind living on an island for nine years. I will admit, though, Kane is a hard man to kill. I know, I tried once and failed."

Madison and Bethany occupied Logan's thoughts, their faces vivid in his mind. If they had indeed been taken, he'd have to strategize on uncovering the whereabouts that Marcus might have chosen for them. Opting for catalyst collective as their destination would provide a higher level of security, yet it would also be the more foreseeable action for hiding them. The thought crossed his mind that Marcus might intentionally lead the girls to that place, hoping that Logan would overlook it due to its apparent obviousness. With little familiarity with Francis, he had no choice but to rely on him to save Madison and Bethany.

"The mother and daughter they have taken, I'm going to get them back. I'll need a hand, if you would be willing?"

Logan had only known the mother and daughter for a short time, but he had already developed a profound affection for them. Their presence brought him immense joy and he couldn't help but feel a strong connection with them. Despite the unfortunate circumstances of their meeting, his affection for them has only deepened, compelling him to protect them from torture and interrogation. He refused to let Damien harm them, fully prepared to take him down if it came to that.

"I'm not going to say no to helping anyone in danger. I'm in. What's the plan?"

The weight of the situation hit Logan as he realised he had no strategy in mind, except for one goal: to rescue Madison and Bethany. The most probable scenario was that they would be brought to the head quarters, where Kane would have full control over their surveillance and access. In order to successfully infiltrate the building, a detailed plan would need to be devised.

"I have an idea of where they would be taken. It would be getting in that would be the problem, they would amp up security, so it would be like breaking into a fortress."

"So our mission is to basically pull off a heist, only not to get money. To save your friends. It's not something I've done before, but there's a first for everything right? Maybe we could use a distraction?"

Logan had already contemplated that, yet he realised that Kane and Marcus would anticipate a tactic to divert their focus. They would be ready and waiting. Madison and Beth were captured, their lives now being used as bait to lead him to his ultimate demise. A smart move. However, he had no intentions of meeting his demise on that particular day.

"They would expect me to try to distract them, I've done it before. I have an idea, but the possibility of both of us being killed are high, unless we can pull it off perfectly." Logan said, mapping out a plan in his head.

"Well, I'm what some people would call an old man. I've lived a good life, I'm not afraid of death. Preferably I'd rather not be killed, as I see taking down this company as my last big case. Every detective has one, well the famous ones definitely do." Francis said, not being deterred by his possible demise.

"We need some gear. I have a place not far from here. Should have the stuff we need there. Let's get going before the cops get here."

Turning left onto the street, the blaring sirens reached their ears, growing louder with each passing second. The authorities would arrive at the scene only to find that they had long since vanished.

# 29

As Kane poured himself a whisky on the rocks, he could smell the rich, smoky aroma of the liquor. Sat at his huge desk, he took small, deliberate sips from his cup, relishing the taste. News spread quickly that the winter's family home had been consumed by a devastating fire. Despite everything, Marcus still hadn't made contact to verify that his target had been eliminated.

Logan's departure from the company left Kane with no other option but to issue the order for his execution. No matter how indispensable he was to the catalyst collective, Kane couldn't allow any loose ends to jeopardise their operations. The thick, imposing oak doors of his office were pushed open. Despair radiated from Damien's face as he approached.

"Damien. I didn't expect to be seeing you. What's the problem?"

"We had word from one of the men who was watching Logan's property. He came out of the house. Marcus did not. I fear that Logan killed him, otherwise we'd have heard something from him."

Kane was disappointed by the unexpected news concerning Logan, but he acknowledged that removing him from the equation would require great effort. Seeking to disrupt their enemy's strategic planning, he made the decision to have Marcus target the family initially, igniting a fiery rage that would hinder any calculated retaliation.

"Go there, find my son!" Kane demanded.

"What will you do?" Damien asked.

"Wait for him. He would know very well who gave the order. Out of anger, he will come here and attempt to take my life. He will fail."

"Was this part of your plan all along?"

"Logan isn't the only man who plans ahead. Now go."

As Damien hurriedly left, he made sure to firmly close the door behind him. Kane stood up from his chair, his eyes drawn to the panoramic window that offered a view of the sprawling London city. It was an amazing sight to behold, with the vast variety of skyscrapers, tower blocks, and bridges stretching as far as the eye could see. The rain started pounding against the window, mirroring the sombre mood that Kane would be in if his son's death was confirmed. From his suit jacket pocket, he carefully pulled out his phone, its sleek design catching the light. His black tailored suit accentuated his short, greying hair. As he entered the number on his mobile and pressed dial, the phone immediately started ringing, and someone picked up on the other end without hesitation. The person on the other end would have been very aware of Kane tapping his foot impatiently, awaiting what was to come.

"Boss. What can I do for you?"

"We are due to have a guest. Mr Winters. Let him up, do not harm him in anyway."

Before he could even utter a word in response to his boss, a gunshot shattered the air, abruptly ending the conversation. This was followed by a series of additional shots, permeating the airwaves. As he listened through the phone speaker, the cacophony of sounds transported him to what could only be described as a war zone. He ended the call, sinking into his chair and eagerly anticipating the imminent arrival of his visitor. His attention was immediately captured by the sound of shots reverberating in the corridor outside his office, indicating that his adversary was getting closer. The sounds of screams and gunshots intertwined as Logan mercilessly slaughtered anyone who stood in his way.

As the doors burst open, Logan strode into the large office, his heavy footsteps resonating in the silence. He came to an abrupt halt, his eyes narrowing in surprise as he noticed Kane seated serenely behind his desk. He was torn between the overwhelming urge to use every bullet left in his possession on the man who had ordered his family's execution and the deep-seated desire to personally strangle him to death. His intention was to gradually extinguish the life from the man who had irrevocably wrecked his own.

"You killed them! Why?! My family did nothing wrong and you took them from me! All because I no longer wanted to work with you?!" He shouted in anger, if he could breathe fire. The room would have been engulfed in flames.

"You were very aware, Mr Winters, that you can't just leave. You know vital information about this company and what we do, some that we couldn't have you speaking about with anyone. You know this. What did you expect?" Kane replied.

"You could have just killed me! They didn't deserve to die!"

Kane rose from his chair, his towering six-foot-four frame dominating the room. Despite his age, his muscles threatened to tear through his suit, a display of his impressive physical prowess. His age didn't deter him from being a force to be reckoned with. Having trained in multiple military outfits throughout his life, he became an exceptional fighter and skilled marksman.

"How do we know that you had not spoken to your wife concerning the company? We couldn't, so she needed to be taken care of. The kids were just collateral. You were supposed to die too. I'm guessing Marcus didn't make it out alive?"

"You are a sick bastard! Marcus is dead. Did you really think he would be the one to take me down? You have been better sending Evan. Oh, wait… he doesn't like violence. You and your family will pay for what you did."

Logan went on the offensive, charging towards the older

gentleman with determination in his eyes. With a powerful leap, Kane soared over the desk and delivered a forceful kick to his enemy's chest, causing him to stagger and retreat.

"Do you truly think that you will best me?" Kane laughed.

Logan's punches and kicks came in quick succession - right hooks, left jabs, leg kicks - but his opponent effortlessly defended against every strike. With a display of brute strength, Kane lifted him off the ground and flung him across the room, crashing into a towering glass casing that housed a mannequin dressed in samurai armour. As the glass shattered, a million tiny fragments covered the entire floor, glinting in the light. As the outfit dropped to the ground, it made a loud clatter, causing the katana, protected by its scabbard, to come crashing down too. The broken glass crunched beneath Logan's palms as he crawled, the pain intensifying with each slice. He firmly grasped the weapon, feeling the weight and power in his hand as he unsheathed it.

"Pathetic. That's not going to help you." He sighed.

With lightning-fast reflexes, Kane skilfully manoeuvred away from his attacker, barely breaking a sweat. With a swift spin, his elbow collided with Logan's face, and a series of punches quickly followed. The contrast between their abilities was stark, with him clearly outshining Logan and making him appear inexperienced.

"I overestimated you. If you call this fighting, then I don't understand how my son couldn't kill you. Hit me. Come on."

Logan's quick and precise motions resulted in a devastating strike to Kane's right arm, causing a deep gash that started just below the elbow. The sting was intense; the blade was designed to effortlessly slice through foes. If he had exerted more strength, the arm would have been severed completely. The blade had such sharpness that it could slice through the bone without any difficulty. With the sight of the older man's hurt expression, Logan's resolve strengthened, and he relentlessly attacked with the katana. After feeling the sting of the blade, Kane was determined to avoid any further contact with it.

Just as the weapon swung down, he turned with impeccable timing, narrowly avoiding being hit by a hair's breadth. With a firm grip, he clutched his enemy's hand, exerting all his strength to immobilise the blade. With a precise strike, he landed a punch directly on Logan's brachial plexus, causing a sharp crack that signified a broken collarbone. Logan's left hand became numb, causing him to suppress a scream of agony. His body filled with anger and adrenaline, he instinctively gripped the katana with his right hand and swung it towards Kane. But with another swift movement, his enemy struck him with a powerful punch to his bicep, the force reverberating through his entire body. Forcing him to drop the weapon. He was rendered defenceless, and it became clear to him that victory was slipping away.

Without any hope of succeeding with additional attacks, he opted to escape. The sensation of paralysis gradually subsided, but deep down, he had a sinking feeling that defeat was inevitable. His boiling anger would be his downfall; he had to disappear completely. The realisation hit Kane like a thunderbolt as he witnessed one of his most formidable killers decide to evade the unavoidable grip of death. With a sense of disbelief, he observed Logan's hasty departure from his office.

"We will find you, Logan. There's no point in running. We will always find you." Kane uttered.

With each step, Logan's pace quickened, his heart pounding in his chest, as he ran towards the promise of future retribution.

# 30

Contrary to popular belief, being a politician was far from enjoyable, with its countless challenges and pressures. Grant Leckie's dream was to see a government where ethics and accountability were valued, unlike the current state of corrupt parliament members. He was one of the rare few who genuinely wanted to make a positive impact on the country and its people's lives. He understood from the start that it would be a challenging endeavour.

Nonetheless, there were those who had selfish motives and were solely interested in filling their own wallets, which added to the difficulty. Rather than appreciating and making slight changes to the infrastructure that had been painstakingly built. They yearned to tear it all down, replacing it with a fresh start where they held dominion over every single detail in the lives of others. The primary motive behind digitising money was to gain control and authority over it. They were determined to establish their new world order, and they had devised strategies to ensure compliance with their rules.

With the deaths of several members of parliament weighing heavily on his mind, he formulated a theory to make sense of the tragedies. Someone was methodically getting rid of them, only to replace them with individuals who could be easily influenced into assisting their agenda of achieving dominance over the United Kingdom, and potentially global control in the future. A nagging suspicion tugged at him constantly, hinting that something was amiss.

Nine months ago, he embarked on a mission to unravel the mystery that had been gnawing at him ever since the untimely passing of the charismatic party leader, Donald Larkin. According to reports, he apparently swerved off the road to avoid an unknown animal and ended up in the River Ouse. Despite his desperate efforts, he was unable to release his seat belt and met a watery grave. That was the story they settled on, despite its flaws and inconsistencies. With a desire to uncover what really happened, he took it upon himself to hire a private detective. After a week of anticipation, he eagerly awaited the detective's report. His discoveries were brought back, and they proved to be incredibly disturbing.

The reported incident of Donald swerving off the road was not accurate. A small piece of tyre rubber was uncovered by the detective, concealed under a bush, adding another puzzle piece to the investigation. The vehicle had been taken and stored in a metal yard, where it sat among a sea of other cars, awaiting its turn to be crushed. Upon closer examination, the small piece revealed itself to be a match, confirming the tire's explosion. He cut through the rest of the rubber, feeling the satisfying resistance of the material as it gave way under his blade. The inner alloy bore an unmistakable indent, evidence of a powerful impact, accompanied by a burn mark. The tyre was targeted and shot, resulting in an explosion that caused the driver to lose control of the vehicle.

The politician's death was not a mere accident; it was a deliberate act of murder.

Equipped with that knowledge, Grant commenced his investigation into the remaining deaths of high-ranking parliament members. He found three cases that stood out as flawless executions, as they had been meticulously concealed. In his search, he found no tangible proof, leading him to ponder if it was not just a single person responsible for all the assassinations. Otherwise, each one would have been untraceable like those three. The individual responsible for taking care of those ones was highly competent and diligent in their clean-up efforts.

Looking into the deaths garnered attention that was not desired. Within a short time, cars started appearing down the road from his house, their occupants always on alert, watching his every move. Questioning their visibility, he pondered whether their purpose was to unsettle him. This made him feel a deep sense of fear for his life. Still, he was resolute in his decision to not let go of his mission to track down the individuals responsible for the deaths of several politicians, including people he had once called friends. Every second felt like a ticking time bomb, as he navigated his life under the constant threat of being killed. In case he met an untimely demise, he made sure that evidence exposing the deaths as targeted assassinations would be shared online and distributed to every news channel.

He had been careful to keep his investigation covert, but it became apparent that someone had uncovered his actions and tipped off the very people he wanted to stay oblivious to his meddling. Among the documents he uncovered, he noticed the recurring initials KH scribbled in several places. But was yet to determine who they belonged to. In the documents, she discovered a group of shady government officials, all sharing the same initials - Kenneth Harvey, Kevin Hendal, and Kaine Hertin - hinting at a potential conspiracy.

He had thoroughly examined their accounts, albeit through means that were not legally sanctioned. But each one was came across as clear of any potential to be having others killed. By surreptitiously diverting funds from several companies, they displayed an uncanny knowledge of each owner's confidential details, which they intended to keep hidden from the public eye. Apart from that, there were no specific details that could identify them as the person he sought.

He took a guess that it wasn't a government official pulling the strings, but rather an unknown puppeteer. With such incriminating knowledge, this individual had the power to blackmail numerous people into obeying their every command. This indicated that the individual possessed exceptional resourcefulness.

When he peeped out his window, he immediately saw that the car was parked significantly closer to his home. Furthermore, he had another realisation. There was no trace of the two men inside the car.

Where were they?

The sound of rustling and quick movement caught his attention from behind. As he started to turn, a sudden, brutal strike from behind jolted him, the unmistakable sensation of cold, hard metal against his head. The force of the impact knocked him down, his body sprawled on the ground, unable to regain his footing. As he lay there, his vision started to blur, and he fought to keep his eyes open. In a matter of seconds, he was engulfed by an impenetrable black void.

# 31

Walking through Sunlight Square, the walls were adorned with graffiti, some of which was truly remarkable. While some parts could be considered perfect artwork, others were nothing more than terrible scribbles of paint. The area lacked charm, with dilapidated structures that were long overdue for a makeover. Unfortunately, the local council showed no interest in allocating funds for much-needed renovations.

Despite not having been in the area for many years, Logan found that not much had improved since nine years ago when he arrived. He could confidently affirm that it was a significant upgrade from its current condition. Francis had witnessed numerous buildings, alleyways, bridges, and walls, each one marred by vandalism. To claim their presence, individuals often spray paint their crew name as a warning to those unfamiliar with their side of London.

"You have a place around here?" Francis asked, his brows furrowed in confusion, why anyone would willingly choose to live in that area, notorious for its lack of amenities and high crime rates.

"I don't live in it. It's more of a stash house. I keep gear, weapons, food and drink there."

The older gentleman found himself constantly mulling over how Logan had acquired the uncanny ability to predict the positions of the snipers surveying the cafe, leaving little space for any other thoughts. The doubts nagged at him, as he couldn't shake the feeling that the man he had only known for a couple of hours was hiding something. Perhaps he was an acquaintance of someone who had once been a foe to Francis? He tried to push the thought aside, but it clung to him stubbornly.

A detective's mind never retires.

"Continuing from my question earlier, well, basically repeating it. How did you know where the snipers would be, you planted explosives in pretty precise locations."

Over a span of six years, Logan's expertise as a marksman rested on his keenness to meticulously observe and track enemy positions for extended periods of time. Diligently scanning the surroundings, he arrived at the cafe well ahead of schedule, searching for potential sniper positions. With careful consideration of trajectory, distance, and wind influence, he thoroughly analysed how the bullet's speed and angle would be altered in each position. Identifying prime spots, perfect for precise and lethal shots.

"I arrived at the cafe an hour and a half before our planned meeting. Determining potential spots for snipers, as with every ambush. If the ones on the ground can't take out the targets, you have the marksman or sometimes two. Just in case one of the best misses his shot. It happens." Logan explained.

Francis couldn't help but admire the proactive mindset of his new comrade, and he was thankful for their well-thought-out strategies. Without taking precautions against a potential ambush, it is probable that both of them would have perished. Excitement coursed through him, his adrenaline pumping as he eagerly anticipated what lay ahead, even if it meant his ultimate demise. He finally felt alive again, his heart beating with newfound energy.

"Well, you are clearly a man with a plan. I've known people similar, but never that good at depicting rough locations of snipers. But then again, I've not had to deal with such an ambush that involved marksmen before. It used to be gang members, so typically just pistols and machine guns. Most couldn't even land a good shot. Where the ones we are up against are much different to what I'm used to."

"From what I saw, you handle yourself very well with a gun. Trust me, even with all the training they receive, some still aren't great shots. So you will be able to handle them easily. Do you go to target practice often? I'm guessing that's what has kept your precision… well so precise. Especially being a retired detective." Logan said.

The apartment complex loomed ahead, its worn-out facade and crumbling exterior hinting at its desperate need for refurbishment. However, the possibility of that occurring in the near future was unlikely, given the notorious hoodlums who call this place their home. Any attempt to restore its appearance would be futile, as graffiti artists would soon deface it and it would become a canvas for bullet holes. The gangs in the vicinity showed no mercy. They would fire an entire magazine into houses, flats, and apartments without a second thought. More often than not, it involves an individual trespassing into a restricted postcode or area, perhaps due to drug-related activities or a personal animosity towards the inhabitants.

Using a key that he had painted blue, Logan opened the door with a satisfying click. To ensure efficiency, he had colour-coded his keys and etched initials on each one, making it effortless to access the different safe houses. This key had SS engraved on it, for sunlight square. Walking towards the stairs, Francis turned and noticed the elevator, its shiny doors beckoning with the promise of a quick ascent.

He guessed that there was a valid reason behind the decision to use the stairs instead. Having reached his limit with stairs, he begrudgingly followed along. As they started to climb, a pungent odour of urine assaulted their senses. The stairs, once a pristine white, complemented the grey walls perfectly. The surfaces of both were now grimy, with dirt, spoiled food, drink spills, and unsightly urine stains. It made Francis wonder if the elevator would have been worse?

"I go two to three times a week. Didn't want my aim to diminish like everything else." Francis replied.

"That makes sense. I'd be the same. Plus, with retirement,

it must be something to focus on. Are you a man with many hobbies?" Logan asked, wanting to know more about the man he was going to be working with.

"I love to read, but then you must have already deduced that. I like doing puzzles, things that keep my mind going. Even dabbled in writing a book myself. But didn't get very far on that. How about yourself? Do anything other than avoiding being killed?" He laughed.

Stepping out of the stairs onto the fifth floor, they found themselves in a narrow corridor flanked by numerous closed doors. The putrid smell lingered, making Francis' eyes sting and leaving a foul taste in the air. The sense of being trapped in an unending corridor only intensified as they continued walking past the countless doors.

Logan's sole focus was on getting inside the apartment, causing him to disregard the question he was asked. With key number 46 in hand, he selected a key that had a slightly lighter blue hue and used it to unlock the door.

As he stepped inside, his ears picked up on the faint sound of movement coming from the living room. The room fell silent as the door creaked open, revealing the young man and woman on the sofa, their expressions shifting from passion to shock in an instant. The girl had been straddling the man, but her panic caused her to lose her footing and crash down onto the ground. In an attempt to maintain her modesty, she hastily grabbed a cushion, though it was clear that she needed something much larger.

"Who the fuck are you?" She asked.

"I'm the owner of this apartment. Wondering why there

are two people living here?" Logan guessed that he'd end up with squatters. They'd bought a television or stolen one. As he hadn't put anything like that within the apartment. Only gear and essential things.

"Well… You haven't ever lived here. This is our apartment, so you should fucking leave." The younger man said, as he stood up from the sofa. Not even attempting to cover himself.

"Wasn't expecting a reception. But I'll give you the choice. Leave now and be able to return later if I allow it. Or we can do this the hard way."

With a resolute look on her face, the woman moved forward to express her thoughts, leaving no doubt that she was prepared for a confrontation. Despite wanting to argue, she bit her tongue when she remembered that they were the ones unlawfully occupying the area. With no alternative accommodations, they were astonished that the owner would even contemplate the idea of allowing them to stay. As long as they left at that moment, to return later.

"Erm… Can we at least get dressed first?" She asked.

"Of course, I'm not going to force anyone to go out with no clothes on. It's cold out there."

*You are losing your edge. Why would you give them an option to return?*

In their rush to get dressed, they both frantically fumbled with their clothes, the man clumsily tripping over himself while trying to pull up his trousers. After a couple of minutes, they were fully dressed, with their shoes on and prepared to depart. As they approached the door, Logan motioned for them to pause by extending his hand. Extracting a handful of bills from his pocket, he displayed a wad of cash. Handing over several hundred pounds, he watched as the girl's eyes widened in surprise.

"Find a hotel, stay there for tonight." He said, being very generous.

With a quick nod exchanged between them, they hastily exited the apartment, their footsteps resonating loudly as they sprinted down the corridor. Francis was taken aback by Logan's unexpected display of kindness. Finding people squatting in his apartment, he'd have been less generous.

"That was… nice of you. I expected it to go a different way. She looked prepared for an argument. Why did you give them the choice to return? Do you not plan on living here at all?"

Taking in the sights, he couldn't ignore the overwhelming sense of squalor that surrounded him. "Saying that… I wouldn't want to live here. Are you going to let them continue squatting though? They've clearly been living here rent free for a while." Francis said, wondering if Logan was just feeling very charitable.

"For me, this place is more for storage than living. I have others, but no, they won't continue living here for free. They will have to pay something for staying here."

The apartment boasted two bedrooms, with the main bedroom showing signs of occupation by the man and woman, while the spare room appeared as though it had never been used. It was evident that the room had been intentionally designed to be smaller than the rest, and there was a logical explanation behind it. The room, as it was viewed, wasn't the full size. Upon entering, Logan's confidence grew as he observed that the people who had been occupying his property had yet to uncover his hidden stash, which had been expertly concealed.

"Open." He said.

As soon as those words left his lips, the entire wall shifted and groaned. With a gentle tilt upward, the mechanism effortlessly lifted it over what resembled a series of wardrobes. Francis couldn't believe his eyes; his jaw dropped in awe as he felt like he had been transported into the thrilling world of James Bond. He'd never have guessed that anything was behind that wall, apart from the other apartments.

"Wow. Who are you? A super spy? I've never seen anything like that before, apart from in movies."

He reached out and touched the sleek, black glass panel positioned on the left side of the wooden framed storage compartment. As his palm was scanned by a green light, the doors swiftly opened. Inside, a small armoury was revealed, with racks of assault rifles, snipers, and machine guns lining the walls. Francis couldn't help but notice a rocket launcher among the weapons. The left side displayed a row of black carry bags, artfully arranged within the racking. It was remarkable how efficiently the small space was utilised and filled.

"I don't believe in over preparation." Logan uttered with a laugh seeping out.

"Clearly." Francis replied.

"So what's the plan?" He continued.

With a plan already forming in his mind, Logan understood that he would need some extra support to ensure his survival.

"We're getting into the catalyst collective. We just need an extra pair of hands." Logan said.

The older man was puzzled, searching for someone who could offer assistance. It seemed that his new friend didn't have many allies. The presence of coded messages in his books suggested his intention to enlist assistance and he was currently the only person who was assisting. Unless there was another who uncovered it all before him.

"Have you got someone in mind? I can't imagine your list of allies is very big. Or you wouldn't have any need for an old man like me." He laughed.

"There is one man who could help. But if he will is another question. I will have to meet him alone though. He has serious trust issues."

The uncertainty in the person's willingness to help made Francis question the feasibility of their mission, fearing it could be a suicidal endeavour.

"What if this man says no?"

It would come as a complete surprise to Logan if this person, who had never turned down a request for help, did so now. However, the man's life had completely transformed, making it possible. Determined to create a better life, he turned away from a world of bullets and death, embracing a future with his wife and children.

"My brother could say no. We shall see."

# 32

The wind howled, causing the trees to sway and creak in response. With determination in his eyes, Lincoln carefully navigated through the woods, his senses heightened as he searched for his target. With his rifle aimed and ready, his prey was doomed as soon as it entered his line of vision.

Throughout his years of service in the army and his shorter stint in the Special air service, he had amassed a collection of medals. He gained a reputation for his exceptional skills with a ranged weapon, as he had a perfect track record of never missing a shot. Amidst the noise surrounding him, he found tranquillity in the wilderness, his second happy place. With the wind blowing through his long, tied back hair, his big, neatly kept beard added to his rugged and distinguished appearance. There was a reason why he no longer resembled the person he once was, and it was evident in his altered appearance.

In the eyes of his enemies, he was nothing more than a memory, and he relished the freedom that came with being presumed dead. His other source of happiness was being with his wife and sons. Their presence always brought a smile to his face. Being in the military meant he was frequently away, which unfortunately limited the amount of time he could spend with them. Nevertheless, he developed the ability to provide for his family through any means necessary.

Beside a towering tree, he observed the tracks that abruptly changed direction, leading off to the left. The gentle glow of the morning sun illuminated the animal, allowing him to spot it easily. A graceful deer came into sight, its majestic antlers catching the sunlight. In the woodlands near Knockholt, there was a remarkable abundance of wildlife to behold.

The fact that their home came with four acres of land was a dream come true, especially since half of it was a dense, untouched forest. The hunting ground was tailor-made for someone like Lincoln, with its rugged terrain and untamed beauty. Moving slowly into a prone position, he felt the rough ground beneath him.

Target in sight.

Dinner was right ahead, yet he couldn't bring himself to take the shot and end the life of an innocent creature. He couldn't quite figure out why he hesitated to take the shot; perhaps a sense of generosity washed over him. Or maybe it was the words of his son that lingered in his mind from the day before.

When Alex turned twelve, his father couldn't help but feel that his intelligence was a double-edged sword. Curiosity consumed him as he interrogated his dad about life and death, particularly the absence of compassion in certain individuals when it comes to ending a life. If the roles were reversed, they would never wish for someone to prematurely end their life.

The sanctity of life was universally recognised, and no one should meet an untimely demise or have their life forcibly taken away. How could anyone claim the right to decide when someone's time on this earth should be over? As his son made a compelling argument, Lincoln couldn't deny the truth behind his own track record of callously extinguishing the lives of numerous individuals. When faced with enemy fire in the military, there's no room for empathy towards the person pulling the trigger - it's all about self-preservation. Consequently, the prevailing sentiment among all is to eliminate potential threats pre-emptively, fearing the consequences of inaction.

As Alex learned about World War, the magnitude of the human cost during those difficult times became a focal point of the conversation. It didn't go in the direction of animals, but made Lincoln reconsider as he felt a chill run down his spine. The animal he had in his sights was grazing peacefully, unaware of his presence. Engrossed in its daily routine, it probably had its own family waiting eagerly for its return.

'Damn it Alex.' He thought to himself.

Despite knowing that having children would make him more emotional, he didn't realise it would influence his ability to take down a deer, which was supposed to be their meal for the night. The absence of a carcass meant that the journey back would be less burdensome, he reasoned.

As he arrived at his home on the edge of Knockholt, he enjoyed the solitude, with the nearest house half a mile away. He had sensors strategically placed around his land, ensuring a peaceful existence. He understood that his enemies wouldn't bother looking for a dead man, yet he stayed on guard, anticipating the day when everything could shift once more.

Though not extravagant, the house offered a warm and inviting atmosphere for him and his family. Both he and his brother shared a distaste for large, extravagant houses. It always made them question why anyone would desire to reside in a mansion, where simply locating your own bedroom could become an arduous task. Such a huge house would be perfect for hide and seek though, it would take hours and hours for kids to find one another.

As far as the eye could see, the land around his home was adorned with endless stretches of vibrant greenery, creating a stunning scene. The evenings were made magical by the breathtaking sight of the sun setting, painting the sky with vibrant hues and creating intricate shadows of the blades of grass.

He had his own farm, where the sound of chickens clucking and cows mooing filled his days. He loved his animals, and though the work was messy, it was also rewarding. He had ten cows, two horses, and three pigs. His wife Stephanie, just like him, cherished every animal with the same love and devotion she had for her children. With its intricate detailing and ornate architecture, his home exuded a timeless Victorian charm, despite its relatively young age. But both he and Steph were enchanted by that vintage aesthetic. Given the context, a modern looking home would have been an odd sight in that area.

Using his key to unlock the front door, he entered the home and was immediately greeted by the sound of laughter and the sight of two young boys rushing over with the happiest of faces. Alex was the older of them. Thomas, a lively seven-year-old, was always bursting with energy, while his brother preferred the company of books, reserving his energy.

"Dad!" Thomas yelled in excitement.

"Boys! You okay?" Lincoln asked, as he embraced them both.

"I found sergeant Shephard! He had fallen down the side of my bed. He is safe now." Thomas said, glad that he had found the toy he thought had been lost forever.

"That's brilliant news! So, Shephard is back reporting for duty huh?"

"Yeah, he has a princess to save." He replied, before running off, heading upstairs to play with his figures.

"You didn't bring anything home from your hunt today." Alex said, puzzled by the lack of anything for dinner. He had seen his father use a rifle several times, even gone hunting with him and although he didn't enjoy it. He was amazed at his fathers skill with a weapon.

"You know what? I thought that the animals can enjoy themselves and live their lives. Your words about choosing to live helped me make that decision. How did I get a son so smart huh?"

A smile illuminated Alex's face, relief flooding over him as he realised the animals were safe from any harm that day. Just like everyone else, they deserved the chance to live.

"The books help. And having the coolest dad ever!" He replied.

Lincoln reached down and lifted his son up and into his arms.

"The coolest? Now that is the best compliment. I will keep it to myself though. Mummy might get jealous." He laughed.

Stephanie approached from the kitchen, her long blonde hair cascading over her shoulders, accentuating her stunning appearance. Covered in a mishmash of cooking ingredients, she somehow managed to maintain her natural beauty. Lincoln had always been drawn in by her captivating, bright blue eyes, which seemed to sparkle in the light. Their initial encounter began with him admiring her eyes, unable to look away.

"Wow! You have amazing eyes." He said.

A blush spread across her cheeks, turning them a rosy hue. Being unaccustomed to compliments, she didn't quite know how to react when someone praised her.

"The rest of you isn't too bad either." Lincoln laughed.

It was on that day that she felt a certainty about him being the right person for her, especially after he had been so kind and attentive all evening, buying her drinks but not going overboard. He escorted her back home to ensure her safety, but rejected her advance when she tried to kiss him. He wanted her to be clear-headed so he could gauge her true desire to proceed.

In his character, he possessed an unwavering commitment to treating women with respect, even when they were inebriated. While her friends had given her stronger drinks, he had only ordered the drinks she had specifically requested. His constant vigilance was directed towards spotting any individuals attempting to spike the beverages. Even with a slight buzz from the drinks, he stayed vigilant and on high alert. Knowing that many predators lurked around bars and pubs. There was no way he would let anyone exploit Stephanie or her friends.

After getting his number the night before, she wasted no time and called him the very next day, hoping to continue the connection they had. Asking if he would be up for meeting for a coffee. Without hesitation, he agreed, excited about the prospect of getting to know her better. From that second meeting onwards, a deep and powerful affection developed between them, binding them together.

He gently placed Alex back down on the floor before crossing over to his wife, showering her with affectionate kisses and warm embraces.

"What are you baking today, my dear?" He asked.

"Just some cookies today. Oh, and gingerbread men. I know you guys seem to eat them the fastest."

"We do love gingerbread men. Especially when you make

them. Yours are the best. What would we do without you?"

"Starve." She laughed.

"I'm sure we wouldn't. We just have very burnt food daily." Lincoln uttered with a smile.

"Didn't find anything out there?" She asked, confused on why he didn't return home with anything.

Without fail, he would return from his hunting expeditions with something to feast on, the result of his skilful butchering and preparation. Not this day.

"I did. I just didn't feel like taking the life of an animal today." He looked down, as if ashamed.

Whenever something was weighing on her husband's mind, Stephanie had an uncanny ability to pick up on it, a skill she had mastered since they first crossed paths. Despite his attempts to hide his feelings, she could still see the vulnerability beneath his facade of strength.

"What's up babe?"

"Just something Alex said. He is too smart for his age."

"He's like his dad."

"That's the first time that you've referred to me as smart." He let out a laugh.

"I mean, he's caring, he see's the good in everybody."

He gave her a grin, but as he did, a wave of regret washed over him, reminding him of all the wrongs he had committed. His remorse ran deep for certain choices he had made, forever haunting him with the knowledge that forgiveness would never come. In order to save hundreds, maybe thousands of lives, he knew there were other tasks that had to be completed. After spending time in the army and then joining the SAS, he eventually ended up working for the man he ultimately desired to eliminate. The sum of his experiences defined his character, leading him to be widely recognised as one of the country's most skilled snipers and soldiers.

Life taught him the value of cherishing moments spent with loved ones, realising that those were the moments that truly mattered. Despite his selfless sacrifice and tireless efforts for his country, he found himself in a cruel twist of fate, being pursued by the authorities for a crime he would never have had the heart to commit. The only method to put an end to their actions was by satisfying their desires. Him dead.

The absence of a body was explained by multiple witnesses who saw him enter the front of the building right before it was engulfed in a devastating explosion. Despite the burn scars that marked his arms and back, he found comfort in the fact that his family remained untouched, making it all worthwhile. In the aftermath of the struggle, he was forced into hiding, and he had to convince his own family that he was dead. It was an unpleasant task to explain what happened when he reappeared.

He spent months in hiding, tormented by the fear that Stephanie would move on and find someone else. He had always made it clear to her that if anything were to happen to him, he would want her to find happiness and continue living. Unbeknownst to him, he had no idea that he would eventually be faced with the unexpected task of faking his own death. As he observed her, he noticed how she used the kids as a shield, trying to hide her sadness behind their innocent laughter. No matter the circumstances, his brother would find a way to offer assistance.

After all was said and done, he couldn't shake the thought of whether his brother had secretly deduced that he was not, in fact, deceased. If he had though, he'd made no attempt to make contact. Following his supposed demise, the very same company that had set him up bestowed Stephanie with millions of pounds, in a deceptive display of mourning for the loss of Lincoln. What he did was a direct result of their involvement, and it was because of them that he took action. In their headquarters, they went as far as putting up a plaque to honour him. Pathetic.

"I've done a lot of bad things that I can never make up for. I can't get past that." He said.

"The thing is babe, you served your country for years and how did they repay you? So don't feel guilty. At the time of doing those things, you were doing your job. I know it's hard, but me and the boys are always here for you. No matter what."

In a display of deep affection, he pulled her into a tight hug, and then gently brushed his lips against hers, savouring the softness.

"I love you." He said.

"I love you too, always." She replied, giving him another kiss.

Just as they were immersed in a caring moment, a sudden, jarring knock at the door startled them. They had no expectations of receiving visitors or deliveries. The unexpected guest had Lincoln on high alert, his senses heightened and ready for any potential threat.

Why had his sensors not picked anything up?

He urgently gestured to Stephanie, indicating that she should gather the children and retreat upstairs. In a rush, she rounded up Alex and Thomas, quietly instructing them to come upstairs with her. Without a word of complaint, they obediently followed their mother up the stairs, their practiced movements showing their familiarity with the routine.

Lincoln made his way to the front door, pausing momentarily to observe a metallic locked cabinet placed strategically nearby. After entering a four digit code, the hallway was filled with a double bleeping sound that reverberated in the air. With a swift motion, he pulled out a glock 17 and disabled the safety, the weight of the gun in his hand giving him a sense of power. Pressing the button to release the magazine, he checked to make sure the weapon still had enough ammunition. Although it hadn't been used, his cautious nature compelled him to inspect it thoroughly. With a satisfying click, the gun was loaded and ready for action.

Another knock came.

He reached into his pocket and retrieved his mobile, quickly opening the security camera app. It loaded up considerably fast. Shock washed over him as he tapped on the front porch camera feed and saw who was standing on the other side of the door.

It couldn’t be.

How was his brother alive?

# 33

The moment Lincoln opened his front door, his eyes widened in disbelief as he found himself staring at a familiar face that he never expected to see again. He had seen the news reports that outlined the heartbreaking story of a father's mental health struggles, culminating in the devastating act of setting his house ablaze, ultimately claiming the lives of his wife and two children. The sombre reality hit hard - there were no survivors to be found.

Assuming the report was false, he experienced immense devastation upon learning the heartbreaking truth: Lilly, Ethan, and Leah had indeed passed away. He attended the funeral from a distance, not daring to approach too closely and risk being recognised as the supposedly deceased man.

"Logan. I thought you were dead." He uttered, his voice

filled with a mixture of surprise and disbelief.

"Says the dead man." Logan laughed.

"Does that mean Lilly and the kids are alive and well?" The moment he saw his brother standing there, alive and unharmed, he instantly suspected that it was a deliberate ploy to throw off Kane and his men.

As Logan looked away, the weight of sadness settled back onto his shoulders. He tried his hardest to keep his spirits up, but frequently found himself succumbing to its negative influence. In an effort to avoid despair, he guarded his emotions carefully, burying them deep within.

"I wish that was the case. I really do, brother."

As Lincoln's eyes welled up, a heavy sadness settled in his heart. He closed the distance between them, pulling his brother into an embrace that conveyed years of unspoken emotions.

"I'm so sorry Logan. " He paused.

"It's good to see you again, though." He said, Before pausing again, he took a deep breath.

There was a moment of indecision as he debated internally whether or not to pose the question to his brother. The one that would consider him a murderer.

He couldn't be.

With a shared upbringing, their understanding of each other was unparalleled - he knew him better than anyone else ever could. For an extended period of time, his brother may have been engaged in a profession that involved the termination of human lives. He had no doubt in his mind that Logan would never commit such a heinous act against his own family.

"Come in." He said embarrassed that he hadn't offered sooner.

Looking behind and around him, his brother meticulously searched for any looming danger. Despite his careful attempts to cover his tracks, he remained vigilant, constantly checking for any signs of pursuit. Everything was clear. Moments later, he entered and was captivated by the interior of Lincoln's home. The walls were painted a bright white and cream, adorned with carefully placed ornaments and photos that added a harmonious burst of colour. The home exuded a warm and welcoming atmosphere, thanks to Stephanie's touch.

Lincoln's intention was to make it less alluring, as he preferred that people did not feel compelled to come back. While he excelled at being an amazing dad and family man, his patience with people in general was limited. For years, he had dreamt of living the life of a lone wolf, secluded in a rustic cabin surrounded by a dense forest, relying on his hunting and farming skills for sustenance. The wilderness would provide.

Then he met Stephanie, and the sight of her smile made him realise that his previous plans were no longer important. Love has a trans-formative effect on a man, leaving him questioning whether he could exist without her. Then she fell ill with sepsis, which resulted in the amputation of her left leg and nearly both. Witnessing her struggle, he couldn't deny the fear of losing her that washed over him, solidifying his understanding that he couldn't go on without her. A few weeks after she came out of the hospital, he got down on one knee and proposed to her. Despite the mental and physical anguish of such a trauma, she couldn't help but feel grateful for the incredible gentleman who had come into her life.

With the press of a button on a small circular device, resembling a detonator, a faint click echoed in the room. Instead, a notification was sent to Stephanie's phone, buzzing softly on the table upstairs. Bringing up an all clear picture on her mobile, to signal that her and the kids were safe to come back down the stairs.

In less than a minute, a series of heavy footsteps descended the stairs. When Logan last saw Alex, he was just a baby, and Thomas was still a stranger to him. Stephanie's eyes widened in shock; she, along with Lincoln, had been under the impression that Logan and his family had been killed.

"Logan? No way! How?" She gasped and clasped her hands against her cheeks, unable to contain her astonishment.

The kids regarded the mysterious man in their house with suspicion, their parents' teachings about the importance of caution echoing in their minds. They stayed by their mother's side, finding solace in her presence. Wondering why his mum was taken aback, Alex glanced up at her and observed her surprise at the sight of the man.

"Who is that mum?" He asked.

"That is your uncle Logan."

As both boys gazed at him, confusion etched across their faces. Puzzled, they questioned why his presence had gone unnoticed until now. Alex surmised that he was likely engrossed in a thrilling job, considering his overwhelming busyness as a reason for him not seeing them.

"Is he a spy?"

A laugh escaped Logan's lips, filling the air with a joyful sound. Along with giggles coming from Lincoln and Steph.

"I wish. I don't think I could pull off the James Bond look."

As Alex observed him, he weighed his physical appearance and demeanour, questioning if he could convincingly wear the attire of an MI6 agent.

"Definitely not. You'd need a shave first, then maybe they would let you join them."

Alex's knowledge of the James Bond franchise extended beyond the movies; he had also read a couple of the books, adding depth to his appreciation. Lincoln would read it in advance, carefully assessing its level of violence before deciding whether it was appropriate for his son. Alex, who possessed a keen intellect, realised that his schoolmates, who were of the same age, faced challenges in distinguishing between fact and fiction in movies and books. Although he acknowledged that others were still in the process of learning, he considered himself a fast and astute learner. Whether in school or not, he constantly immersed himself in books, absorbing knowledge like a sponge. He had an insatiable thirst for knowledge, constantly seeking to quench it.

"Well, I better work on getting rid of this beard, then." He laughed.

"You call that a beard?" Lincoln joked.

They shared a moment of amusement, their hearty laughs ringing out in unison. Logan couldn't help but admire the majestic beauty of his brother's well-groomed beard. It was impeccably groomed, flowing all the way down to the stomach. Growing his facial hair to a similar length was something he desired, but the high maintenance involved in caring for such a long beard was not something he was willing to put up with.

"Trust me, I wish mine could look like yours. But to be honest, I have been hoping to trim it all down. Look a bit more presentable and less like a caveman."

Stephanie moved closer. With years of experience as a hairdresser, she was always eager to help people feel more at ease with their hair, or, in Logan's case, his beard.

"I can help you with that. If you'd let me. It wouldn't take long. Promise. Then you can speak to Linc." She said, relishing the opportunity to bring out the clippers.

Contemplating a beard trim, Logan realised it would allow him to savour their company a bit longer. Before embarking on a perilous quest that could lead to his demise. Believing he might not survive, he opted for a well-groomed appearance.

"Yeah, okay. That would help. I mean, look at this." He ruffled his beard.

Logan watched as Stephanie hastily made her way into what he presumed to be a spare room, the sound of her rapid footsteps reverberating in the air. With a container in hand, she briskly walked back, carrying a couple of clippers, each with a different head for various uses. Among the combs, there was a spray bottle on top, ready to mist the hair. The thought of Madison's reaction to his newly clean-shaven face filled him with curiosity. Steph gestured for him to follow her, and he obediently trailed behind.

Stepping into the converted garage, he was greeted by the sight of hair-styling stations and manicure tables, giving it the appearance of a whimsical cross between a hairdressers and a nail salon.

"You do nails too?" He asked.

"Yeah, hair and nails, I do it to help about the people in the village. Offering affordable prices, compared to those further out. It gives me something to do."

"I get that, keeps you busy."

"Exactly. Take a seat." She said, pointing to one of the swivel chairs positioned opposite one of the mirrors on the wall.

Taking a seat, he couldn't help but notice the unexpected comfort of the cushioned chair, as if he had settled into the embrace of a soft, cosy sofa. It was a chair so relaxing that he could easily fall into a deep slumber on it.

To prevent any hair from getting on his clothes, Stephanie carefully placed a barber cover over him. With a quick motion, she produced the beard clippers and connected them to the electrical socket on the wall. Prepared to demolish the facial hair that made him look scruffy, even with the nice clothes on, he kept his brown leather jacket on, feeling its familiar warmth and scent. Not wanting to part with it, feeling like he'd forget it, should he take it off.

"What number you thinking?"

"I'd say three, so it looks neater. Then just straighten it up, if that's okay."

"I was thinking the same. Of course it is."

With the clippers humming in her hand, she got to work and finished in no time. In a blink of an eye, the dishevelled look he had before had completely disappeared. As she carefully shaped the remaining facial hair, he couldn't help but marvel at the transformation in his appearance. Something plagued her mind, a question that she'd had since she walked down the stairs and laid eyes on the man that she thought was dead. The weight of uncertainty settled in her chest, like a heavy stone.

"Where have you been all these years?" She asked.

He was determined to be honest, no matter what. Trusting her and his brother was something he never questioned; it was a certainty. In his eyes, they were the epitome of trustworthiness.

"I remained off the grid, living on an island off the coast of Cornwall. I needed to be somewhere, where I could be left alone. London was too dangerous and too close to home, which I just couldn't deal with at the time. Not after…" He paused, unable to say what happened.

The sadness in his eyes spoke volumes to Stephanie, revealing the lingering wounds of his past and the weight of his family's absence. No matter how hard he tried, he couldn't find a way to heal from the loss of his family. Who could? Especially after what happened to them.

"Living on an island is smart. You know that you've always got us."

He gave a nod of understanding. She could easily discern his lack of desire to be there, as it seemed he had been left with few options. The thought of attempting the task without his brother filled him with a sense of dread and uncertainty.

"He's missed you. Ever since all of that happened with him and you. He was in hiding, then we thought you were gone. It broke him. He tries not to let it on that it did, but I can tell."

"You were always observant, Steph. He is like me in that aspect. Even in pain, we try to be strong. Suppose it was the way we were brought up. Our father always told us that men don't cry. We are the armour for the family. Suck it up, move on and protect the family at all costs."

Their dad's passing came shortly after she met Lincoln, leaving her with the regret of never getting to meet him. According to her husband, Frank had a reputation for being a pleasant person, which made her think that Lincoln must have inherited his amiable nature from him. She was taken aback by his unexpected perspective on men and their relationship with sadness.

"I didn't know he was like that. But then in his day, that was the attitude that men don't cry. Many people looked down on such things. So I suppose he was passing down what he learnt."

"Yeah, he never made him a bad father. He was a military man, so was strict, but was always a good father to us. If he was home, then his attention was on us and mum."

Right as Stephanie was putting the finishing touches on his facial hair shape up, Lincoln walked in to see the final result.

"All done?" He asked.

Meeting his gaze, she couldn't help but break into a smile. It was as if he had a sixth sense for perfect timing.

"Just finished. Perfect timing. You two can have a catch

up."

As Logan stood up from the chair, he couldn't resist glancing at his reflection in the mirror and feeling a sense of satisfaction at how good he looked. It was a rare sensation, but he couldn't help but smile as a sense of pride welled up inside him, dispelling years of self-hate towards himself.

*Looking good. I suppose we can pull off an MI6 look. Fuck me, we look sexy. Don't deny it. You know I'm right.*

Surprisingly, Logan and Magnus were finally on the same page for the first time in a while.

The mirror became his enemy after his family's demise, reflecting back a distorted image that haunted him with the guilt of their deaths. Without hesitation, he turned to her and pulled her into a comforting embrace.

"Thank you Steph. It's great to see you."

Lincoln led them into the brick built conservatory at the back of the house. The moment they stepped inside, they were captivated by the view from the large bullet proof window, which showcased the beautiful fields surrounding the home. Inside, the two-seat sofa provided an incredible vantage point for admiring the awe-inspiring view. Logan daydreamed about starting his day with a cup of coffee, gazing at the majestic sunrise. In the office, Lincoln took a seat on the opposite side, their chairs forming a symbolic divide between them.

"So how are you alive?" Lincoln asked.

"Marcus killed Lilly and…" He couldn't finish the rest of the sentence, his voice choked with suppressed tears.

"Because you wanted out of the business?"

"Yeah, as if they believed I'd have spoken about any of the missions I'd done or spilt any details about the company's business. Kane has always been a man who hated loose ends. Some I agreed with, that is until me and my family became one." Logan uttered.

His brother was well-acquainted with Kane's approach to dealing with people who wanted to leave Catalyst Collective, and it baffled him. Why sign a nondisclosure agreement? The moment you indicate your intention to depart, they will devise a plan to eliminate you, fearing that you may pose a threat to their safety. Kane vehemently denied any involvement in sending men to harm Lincoln, fully aware that Logan was still employed by them during that time. They didn't want both brothers standing in opposition to them, presenting a formidable challenge.

"I hoped you killed that evil bastard. I never really liked Marcus."

The room fell into an uneasy silence as Logan wrestled with the notion that he had somehow fallen short in his mission to ensure Marcus's demise. Instead, he left him behind, lying motionless amidst the flames engulfing Logan's home. The brutal assault left the man barely recognisable, his eye socket now home to a gaping hole.

"I thought I had. But somehow… he survived."

"Well, he always joked about how death avoided him. Maybe it's true." Lincoln said.

Logan was filled with a steely determination, knowing that his enemy would not make it out alive in their next encounter. He was determined to avenge his family, even if it meant risking his own life in the process. With a burning desire for vengeance, he fought to suppress the rage that consumed him. If he let himself succumb to an anger outburst, Magnus could seize the chance to take over.

"He won't survive next time. I'm going to make sure about that."

One thing lingered in Lincoln's mind. How did his brother know he was alive and where he was?

"Can I ask? How did you know I was alive and where I was?" He asked inquisitively.

"Did you really think that I didn't know you were alive? You aren't an easy man to kill, we are similar like that. I'd have reached out sooner, but I didn't want to risk the chance of them discovering that you were alive."

"What's changed then? You wouldn't take such a risk without a very good reason."

Looking out of the window, Logan was greeted by a picturesque view of vibrant green foliage. The thought of his presence at his brother's home filled Logan with worry, fearing that it might have jeopardised the safety of his brother's family.

"It took them many years. But they found me. Now they have taken two people I have come to care for and I don't want them being hurt because of me."

"You need my help to get them back?"

"If you would be willing. But I understand if you can't and wouldn't hold it against you. You have to protect what you have. I wish I had come to say that Kane and his vile company were gone forever. But they only seem to be growing in power."

Lincoln could sense the desperation in his brother's eyes, knowing he wouldn't have sought him out if he wasn't in dire need. He began going through scenarios in his head, each one more terrifying than the last, with images of his loved one's suffering or worse.

"I don't know Logan. I want to help, but I haven't done anything like that in a long time and I fear for my family's safety. I'm guessing time is of the essence and all that, palaver?"

"If I don't save them, I fear the mother will be killed. Her ex husband, well technically they are still married, is Damien." He revealed.

Not the revelation that Lincoln expected. From the moment they met, there was an instant clash between him and Damien. Together, they accomplished multiple missions, always teetering on the edge of success. His partner was known for his independent nature, frequently disregarding orders and doing his own thing. Believing that he did not need anyone else. On a couple of missions, Logan had a problem with the maniac - a code name for someone who was completely unhinged. His unpredictability turned him into a highly dangerous individual.

"Damien? You mean that crazy lunatic? Why would someone even want to marry him?"

"She has told me that at one point, he came across as a loving man. That changed. It's a long story for another time. Trust me, he will not keep her alive. She took his kid from him for very good reason and he vowed to kill her. Kane will probably hold him off for a while."

Shocked. Lincoln, usually quick with words, was unexpectedly at a loss for what to say.

"Will you help me Linc? I need that snipers eye. The best one in the world."

The gravity of the decision weighed heavily on Lincoln, as he understood the life-threatening implications it could have for his wife and children. Yet, it was his brother who was reaching out, the sibling who had proven time and time again to be a reliable source of support. The risk was so high that it felt like he would be walking on a tightrope without a safety net. He had been left alone for almost eleven years. The thought of not having enough time to set up contingencies for his family's protection weighed heavily on his mind as he contemplated the situation.

Would he risk his wife and children's lives, to save the lives of two people he'd never met?

"I… I can't give you an answer right now. I'm worried about the safety of my family. I know you are family too, but I mean us two can defend ourselves. They can't. If I have to give you an answer here and now. Then it's going to be a no. I'm sorry, brother. It's the consequences that come with the risks that worry me."

Such a response was exactly what Logan was expecting. He'd have probably said the same, if it was the other way around. But he would never know, his wife and kids were already taken from him. Asking for Lincoln's help was a long shot, but despite the rejection, the warmth of seeing and conversing with his brother again filled Logan with contentment.

"It's okay. If it was the other way around, I'd have been the same. Protect them at all costs. I'm just glad I got to see you all again."

The feeling that his brother was saying goodbye in a permanent manner weighed heavily on Lincoln, causing his heart to plummet into the pit of his stomach.

"Why do you say that like we aren't ever going to see you again?" He asked, worried for Logan.

His brother rose to his feet, placing his hand on Lincoln's shoulder, and smiled.

"I love you Linc. Look after them, okay? I'll see you again." He uttered, still giving off a tone of finality.

Without waiting for any further conversation, Logan swiftly departed from the house. He disappeared into the woods, leaving his brother standing there, watching his figure slowly fade into the trees. Lost in his thoughts, he couldn't help but question the correctness of his decision. Stephanie approached him stealthily from behind and gently enveloped him in a warm embrace.

"You decided not to help him?"

"It's that obvious?" He said, regret taking over him.

"He's your brother. You are both smart men. Together you could beat these ass-holes. Think it over. We love you no matter what."

Standing at his front door, he was serenaded by the symphony of chirping birds and rustling leaves. Despite his wife's encouragement, he understood the undesirable consequences that would accompany assisting his brother.

His devotion to safeguarding his family was so strong that he was willing to put his own brother at risk.

# 34

Madison and Bethany sat in the corner of the well-furnished room, surrounded by plush cushions and ornate decorations. The room had a calming atmosphere, with its harmonious blend of white, grey, and blue on every surface - walls, ceiling, and floor. Which reminded both of them of hospital rooms and corridors.

Fear had its grip tight around Madison, suffocating her with the anticipation of what might be her final day in the world of the living. The threat of Damien's murderous intentions loomed over her, as he had sworn to eliminate her and swiftly turn Bethany against her. She began to wonder if he would be able to influence their daughter's decisions so effortlessly. Beth had grown into a force to be reckoned with, her strong will emanating from every fibre of her being.

While her mother was overcome with tears in the face of death, she was the one who stayed calm and collected.

"Are they just going to keep us in here?" Beth asked.

"For now, I can imagine that they are biding their time. Waiting for Logan to fall into the trap that they have set."

"Well, I think that he is going to kick their asses when he does get here." Beth uttered.

Before Kane entered, the heavily fortified door to the room emitted two distinct bleeps, creating an atmosphere of heightened security. The girls were amazed by his towering height and robust build. His eyes were filled with a sinister darkness, reminiscent of Damien. If only Madison had been more observant and taken note of the details when she met Damien and began dating him. She was young, inexperienced, and often made poor decisions. He turned out to be one of them.

"So this is the wife and daughter of Damien." Kane said.

"Fuck you! Let us go." Bethany shouted.

"Let you go? Okay. The door is right there. Leave."

Bethany rose to her feet, but before taking a step, she couldn't help but notice the mischievous smirk on his face.

"I have to point out, though. You won't get very far. Maybe twenty, possibly thirty feet down the corridor before you are shot in the legs. Disabling you from any further attempts to escape."

Choosing the path that allowed her to retain the use of her legs, she sat back down next to her mother.

"Who are you?" Madison asked.

"Kane, the man who is keeping your head on your

shoulders." He replied.

"What do you want with us?" Madison questioned.

"You are the perfect bait. Logan will come for you, I know he will. He always has to be the hero, even though he is a cold blooded killer."

Madison and Beth exchanged confused glances, their brows furrowed in unison. Was this man telling the truth? Observing their bewildered faces, he chose to compound their confusion by divulging a surprising revelation of his own.

"Oh, he didn't tell you? It wasn't us who killed his family. Logan Winters killed his own family."

Their heads shook in disbelief, their mouths agape as they tried to process what they had just heard. The man's words were met with resistance as neither of them wanted to believe what they were hearing. Not only did they lack any knowledge about him, but they also harboured a deep scepticism towards anything he claimed.

"Why lie? He informed me of what happened. Why would we believe anything that comes out of your mouth?" Madison said begrudgingly.

Kane reached for one of the wooden chairs, positioned neatly on the right side of the room. Placing it opposite the girls, who had been huddled in the corner of the room, they now stood tall, no longer cowering.

"Okay, I understand why you would wouldn't trust me. But that doesn't mean that Logan is a man to put your trust in. He was trained in the art of deception. Do you really think that he wouldn't just tell you what you want to hear?"

Madison was adamant about not letting Kane influence her perception of Logan. She couldn't help but feel grateful for the man who had saved her from a certain death and had only ever tried to protect her and Bethany. Her daughter's focus shifted as she started considering the man's words. Could Logan truly be trusted?

"I won't allow you to try and make us believe that he is some kind of bad guy. I know he did bad things in his past, but I can tell that he is not a man who would murder his own family."

Kane's gaze lingered on Madison, assessing her every expression, as he contemplated which side her daughter would choose once the complete truth was exposed. When he looked at her, there was a sense of recognition that washed over him.

"You look like her." He said.

"Who?"

"Lilly."

"Logan's wife?" she asked.

"I can see why he was drawn to you. You have many similarities to her. I can tell that you have fallen for him to, for a killer."

She was taken aback, her eyes widening in surprise. Unsure whether Kane was speaking the truth, she scrutinised his every word and gesture. Had he met Lilly? Since she didn't have much knowledge about Logan's past, it was difficult for her to ascertain the veracity of the person labelled as the enemy. Or was he merely crafting an intricate fabric of falsehoods to manipulate her perception of the man who had risked everything to keep her safe?

As Kane observed her, he could see the wheels turning in her mind, contemplating whether or not she should place her trust in him. Seeing people struggle with the truth brought him a twisted sense of satisfaction. The weight of his revelation lingered in her mind, causing her to question if Logan's protection was driven by something more than what she initially thought. Was his protection solely driven by her uncanny resemblance to his late wife, prompting him to shield her from harm?

"I could sit here and say that Logan is truly a bad man, but he does have good in him. Only his dark side tends to win over most of the time. One question I have is this. Why did he leave you in that house? He would have had a good idea that we had men watching it. Unless he left you there on purpose, wanting you to get captured."

A moment of hesitation passed, and then a wide smile broke out on his face.

"You see, Logan never stopped working for me. He is the reason we found you. Damien has searched for you, for a long time."

Just as they were about to gather their thoughts, the door swung open, and Damien strode into the room with a determined look on his face. Despite his best efforts, his daughter did not return the smile he gave her, leaving him feeling a tinge of disappointment.

"Hey baby girl. Not gonna give your dad a hug?" Damien asked, puzzled by the way his daughter just stared at him like a monster just entered the room.

"I'm not going near you. Why would I go near the wife beater? Yeah, mum told me what you did."

His face was instantly consumed by shock. Madison's admission caught him off guard; he never expected her to speak up, fearing that it would give him no incentive to spare them both. His eyes locked with Madison's, and a deathly glare sent shivers down her spine.

"Really? I'm the wife beater? Are you for real Maddie?! The only time I lost my shit and hit you was when I found out about you and Jack. I shouldn't have hit you and I have never forgiven myself for it. I should have walked out that day, but I forgave you and wanted to make it work. You were the one who then fled with my daughter and decided to start pinning me as the bad guy." He uttered.

Bethany's mind was a jumbled mess of confusion. Despite her father's convincing tone, she couldn't ignore the deep understanding she had of her mother's character. There was no way she would fabricate something of that nature. Would she? Did she truly know her mother?

With Madison's expectations high, she braced herself for his well-crafted defence, fully aware of his quick wits and deceptive nature. She felt a pang of fear, knowing that no matter what she said, he would always have the perfect response. Having had years to prepare, he was undoubtedly equipped to handle any secret she might reveal.

"Trust you to immediately lie through your teeth. She knows about Jack because I told her the entire truth. Not just what she wanted to hear." Madison moaned.

Kane stood, a wide grin stretching across his face as he

found the ongoing feud between the husband and wife highly entertaining. He knew exactly who was speaking the truth and could easily settle the argument, but couldn't help but find humour in the situation.

"This is a good family reunion, isn't it?" He laughed.

As Damien turned to him, his fists clenched, the tension in the air was palpable. The idea of lashing out at his boss with a rapid succession of punches crossed his mind, but he promptly suppressed the urge.

"Maddie, I'm sorry about what happened in the past. I wasn't a good husband or father, but I would love to be given a second chance. At least at being a father. Please." Damien said sincerely.

Despite being nearly convinced, Madison's intuition allowed her to see beyond his words. She knew that he was concealing his true monstrous nature, opting instead to present a fabricated version of himself that appeared caring to elicit sympathy. The sight of her daughter's worried face made her fear that it could have an effect on Bethany.

"Beth, trust me, this isn't the real him. He has a way of convincing people that he is a good man, I was stupid enough to fall for it before. But I can't go through that again, I'd rather die than give that man a second chance."

"Mum, I don't know how I feel. All I have to go on is your words and his. Both are conflicting and I don't know who I can trust. I know you better than anyone. But you lied to me about what dad had done and that you had an affair. How do I know you aren't hiding anything else from me?" Beth asked, a tear forming in her left eye.

"I told you everything, I promise. I know it's all confusing, but you cannot trust him. He lied to me for years, telling me he worked security. When in reality he was killing people for a living. I love you and just don't want you making the wrong decision, baby girl."

"Did you tell her everything about Jack? Like how you argued with him and something happened that resulted in his death. He was found days after you left. Is that really why you left? But you wouldn't have revealed that to her would you? Don't want your daughter thinking that you are a killer. I mean... look at your mother and her accident." Damien said with a smirk, like he'd just put her in a coffin and nailed it shut.

Madison stood, her eyes wide with shock, her hands instinctively covering her mouth. Her breathing became laboured, and her legs turned into wobbly pillars beneath her. Tears streamed from her eyes as she crumpled to the ground, the weight of her emotions overwhelming her.

"So you hadn't told her."

Puzzlement washed over Bethany as the revelation sank in, leaving her with more questions than answers. Why would her mother kill Jack? What happened with her grandmother? Was Madison responsible for her death, disguising it as a mere accident?

"Mum, what does he mean?" Beth asked, her mind reeling with confusion, as if she had been struck by a baseball bat.

Tears welled up in Madison's eyes as she struggled to find her voice, utterly speechless. What had he done? Even though she expected him to be prepared, this lie took her by surprise with its audacity.

"I… I didn't." She cried, unable to get the words out that she wanted to.

It was incomprehensible to Bethany. She observed her mother's breakdown as the fear of death loomed overhead. How could that person, also be a killer? Or was that all an act?

"I don't understand. You killed Jack, and that's really why we left in such a hurry? Please explain it to me, mum, as I just can't see you as a killer."

Despite her best efforts to compose herself, Madison couldn't help but feel inundated by the weight of everything that had unfolded and the shocking revelation. Her breathing was erratic, and the tears flowed freely, unstoppable and overwhelming. The weight of her world closing in on her was crushing, and she felt utterly overwhelmed and unable to cope.

Madison's silence did nothing to quell her daughter's growing anger; instead, it deepened her confusion about the unsettling notion that her own mother might be a killer. Nevertheless, she understood that her father's profession had required him to take countless lives. Could neither parent be trusted?

"I need answers, mum! Are you a killer?! Did you kill Jack? Tell me!" Bethany yelled in frustration.

"Beth, I can protect you. I promise I am not the man your mother perceived me to be. Please trust me." Damien said.

With a look of fury in her eyes, she turned to her father. Kane observed everything unfolding before his eyes, and there was a certain aura about the young girl that caught his attention. Potential.

"Trust you? At the moment, I can't trust either of you. Both of you are full of lies!"

Damien had imagined a different outcome for the situation. He had anticipated her coming alongside him, providing the opportunity to take care of Madison.

"You can trust me. I promise. I would never hurt you." He muttered.

"No. I can't. You both lied to me for years. I know mum better than anyone and that whatever you done to her, broke her. I don't know if you did beat her half to death several times. But you admitted to hitting her once and that makes me think that you wouldn't have thought twice about doing it other times. You kill people for a living, so clearly have something evil inside you. Even Logan called you a psycho and he kills people too. I seem to be surrounded by murderers. I need time, as right now I have no trust in either of you."

Seizing his chance amidst the chaos, Kane rose to his feet, ready to interject.

"I can have you moved to a private room. Give you time to go over this all. If you need to speak to either of them, I can arrange this." Kane said.

Bethany was puzzled by the captor's sudden change in behaviour, unable to grasp his motives for being kind.

"Why are you being nice? We are your captives, are we not?" She asked.

"You are. But that doesn't mean I cannot take care of you.

Once Logan has come and we have him. You and your mother will be free to go."

Kane extended his arm, signalling for Bethany to make her way out of the room. Despite the circumstances, she stood motionless, rooted to the spot. Suspicion filled her as she glanced around the room, not trusting a single person, especially in that particular moment. But one thing she was sure of, was that there was no chance that she was leaving her mother alone in that room with who she now knows as a killer, feeling a surge of protectiveness. Despite her uncertainty about her own mother's trustworthiness, she couldn't deny that she knew her better than anyone else. She resolved to stay by her side, even in moments of intense animosity.

"I'm not leaving my mother. She lied and I don't know who is telling the truth. But I will not leave her. She has always stuck by me, no matter how much of a pain in the ass I've been. So I'm not going anywhere." Bethany uttered.

The tension in the room had reached a breaking point, so Kane's surprise was even more pronounced. He was confident that she would have desired a tranquil environment to contemplate. It was clear that he wasn't always right.

"We will leave you guys alone." Kane said.

Damien did not think that meant he was to leave, until he noticed his boss giving him a stern look. The mere glance from him was enough to send a clear message: obey or suffer his wrath. He shook his head in disbelief, determined to mend his relationship with his daughter and earn her trust.

Despite the circumstances, she couldn't bring herself to trust any of them.

With a discontented expression, Damien begrudgingly left the room alongside the boss. Witnessing the repercussions faced by those who dared to cross Kane, he was determined to avoid his wrath at all costs. Soon enough, he would have the opportunity to engage in conversation with Bethany once more.

The room was devoid of any presence except for Madison and her daughter. Beth approached her mother, her heart pounding, knowing that only the truth would satisfy her.

"Mum, tell me honestly. Did you kill Jack?" She asked.

# 35

The clock ticked, and it had been nearly five hours since Logan's departure. Francis remained on high alert due to the persistent noises outside. He couldn't shake the feeling that the front door to the flat might suddenly burst open and hostile intruders would swarm in, taking him prisoner or killing him. While he had the capability to take on anyone who posed a danger to him, the presence of Logan provided an extra sense of security. Though he was a stranger, there was an aura of honesty and reliability about him that made him seem like a good and trustworthy man.

With a gentle motion, he retrieved his wallet from his pocket and unfolded it, revealing a cherished picture of his wife Claudia, a radiant African woman. As he reminisced, a cascade of happy memories flooded his mind, each one eliciting a smile.

"If only you were here Claud. You'd be telling me that this crusade is gonna get me killed. If I'm honest, you'd be correct. You always were."

In his thoughts, he travelled back to the cherished memories - the adventures to Cornwall, the mesmerising sunsets they experienced while standing on the beach at Torquay. The view was absolutely breathtaking, and the company he had made it all the more enjoyable.

Memories of his wife's hospital appointments and the dark days came rushing back as he began to recall the sad times, and his once bright smile slowly disappeared. Claudia's unwavering spirit shone through even after learning about her terminal illness, as she made it her mission to bring light and joy to every room she entered.

Her constant reminder to focus on the positive remained unwavering, reminding him that even in the darkest of times, there was a flicker of light.

The memories came rushing back, each one vividly depicting the happiness they experienced while purchasing their first house and receiving the news of their impending parenthood. Francis' promotion to superintendent was met with overwhelming joy from Claudia, who eagerly embraced him with a heartfelt hug and a passionate kiss, recognising his talent and dedication for the role. A tapestry of happiness and sorrow, woven together in dozens of moments.

She began shedding pounds rapidly, her body growing frail. Most evenings were spent in tears, grieving the loss of a future that would never include reaching her sixties or meeting her grandchildren. As sadness consumed Francis, a solitary tear trickled down his cheek.

"Hey. Why are you crying? You are still alive!"

Startled, he turned to find Claudia standing next to him, her sudden presence catching him off guard. He hadn't seen her since shortly after her death, and her sudden appearance sent shivers down his spine. He had put it down as his mind struggling to comprehend her absence, a void that seemed to grow larger every day. Their lives had been filled with love and companionship for four decades until the day he was left to navigate the world alone.

"I… I'm not. It was a tear is all." He replied.

"Just remember that you are strong and obviously alive. Don't take that for granted and also, don't be stupid and get yourself killed. I know you have many years left, so don't get yourself shot for some mans crusade."

Even in the afterlife, she persisted in criticising him for constantly sacrificing his own life. Selflessness was his defining trait; he rarely considered his own well-being as he prioritised the lives of others. She had frequently expressed to him the importance of taking care of his own needs and desires. He had a track record of helping others, but it was rare for him to be on the receiving end of any assistance, despite his good character. Still, he never allowed it to bother him; an inner conviction assured him that he didn't need any reciprocation for his kind gestures. Since childhood, he had an innate desire to lend a hand to those in need.

"He is fighting to protect the country from bad men, ones who want to take control of everyone and everything. They will kill anyone who gets in their path, but need to be stopped. If I can help him stop them and not die, then I am happy to help. If I die taking them down, then I die. I'd be with you again."

Her head shook with disappointment, a silent expression of her disapproval. It was clear to her that he was set in his ways and would never change, yet she couldn't help but continue to try.

"I understand that. But don't get yourself killed. You don't need to be joining me yet, I can wait. I'm always happy to wait for you. Promise me that you won't get yourself killed?"

He smiled at her, his eyes twinkling with warmth, but his attention was quickly drawn to the sound of the door opening. Removing the Glock 17 from the back of his trousers, he felt the weight of the weapon in his hand, knowing it was his last line of defence against any imminent danger.

"It's me." Logan uttered, already aware that if he were in the same situation, he would have a weapon at the ready, prepared to unleash a hail of bullets on anyone who dared to enter.

Logan stuck his head around the door, ensuring Francis could see him and recognise his face. Hoping that the man he barely knew wouldn't blow his head off. There was never an instance where he made an effort to verify Francis's mental stability. Especially with twenty-plus years in the force and then the death of his wife. The accumulation of witnessing disturbing events can make even the loss of a loved one enough to push someone over the edge. Instead, Logan had trusted his instincts.

Entering with a jovial spirit, he threw his hands up in the air and let out a hearty laugh.

"Don't shoot officer. I'm innocent." He joked.

As he lowered his weapon, Francis couldn't suppress a giggle that escaped from his lips. Sometimes, amidst tense moments, a simple joke can bring much-needed laughter and relief. The outcome of something comedic can differ based on the situation and the individuals involved.

"Damn, I should have shot you. I mean, you have a weapon in your hand. Some officers may have shot you. Luckily, I'm in a good mood." He replied, laughing.

"I've seen how good of a shot you are, so I don't think I want to be at the end of your gun."

The absence of any companions with Logan led Francis to deduce that the person had chosen not to assist.

"Your brother couldn't help?" Francis asked, to confirm his suspicions.

"He didn't want to risk it coming back on his wife and kids, which I understand. It was a long shot."

Francis couldn't help but notice the shift in his new comrades' demeanour. As he spoke, his voice carried a hint of defeat, as if he already anticipated the dangerous outcome of their mission to save Bethany and Madison.

"You don't think we can do it without him do you?"

Hesitation flickered in Logan's eyes before he finally spoke. He found himself in unfamiliar territory, unsure of the outcome, a departure from his usual ability to anticipate how things would go. In most scenarios that he played out in his head, the outcome always led to their untimely demise. His mindset regarding the rescue attempt had undergone a significant transformation. His gaze fixated on the man in front of him, and a wave of reluctance crashed over him, realising the risk of sacrificing his life for two unfamiliar individuals.

"The possibility of survival isn't high. It could still be done, I'm just uncertain of how. Are you certain you want to help? I'd never be able to live with myself if you were killed helping me rescue two people that you haven't even met."

Being someone who never backed down from a challenge, Francis had no intention of withdrawing. He was eager to lend a hand to those in need, offering his assistance in any way possible. Regardless of the potential consequences, even if it meant losing one's life. One characteristic his wife never failed to mention was his relentless stubbornness. When he is determined to achieve something, there is no obstacle that can discourage him.

"I'm not leaving you to do it alone. People are in danger and I will help however I can. Let's get to planning. I'm sure we can figure out an approach that maybe has at least a seventy percent chance of success."

Logan was glad to have a companion who matched his level of stubbornness. As he pondered, his mind became a playground for fresh ideas, each one vying for attention. Implementing one idea would require devising a plan to extract Madison and Beth from their predicament and dismantle the company by targeting its boss, Kane. It had been a while since their last encounter, and now the time had come for their rematch. Along with one with his son, Marcus.

"A man as stubborn as me. Well, I have a couple ideas. We need the blueprints for the building to determine the best entry point."

"Now I can help with that. Do you have a computer?" Francis asked.

With a nod from Logan, the older man was directed into the bedroom, where a computer awaited in the corner of the room. He couldn't believe it was still there, especially with the people squatting in the flat, making it even more surprising. Contrary to his expectations, they didn't sell it. It was obvious that they had been utilising it for their own private use.

"I half expected it to no longer be here."

Upon turning it on, Logan's attention was immediately drawn to the log in section, where he noticed that there was only one user, impressing him as it meant the original had been removed. James, the person who had accessed it, had neglected to set a password. The speed of the high-end computer was slightly slower than Logan remembered. As he clicked on the start menu, a plethora of programs popped up, creating a visual overload. Among them, he selected Armoury. Upon opening, the computer prompted him to press the green button to ensure its security. With that, he stood up from the chair and gestured for Francis to take his place.

"Impressive software. Guessing it stops anyone being able to track you or breakthrough your firewall at all?"

"Exactly."

The older gentleman sat down, his fingers hovering over the mouse, and with a click, the internet symbol came to life. He was taken aback when thirteen tabs suddenly filled the screen, each displaying explicit content. It seemed as though someone had developed an intense fixation, which accounted for the machine's slower-than-expected performance. Fortunately, once activated, the software not only cleaned the computer of viruses but also provided protection against potential hackers or bugs.

He diligently searched through numerous London archives in his quest to find the blueprints for the Catalyst collective, but all he could find were plans for the neighbouring buildings.

"They must have buried it deep, or done what they could to ensure that it wasn't easy to access."

"So we can't get them?" Logan asked

"I didn't t say that, my friend. I may have to make a phone call to someone who can get hold of them. This person will get them easily. Only thing is, it wouldn't technically be legal." He replied.

*Wow. Is he for real? Worrying about what's legal and what's not. He isn't a copper anymore.*

"You are worried about what's legal? We are planning on breaking into a private company building. I think legal fell out of the window." Logan laughed.

We aren't just breaking in; we are gonna burn the place to the fucking ground!

As Francis nodded, he carefully registered their intentions and the fact that their chosen course of action was far from lawful. He came to the realisation that in order to make a positive impact on the world, one may need to make some morally compromising choices to achieve their goal. With full assurance, Logan relinquished his mobile, aware that its level of security far exceeded that of the former detectives. As he took the phone, the older man's fingers danced across the screen, typing in a number. He then paused, his gaze shifting towards the man he knew as Lance. However, he knew that Lance was merely a pseudonym, and it was crucial for him to establish a sense of trust.

"Before I do this. I need to know something."

As Logan waited, his curiosity grew, and he couldn't help but shoot a perplexed look at the man in front of him.

"What is it that you need to know?" He asked.

"Your real name. I need to know there is a degree of trust between us. I mean, we barely know each other, but it would be nice to know the true name of the man that I may die beside."

*Who gives a shit about names? Shut up, old man, and make the call.*

After spending enough time with Francis, he concluded that the older man posed no threat and did not view him as dangerous. His thoughts were constantly plagued by a faint trace of doubt, an intrinsic part of his being. Apart from his perfect aim, Francis showed no signs of suspicious behaviour and posed no threat to Logan. If he wanted to, he could have easily confronted him in the car park, but instead, he chose to lend a hand in bringing down their enemies.

"Logan. Logan Winters." He uttered.

*Who are you, James fucking bond? You never say you name like that.*

As soon as Francis heard the name, a sense of recognition washed over him - he had definitely come across it before. The news reports detail the harrowing incident of a man who not only took the lives of his family but also reportedly met his own demise in the ensuing fire.

"The house fire, that was you?" He questioned.

"I did not start that fire or kill my family. That was Marcus. I tried to save them and fail…"

With a touch of sadness, his voice cracked and he couldn't bring himself to complete the sentence. In his mind, the memories of that night played out like a series of camera flashes, with the images of flames and the sounds of piercing screams. As Lilly's desperate pleas for help echoed through the air, he found himself helpless, unable to reach her in time because of Marcus. As she was trapped behind the door, her final words echoed in his mind - a haunting cry for the well-being of the children. As he made his way towards their rooms, his enemy viciously thrust a knife into his shoulder.

"They framed you, didn't they?"

Logan's mood had changed, evident by the nod he gave. Like a broken record, his dying wife's cries reverberated in his head, refusing to fade away.

"Why?" Francis asked.

"I knew too much about the company business and no longer wanted to work for them. They don't take kindly to people wanting to part ways with them."

"Wow, could they not have just made you sign an NDA?"

"That's the thing. When you join them, you have to sign one. But clearly their trust issues mean that even a non disclosure agreement means nothing to them. Because of their plans, they aren't willing to allow anyone to leak such information." Logan revealed.

"Why didn't you just leak it all?"

"I considered it, but somehow they would bury it. I knew I had to go about it differently. I needed more people on my side to truly take them down for good. Leaking their secrets would slow their plans, but not stop them. We need to cut the head off the snake."

"That Kane fella?"

"Precisely. Take him down and the company will begin to crumble."

"Just need to get to him first and rescue… the girls. What is there names?"

"Madison and Bethany. Kane will not be an easy man to take down, but it is the only way to end their reign of terror. Let's get that blueprint first."

Francis gave a small nod, his finger hovering over the mobile screen, ready to initiate the call to the number he had just entered. Pressing it. The incessant ringing seemed to go on forever, until at last, a voice broke the silence. A woman's voice. Which surprised Logan. For some reason, he expected a man to be on the other end.

"Hello darling. You okay?" Francis said.

"Yeah, I'm okay dad. How are you? How come you are calling? Never usually ring in the evening."

Logan was taken aback when the older man unexpectedly

called his daughter, a person he never would have anticipated to be on the other end of the line. Logan had always been curious about his children, but he respected his new friend's privacy and had refrained from asking.

"I need your help with something and I'd rather not have to ask you, but I know you are more than capable."

"My help. I thought you didn't like what I did?"

Francis paused, his heart sinking as he realised his daughter's words held an undeniable truth. He had always harboured a distaste for what she did in the past. Still, he couldn't overlook the fact that her skill set was the missing piece they desperately needed.

"Your skills and what you used them for in the past, I wasn't happy with. I won't deny that, but right now those skills are needed and I promise that I won't ever ask for such a request again."

The sound of a deep, exasperated sigh echoed through the phone's speaker, audible even to Logan.

"So when you need help, my hacking abilities are perfectly fine? I don't get it dad, you literally said to me before that if I used them wrongly again, that you would no longer speak with me. Yet you are the one who wants me to use them. I mean, that's very hypocritical."

He could feel the tension in the air, knowing he had struck a nerve with his daughter by asking her to do the one thing he explicitly warned her against.

"I'll be honest, Remi. We are in a predicament, we need blueprints, and I have been unable to obtain them through my usual channels. I didn't want to ask you, because I'd rather you didn't do it. But doing it now could save two peoples lives. So, it is literally a life and death situation."

He preferred not to mention the peril, as he didn't want her to become anxious about his well-being. The silence stretched out, and then her reply resonated, filling the space.

"Okay. But if you are putting yourself in danger, I need to know the time and location. So, if I haven't heard from you by a certain time. I will have officers sent to your location. Don't get yourself hurt or worse, dad. Please." She pleaded.

"I promise you, I won't. I can send you details of time and location, once we have the blueprints and work out a foolproof plan. That okay?"

"Okay. Make sure to be careful, dad. Me and Roman need our father. I'm sure he doesn't want to find out that you were killed, while he was stuck in there."

"I will. I'm not leaving you two anytime soon." He replied.

"So, what are the blueprints you want me to get hold of?" She asked.

"Have you heard of The Catalyst Collective?"

"Woah! You're for real? You want blueprints for that place?! Why?"

Confusion overwhelmed her as she tried to comprehend why her father had such a strong need to enter the company building. From her perspective, this one was not a threat whatsoever to the world. She had no idea of the obliviousness that surrounded her.

"Me and my friend need to get in there. We have a strong reason to believe that two people are being held captive inside. I can't reveal much more than that and you really cannot speak of this with anyone. Okay?"

"Wow. Okay, I promise I won't. I'll try and get them for you now. Give me a few minutes."

He could hear the rapid tapping of her fingers on the keyboard, accompanied by the occasional click of the mouse. As time passed, she emitted a sound that could only be described as a grunt, expressing her growing frustration through a chorus of heavy sighs. It was the sudden silence that alerted him to her discovery.

"Got it. That was harder to find than I expected. It was like a ghost file. Someone had worked hard to erase it from existence. I'll email it over to you."

"Perfect. Thank you baby girl. I appreciate it a lot. I'll send you details shortly."

"Okay, speak soon. Love you dad."

"Love you too sweetie." He replied lovingly.

With those final words, the call came to an abrupt halt, leaving a void of sound. The thought of someone else having a general notion of their plans made Logan feel uneasy and uncertain. She lacked a lot of information. However, if she allowed worry to consume her, she risked compromising the entire mission. Something that he could not allow.

"I don't think we should give her an exact time. That could prove dangerous for us, especially if we end up delayed and suddenly she is sending police in. A lot of people could end up killed. We need to think about our strategy."

Francis acknowledged that if Remi had the exact time, it had the potential to backfire on them. He did not give an immediate reply. Instead, he logged into his email account and saw that his daughter had encrypted all the sensitive information, making it impossible to trace her activities. She had emailed her father, sounding eager to plan a lunch meet up, and even included a list of recommended restaurants as an attachment. Her ingenuity was so remarkable that it even caught Logan's attention.

"Smart." He said.

"That's Remi. Don't worry about the time thing. We can give her time that is an hour off from our actual time. So even if we are delayed, it should be okay."

Opening the attachment containing the catalyst collective blueprints, they examined it closely, realising the immense task ahead of them. It was time to plan out their approach, one that would minimise the risk of harm or danger.

While their attention was focused on the blueprints, they were suddenly interrupted by the sound of their mobile pinging, indicating a new message. Surprisingly, what Logan found when he checked it was not what he had been expecting.

"She got into their surveillance systems. Giving us access to it. I have to admit, your daughter is good."

A mix of frustration and disappointment welled up inside Francis as he contemplated his daughter's actions, hacking into the company's systems. However, he was aware that she was unmistakably doing it, in order for them to scout the location of security, estimate the number of people on each floor, and, most importantly, gather valuable information. Along with discovering the location of keeping Madison and Bethany.

"That is truly going to help us. We can now plan accordingly. Being able to locate where the girls are and, better yet, where the enemies are."

A surge of confidence returned to Logan, a feeling he believed he had lost forever. It seemed that their mission was no longer filled with the same sense of impending doom. By coming up with a strategy and executing their plans with precision, there is a possibility that both of them will make it through.

# 36

Evan sat in the surveillance room, listening to the hum of the monitors and observing the live feeds from the outside and inside cameras. With anticipation, he meticulously scanned the screens, hoping to catch a glimpse of Mr Winters. With his cunning intellect, Logan had become a master at avoiding cameras, skill-fully evading all forms of surveillance for an extensive period of time.

Despite not being assigned the role, Evan felt a surge of importance as he kept a vigilant eye on the monitors for any indication of enemy movement. His family primarily viewed him as the accountant, relying on his intelligence for financial matters, but his intellectual abilities remained untapped elsewhere. He understood the value of his photographic memory, knowing it could play a crucial role in mission planning. While his memory and knowledge had greatly benefited him in matters of money, he couldn't help but feel their potential extended far beyond financial matters.

Evan wished his father viewed him as a military expert, but unfortunately, that was not the case. As a result of his years of service with his brother in the army, he became acutely aware of the stark contrast in their approaches - his brother's brutal and bloodthirsty nature, and his own more reserved demeanour. His mother, the unwavering believer in his abilities, was the source of his knowledge and guidance. Her intelligence and strategic thinking shaped his own approach to life. Whenever she talked about Kane and Marcus, she would playfully tease them as the family's brutes, emphasising their physical prowess over their mental abilities.

Memories of his mother's joyful face flashed before him, especially when he would proudly display his school awards for his inventions. In the aftermath of his best friend's tragic loss, she was always there, ready to give him the biggest hug, a symbol of unwavering support. She was there for him every step of the way, helping him navigate the overwhelming waves of grief. And then, suddenly, she was gone.

One day, he came home from school and his father delivered the devastating news that Maggie was now classified as MIA, missing in action according to military terminology. As part of a rescue team, she embarked on a mission to retrieve four British prisoners from South Africa. The team was caught off guard, while the captors, fully prepared, successfully took them captive. They fled with them all, leaving a trail of body parts that were discovered one by one. Maggie was believed to have perished.

Evan couldn't comprehend how he lost such an influential and formidable woman. The fact that her body was never recovered fuelled his optimism that she might still be out there. Despite the efforts of search teams, she remained elusive for years, never to be seen again. His fear that she was truly dead sank in, weighing heavily on his heart. Ever since she disappeared, he has felt like a stranger within his own family. Out of everyone in his life, it was his mother who had the power to make him feel like he truly belonged.

Thoughts of Logan's inevitable grand entrance flooded Evan's mind, each scenario more vivid and unpredictable than the next. As Evan fantasised about his heroic role in taking down the infamous assassin, he could almost hear the resounding applause and words of admiration from his brother and father echoing in his mind. However, those thoughts quickly disappeared as his mind dismissed them as a mere jest. Instead of acknowledging the truth, they would always find a way to cast him in a negative light, as they did repeatedly. In the face of constant doubt, he persevered, determined to earn their approval. There was always a part of him that yearned for a certain affection from them, an affection they seemed hesitant to provide.

While closely monitoring the screens, he suddenly spotted someone, causing him to doubt his own eyesight. Dismissing it as a figment of his imagination, he shook off the unsettling feeling. It was impossible to ignore the shock of seeing a person who had been dead for years casually strolling through the building lobby. Another screen caught his eye, revealing a clear view of his target and diverting his attention. Why was Logan stood in the open? He was more cautious than that.

Should Evan inform his father about the enemies' arrival? The question lingered in his mind, causing him to hesitate. Contemplating the possibility of confronting the man directly. Evan's concern grew as he observed that Logan was positioned directly in front of the camera. Adding to the alarm, his eyes were locked directly onto the recording device, intensifying the unease. Something wasn't right. He stood motionless, prompting the question of whether his intention was to allow himself to be captured. It would get him inside, but Logan would be aware he was up against an insurmountable number of armed men; nobody could handle such a challenge.

Pulling the walkie talkie to his mouth, he urgently called for both security and his father.

"Our visitor has arrived. I repeat, Logan Winters has arrived. He is outside, at the south side of the building. Possibly considering a back door entry."

"Confirmed. I'll send men there now." Gerard, the security commander, replied.

After tearing his eyes away from the screens for a few moments, he glanced up to find that Logan had vanished from sight. Had he managed to get inside? With each passing moment, panic grew stronger within him. Not only was the man who vanished from the screens highly skilled in combat, but he also demonstrated impressive cunning. If he could find a way past the security and incapacitate enough guards, he might have a shot at reaching the upper floors, but it would undoubtedly be a suicide mission.

"Erm… he's gone."

"What do you mean, he's gone?" Over the radio, Kane's voice crackled with anger as he asked.

"He was literally there, then he… wasn't. No one can move that fast, though. My eyes came off the screen for maybe a second."

"You are fucking useless! You know that?!" Kane snapped back.

He grew accustomed to the words, hearing them so often that he no longer anticipated anything different. No matter how hard he tried to deny it, he couldn't escape the fact that his father's words still cut deep.

"I'll find him." Evan replied.

"Don't bother. You'll just lose him again. I'll get your brother to find him."

As he stood from the chair, he could feel his heart pounding in his chest, fuelled by the desire to prove himself to his father. His sole objective was to take down Logan Winters and show his family that he possessed far more capability than they gave him credit for. They only see him as the family's financial wizard, overlooking his other talents. That was going to change.

"I'll show you. I'll show you all." He mumbled to himself.

The moment he turned to leave the surveillance room, his breath caught in his throat as he locked eyes with the man he had sworn to take down. With a swift motion, Logan struck

Evan on the head using the butt of his Glock 17, causing him to lose consciousness.

*It appears the retired detective's daughter is more useful than the old man.*

"I wouldn't underestimate Francis." Logan uttered.

*Do you really think that he will pull off his part of the plan?*

"I do. He is skilled with a weapon and is smart. I trust he will do his part. He's a good man, he won't let two innocent people get hurt."

# 37

The force of Kane's rage caused his fists to collide with the desk, leaving behind a small crack on the unyielding marble surface. This only served to further ignite his anger. In the chair opposite his father, Marcus couldn't help but smirk, anticipation evident in his eyes. Despite it being a simple task, his brother had failed to fulfil his duty of monitoring and reporting.

"I swear, sometimes your brother makes me want to put a bullet in his head."

Marcus was taken aback by the unexpected words that spilled out of Kane's mouth. Despite acknowledging Evan's occasional uselessness, he recognised him as the financial mastermind responsible for the company's increased profitability. His intelligence shone through in every conversation, leaving no doubt in anyone's mind. Despite his lack of skill in displaying emotions, Marcus's love for his brother ran deep.

"That's a tad harsh, dad." He couldn't allow his father to say such a horrid thing.

It dawned on Kane just how cruel he had been towards his own flesh and blood. Consumed by anger, he unleashed an outburst that was unjustified and directed towards Evan.

"Sorry. I didn't mean it. I just need Logan taken care of. That bastard needs to die. Find him, and when you do, kill that fucker!"

Marcus could feel the burning desire for revenge surging through his veins as he realised that this was his moment to settle the score with the man who had robbed him of his sight in his left eye and left him for dead.

"Oh, don't worry. He won't survive the night. I'm gonna take his eye, like he took mine. Then I'll set the bastard on fire and kick him from the rooftop. He won't survive that."

Kane, fully aware of his son's previous encounter with Mr. Winters, felt a deep sense of responsibility to assist him in any way possible.

"Don't underestimate him Marcus. He has bested you before. I will join you shortly, he will not be able to take us both on. He hasn't beat me yet. I'll give you some men until I join you."

His pride often got the best of him, but deep down, he couldn't help but feel the urge to show his father that he could triumph over Logan on his own. Kane raised a valid argument - if they joined forces, their enemy would be caught off guard by their unexpected collaboration.

"I won't. He dies tonight." In agreement, he gave a nod, acknowledging his father's assistance.

Exiting the room, he headed towards the two security team members who were positioned nearest to him. The weight of the MP5 machine guns in their hands gave both men a sense of power and control.

"Where's my brother?" He asked.

A brief moment passed as the men locked eyes, silently deliberating on who would break the silence.

"The surveillance room was his last reported location." The man on the left replied, his voice filled with a palpable sense of fear.

Marcus's unstable nature struck fear into the hearts of most security teams; they knew all too well that he had brutally ended the lives of several members who no longer met his approval. Frustrated by the lack of information within the given time frame, Marcus resorted to killing one person. Giving him a mere two minutes, he was tasked with obtaining an extensive amount of intelligence. The man's failure to complete the task in the given time led to Marcus brutally assaulting him until he ceased to breathe.

"Thank you. Does he have a team with him?"

"He refused a team, said he didn't need people with him to stare at monitors."

"Men could have remained stationed outside the door. Fucking useless. If he's hurt, you and your team are dead!"

With every step he took towards the stairs, his anger intensified, clouding his mind. His brother's intelligence was overshadowed by his frequent displays of utter stupidity. He was known for his careful nature in the family, so it was out of character for him to willingly put himself in harm's way. The thought of his brother's actions left Marcus curious. Would he be foolish enough to challenge Logan single-handedly? Would he be that stupid?

Glancing behind him, he observed that security was still stationed in the exact same position, un-moving. They remained perfectly still, as if their bodies were unwilling to venture towards the impending danger. The tales circulating about Logan were sufficient to discourage them from ever wanting to encounter him.

"What are you doing? Come on. Chop chop!" Marcus yelled.

Pausing by the elevator, he came up with a plan in his head. If his enemy was present in the building, they would predictably assume he would opt for the lift. Logan was fully aware of Marcus' strong aversion to stairs. Whether it was going up or down, Marcus simply couldn't tolerate them. But on this particular day, he decided to forgo the elevator and opted to climb the stairs instead, although that didn't mean someone else couldn't still take the lift. As the doors opened, two men in impeccably tailored suits stood inside, exuding an air of authority. Marcus paid no attention.

"Out, now!" He demanded.

He directed his gaze towards the security team, fully aware that any member he dispatched would almost certainly meet their end without even having a chance to pull the trigger. Especially if Logan was going to execute his approach exactly as Marcus had anticipated. As it would be the smartest approach. A persistent unease tugged at him, like a loose thread that he couldn't quite pull.

Why did Logan reveal his arrival so quickly?

Why had Evan gone radio silent?

As he lifted the walkie talkie to his mouth, a sense of unease washed over him, prompting him to check on his brother once more.

"Evan, you there?"

"Evan."

A tense silence hung in the air before it was broken by a crackling sound and a reply emerged. Much to his surprise, the response he got was unexpected.

"I got him. He had caught me by surprise, but I got him. I fucking got him. Logan is down. I repeat, Logan Winters is down."

# 38

As Logan looked up at the towering forty-eight story building, memories of his countless visits flooded back to him. Until now, he had never felt compelled to attempt a break-in. The blueprints that Remi managed to obtain provided crucial guidance in devising their plan of action. Adding to her advantage was the fact that she had managed to breach their security systems, granting her the ability to closely monitor the CCTV and keep them informed about the enemy's positions.

"This is so cool. I'm part of a mission! Never thought I'd be doing something like this." Remi said gratefully through Logan's earpiece.

"Don't get too excited, Rem. You are purely over-watch, that's it. I'd rather you not be involved at all. But you have the stubbornness of your mother." Francis uttered through the audio device.

"I mean, mum wasn't the only stubborn one." She laughed.

"Thank you for assisting Remi. I appreciate it. Usually I'd have just broke in with force. Taking down a few men in the process. Your way is smart, they won't expect it." Logan said.

*I can't believe we aren't just going for our way, get in and kill everyone. This way is boring.*

'You mean your way? I'd rather not have to kill loads of people who don't need to die.' Logan thought, replying to the voice in his head.'

*Once you get in there, they will come at you hard. You won't be able to take on an army alone. You'll need me.*

'If the plan goes they way it's supposed to, there won't be any need to fight through any armies.'

As Logan arrived at the south side of the building, he positioned himself in front of the camera, making eye contact with it to ensure maximum visibility. He was aware that upon entering through the back door, a multitude of security members would be positioned, ready and waiting. That's why he had no intention of using that door to enter.

*That's if the plan goes your way.*

"Got you on CCTV. Footage being looped now. Done." Remi said.

The person monitoring the screens in the surveillance room would have swiftly alerted security, prompting them to relocate to that specific location. With a sense of urgency, Logan headed towards the west side of the building, where he knew the fire exit was located. The broken door, a result of

Damien's actions long ago, had been patched up as a temporary solution. One that became permanent. Consumed by anger, he unleashed a powerful kick on the door, resulting in the loosening of the latch. The maintenance man, displaying laziness, used a cable tie to seal the door shut. The plastic had been specifically chosen for its easy break-ability, guaranteeing a quick exit in case of any emergency. It clearly hadn't crossed the man's mind that someone might try to gain entry.

After unburdening himself from the large duffle bag, he retrieved a sturdy crowbar. With precision, he slid it into the small space between the door and the wall. With a sudden jerk, the cable ties broke free from the handle. The open door would serve as a grim reminder to Kane of his negligence. Now his enemy had infiltrated his domain. Logan couldn't comprehend why, after all these years, they had chosen to leave it untouched. Yet, he found solace in their indolence, as it greatly facilitated his work.

Inside, the cacophony of footsteps and urgent whispers revealed the presence of a large number of security personnel rushing towards the back entrance. The clock was ticking, and he knew he had up to ten minutes to act before they became aware of the situation. As he hurried through the corridors, he caught a glimpse of the sign for the surveillance room out of the corner of his eye. He was desperate to get a visual on Madison and Bethany's location. Remi had access to the first set of floors, but the ones above floor ten were protected by a formidable encryption that even she found challenging to bypass.

With the surveillance room in sight, he prepared for the encounter by attaching a silencer to the barrel of his Glock 17, anticipating the presence of two guards. However, there was no sign of anyone standing guard. Had they sent all of their security to Logan's reported location? Slowly, he opened the door, his finger poised on the trigger, prepared to shoot at any potential threat. He was taken aback by the individual who was sitting, completely absorbed in monitoring the screens. Evan Hunt.

"I'll show you. I'll show you all."

His face painted a picture of astonishment when he stood up and found Logan staring right at him. With a forceful blow from the butt of his gun, the man rendered him unconscious. This unforeseen situation was not accounted for in the main plan, but he had foreseen the need to secure a Hunt family member and had made the necessary arrangements. A bargaining chip

"It seems that the plan is being changed. I have Kane's son. Plan C is now in motion." Logan uttered.

"That changed quickly." Francis replied.

"He could be useful in helping us get Madison and Beth out safely."

"You're thinking an exchange?" Remi said, feeling a little left out of the conversation.

"Exactly."

He wondered if Kane, known for his brutal nature, would be willing to take the risk. There was no doubt in Logan's mind that he would do whatever it took to protect and support his family.

"If you can get me access to all the levels, then I can be yours eyes. Did dad give you the usb stick I gave him?"

With a smile on his face, he reached into his jean pocket and retrieved a small, black metallic device. It bore a striking resemblance to a memory stick, but its power far surpassed that as he plugged it into the computer system in front of him.

"He did indeed. I just plugged it in, so you should be able to get in now."

Behind him, Evan's moans grew louder, a visceral response to his sudden awareness of the situation. Holding his nose with one hand, he grimaced as the throbbing sensation grew stronger.

"Ouch. That fucking hurt. Did you really have to knock me out? Not a nice way to say hello." Evan asked.

*Luckily it wasn't me. Or he'd have been shot in the face instead.*

"Well, I could have just shot you."

*Should have.*

Evan's realisation of what Logan had done to the footage left him impressed; it was a departure from the man's usual style. It indicated to him that he was not alone and had someone supporting him. He had his doubts about the older gentleman's knowledge and experience in such matters. So it meant that there was another person implicated in the situation.

"Looping the footage was a smart move. Not something you'd usually do. Who's helping you? Apart from that ex cop, who definitely isn't a person skilled in technology."

Logan was aware that it wouldn't take long for Evan to

uncover the truth - that he wasn't acting alone. While he may not have inherited the same violent tendencies as his father and brother, his intelligence more than compensated for his lack of strength.

"I always liked you Evan. Your family underestimate you. They always have." Logan said, avoiding the question that he was asked.

Evan grappled with the temptation to fully embrace the man's words, even though deep down, he agreed with every single one. As he faced the enemy, memories of Kane and Marcus's cruel treatment resurfaced. However, he couldn't help but acknowledge that they were his best chance of rescue in a dangerous situation. Dysfunction is a part of many families, but they find a way to navigate through it and still function. Despite the challenges, he remained determined to make it work.

"Do you actually think that you are going to win? My father beat you before. You literally ran away from him." Evan laughed.

"I don't need to win. This isn't a game. Your father and brother need to be stopped."

Not just stopped, they need to be torn limb from limb. We took Marcus' eye before, this time he will lose everything and then we kill him. Make him suffer!

"I won't let you hurt them. I'll stop you."

As Logan glanced down, he observed the man on the floor, wincing in pain as his nose bled uncontrollably, his hand desperately trying to stem the flow.

"How's that working out for you so far?"

*Fuck an exchange. That won't work out. Let's just blow this bastards brains out.*

Evan was well aware that if he were to engage in a battle against Logan, defeat would be inevitable. However, another approach could play to his advantage, increasing his chances of success.

"You know, Madison kind of looks like Lilly. Apart from the hair."

Immediately, Logan shot a piercing glance that spoke volumes, as if commanding someone to be silent. The man's intense stare sent shivers down Evan's spine, as if he could feel the daggers piercing into his soul.

"Maybe Marcus will kill her too. Or Maybe my father might let Damien have his way with her. Now that man is a psycho."

Logan moved with such lightning speed that it struck fear into his enemy's heart. With a firm grip, he wrapped his hand around the man's throat, exerting his dominance. Evan had tugged at the heartstrings, understanding that the man in front of him had a deep sense of guardianship over those he cherished. It was now very clear that his feelings for Madison ran deep.

"If I was you. I'd keep my mouth shut." Logan uttered, his voice deep and scary.

"You like her." Evan said, struggling to breath.

*He's not wrong.*

Letting go of his grip, he could sense the man's attempt to unsettle him, his words hanging in the tense silence. Utilise past trauma to disorient the enemy. He needed to carefully consider his next move, weighing the potential consequences.

"I can see that the lady and her daughter are being held in a room on the twenty-third floor."

"You won't get to them. Even if you did, how do you expect to get back down alive? You'd all be killed."

His point was valid - the ease of getting up while still holding Kane's son hostage was undeniable. But coming back down, following the exchange, was an entirely new challenge. Kane wouldn't let them leave the building.

"Who said we are going up?"

A worried look crept across Evan's face as he anticipated that the exchange would not unfold as expected, and a sense of impending doom hung in the air. No matter the scenario he imagined, the sound of gunfire filled his ears as he desperately tried to dodge the flying bullets, only to be struck down in the end.

"Francis, the exchange will happen outside, close to vehicles and overall, better for us. They haven't got enough time to get a chopper team ready to take us out."

"Smart. You sure they won't have any snipers already placed on buildings in the area, as a safety precaution?"

Doubt lingered in Logan's mind as he grappled with something he was unsure of. The company had failed to foresee the specifics of the situation, leaving them unprepared. Kane would have predicted a conflict within the building, leading to Logan's demise. Not fully aware of the people assisting his enemy, he would definitely not approve of conducting the exchange outside.

"We will be outside in a few minutes. Can you have a

vehicle at the ready?"

"I can and will be outside waiting." Francis replied.

Turning his attention back to Evan, who was furrowing his brow in deep concentration as he considered how to outsmart Logan and make his escape. Despite his quick-thinking mind and sharp intellect, his every endeavour would prove futile.

"Now, I need you to do something. If you do it correctly, then everything will be fine and you will be safe."

"What do I have to do?"

"Radio over that, you managed to knock me out and have me outside."

It didn't make any sense to Evan, believing it to be an odd approach.

"But how would that get Madison and Bethany outside?"

"You inform them to bring the girls, so you can make a statement by killing me in front of them."

"Do you think they will believe it? I don't know. I don't think they will."

"Make them believe it. If not, it goes the other way and a lot of people end up dead. I'm sure like me, you'd rather the less violent approach."

Nodding in agreement, he reaffirmed his commitment to resolving conflicts peacefully, rather than resorting to violence. Opting for a path that prioritises safety and avoids any fatal risks. The thought that kept haunting him was the inevitability of violence, regardless of the situation. Because his father and brother were the reason behind Logan's family's deaths, he wasn't just going to let them live.

"I'd prefer no violence yes. But either way, people are

going to die. I know my father and brother, aren't so easily going to let you walk away and I also know that you would probably like to kill them both. I don't agree with what they did with you and your family. But then, I am always told that I'm too trusting of people and that's my downfall."

The haunting sounds of his wife's screams of pain played over and over in his mind, a constant torment of his inability to rescue them in time. Before he could reach them, the flames had mercilessly snatched away his children. The actions of Kane and Marcus were unforgivable in his eyes.

"I wish I could go back and stop it from happening. But it's in the past. The pain though, that lives with me forever. Your father knew for a while that I wanted out, he was also aware that I was good at keeping secrets. I'd have never shared information about the company. His trust issues are the downfall of the entire company. You should be the man running things. You have the right mind and attitude."

Having worked together on numerous occasions, the men had cultivated a professional rapport that was characterised by a neutral respect. In the past, Logan had expressed his belief in Evan's ability to successfully manage the company. Despite the passage of time, he refrained from directly questioning Kane's leadership, yet he still held some reservations. The man was notorious for his brutality, leaving a trail of fear and destruction in his wake.

"My father isn't the nicest of men. But at the end of the day, he is my father and I will always stick by him. Even when he makes that hard to do sometimes. I wish what happened with your family never happened. They didn't deserve that and either did you. You was the company's best asset and they did they to you, because you wanted to retire. No matter what happens, just know that I was never a part of that and as a man, I do respect you. Even if you do scare me a little."

In a moment of clarity, he entertained a thought that could spare his father, brother, and Logan from their untimely demise. Though not an ideal solution, it would minimise the loss of life.

"What if no one had to die?" He asked.

Logan's interest was piqued. He couldn't help but wonder what Evan's alternative solution could be, one that didn't involve violence. The thought of people potentially getting shot lingered in his mind, which would make him hyper-vigilant during the exchange, even though it took place outdoors.

"What are you thinking?"

"Now, I know you can't fully trust me because of what my family done to you. But there's information hidden even from my father. That implicates all of them in various crimes, that would have them imprisoned for many, many years. I was suppose to destroy it all, but I couldn't bring myself to do it. Call it an insurance policy. I just don't want them to die."

The idea was undeniably good, and Logan couldn't help but acknowledge it. But he knew that both men, stubborn as they were, wouldn't go willingly. It was almost certain that they would take down numerous officers in their daring escapade, their names forever etched in the annals of glory.

"It could work. But even you have to agree, they won't go

with police easily. They'd probably get themselves killed trying to fight. For now, we will go forward with the exchange. If you play your part, I promise you won't be hurt or worse."

*Thank god for that. Can we get on with this shit. I'm fed up with the chit chatting. Let's kill some people.*

With a single nod, Evan conveyed his agreement. Praying for a smooth operation, hoping he would avoid any stray bullets. Logan passed over the walkie talkie.

# 39

Doubt, a merciless destroyer, left a trail of broken dreams, abandoned plans, and lost lives in its wake.

"I'm taking him out the front. Bring the girls down, let's make a statement. People don't fuck with us. Hunts don't play games." Evan said over the walkie talkie.

There was a lingering doubt in Marcus's mind about his brother's capability to defeat someone as formidable as Logan. Was his brother using this as an opportunity to demonstrate something? With a burning desire to prove himself to his family, he set out on a mission to show them that he was more than capable of taking down the man they had failed to, leaving no room for doubt.

Marcus couldn't shake off his severe doubt, fully aware of the enemy's exceptional abilities. With his brother and father frequently deeming him useless, Evan was well aware that they were probably doubting whether he would actually have the audacity to try such a task. Doubt gnawed at Marcus as he questioned whether his brother's claim of taking down Logan Winters was genuine.

"You actually got him? Like killed him?" He asked.

"No. I managed to knock him out, though. Wasn't easy."

Although Marcus struggled to believe it, he didn't want to constantly question his brother's credibility. Despite having done it countless times before, Evan's continued respect for him and their father never failed to amaze him. Despite numerous challenges, he persevered in his quest for admiration and respect.

"I can imagine. He is a hard man to kill. I'm impressed, brother." He said convincingly.

Despite his scepticism, he chose to play along, entertaining the idea that his brother's claims might be valid. His gut feeling urged him to stay alert, as if sensing a trap waiting to be sprung. He couldn't put his finger on it, but a sense of unease washed over him, making him feel on edge. With a swift motion, he retrieved his mobile from his pocket and dialled his father's number, the soft tap of his fingers against the screen breaking the silence. Within seconds of the ringing, a voice came through the speaker.

"Tell me that you've got good news." Kane said.

"Well… It seems that Evan somehow got the better of Logan. He radioed over to say that he has him unconscious and is taking him out front. Wants us to kill him out there, take the girls down for them to see their protectors death."

Like a sudden onslaught of blades to the face, shock hit Kane, leaving a long pause in its wake.

"Our Evan bested Logan Winters? I don't believe it. How?"

"Apparently so. The thing is, I just don't believe him. Something is up. Evan said Hunts don't play games."

"Our old saying. Maybe that's code for help?" Kane recalled saying those words many times over the years. But hadn't uttered those words for almost a decade.

"Take several men down with you. Also, have a couple guys get into sniper positions on the outer buildings. We need to make sure that if Evan has Mr Winters, or vice versa. That our enemy is not able to escape. Logan is very resourceful, as you know very well."

It was clear that their enemy had managed to escape death every time they tried to kill them. Kane was the only man who came close to ending the man's life all those years. Nevertheless, he chose to let Logan escape. Since that fateful event, he had been haunted by deep remorse.

"It will be done father. That bastard will not survive the day."

"He better not. Or I will handle it myself." Kane uttered begrudgingly.

Marcus ended the call. Hastily returning the walkie talkie to his mouth, he swiftly switched to a clandestine channel, reserved exclusively for select security personnel. He couldn't risk Logan catching wind of the plan.

"I need a team with me. Position the best snipers on the buildings opposite the front entrance. Logan Winters does not escape. It is possible that he has my brother and will be holding him hostage. So be vigilant and do not shoot to kill. Arms and legs, wound, but don't kill."

"Copy." A voice replied through the radio.

Another decision loomed before him, casting a shadow over his thoughts. The question was whether to bring Madison and Beth down to witness the potential demise of Logan. Despite the attempt to set a trap to lure Marcus out and bring them with him, it wasn't going to work so well, not with their ability to see through such schemes. He would not give his captives up so easily. Madison's presence, with her undeniable chemistry with Logan, made him wonder if there was something more between them. He contemplated ways to confirm his suspicions.

In order to get his message across, he reached for the radio and dialled the channel that Evan and Logan were on, hoping they would be listening. He wouldn't reveal his true plan. Doubt lingered in his mind as he pondered whether Logan would be prepared for a possible double cross. Was everything they doing part of his plan? Logan's planning expertise made him constantly doubt his own decisions, which he despised. The thought of finally defeating the man who had taken his eye filled him with determination. With a clear plan in mind, he was ready to take action and execute his decision.

"I will come and retrieve the girls myself. Have them ready."

Before speaking directly to Evan, he paused for a moment, torn between the possibility that Logan was genuinely unconscious and the suspicion that his brother was manipulating him through life-threatening coercion. Doubt clouded his mind as he tried to discern the truth. Logan, a clever and cunning man, was always armed with multiple plans.

"Evan. Have you got him outside already? I will be with you shortly."

As he waited for a response, he began to understand the true nature of what was happening. He was willing to play the game until he achieved his goal. It was a delicate task, much like threading a needle.

"Yeah, we are ready and waiting. Hurry up, it won't be long before he wakes up." Evan replied.

"If he begins to come around, just kick him in the head. Make sure he doesn't get back up."

If his brother was being coerced, he expected to hear a hint of fear in his voice, but instead, his words flowed smoothly and convincingly. Logan's mere existence had him doubting every decision, causing frustration to build, but he realised that giving in to anger would be playing right into the enemy's trap. His mind raced with possibilities, considering both the actions of his brother and the manipulations of their enemy.

His attention was drawn to the sound of the radio crackling, and soon after, a voice could be heard.

"Boss, we have a problem. There are multiple armed response officers surrounding the building. What should we do?" Parker, the security commander asked.

It blindsided him, leaving him speechless and in disbelief. The retired detective evidently maintained many connections within the police force. The question of why they would show up puzzled him, as he couldn't think of any valid grounds for their presence. With great caution, his father made certain that any potentially damning information was wiped clean and destroyed. Logan's testimony held little weight with the cops, who had already labelled him as a murderer.

"Do nothing. Wait on orders from my father. He…" Before getting to finish his sentence. A voice came through.

"Leave it to me. They will leave, it is a fools errand to send them here. Marcus, get to the girls and do not let them out of your sight." Kane said.

"I'll keep my one good eye on them."

Suddenly, it dawned on him - the commander had only spoken about the presence of police, conveniently leaving out any mention of Evan and Logan. With a quick motion, they seamlessly switched back to the private security channel, avoiding any potential eavesdroppers.

"Parker. Do you have eyes on Evan and Logan? Are they outside?"

"No. Just police out there. Need me to put out a search of the building?"

Panic slowly crept in as he began to comprehend the gravity of the situation. How?

"No. I know where they are. We've been played. He is on the twenty third floor! This was all a fucking distraction!"

# 40

With the gun pressing into Evan's back, Logan firmly directed him towards the stairs, their footsteps echoing in the silence. The confusion on the part of the younger Hunt family member was palpable.

"I thought the exchange was happening outside?" He asked.

"Do you really think I'm that stupid? I needed the security elsewhere. Your brother, being predictable. Would have got snipers positioned on the rooftops opposite the building and an army waiting for us. Because he'd have guessed that you wouldn't have actually bested me in combat. No offence."

*What do you mean no offence?! Fuck this guy, is he that stupid that he believed your story that even I have to admit was pretty shit. Decent enough within the time frame. But still not very believable.*

"Non taken. I have to ask, how do you expect to get out?"

"There is always a way out. I didn't come here with just one plan." Logan uttered.

A laugh escaped from Evan's lips involuntarily, even though he found himself in the unexpected situation of being a hostage to the contingency man.

"Living up to name. The contingency man. It's a good title."

Even though he had earned the name, Logan had a strong aversion towards it. Every time someone referred to him using it, he felt a pang of annoyance. It was Kane who had given him the name, recognising his meticulous planning and multiple contingency plans for each mission.

"I hate that name."

"You earned it, though. Your record is impeccable because of your diligent planning. Except that last mission, but we know that was your doing. You wanted out. I mean, I would too. You worked for my father for long enough. He's never been too good at letting things go."

As they made their way up the stairs, a cacophony of footsteps reverberated from the levels above. Without wasting a moment, they swiftly passed through the level two door, anticipation filling the air. Hoping for an unoccupied space, Logan sent a quick prayer to the heavens and was grateful to discover no one there. The hallway stretched out before them, empty and quiet, while the sound of voices and typing drifted from the offices on either side. The situation could change in an instant if one of them suddenly had to go to the bathroom, potentially forcing Logan to make a decision. The last thing he wanted was for anyone to find out which level he was on.

"Make a sound and I'll give you a slow and painful death." Logan whispered.

Evan nodded in agreement. Realising he wasn't foolish, he had no desire to meet his demise and would do everything possible to prolong his life. Among the swarm of armed personnel that passed by the door, Marcus stood out with his determined gaze and confident stride. Logan peered through the small mirrored glass panel, catching a glimpse of his own reflection. While his enemy remained oblivious, Logan fixed his gaze upon him, his eyes filled with a deadly resolve. The impending eruption of Logan's anger frightened him, knowing that the man who killed his family would soon face the consequences. For an extended period, he had concealed his boiling rage, meticulously biding his time and plotting his revenge.

With the coast clear, Evan's captor urged him to continue their ascent to the twenty third floor, and the feeling of anticipation grew stronger with each step they took. He knew the risks involved, but he was willing to face any danger to ensure Madison and Bethany reached safety. He couldn't shake off the guilt of placing them in what he thought was a secure house, only to have Kane and his men effortlessly capture them.

"So, what is your plan, Logan?"

*Please shoot this bastard already.*

'Have patience.' Logan thought to himself, answering Magnus.

*You have too much of that. Let me take over, I'll kill all of these bastards. Stop fighting me, you need that strength to take these fuckers down.*

"I don't know why you think that I'd tell you what it is. You've known me for how long now?"

His point was valid - it seemed illogical for him to confide in someone he regarded as his enemy. It would take a delusional mind to even entertain the thought of doing that. In terms of his mental state, he was far from being sane. If Evan and his family were aware of the monstrous entity lurking within him, thirsting for destruction, they would be filled with terror. Logan was known to be a man of great danger. Magnus, on the other hand, personified death.

"Almost twenty years, if I remember correctly. You do realise that my father and brother won't stop hunting you? If it wasn't for me, they'd have found you much sooner. I've known that you were hiding out in Cornwall for a while now."

Despite the expectation of surprise, Logan wasn't caught off guard by Evan's intelligence. Despite his talents and contributions, he was often disregarded within the Hunt family. A part of him regretted not being found sooner, as it would have spared Madison and Beth from the imminent danger, and he wouldn't have crossed paths with them. However, his heart longed for the contrary. Meeting Madison left him with a strong desire to fast-forward through everything else so that he could spend more time getting to know her. The primary goal, however, was to save them and stop Kane from carrying out his plans.

"Why didn't you tell them sooner?" Logan asked, wondering who Evan's loyalties were towards.

Evan didn't answer immediately; instead, he furrowed his brow and contemplated the multitude of thoughts swirling in his mind. Despite his accomplishments, his brother and father consistently failed to recognise his efforts. Their willingness to kill anyone who stood in their path was a constant source of debate for him, making him question his allegiance. The chilling reality was that their own family was not excluded - if they posed a hindrance, they would be swiftly taken care of. The terror it evoked in him was indescribable. How could he ever fully be onboard with everything they do? No matter what, he always arrived at the conclusion that they were family, making any thought of betraying them an immense struggle.

The reason for not disclosing Logan's whereabouts when he first discovered them wasn't solely about his loyalty, but also because he knew his efforts would go unnoticed and unappreciated. He also didn't understand why his father had set in motion the brutal murder of Logan's entire family and targeted him, especially considering his unwavering loyalty and exceptional skill at safeguarding classified information. He'd never have uttered a word about any of the business the company was undertaking. Despite knowing it, Kane still desired his removal.

Evan often questioned whether Kane's fear of the catalyst collectives secrets being revealed was merely a cover for a more personal motive - a feeling of being disrespected by the man deemed the most valuable. His father was a man who clung tightly to grudges, never willing to release them. Betrayal or failure towards him leaves an indelible mark, never to be forgotten. Logan's longing for freedom felt like a personal betrayal to Kane, leaving him feeling hurt and deceived.

"They didn't need to know at the time. You'd seen enough death." He replied.

Their silence spoke volumes, a quiet understanding that gave space for introspection. They delved into the past, examining every detail and pondering whether the journey had been worthwhile.

"You could have attacked us and taken us out at any point over the years. Why didn't you? I mean, if I had your skills and with what my father and brother did, I'd have waited a little while for them to think that they were safe and then I'd strike." Evan asked, puzzled to why Logan hadn't acted sooner.

On that island, he had contemplated the matter numerous times, going over it again and again in his mind. Despite his intentions, he never took any action on the plans he had made to eliminate Kane. Rather than taking the conventional route, he opted to write books embedded with secret codes, exposing the company's operations and the extensive list of misdeeds they had perpetrated. Which Kane had always claimed was in pursuit of the 'greater good.' Logan had been aware that his way was playing the long game, but in his perspective, he had all the time in the world to spare. The enemy hadn't found him, so he was safe for the time being.

"Your father had my family killed. I will never forget that. He will pay for what he done. I thought I'd got rid of your brother, but apparently, he is more resistant to die than I originally thought. I could have made attempt to kill Kane, but one thing I will say about your dad. He'd have seen me coming, I'll give him that, he is a smart and resourceful man."

Neither man relished the challenging journey of walking up the stairs, as it left them feeling fatigued and unenthusiastic. But Logan understood that opting for the stairs was the wiser decision. By avoiding the elevator, they minimised the risk of the enemy anticipating their destination and setting up an ambush. Although the security teams were currently occupied, searching for both men outside.

As they reached the twenty-third floor, Evan couldn't help but wonder if his captor had any intention of letting him live. Once he had the girls, Logan wouldn't have much use for him, leaving him feeling disposable and insignificant. Unless he was still going to be used as a means for them to get away without harm. The fear gnawed at him, casting a shadow over his hope of witnessing the day's conclusion. Would Logan kill him to anger Kane? Acting impulsively, just like Logan did after his family's tragic fate, which ultimately led to his defeat in combat against the boss.

"I'm guessing that you have a plan to get out?"

His question hung in the air, met only by a deafening silence. In his single-minded determination, Logan's sole objective was to rescue Madison and Bethany and bring them to safety.

"They should be six doors down. Room 316 if my

calculations are correct." Remi said through the earpiece.

"Copy." Logan replied.

It was clear to Evan that Logan's conversation was meant for someone else, not him. The person he was communicating with had infiltrated the building's systems. Which meant that their hacking abilities were top tier. He had poured countless hours into making the security systems and software impervious, but somehow, someone had found a way to bypass them. Whoever the person was, Evan knew that Kane would prefer them to be working for him.

"Who is the person who got into our systems?" He asked.

*Kill this nosy piece of shit. He is jealous of the fact that you have someone who hacked into their supposed extremely secure systems.*

"You like talking when your nervous don't you?" Logan replied.

"I'm just curious. They are made to be impenetrable. Yet you have someone who didn't take long to break through. How?"

Upon reaching the room where the girls were held captive, Logan carefully scanned the area around the door, on the lookout for any hidden traps or alarm triggers. Due to the electronic lock, kicking the door open would require an immense amount of force. Remi's presence was invaluable in that moment; he had never been more grateful for the assistance of a stranger. Francis' daughter was proving vital to the mission. Her presence prevented what could have been a highly volatile and potentially deadly encounter.

He anxiously anticipated the sound of hurried footsteps as Marcus and his men realised, they had been tricked. It was a situation his enemy should be well-versed in by now, as familiar as the sound of their own heartbeat.

"Can you open the door?" Logan asked.

"I can indeed. Easy peasy." Remi replied.

A loud bleep echoed through the room, followed by the distinct sound of two locks unlocking simultaneously. Within seconds of the locks releasing, Logan motioned for Evan to go in ahead. Just in case there was any kind of security measure. He walked through and nothing happened. Madison and Bethany shot him a deadly stare, but their expressions quickly transformed into huge grins when they saw Logan trailing behind him.

"Logan! I knew you'd come!" Bethany shouted with joy.

Beth rushed over and hugged him with such intensity that it felt like every ounce of air was being squeezed out of him. Gladness washed over Madison as she saw his face again, a smile spreading across her lips and lighting up her eyes. Relief washed over him as he saw them both unharmed, and his gaze locked with Madison's as she slowly made her way towards him. Beth moved to the side, shooting Evan a look that sent shivers down his spine.

Logan and Madison closed the distance between them, their arms stretching out to embrace one another. In that moment, their lips met, and he was transported to a world where troubles ceased to exist. For those precious seconds, he was filled with an overwhelming feeling of contentment and bliss.

Beth watched on, her face twisted in slight disgust, knowing deep down that it was an inevitable occurrence.

Witnessing their togetherness, Evan couldn't help but feel a glimmer of relief for the man who had suffered greatly at the hands of the Hunt family. It made him realise something, he was different from Kane and Marcus, and that was okay.

Unlike others, Evan possessed a genuine desire to aid those in need, to heal rather than harm the world. Logan had given him hope. In the midst of our darkest moments, there is always a flicker of hope that will eventually illuminate our path. The actions of one person should never condemn another to a state of ignorance. Logan's family would have wanted him to move on, but their memories continue to live within him.

"Logan?"

As the man turned to face Evan, his hand intertwined with Madison's, a sense of unity filled the air.

"I can't do this anymore. They took your family from you and I did nothing. You didn't deserve that. You are a good man."

*What a soppy bastard.*

He took a moment to collect his thoughts, his mind buzzing with different scenarios and possibilities. It took him years to gather the courage, but he finally decided to step up and play an active role in putting a stop to what was happening. It was time for him to stand up to his family.

"Let me help you. I can get you out. Even if it gets me killed."

*Nope. You're useless.*

Logan was astonished by the man's change of heart, a moment he had anticipated and waited for over the course of several years. Evan had always cowered under the weight of his family's disapproval, doubting his own abilities and never finding the courage to assert himself. The man they considered their enemy had frequently acknowledged his intelligence, insisting that he was capable of much more than being a mere accountant for Kane and the business.

"What's with the change of heart?" Logan asked.

*He realised he was going to die. That changes peoples perspectives very quickly.*

As Evan's decision weighed heavily on him, a single tear escaped down his cheek, signifying the gravity of the situation. He realised that once he made his choice, he would become a target, and he questioned his own combat skills against formidable opponents like Kane or Marcus.

"You lost everything. Yet in all that darkness, you found these two wonderful women. Who, I have to say, didn't deserve to be kidnapped. I'm sorry about my family's actions and hope that what I'm going to do will make up for my inaction before."

"What are you going to do?" Logan asked.

"Buy you some time."

"You don't need to." Logan replied.

Evan looked at him, a mixture of bewilderment and uncertainty written across his face.

"What do you mean?"

"This was one of my plans, I have a way to escape and you are part of that plan. So I can't let you just go off and do your own thing. You'd get yourself killed and then what use are you, if you're dead?"

"Oh. So what's the plan?" Evan asked. Surprised that he had been a part of Logan's plan.

"Up. Get to the roof."

Evan's face contorted into a puzzled expression as he tried to make sense of the illogical situation. How were they planning to descend from the roof? Logan definitely didn't have a spare helicopter.

"The roof? You got a secret helicopter that we don't know about?"

*Is he for real? I really don't like this guy.*

The sound of Logan's laughter filled the room, a clear indication of his amusement at the man's obliviousness, especially considering his many years of working in the building.

"No. Your father does." He paused, looking at the time on his black aluminium watch.

"In precisely nine minutes. The helicopter that he takes every day at precisely six o clock will land and instead of him getting on it. We will be."

Despite being impressed by the level of planning involved, Evan couldn't shake off the shock of realising that his father's enemy had specifically accounted for his willingness to assist Logan.

"Well, we better get up there fast. If you will have me I mean?"

Logan placed his hand on Evan's shoulder. They had never been true enemies, their bond was broken only by the actions of others. Before that, they had become like brothers. Their relationship extended beyond the workplace, as they had become like a family, sharing meals and frequently supporting each other.

"You never stopped being a brother to me. I lost respect for your father and brother. I knew that what happened wasn't anything to do with you. I know you and how you have never liked their violent approach to everything. I'm not saying I trust you completely, but you know that if you tried anything. I'd kill you myself."

As they embraced each other, Evan couldn't help but feel a sense of warmth and acceptance from the man who was often misunderstood as an enemy.

"I'm with you Logan. I will do everything I can to earn your trust."

"Well, first, we need to get to that helicopter." Logan said.

Evan approached the door, but before he could exit. With a group of armed men trailing behind him, Marcus emerged, his face twisted with displeasure.

# 41

As Kane stood in the lift, a cheerful melody played throughout his descent to the ground floor, a tune that grated on his ears greeted him. The police were around his building, indicating that they were working with the man who was collaborating with Logan. Francis Kingsley, a man who clearly had an extensive network of loyal officers, even after retiring several years ago. It was yet to be decided whether their situation would change after Kane spoke to them. As the lift gradually slowed down, it eventually came to a complete stop.

As the lift doors opened, a pleasant ding filled the air, signalling his arrival as he walked towards the entrance of the building. Through the massive glass panels surrounding the main entrance door, he could make out the figures of several armed police officers. As he approached, he noticed a group of guards, their fingers tightly gripping baretta m9 pistols and MP5's, their presence exuding an aura of readiness for battle.

"You won't be needing them. Trust me. These bastards won't be here for long." He uttered.

With a collective sigh, each man cautiously lowered their weapon, their attention fully on the boss who emerged from the building, his expression revealing his annoyance at having to handle the situation personally. It didn't take long for an officer to approach him after he stepped outside, their footsteps echoing on the pavement.

"What can I do for you officer?" Kane asked, remaining polite.

"Hi, I'm detective Pilton. We have reason to believe that you have a bomb in your building. Along with several dangerous individuals. We need you to evacuate your staff and allow us to send a team in to locate and disarm it. And capture the people responsible, they could be in on level." Officer Pilton said.

Kane chuckled, recognising the cleverness of Logan and his new companion. The seriousness of a bomb threat, with its potential for loss of life, ensured that the police would respond swiftly. Considering the possible threat of dangerous individuals, the authorities would undoubtedly mobilise with great urgency, ensuring a rapid response.

"A bomb threat and terrorists. Smart." He mumbled.

A look of confusion washed over the policeman's face, clearly indicating his lack of understanding.

"Are you suggesting that there is no threat Sir?"

"There is no bomb threat. The person who provided this information has sent you on a wild goose chase."

With his face twisted in anger, Kane turned around and started walking back inside. His time had been wasted, and now he was determined to make the man responsible suffer the consequences.

"Do you mind if we do a quick sweep of the building, just to be sure?" The officer asked.

Spinning on his heel, he hastily approached the officer with his right fist clenched, the tension palpable in the air.

"There is no threat in that building. So, if I was you, I'd leave. Now! Or you will have a threat on your hands. Me. You seriously do not want to piss me off, trust me. That job of yours wouldn't be safe if you do. You and all of your men are to leave immediately." With a loud yell, he stormed back off into the building, leaving a trail of tension in his wake.

Compared to Kane, the policeman was noticeably shorter, a stark contrast in stature. With his imposing stature and intense gaze, Kane exuded an aura of intimidation. With a terrified expression, the officer slowly began to withdraw. However, when he glanced back at the large man, a sense of uneasiness washed over him, sensing that something was amiss. Despite being aware of the larger man's identity and not wanting to provoke him, he refused to back down easily if there was a hint of something unusual occurring. Kane had made appearances in news articles before, typically for his supposedly commendable actions. However, many were always aware that something sinister lurked behind his friendly demeanour.

In hushed tones, rumours of secret government dealings that implicated Kane and his business had made their way to Mr. Pilton more than a few times. However, locating evidence against him proved to be an almost impossible task, as a detective had tirelessly worked on bringing the man to justice a couple of years ago. With the goal of taking down Catalyst collective, he embarked on a mission to compile enough evidence to lock Kane away. Detective Wright mysteriously disappeared, and no one had laid eyes on him since. He had clearly unearthed a revelation that they were intent on concealing from the world.

Receiving a call from Francis had shocked detective Pilton; the familiar tone of his former partner's voice instantly transported him back to their days of working side by side. The retired detective informed him about the potential explosive device in the building, leaving him with no option but to take immediate action.

"We not going in boss?" Another officer asked.

"It appears they don't want us going in there at all. It seemed to anger him when I asked." Pilton responded.

"Odd, you'd think they would want to get everyone out. Especially if there is a bomb inside."

"I don't think there is a bomb inside. But someone wanted us here for a reason. Something is going on in there"

Retrieving his mobile from his trouser pocket, he dialled the same number Francis had used to contact him. The incessant ringing of the phone seemed to stretch on for an eternity, leaving him wondering if anyone would ever pick up. Then they did.

"Michael. Everything okay?" Francis asked.

"Well, apparently there is no bomb threat. Mr Hunt was extremely irritated by our arrival. Which now has me wondering what is actually going on. Why did you tell me that there was a bomb in the building?"

"We needed you guys here as back up. It's why I got you to assemble your most trusted officers."

"What do you mean we?" Officer Pilton asked.

"I have a man inside, one who has intel that can bring this company down."

"He works for them?"

"Kind of. Well, he used to." Francis replied.

Now he was confused, wondering why someone with insider knowledge and a past connection to their organisation was present inside the building, putting themselves at risk of being killed. Why do that? Especially when he no longer worked for them.

"So, why is he in the building then?" Pilton questioned.

"He's on a rescue mission. Once he has them safe, he has agreed to give over all the information that we need to take these bastards down. Get justice for detective Wright. I knew he'd been looking into a company when he disappeared. But didn't know it was this one. After stuff I have found out about them, I can see why they didn't want anyone poking around."

His confusion only grew when she learned that there was a man inside, risking his life to rescue people. Dozens of well-armed security members could be seen throughout the building, leaving no doubt about the level of protection. How was one man getting passed or through all of them? It also troubled him that there were no reports about the alleged kidnappings, adding to his concern.

"How is one man getting through all of that security? Also, are you saying people have been kidnapped? Why was this not reported?"

"Trust me, if you knew the man. You wouldn't ask. Reporting it wouldn't have got us anywhere. From what I understand, Kane has control over most of the government. Maybe all of it by now. Once you have the intel, you will understand more. But I need you and your guys to stay in the area and remain vigilant. These guys will not hesitate to kill you. Be ready"

"I can have my guys patrol the area for a while, maybe an hour. Then my boss is going to start questioning why we are still here, if there is no bomb threat. I'll do my best to stall him. You better be right on this Francis, I'm putting my job on the line here. Who is this man?"

"His name is Logan and he is a force to be reckoned with."

# 42

*Who invited him to the party?*

"Aren't you all looking cosy in here." Marcus laughed.

*Blow that bastards head off. He doesn't need it anymore.*

"Marcus." Logan said. The room fell silent as he locked eyes with his opponent, unleashing the deadliest stare in the world.

As Marcus gazed at his brother standing next to the enemy, a fiery rage consumed him. The thought of blowing Evan's brains over the ceiling crossed his mind, but he held himself back, for now. He walked into the room; his mischievous grin directed towards Logan. The room was filled with an undeniable sense of hatred, causing an atmosphere of tension to settle in. As he walked ahead, Damien trailed behind with a disturbing smile that bore an uncanny resemblance to that of a remorseless serial killer.

"Girls." Damien uttered.

"So you managed to trick us once again. I'm guessing that you thought we would have taken longer to realise and by the time we did. You and these lovely women would have been gone. Along with my brother apparently." Marcus said, his stare moving to Evan.

"Nope. Your timing was how I expected."

"Marcus, I…"

Before Evan could finish his sentence, his brother's fist collided with his cheek, sending him sprawling to the ground. He placed his trembling hand on his face and looked up, his eyes wide with shock.

"I don't want to hear from you right now. I always knew that you were a snake. You always had more respect for Logan, treated him more like a brother than you did me. Traitor! How could you!?"

Stepping forward, Logan positioned himself between the girls and Evan and Marcus, asserting his protective presence. He was determined to protect them all, ensuring that no harm would come to them under his watch.

"Leave him be Marcus. You never respected him. That man is the reason the company continued to run. You and your father haven't ever shown him the gratitude he deserves. He is free to choose what he wants to do. How long has he stuck by you? Even when you have treated him like a waste of space."

Fixing his gaze upon the man he despised, Marcus's mind began to wander, concocting a plethora of gruesome scenarios for his enemy's demise. He wished for Logan to experience a prolonged and agonising end.

"Do not tell me what to do. You know nothing! Where have you been for all these years? Hiding! My father could have killed you that night, yet he let you live. I will not be doing the same. You die today! You took my eye and left me to die, you should have made sure I was fucking dead!"

Logan prepared himself for a fight, feeling his heart rate quicken and his muscles tense.

"Try it and this time, I'll make sure you are dead."

Frustration consumed Marcus, causing him to restlessly pace, his footsteps reverberating with each step. He glanced at his security team, which consisted of six individuals. He carefully chose each individual based on their unparalleled abilities, making sure they were the best of the best.

"It seems you can't count, Mr Winters. You are outnumbered." Marcus uttered.

"I've heard that before." Logan laughed.

Disappointment washed over Damien as he shook his head in disbelief. Observing the man ahead of him, he couldn't shake the feeling that his unwavering self-assurance was misplaced.

"You must have gone crazy living on that island. It's given you some kind of superman self-confidence. You have no chance against us. You've been out of work for a while."

Examining the opponents who stood before him, Logan's confidence grew. His father's constant reminders to trust in his own skills resonated in his mind, strengthening his resolve. Despite his unwavering self-confidence, he frequently questioned the capabilities of his adversaries, reflecting on whether the fight was unjust for them.

"It's not just confidence in myself. I favour my odds here." He said with a smirk.

With a determined look on his face, Evan picked himself up from the floor and dusted off his clothes. The nervousness in his eyes betrayed his concern for what was about to unfold. He couldn't bear the thought of his brother getting injured or, God forbid, facing a more disastrous outcome. Yet felt the same for Logan. Regardless, he felt no sympathy for Damien. As far as he was concerned, Damien was a devil in human form.

"You don't have to do this Marcus." Evan pleaded.

Despite having only one eye, he shot his brother a menacing glare that could kill. Forgiveness was no longer an option, as too much had unfolded. Logan's heart hardened, refusing to forgive them for their actions, just as they refused to forgive him for his. Evan had concealed a truth, a truth that would inevitably shatter his soul.

"You're wrong. This is exactly what I have to do. And for you to side with him, that is the ultimate betrayal. Especially after what he done."

Evan's face twisted in bewilderment as he gazed at his brother.

"All he did was want to leave the company. You and our father had his family killed for it! That is not how mother raised us. She would turn in her grave at the sight of seeing the monster that dad made you into!" Evan shouted.

"The grave that he put her in!" Marcus replied in anger.

Madison and Bethany exchanged wide-eyed glances, unable to comprehend what they were witnessing. Was the man speaking the truth? The question lingered: had Logan actually committed the unspeakable act of killing Evan and Marcus' mother? The shocking sound echoed in Madison's ears, and as she glanced at Logan, she realised he hadn't made a single movement. The silence stretched on as he didn't immediately deny it, adding to the suspicion. The fear intensified as she considered Logan's violent history, yet she couldn't bring herself to believe that he would be capable of killing their mother. Had she put her trust in someone who didn't deserve it?

It couldn't be true, Evan stood frozen in awe. Logan held their mother, Maggie, in high regard for her consistent acts of making him tea or any beverage he craved whenever she spotted him and just being a lovely, caring woman. There was no way he would have snuffed out her life. However, when he turned to look at Logan's face, he found it inscrutable, making it difficult to determine what the man was thinking. An angry expression consumed his face, resembling the unsettling look Damien would wear before committing heinous acts.

"Is it true?" He asked.

No reply came. The room fell eerily silent, and the intensity of the evil look on Logan's face only grew. Suddenly, laughter erupted from him, echoing through the room. Everyone who knew him was taken aback by the sound of his laughter, as it was unlike anything they had ever heard before.

"You are pathetic. Yes, I killed that bitch. She asked for it. You boys don't know everything."

*Stop. What are you doing?*

"Oh Logy boy. You really should learn to control that anger." He laughed.

The room was filled with a collective sense of perplexity as everyone struggled to comprehend the unfolding events. While everyone else remained clueless, Madison had a keen insight into what was going on. Thinking back to those unsettling moments with her brother, she could almost hear the distinct change in his voice and see the eerie transformation in his eyes. He often described it as his shadowy alter ego, and eventually, that side triumphed in the battle for dominance.

"That's not Logan." Madison revealed.

The confusion was evident on Bethany's face as she tried to make sense of the situation, realising that the man standing before them was not their previous protector.

With a clown-like smile spread across his face, Logan twirled around, his laughter filling the air.

"That is correct. Logan is a little pre-occupied right now."

Marcus had never seen his former friend in such a state, making him uncertain about how to handle the situation. This could be a grittier and more menacing adaptation of Logan, where the danger knows no bounds. Knowing the consequences, he bravely gestured for three of his men to launch an attack, fully aware that it might be a fatal misstep. But if the person ahead of him was this unhinged, it would have been a matter of time before he attempted to kill them all.

With caution, the three security officers advanced towards their enemy, brandishing metal batons. His smile stretched further as he turned his head, reaching a point where his cheek muscles were sure to protest.

*Don't do it Magnus.*

"Time to play a little game," Logan laughed.

One of the men lunged forward, his baton whistling through the air as he aimed for his target, but Logan skilfully evaded the strike. Despite his best efforts, his attempt to strike again was met with a devastating punch to the wrist, causing the bone to break with a resounding snap. The baton slipped through the man's fingers, but Logan was there to snatch it before it could hit the ground.

"This little piggy doesn't know how to play."

With a tight grip on the weapon, Logan exerted all his strength, driving it forcefully into the man's mouth, causing it to explode out the back of his throat. In a sudden motion, the body fell limply to the ground, leaving a disturbing silence in its wake.

With a sense of desperation, the next two men attacked their target, their swings wild and uncoordinated, as if their adversary had the power to foresee their every action. Logan's forceful kick landed on the left side of his opponent's right knee, instantly causing him to buckle under the impact.

As he descended, a forceful uppercut found its mark on the man's nose, causing a jarring impact. The nose-breaking blow was so powerful that it caused the broken bone to penetrate deep into the man's brain. Without warning, his life was abruptly snuffed out.

"This little piggy died on the same day." He continued to sing.

"And this little piggy."

With a firm grasp on the third man's head, he mercilessly dug his thumbs deep into his eye sockets. The man desperately tried to restrain him, but to no avail, resulting in a blood-curdling scream as his eyes burst inside his skull.

"Couldn't see another way."

Leaving the man writhing in agony on the floor, he felt no remorse. As Logan looked up at Marcus, his face marred by blood, a chilling and sadistic smile played on his lips.

"It seems that you are three men down. Whose next?"

Evan stood there, staring in disbelief at what his eyes were witnessing. The room was filled with a collective gasp as everyone else stared in awe.

"What happened to you?" Evan asked.

"Me? I'm better than I ever was. Now, are we going to rumble or not? Oh and Evan, Logan may have been willing to work with you. I am not. Why would I trust a man who would betray his own family?" Once again, he burst into fits of uncontrollable, hysterical laughter.

With a subtle hand gesture, Marcus signalled his remaining men to launch their assault. As he observed the man in front of him, a nagging thought crossed his mind - was this all an act? As Damien stood, his gaze was fixated on his target, his body poised for a powerful leap. It wasn't Logan who those murderous eyes were aimed at, but rather Madison.

In an aggressive onslaught, the first attacker sprinted towards his target, unleashing a relentless combination of punches - a rapid series of rights, lefts, and a forceful right hook. The third punch swung at Logan, grazing his nose by a hair's breadth and causing a gust of air to brush against his face. With a single, precise strike to the man's chest, the force behind the hit reverberated through the air, leaving no doubt of its lethal impact. With precision, the blow landed on the left side of the chest, shattering a rib. As the fractured bone pierced his heart, the man's body convulsed with excruciating pain and a profound understanding that his existence was fading. With each thump of his heart, crimson blood gushed from the wound, pooling inside his chest. In a matter of minutes, he fell to the floor, his body wracked with convulsions as he struggled to catch his breath. The air was heavy with the smell of blood as he coughed, his coughs splattering the floor with crimson.

Uncertainty filled the air as the other two security members paused, contemplating whether they were prepared to confront their mortality that day. Both had families of their own, and it was evident from the way he carried himself that the man in front of them was highly proficient in close quarters combat. Giving their boss a hesitant glance, one of them expressed their uncertainty.

"What are you doing? Kill him! Or I'll kill you!" Marcus yelled.

Both men knew that Marcus would follow through on his words, willing to sacrifice their pride, they lunged at Logan. If they were going down, they were determined to bring him down as well. The wide smile suddenly disappeared from Logan's face. His attackers swung their batons, along with throwing punches and kicks. He managed to avoid most of the hits, but a kick caught his leg and one of them managed to hit him in his side with their weapon.

"Stop. Please don't make me hurt you." Logan pleaded.

*What the fuck are you doing? Give me back control!*

Confusion hung in the room, wrapping its tendrils around each person's mind, dragging them deeper into a bewildering abyss. What was happening with Logan? In the midst of the puzzled crowd, Damien's curiosity shone brightly, setting him apart from the rest. The desire to confront this alternate version of Logan burned within him, fuelling his determination to engage in combat.

Logan expertly manoeuvred to avoid the punches and baton swings of the two men, who showed no signs of slowing down their assault. Employing a counter punch, he skilfully disarmed her opponent and sent them sprawling onto the floor. Following that, he delivered a forceful blow to the stomach of the second security member, followed by a powerful uppercut. They both lay on the floor, feeling the impact of being knocked down, while their attacker displayed obvious restraint. The mere idea of him unleashing his full power and making a genuine attempt to kill them sent shivers down their spines.

The sight of the three corpses on the floor was chilling, and his attention was drawn to the two men, clutching their faces in pain from the force of the strikes. Marcus was well aware that his enemy possessed the skills to swiftly eliminate both men. The frustration of wasting time had finally got to him. With his baretta pistol drawn, he skilfully aimed at Logan's head, ready to pull the trigger. With a victorious smirk on Marcus' face, he let him know he had won.

"Did you really think that I would just have a fist fight with you? When I can just put a bullet it your head." Marcus laughed.

*Let me kill this bastard! Give me back control Logan. If you get yourself killed, I die with you. Don't get yourself killed.*

"I also forgot to tell you. I had a sniper position himself opposite the building, so if you managed to get in and get to this room. He could eliminate you on my call. You see Logan, I adapted. Always have a contingency plan, along with more to back that one up right?"

Logan was impressed to see that the man he once considered his friend had learned from his numerous mistakes. He gave his all, determined to emerge victorious over Mr. Winters. Kane consistently favoured Logan over Marcus for every mission, always appointing him as the leader and showering him with constant praise. Over time, that drove him to despise the man he had once considered a brother.

"Marcus, you don't have to do this. Be the better man, let them go and you can have me."

"No Logan." Madison cried.

"The thing is. I don't care about them. They are Damien's problem." Marcus said.

Damien's face beamed with a wide smile as he stood there. The anticipation had been building up inside him, as he waited for those words to be spoken. With Madison in grave danger, Logan's determination to keep her and Bethany safe intensified.

"I won't let you or him, hurt them."

*Let me handle this.*

Logan desperately tried to block out Magnus, terrified that his mere presence would result in a bloodbath. He wouldn't just stop the ones who posed the biggest threat; he would go after anyone who appeared even slightly suspicious. Three people had already lost their lives at his hands.

"I have the gun pointed at you. If you move even a muscle, I'll blow your brains out. You lose Logan. Just accept it." Marcus uttered.

Both men locked eyes, their intense gaze mirroring a classic western duel. Except one man stood out from the other, empty-handed. Knowing that he didn't want either man to kill the other, Evan watched on in dismay, his stomach churning with anxiety. His deepest desire was for a gentle and peaceful resolution to all the turmoil. Aware that peace was not a value his family upheld, he still sought moments of calm amidst the chaos. Carefully manoeuvring himself between his brother and Logan, he silently hoped that Marcus wouldn't take a drastic step like shooting him in order to confront his enemy.

"What are you doing? Move!" Marcus yelled in anger, confused by his brothers actions.

"It doesn't need to end like this. Please. Why is your answer to everything death? That just results in further death. When does it end?"

"Move, Evan, or I will put a bullet in you. I'm fed up with your shit. You are a needy little bastard. You've always hated the fact that dad chooses me over you. Is this how you want to die? Protecting that bastard."

Evan stood his ground, rooted to the spot like an immovable tree. Not a muscle twitched as he remained motionless. Fear of his brother and father had always consumed him, but he had finally broken free from its grip. He couldn't handle the constant feeling of being belittled anymore. He believed that if he died, they would bear the burden of remorse. The family would be torn apart by their father's hatred towards Marcus, leading to their downfall. They would go to war with each other over it and most likely kill one another.

"Do it." Evan said.

Marcus looked at him, his shock barely concealed beneath a thin veneer of composure. Anticipating his brother's compliance, he expected him to step aside, only to be met with resistance. According to Logan, they fail to fully comprehend Evan's potential. The evidence suggested that his enemy's claim was right.

"Move. Last warning."

In spite of it all, he refused to move, resolute in his spot.

"Target in sight. Do I take the shot? Please confirm. "A voice said through Marcus' earpiece.

With a wide grin forming, he met his brother's gaze, a playful spark in his eyes.

"Confirm."

# 43

With a quick squeeze of the trigger, the bullet was unleashed from the barrel of the L115A3 sniper rifle. Travelling at an incredible speed of approximately three thousand square feet per second. The sound of breaking glass echoed through the air as the bullet punched through and found its mark. In a violent burst, the end of Marcus' pistol shattered into fragments, sending a shock-wave through his hand. He stood there, frozen, as a wave of utter shock crashed through his body.

Why had the marksman not taken out Logan?

"What the fuck are you doing?" Marcus asked.

"Oh sorry, I missed." The man laughed.

The moment Marcus heard the laugh, he had a sudden realisation about the identity of the person on the other end.

Lincoln Winters.

"You… You are dead."

"How did a dead man just blow your gun up?"

Logan turned his gaze towards the window, his face lighting up with a grateful smile. He knew who was out there. His brother's selfless act of endangering himself and his family to aid him left Logan forever indebted. The room was filled with a perplexed silence as Damien, along with everyone else, struggled to comprehend what was unfolding before them. The tension in the air was palpable as he anxiously contemplated if the sniper's next victim would be him or Marcus.

"How are you alive?" Marcus asked.

"That doesn't matter. What does, is you letting my brother and those women go. If you don't, I'd be more than happy to put a bullet through your good eye."

Marcus weighed his options, with the idea of relinquishing them not ranking high on his agenda. Marcus knew that even if he released his captives, he would still be in danger of being shot by Lincoln, creating a lose-lose situation. Rather than simply watching his enemy leave, he'd choose death as the alternative. His eyes darted around the room, searching for any objects that could offer protection or obstruct Lincoln's line of sight.

"Your brother is not leaving this room." Marcus said.

Using a wordless gaze, he signalled to Damien to look towards the left side of the room, where the fire extinguisher was mounted on the wall. Advancing slowly towards the extinguisher, Damien kept a vigilant eye on Madison and

Bethany, his attention fully focused on them.

"My father will be happy to know that he can capture and kill both the Winters brothers. Then he will find your family and just like Logan's, they will die. Only I don't think we will burn them this time. Maybe drowning will be the best option." He laughed.

"Now!" Marcus shouted.

With lightning speed, Damien snatched the fire extinguisher and doused the window with foam, effectively blocking the sniper's view. Lincoln's shot went awry, the restricted view and Marcus' sudden movement to the right causing him to miss his mark.

With urgency, Marcus sprinted towards Logan, shoving Evan out of his path. The air crackled with energy as he threw a left hook, a rapid succession of jabs, a powerful right hook, and a symphony of kicks. The intensity of their fight mirrored the fierce competition between Lions, each determined to claim the throne of the pride.

With a burst of energy, Damien sprinted towards Madison, yanking her hair and forcefully slamming her against the wall. In the midst of the chaos, Evan found a moment of stillness, as if time itself had halted. He watched as his brother and Logan fiercely exchanged blows. Madison's back was pressed firmly against the wall as Damien loomed over her, his face contorted with a menacing expression. Who would he help first? While Logan had the skills to protect himself, Evan's love for his brother made him hesitant to witness his demise. The two security members hastily made their escape from the room, fully aware of the potential outcome if Marcus prevailed. Faced with the looming threat of the coming days, they fervently prayed for his defeat in the battle.

Bethany desperately tried to wrench her father away from her mother's grip, but he forcefully shoved her aside, causing her to crash onto the floor. Each blow against the wall intensified Damien's sadistic pleasure, until he finally turned his attention to strangling Madison, his depravity on full display. He did not care if it was a woman or man that he was hitting. Desperate to break free, she clawed at his face and hands, but his grip remained unyielding.

As Madison's life slipped away, she could feel the suffocating grip of darkness tightening around her. In an instant, Damien was forcefully pushed away from her, his body colliding with the window and shattering it with a loud crack. In the midst of the attack, he spun around, only to come face-to-face with Evan, who was glaring at him with a mix of determination and fury.

"Leave them alone!" He yelled.

Bethany quickly climbed back to her feet and hurried over to help her mother, who was struggling to get up. Every time Madison tried to rise, she fell back down, her consciousness flickering like a dying light. Evan harboured a deep loathing for the maniac, who showed no regard for the lives he took. Damien couldn't help but laugh at the irony of Evan, the least confrontational person, standing up to him.

"Really Evan? Do you want to die?"

"Get your mum and get out of here. Quickly." Evan said.

With a caring touch, Bethany offered her arm to help her

mum, leading Madison towards the door. Damien's frustration boiled over as he saw them trying to leave, and he made a desperate grab for Beth. The impact of Evan's powerful right hook jolted him backwards. Just as another punch was about to connect, Damien skilfully evaded it, swiftly manoeuvring Evan and propelling him into the wall. With precision and power, the Damien began a rapid assault, landing a series of punches to their opponent's face and body.

Every desperate attempt to halt the maniac's relentless attack on Evan proved futile. Damien's punches to Evan's chest were forceful and targeted, each strike packed with maximum strength. The sound of breaking ribs filled the air as he let out a piercing scream of agony.

"Did you really think you would beat me? Pathetic." Damien said, his evil eyes piercing through his victims soul.

Just as he least expected it, a forceful kick sent him sprawling, and he looked up to find Madison, the source of the attack. Tired and frustrated, she had reached her breaking point, running endlessly from the clutches of a vile man. With a deep breath, she steeled herself to confront her fear, and there he stood, the one she had dreaded facing for years.

"You came back to die. You should have run." He laughed.

"I'm not running anymore and you should never be allowed to hurt anyone ever again."

Bethany appeared from behind her, gripping a baton tightly in her hand. The fact that Madison was going to put up a fight had left him in a state of disbelief. His soul shattered as he realised that his own daughter was now his adversary.

"You are a monster. Not my father. You have never been my father." Beth said, gripping the weapon tightly.

Realising that he no longer needed to conceal that part of himself, he tore off his shirt. His torso, marred by deep scars, was exposed for all to see. The scars on his body resembled tally charts, with each one tallying up to five, and he had accumulated hundreds of them. Confusion filled Madison and Bethany's eyes as they took in the sight of his scarred body. What had happened to him?

"I am a fucking monster! Do you wanna know what these scars are for?"

Their intrigued expressions spoke volumes, even though they didn't utter a word in response.

"It's the amount of lives I've taken. You see, I didn't want a record on a computer or anywhere. I wanted it on me. After every kill, I added to it. After today, I'll be adding a few more. You think I'm a monster. You've not seen anything yet."

In a sudden burst of aggression, he charged at the women, but Evan managed to swiftly grab hold of him, struggling to maintain a tight grip. He held Damien close, skilfully dodging the powerful backwards headbutts that the man was unleashing.

"Now!" Evan yelled.

The impact of Madison's kick landed directly on Damien's testicles, sending waves of intense pain through his body. As his strength gave out, he fell to his knees and clasped them tightly, seeking support. Evan moved off of him. Madison's kick landed squarely on the man's face, adding to the intensity of the altercation. As she continued to attack him, a chill ran down her spine when his laughter filled the air. His face was a gruesome sight, with blood trickling down from several cuts, creating a macabre pattern. Nevertheless, a smile crept across his face as he found it humorous.

While attempting to kick him again, he skilfully seized her leg and effortlessly swept her other leg off the ground. Collapsing to the ground, she felt his weight instantly press down on her, his wounds oozing blood onto her skin. He locked his gaze with hers, their eyes connecting in a deadly exchange.

"I never told you how I killed that bastard Jack. I caught him coming back from the school after he finished. Tortured him for days. Removing each one of his toes and fingers. Then I took his eyes and fed them to him. After that, I removed his tongue."

Fuelled by his words, she lashed out, attempting to strike him and forcefully push him aside, only to come up empty-handed.

"Shut up! You are a disgusting human being! I can't believe at one point in my life, I actually loved you. You never deserved it!"

As he leaned in, his face contorted into a menacing expression, and she could feel his hot breath on her skin, as if he were about to trace his tongue along her. A powerful blow to the head sent him tumbling off Madison. Beside them, Bethany stood with the baton now stained with blood.

"Touch my mum again and I will fucking kill you!"

With a gentle gesture, Evan moved beside her and assisted

Madison in standing up, ensuring she was steady on her feet. The agony in his ribs intensified, but his determination to help outweighed the pain. She looked up at him, her eyes filled with gratitude for his presence. Looking over, she saw Logan and Marcus, their faces covered in blood and bruises, but still fighting with unwavering determination.

Slowly rising up off the floor, Damien felt a wave of dizziness engulf him after the blow to his head. The fire in his eyes showed that he wasn't ready to surrender the fight. With a forceful kick, he struck Evan in the side of his right knee, causing it to give way. The older Hunt family member landed a powerful uppercut, causing the younger family member to stagger backwards and collapse onto the floor. With his attention now fixed on the girls, he was moments away from demonstrating just how bone-chilling he could be.

Bethany swung the baton towards him, the whooshing sound filling the air, but he agilely evaded the attack and swiftly retaliated with a forceful jab to her nose, resulting in a sudden gush of blood. Clutching her face, she couldn't fathom how he could have done something so terrible to his own flesh and blood. He wasted no time and swiftly seized Madison by the hair, forcefully dragging her towards the already cracked window. No matter how hard she tried, she couldn't escape his vice-like grip; his strength was insurmountable.

"You used to like watching the birds fly all those years ago. Now I'm gonna let you be a bird. Minus the flying."

Despite the pain shooting through his ribs and the persistent ache in his knee, Evan mustered the strength to rise from the ground. He wasn't about to let Damien have his way. Despite his aversion to violence and death, he couldn't ignore the fact that the man standing before him was the most dangerous threat in the room, particularly to the mother and daughter. He gritted his teeth, fighting through the pain, as he rushed towards Damien. With a swift move, Evan tackled the man away from Madison, successfully dislodging his grip and bringing him down to the ground. As Madison fell away from them, she landed on the floor with a heavy thud, the impact sending a jolt of pain through her body. A torrent of anger surged through Evan, its intensity revealing how tightly he had held it back. His fists relentlessly hammered into the man's face, the sight of blood splattering across the ground a testament to the force behind his blows.

The maniac lay there, barely conscious, his defeated and disappointed expression speaking volumes. The weight of his failures as a husband, a father, and a man descended upon him like a suffocating fog, dragging him into a new kind of hell.

Memories of his laughter-filled adventures with Madison filled his mind, but also brought a pang of regret for not giving it his all. Rather than offering support, he frequently directed his anger towards his wife. Driven by his failure to love Madison as she deserved, she found comfort in the embrace of another man. In that moment, as he endured the physical pain from his failed attempt to harm his wife, he finally understood the ripple effect his actions had on his family.

With a struggle, he managed to rise up from the ground

and turned his gaze towards Madison and his daughter. A single tear escaped from his eye and trailed down his cheek. He knew deep down in his heart that they were worthy of a better life.

"I'm… sorry." He mumbled.

Madison looked at him with concern, aware of his usual reluctance to apologise. In a split second, Damien lunged through the glass window, leaving behind a trail of shattered fragments. As if driven by an innate instinct, she extended her hand towards him, her heart filled with a fierce determination to save him. He was gone. But her mind or heart did not feel at peace, as conflicting emotions swirled within her. Part of her wished for him to cease to exist, while another part struggled with those dark thoughts. Regardless of his inclination towards violence, he remained Bethany's biological father.

The intense fight between Marcus and Logan came to an abrupt stop, leaving them both stunned by the unexpected turn of events. Marcus's expectations were shattered when he realised he was alone in the room, pitted against them. They were fortunate to have his own brother standing with them. The man's surprising action caught Logan off guard, as he had never expected such behaviour from someone he thought was heartless. Ultimately, he came to the realisation that he did possess a heart, and this newfound awareness compelled him to acknowledge the danger he posed to his own family.

Seizing the opportunity amidst the turmoil, Marcus pushed Logan aside with a sense of urgency and hastily escaped through the door.

He needed help.

He needed Kane.

# 44

The doors of the elevator chimed, and Kane's heart skipped a beat when he saw his son, a haunting image of blood and bruises. With each stride, Marcus could feel the anticipation building, knowing that his father's presence would bring a sense of balance to the situation. Curiosity compelled Kane to look behind his son, eager to see if Damien or his other son would join them. Fearing the worst, he felt a burning sensation growing inside him, like a raging fire.

"Where is Evan?" He asked aggressively, his voice tinged with an underlying concern.

"He… he is with them now. He betrayed us!"

The impact of shock on Kane was as powerful as being struck by a freight train. Evan, although not the strongest, had always been known for his unwavering loyalty within the family. Like an unexpected storm, disappointment poured down on him as he realised Evan had betrayed them.

"He wouldn't." He replied, lost for words.

"He did. He fought Damien."

"And?" He asked, wondering whether his weakest son, beat the maniac.

"Well, Damien isn't here is he? I don't know what came over him, he was beaten and then jumped through the window to his death. Logan was wrong. Apparently, the man did have a heart."

Kane couldn't help but smile as he thought about Evan's accomplishment - taking down one of the most terrifying killers was truly impressive in his eyes. The fact that one of his assets was dead didn't bother him; after all, Damien had always been a difficult person to collaborate with. Suddenly, a nefarious scheme materialised in his thoughts, one that had the potential to bring about Logan's downfall.

"Get them to my office. I'll meet you there."

"Yes, father." Marcus said with a nod.

"There was something else." He quickly uttered.

"What?" Kane asked.

Aware of the limited time available, he quickly let go of his intention to share something with his father.

"Never mind. I'll get him to you."

Kane stepped back into the lift, and as the doors closed, he caught a glimpse of Logan emerging from the room. Just as he looked up, she saw Kane for a split second before he swiftly vanished behind the doors. Logan couldn't help but ponder if Kane had witnessed the distressing image of his own son, battered and covered in blood, and deliberately turned his back on him. Peering at his brother's expression, Evan emerged from behind him, questioning whether joining forces with Logan had been a wise decision. The point of no return had been reached, and there was no choice but to move forward.

"Why is he just standing there?" Beth asked, as she poked her head around the door.

"He wants me to follow." Logan replied.

"I wouldn't. It's a trap." Evan said, knowing that his brother would want just Logan to follow, take him down once and for all.

"If it ends it, once and for all. Then I'm willing to walk into it. I want to finish it."

As Evan glanced at him, his worry for his brother's safety consumed him. He braced himself for the inevitable, knowing the possibility of only one of them would walk away from this fight. It was a life-or-death situation, where either both men would meet their demise or one would emerge victorious. He couldn't predict the outcome, unsure of which one would be the survivor.

"Will you kill him?" Evan asked.

Logan let out a heavy sigh, the weight of uncertainty settling in his chest. On one hand, he craved the satisfaction of ending the life of the man who murdered his family. On the other hand, he desired to witness the man's prolonged misery behind bars.

"I don't know. I'm not going to lie and say I don't want to see him dead."

"I get that and because they are family, I don't want them to die. But I know what they've done."

As Evan dropped his head in shame, he could feel the weight of his actions settle on his shoulders, and he turned his head slightly to catch a glimpse of his brother's disapproving expression. Marcus, with his one eye fixed on Evan, stood surprisingly patient, emanating an intense and unsettling aura. Mouthing the words 'You're dead.' With a sense of conviction, he made the decision to stick with Logan, the one person who had consistently shown him more respect than anyone in his own family.

Evan couldn't shake the thought that plagued his mind, especially after his brother's shocking revelation. He had tried his best to ignore it, even after Logan's strange alter ego made an unexpected appearance.

"Did you really kill her? My mother." Evan questioned.

Deep in thought, Logan pondered his response, fully aware that his words wouldn't bring clarity to the younger Hunt's mind.

"Your mother was a lovely woman, one who had always been kind to me. No, I didn't kill her."

"You said was. So she is dead then?"

"There's things that you aren't aware of. Things that Maggie, had forbid me to tell you. I don't know if she is dead or not. What that part of me said before… well, he knew that would get to you."

It worked.

As Evan's curiosity grew, he couldn't help but wonder about the forbidden knowledge his mother guarded, but the ticking clock added urgency to his thoughts.

"If we survive this, would you be willing to tell me more? I just want to have a better idea of what happened to her."

Studying the man's face, Logan recognised the sincerity and earnestness that warranted sharing some of the truth with him. He'd earned it.

"I will tell you everything I can, when this is all over. Okay?"

"Okay and Thank you. What do you want me to do?" Evan asked.

"Get Madison and Beth outside, to Francis. He knows what to do. He will protect them."

Standing by the door, Madison's expression conveyed a profound sadness as she locked eyes with Logan. The way he kept talking unsettled her, his voice filled with a sense of determination and purpose, as if he was on a mission with no plans of ever coming back. The more time she spent with him, the stronger her affection grew; the mere thought of losing him made her heart ache. She yearned to build a stronger bond with him, eager to uncover the depths of his character.

"You make it sound like you aren't coming back." She said, a single tear threatened to spill over as it swelled up in her eye.

He acknowledged her sadness and refused to deceive himself; he'd rather be with her and Beth, but he couldn't until he brought closure to everything. With their fair share of close calls, his main priority was to eradicate any lingering danger. He knew the risks involved, but was prepared to give his life for it. He was willing to do whatever it took to keep them out of harm's way.

"I can't stand here and promise that I will come back. But I will promise that I will do everything in my power to come back to you." He said, brushing his hand over her cheek.

Leaning in, he pressed his lips gently against hers, savouring the intimate moment. Their arms wrapped around each other, and they held on tightly, cherishing the moment. With a heavy heart, he moved away, his eyes reflecting the sorrow within. The warmth of happiness slowly enveloped his heart, a feeling that had been absent for so long since his family's untimely departure.

"I like you." He said.

"And I like you too." She replied happily.

Observing the scene, Bethany couldn't help but shed a tear of happiness, knowing that her mother had found someone who could make her smile again.

"You're pretty cool, Logan." Beth uttered.

As Logan smiled at her, he couldn't help but remember how sceptical she had been of him when they first met.

"You're pretty cool yourself."

As he shifted his focus to Evan, he couldn't help but notice the sorrowful expression on his brother's face. But all he received in return were hostile glares.

"You've gotta go. Get them to safety. Promise me that you will keep them safe."

*What is with all the soppy bollocks?*

"I will. I'll get them to your friend." Evan nodded.

Evan began walking off, and Beth could feel a sense of

urgency building within her. She turned abruptly, and rushed over to Logan and gave him an enormous hug.

"Come back please." She whispered.

"I'll do my best."

Eager to catch up with Evan, she hurriedly made her way towards him. Madison embraced Logan once more, her heart pounding as she held him even closer than before. Unsure if it was the last time. Instead of getting mushy about it, she resolved to be his source of motivation.

"Go and kick his ass." She said, giving him a smile.

With each step she took, she could feel the tug of his hand, as if it was unwilling to let her go. He couldn't help but give her one more heartfelt grin.

"He won't know what hit him."

Following her daughter and Evan, she reached the end of the corridor and made her way out the door. They were gone. Logan spun around, his heart pounding, to find Marcus standing there, his fists clenched and determination in his eyes.

"Prepare to die Logan!"

Logan's face broke into a grin as he walked towards him. Dying was not on his agenda for the evening; he had discovered a renewed sense of purpose and determination.

"Your confidence will get you killed Marcus."

"Remi, disable all cameras in the building and the lifts please."

"Yes, sir. Although I will not be able to provide over watch for any approaching threats." She replied, her voice echoing through the earpiece.

"If you can see where they are. They probably have someone monitoring where I am. Disable them from being able to see at all or get to me quickly." He said.

"Will do."

As he quickened his stride, he closed the distance between himself and his adversary. Without warning, Marcus burst through the stairway door and started climbing the stairs, his hurried steps echoing through the building. Immediately, he could sense Marcus's reluctance to engage in a one-on-one battle. Aware that alone, he'd probably lose.

*You know it's a trap right? He is luring you to him.*

"I know he is." He mumbled to himself.

*Think we can take them both? I mean, the man beat you before. Let me take care of it, you hold back too much.*

"Take Kane down and Marcus will flee. His father is the target, not him. Kane put everything in motion, he started all of this and it will end with him."

*Just don't die. I like living. Now this isn't me being all soppy. But if you need me at any point in this fight, give me control and let me help. We've worked against each other for so long. Maybe it's time we worked as one.*

The realisation dawned on Logan that Magnus, his darker self, had a valid point. It seemed logical to join forces rather than oppose each other. He was exhausted from constantly battling to prevent Magnus from seizing control; they desperately needed to find a way to collaborate harmoniously.

"You've not exactly earned my trust. How can I trust that you won't take over permanently and just kill everyone? You aren't exactly stable."

*I mean, your are currently having a conversation with yourself. Neither of us are stable.*

"Let's just get up there and put an end to this."

# 45

As Marcus burst through the doors to Kane's office, he was met with the unexpected sight of his father, relaxed and at ease in his chair. Despite the impending event, he appeared completely unfazed, with a relaxed expression on his face.

"He's coming. Logan's coming." Marcus said.

A mischievous smile played on Kane's lips, determined not to let Logan slip away again. He had predicted that Marcus would not be able to defeat his enemy on his own. Though his son was skilled in combat, Logan had always possessed an undeniable edge.

"Good." Kane uttered.

"There's something…" Marcus said.

Before he could utter another word, the sound of Logan's footsteps echoed towards them. He spun on his heel, his gaze locking onto the man who had taken his eye. Kane remained firmly planted in his seat, exuding an air of tranquillity and composure. Dismissing the man ahead as insignificant, he didn't regard him as a serious threat.

"Mr Winters." Kane grinned.

Without uttering a word, Logan's gaze pierced through both men, his expression conveying a deadly determination despite his doubts about facing them alone. When it came to combat, Kane was in a league of his own, his reputation as a formidable fighter preceding him. If he were to face each of them individually, he believed his odds of defeating them would increase.

*Have faith Logan. We've got this. Trust me.*

Unexpectedly, Magnus's voice echoed in his mind, saying words he never thought he would hear - a stark contrast to his usual bloodthirsty desires. Logan couldn't shake the lingering suspicion towards his darker half, the personality that embodied a killer instinct, even though he recognised its current role in keeping him alive. If his life is taken, they both perish.

"You won't survive this Logan." Marcus had his confidence once again, due to his father's presence.

"You overestimate your odds." Logan laughed.

With a thunderous clash, both men charged towards each other, their fists flying. Logan unleashed a powerful right hook while Marcus retaliated with a lightning-fast left punch. The impact of their punches was synchronised, propelling them both backwards with equal force. Marcus's fists flew in a rapid succession, one blow finding its mark on Logan's left side, causing a sharp pain in his ribs. Though it didn't fracture his ribs, the impact of the punch left him with unmistakable bruising.

Kane observed, biding his time, saving his energy. Much to his surprise, his son displayed impressive fighting skills, exceeding his initial expectations. As he watched, Logan skilfully dodged and parried a barrage of punches and kicks, retaliating with his own powerful strikes. The impact of a well-aimed kick to Marcus' left inner thigh caused his leg to collapse beneath him. Taking advantage of the opening, Logan unleashed a relentless assault on his opponent's face, raining down a barrage of jabs, hooks, and a spinning kick with the sole purpose of incapacitating his foe.

In a split second, Kane's punch intercepted Logan's kick, knocking him down with such impact that he hit the floor. Now, the real fight was about to start.

With determination in his eyes, Logan dusted himself off and readied himself for what would be the most intense fight he had ever faced. Moving swiftly towards Kane, he feigned a left hook before swiftly delivering a powerful blow to the man's chest with his right fist. He wasted no time, throwing one punch after another, each one finding its mark with a powerful impact to the stomach and a solid strike to the ribs. The impact of the blows was strong, but Kane barely reacted, displaying his remarkable stoicism. His gaze locked with Logan's, and in that moment, Logan realised with astonishment that this man had grown even stronger than he had been previously.

*Tickle him, maybe he's ticklish.*

Despite the urge to burst into laughter, Logan managed to maintain a serious expression, suppressing his amusement. Kane swiftly caught the powerful overhand hook, halting its trajectory. With a tight grip on his wrist, he could feel the bones threatening to shatter with any additional force. With each punch, the sound of impact reverberated through the air as he unleashed a dozen powerful strikes on Logan's face. Remembering something that his enemy had done to him during their last battle. Using his left hand, Logan exerted maximum force as he landed a powerful blow to Kane's left upper inner arm, effectively forcing him to relinquish his grip and disabling his arm briefly.

"You remembered." Kane uttered.

With determination in his eyes, Marcus rose up and positioned himself next to his father, ready to face their adversary as a united front. The realisation hit Logan hard - he knew he couldn't effectively fight them both together and achieve his goal.

*Let me have a crack at them.*

Could Magnus the maniac side of Logan, really best both men? He doubted it, knowing that Kane alone possessed an undeniable power. The odds were stacked against him when facing both him and his son, and he knew that it could be a one-way journey when he followed Marcus.

'Okay. Give it your best shot.' Logan replied in his head.

That big, crazy grin reappeared on his face, making him look like a total maniac. Marcus noticed it immediately; a chilling sensation crept up his spine, signalling the arrival of his enemy's deranged alter ego.

"Well, boys, give me your best shot. Or was what you just did your best?" Magnus laughed.

He started pacing back and forth, taking a different approach than Logan had anticipated. While waiting for them, his darker half played the defensive strategy, which turned out to be a smart move. Logan was astonished.

"Take him together." Kane said.

"Two of you, for little old me. I'm flattered." Magnus laughed.

Approaching their enemy, Marcus nodded and stayed by his father's side. Marcus swung a right hook to start the assault but failed to hit his intended target. As a response, a quick left jab landed squarely on his face. Kane's kick missed its target, nearly striking his own son in the process. Their punches and kicks were fierce, landing a couple of hits, but it wasn't sufficient to overpower their opponent. Swiftly and skilfully, most of the attacks were evaded.

"I thought you'd do better than that. Well not you Marcus. You punch without thinking, but then again, with a brain as small as yours, I'm not surprised." Magnus laughed.

Kane was discovering a previously unseen facet of Logan's character, one that intrigued and surprised him. His serious demeanour during fights never lent itself to playfulness or jokes, which is why he was taken aback by the surprising comments. Magnus's attention was caught by Kane's puzzled look, indicating his confusion.

"You must be confused? Logan doesn't laugh and joke. He is Mr fucking serious. Well, here's the kicker. I'm not Logan. He is residing in my usual home, having a rest. Maybe a cup of tea. I wonder if he will make me one? Logan, if you're listening, make me a cuppa." His laughter continued.

As the big man stared at him, a bewildered expression crossed his face, unable to comprehend the bizarre manner in which he spoke. Had the extended period of solitude fractured the man who was once his top-performing and deadliest asset?

"What happened to the great Mr Winters? Finally snapped I see." Kane said.

"First of all. When I'm in control, call me Magnus. Logan is basically an entirely different person to me. He holds back, stops himself from doing things that would hurt others. I'm not the holding back type."

*I'm sure you saying all of this will actually scare them away. Although Kane will probably want you in a mental hospital, rather than kill you. He always considered those who were mentally ill, to be weaker. Time to prove the bastard wrong.*

"Pathetic. Your mind crumbled. You are weaker than I thought." Kane uttered.

"Do you really believe that it was the time living alone that broke Logan? I've always been here. He just ignored me for years and years. The time alone, meant that he needed someone to talk to and that was where I came in. I was there when no one else was. So you believing us to be weaker. What, because we are considered mentally unstable? A lot of those big missions you gave him, if he couldn't take the shot. Who do you think took over? We are much stronger than you realise."

Logan's mind was flooded with countless memories, all

revealing that it was Magnus who had propelled him to become one of the most renowned assassins of his generation. Watching the scenes unfold once more, he witnessed his darker side effortlessly assume control during various missions, efficiently eliminating the target before relinquishing command to Logan. This was something he did frequently, on many occasions. Every step of the way, he had accompanied Logan, utilising his insatiable desire to kill in order to assist the individual who possessed complete authority over their joint existence.

Dumbfounded, Kane was left without any words to express his astonishment. In a whirlwind of thoughts, he tried to fathom the astonishing ability of someone with two personalities to seamlessly harness them, completely unnoticed by others.

*You've been here the entire time? How did I not know?*

'Because you didn't need to know. All that time alone didn't help your mind. My presence became stronger. You needed a friend, I'm sure you'd have preferred a less psychotic one, but you got me. I've always been around, part of you. Your memories are my memories. Only sometimes if I force the take over, you don't remember anything I did. Which I why there was a few missions that you did, where you couldn't recall taking the shot. You would receive the call to confirm if the news reports are true and often you'd quickly agree, because you didn't want to disappoint this big lump of muscle. You now knowing about it all, has clearly released all of those memories to you. So you now remember every moment.'

*It appears I was wrong about you. I thought you only ever wanted to kill. But you've been helping me for my whole life. Thank you.*

'Trust me, you weren't wrong about me. I do like killing. But maybe a bit of your humanity has broke it's way into me. Don't get all soppy though. We have business to attend to. Let's finish this.'

*Let's do it. Together.*

Catching Kane's right hook took immense strength, and Logan winced as the force of the blow sent a sharp pain through his hand. The huge man was astonished when his opponent skilfully stopped his punch, something that had never happened before. Magnus then launched a swift uppercut, connecting with Kane's chin and causing him to stagger backwards.

With a sudden burst of energy, Marcus launched himself forward, his fist aimed at Logan's chest. However, his attack was intercepted as Logan effortlessly caught his arm and effortlessly tossed him over his shoulder. In a fit of rage, Kane charged at and tackled Logan to the ground. Because of his size and weight, he wasn't the easiest of people to move off. He began to pummel his fists into Logan's face, along with hitting his chest.

With a forceful blow to the side of his head, Kane was knocked off balance and crashed onto the floor. As he looked up, his mind foggy and confused, he couldn't help but question the reality before him. The man standing before him couldn't be.

"You should be dead." He mumbled.

"You're the second person to say that today." Lincoln replied.

As Lincoln helped his brother up off the floor, a warm smile spread across his face, filling Logan with an overwhelming sense of relief.

"Took your time." Logan said.

"You seen those stairs? Why is there so many? Also, the bloody lift is broken." His brother laughed.

"Sorry, that was my doing."

"I thought it would be."

"I'm glad you came." Logan smiled.

Lincoln embraced his brother, feeling a pang of worry as he saw the faint wince on his face. He gently held him, careful not to apply too much pressure, as he could sense the pain radiating from his injured body.

"Always." Lincoln replied.

As they both turned, their eyes locked onto Kane and Marcus, who were gearing up for a fierce and deadly confrontation. Marcus's fist crashed through the glass casing on the left side of the room, revealing a lethal mace and a sturdy battle axe. He deftly retrieved both weapons, handing the battle-axe over to his father with a determined look in his eyes. They were deliberately eschewing fair play in favour of a more aggressive approach. As they looked at each other, their grins mirrored in perfect synchrony, a palpable aura of increased power surrounded the brothers.

"You ready?" Lincoln asked.

"Always." Logan grinned.

As the four men charged at each other, their heavy

breathing created a symphony of sound that filled the air.

# 46

With each step down the stairs, Evan's eyes revealed a torment that Madison and Bethany couldn't ignore, a constant reminder of his betrayal. They understood that what he did was not easy. He had the option to let Damien end them and stay with his brother, but he made the brave decision to stand up and fight. Despite the potential harm to himself, he selflessly put his life on the line to save them.

"What you did back there. Thank you. It couldn't have been easy." Madison said.

The weight of uncertainty burdened him as he pondered whether his actions constituted a monumental blunder. Yet, a strong intuition reassured him that he had made the right decision. The memory of what his father and brother did to Logan's family haunted him, and he couldn't shake the belief that innocent lives could have been spared. He never had the chance to get to know them well, as he had only crossed paths with them a few times. Nevertheless, their friendly demeanour never faltered, ensuring that everyone felt welcome. All because Logan wanted out, their lives were abruptly ended in a tragic murder.

"He would have killed you. I couldn't… I don't want innocent people being hurt. It's not fair." He mumbled.

As Bethany walked, the image of what happened with Logan plagued her thoughts, leaving her confused as to why no one seemed to be discussing it.

"Are we not going to talk about how Logan changed back there? What was that? He turned full psycho."

Madison had sensed that Logan was grappling with his own demons; his vacant stares and occasional moments of unease hinted at the inner battle he was fighting. It became clear that the thing he was up against had succeeded, albeit momentarily. It was a terrifying sight, evoking vivid memories of the incident with her brother.

"Do you remember what happened with uncle Luke?"

Beth looked at her mother. Suddenly, the memories of her uncle flooded her mind, recalling his drastic transformation from a cheerful individual to an aggressive, unhinged man. He would transition from a state of tranquillity to erupting in a frenzy of yelling, passionately warning everyone about their impending doom and eternal damnation.

"That's not what's wrong with Logan is it? Is he going to need to go to a mental hospital? Luke never came back out since he got put in there." Beth asked, concern in her voice.

"I don't think so." Madison did not fully know how to reply.

With a heavy heart, she grappled with the unknown, her primary concern being Logan's chances of making it through the night. She feared that he might not, and the thought sent shivers down her spine. She turned her attention back to Evan, noticing the intensity in his eyes.

"Do you think Logan can beat your brother?" Madison questioned.

Peering back, Evan wrestled with his thoughts, unsure of how to respond. While Logan was highly capable, his brother had a knack for being deceptive. His concern stemmed from the unknown nature of the other variable.

"In a fair fight, yeah. My brother isn't my concern. Logan has beat him before. He couldn't beat my father last time."

Madison stopped walking, her heart pounding in her chest with worry.

"Last time? Are you telling me that Logan is taking on your brother and father at the same time?"

"Possibly. I don't know. His brother is nearby. Maybe he made it inside to help. We need to get downstairs and outside."

"But if he didn't, Logan would be killed." She cried.

Evan halted his steps abruptly, pivoting to face the girls directly. Wanting to provide reassurance to both of them.

"As long as I have known Logan Winters, he has been able to get out of dangerous situations, that even regular military people would have been killed in. That man always has a plan, I've learnt to never underestimate him. Trust me, if I know him, he will be fine. Once I get you outside and to safety, I will go back up myself to make sure he is okay."

Despite her reservations, Madison nodded reluctantly, fully aware that her involvement would likely result in his untimely demise. Nevertheless, an inexplicable force held her back, forbidding her from hastily retreating up the stairs, all in the pursuit of her daughter's safety. As they turned their heads, they noticed swift movement on the stairs, grabbing their attention immediately. A group of armed police officers, led by a distinguished older gentleman, marched with determination. When he looked at Madison and Beth, it was as if he saw them as nothing more than his intended targets.

"You must be Madison and this must be Bethany." Francis said.

"Yeah. Who are you?" Madison asked.

"Francis. I'm a friend of Logan's. Here to get you to safety."

"What about Logan? He is up there now. He needs help." She pleaded.

Looking at her, Francis couldn't help but smile, appreciating the genuine concern she had for the man he had not long become acquainted with.

"My men will head up to help him. My orders are to get you and your daughter to safety. Logan had very strict instructions for me."

Francis turned his gaze towards Evan, his mind buzzing with uncertainty about his true intentions.

"I'm unsure who you are. Care to enlighten me?" Francis questioned, puzzled on why the man was with the girls.

"He saved us." Bethany said, before Evan could speak.

"Well, okay then. Come with me, I'll get you to a safe place that was chosen by Logan. He said he'd meet us there after."

With a quick glance, Evan took in the sight of the girls, then turned his attention to Francis and the other officers. Wrestling with a difficult decision, he engaged in a back-and-forth debate within his own mind. Madison observed the man lost in contemplation, his gaze fixed on the distant horizon.

"You want to go back up and help?" She asked.

"Maybe I can stop any of them being killed. I'd rather my brother and father hate me from a prison cell, then both be dead." He uttered.

Just like with Logan, she could sense the goodness emanating from him, comforting and familiar. Both of them possessed kind hearts that radiated warmth and compassion.

"Go. Don't get yourself killed. You seem to be one of the good ones."

With a smile, he silently conveyed his appreciation for the unexpected gesture of concern. It was a pleasant sensation for him, breaking free from the lifelong pattern of obeying his father or brothers. Finally, he felt empowered to make his own decisions, choosing to do what he knew was right. The cessation of death was imperative. He sprinted up the stairs.

"Him going back up there is dangerous, they will kill him." Francis said, unsure on if the man's decision was the right one.

"From what we saw up there, they had no respect for him. Yet he had always followed their orders, even when he disagreed. I suppose this is his way of trying to make things right. Make up for the wrongdoings of the past." Madison uttered.

With a hand motion, Francis directed the group of men to move upward, indicating that they should follow Evan. The clatter of the armed officers' boots echoing as they moved up the stairs.

# 47

The battle axe sliced through the air as Kane swung it towards Logan's head, narrowly missing him but leaving a rush of wind in its wake. The weight of the weapon, meant that the attacks were a little slower. Logan's slight advantage in speed meant that if he timed it perfectly, he could disarm the big man, minimising the possibility of losing his head. Each swing came closer and closer to severing a limb.

Marcus tightly gripped the mace, its weight pressing against his palm. With a mighty swing, he released the weapon, the force behind it creating a whoosh that echoed through the air. The whooshing sound reverberated, filling the area as the mace cut through the atmosphere. But Lincoln, nimble and quick, effortlessly evaded the attack, his movements a testament to his skill. The spiked weapon struck the concrete floor with a powerful force, creating a resounding crash and causing cracks to spiderweb across the surface. Seizing the opportunity, the vigilant man deftly delivered an uppercut to Marcus' upper left arm, unleashing a powerful blow that forcefully dislocated it from its socket. The impact resonated with a bone-crunching thud, leaving Marcus reeling in agonising pain.

"If you had two eyes, you might have seen that coming." Lincoln laughed.

With a swift motion, Marcus lunged at the man who had made the comedic remark, his right arm poised to deliver a powerful punch. However, his attempt fell short as he failed to make contact.

"Shut your mouth! You and your brother will die!" Anger overwhelmed Marcus as he yelled at the top of his lungs.

"Typical Marcus. Always letting your anger guide you. Should I get you a chill pill?" Lincoln enjoyed irritating his enemy.

The sound of Lincoln's fists connecting with Marcus's body echoed through the room as he unleashed a series of jabs and hooks, leaving Marcus staggering and struggling to regain his balance. The man who had killed many and was notorious for being relentless and merciless, finally gave up; his enemy could see it in the way his one good arm dropped to his side.

"Finish it." He mumbled.

Marcus had changed since the last time Lincoln saw him; he had always been resilient, never one to easily surrender. Despite his reputation, the dangerous man didn't offer much resistance, disappointing him. Logan, however, was the one who truly deserved the honour of putting an end to him.

"No."

The force behind Lincoln's kick was enough to knock Marcus to the ground, the sharp intake of breath indicating the pain he felt. He wanted the man to witness the brutal punishment his father rightfully deserved. For a long time, Kane had been a terrifying figure, instilling fear in the hearts of many, including the Winters brothers who wouldn't dare to cross his path. The situation had since shifted.

With a quick reflex, Logan narrowly avoided the axe swing and made a calculated move to break Kane's wrist, hoping to disarm him. The moment he failed, his enemy anticipated his move and swiftly counterattacked, landing a powerful blow to Logan's face with the butt of the axe, resulting in a broken nose. The impact sent him reeling, disoriented and determined to pry the weapon away from Kane, a task that seemed increasingly arduous.

The ticking of the large clock on the wall caught Logan's attention, prompting them to check the time. Nine in the evening, it would be on. Recognising that Kane had the advantage in a direct confrontation, he realised it was time to shift the balance.

"Is that the time? You better turn on the news." Logan uttered.

As Kane looked at him, a puzzled look spread across his face. As Lincoln scoured the room for the television remote, his eyes landed on it, sitting prominently on the desk of the big man. He hurriedly crossed the room, reaching for the remote to turn on the television and quickly changing the channel to the news. With a sense of urgency, the reporter relayed the breaking news to the audience. From the floor, Marcus peered up at the screen, his one eye swollen and barely able to open. Despite the pain, he could sense the anticipation of what was about to come. His father did not want to watch, certain it was a distraction.

"You think you can distract me?" Kane said.

With uncertainty looming, Lincoln's intrigue grew as he eagerly awaited the report. Logan smirked at his enemy, relishing the anticipation of the big man's inevitable shock.

"I don't think it's a distraction." Logan said.

The reporter had a picture up of the Catalyst Collective building, capturing its striking presence against the city skyline. Unbeknownst to many, the leaders of the company were secretly plotting to overthrow the government and establish their own rule. The evidence, detailing how it had been obtained and sent to the police, pointed unequivocally to Kane Hunt as the mastermind behind it all. He had orchestrated the demise of numerous politicians, ensuring their replacements were under his influence.

Kane heard every word, but his expression remained unchanged.

"Do you really think that will work? That is old information. We aren't trying to take control of the government. We already have control of it. None of it will stick. We can spin an entirely new story, one that puts you and your brother as the ones responsible for all of the killings."

Logan was taken aback, the speed at which they had worked surpassed his expectations. However, the report wasn't finished. The truth slowly emerged, exposing Marcus Hunt as the culprit responsible for the deaths of countless individuals, including Lilly Winters, Ethan Winters, and Leah Winters. The screen displayed a solemn list of politicians who had lost their lives, accompanied by the names of those who had taken their place. It was gut-wrenching for Marcus to watch it all unfold, and he had no desire to end up behind bars. Despite everything, he couldn't deny his admiration for Logan and all of his achievements.

"The thing is, Kane, you may get away with it. But the people of the country are going to cause an uproar, they won't trust the government. You will have riots, civil war, you will have a target on your back. I didn't want to do it this way, but you and your family forced my hand."

In the stillness, Kane's eyes betrayed the growing fury within him. It was as if he were a dormant volcano, simmering with rage, ready to explode at any given moment.

"You took my family from me. I waited and plotted for all these years and you maybe had a few more months, until I would have began to put my plan into motion. But your men showed up, tried to kill me. That fast tracked things. Now I will get to watch you fall." Logan said.

"You bastard. I should have killed you."

"Yes. You should have."

In a furious charge, Kane stormed towards Logan, flinging the axe with a deadly precision. The sharp-edged blade came dangerously close to slicing through his arm, but with a swift motion, he managed to dodge it, the blade instead grazing his jacket and embedding into the wall with a powerful force. He attacked Logan with a vengeance, his punches and kicks filled with a lethal power that was amplified by his uncontrollable rage. A single blow to his face could prove to be deadly.

Logan skilfully evaded most of Kane's attacks, so Kane took hold of the enemy's arm and forcefully struck Logan's wrist, causing it to shatter. Overwhelmed by pain, he couldn't suppress his agonised scream. The force of the big man's punch collided with his cheek bone, causing it to fracture. With a burst of energy, Lincoln leaped onto Kane's back, causing the large man to momentarily lose balance. Employing a barrage of punches to his face, he was able to successfully intervene and separate him from his brother.

*Fuck me this fella is strong. It's like trying to fight an actual tank.*

The large man forcefully flipped him off his back, causing him to crash onto Logan, who was sprawled on the floor. With a burst of aggression, Kane initiated a series of kicks, targeting Lincoln's face twice and then relentlessly assaulting his stomach. He then lifted him from the floor and forcefully hurled him across the room, causing a violent collision with the fireplace. The impact sent several pieces of burning wood careening across the room. As the fire crackled, a burning log unexpectedly rolled towards the bear fur rug, located ten feet to the left of the entrance. As the final one made contact with the wallpapered wall, a sudden burst of flames erupted, quickly engulfing the area.

As the entrance swung open, Evan sprinted inside, narrowly escaping the flames that consumed the door. As the fire rapidly spread throughout the room, the heat intensified, preventing the police officers from entering without suffering severe burns. Evan's heart sank as he witnessed the brutal marks of violence on Marcus, who miraculously clung to life. He was left feeling both confused and relieved, a whirlwind of emotions swirling inside him. The anger that filled his father was a sight he hadn't witnessed in years. He relentlessly attacked Logan, his fists repeatedly striking Logan's face. Logan's left eye was so swollen that his vision became completely obscured.

"Father stop!" Evan yelled.

His rage-filled onslaught abruptly ceased as Kane's gaze shifted towards his son, who held a Glock 17 with unwavering aim. He had concealed the weapon the entire time, not wanting to rely on it as a last resort. However, he knew deep down that it might be the sole solution to halt his father's actions.

"Evan. What are you doing?" Kane asked.

"You need to stop this. Now! This doesn't need to end in death. Please."

Marcus looked at his brother, and the disappointment he once felt faded away, replaced by a sense of pride. Seeing Evan summon the bravery to stand up to their father filled him with a sense of pride, as he had been too afraid to do the same.

"That is the only way this ends. Have you not seen what that bastard has done?!" He yelled, pointing at the television.

As Evan looked at the news report, he felt a sense of satisfaction knowing that it was now public knowledge. His father's sole focus was on gaining power, and he didn't hesitate to do horrible things to achieve it.

"Good. Someone needed to stop you. I'm sorry dad, but you are a fucking monster! You have never cared about us. You use us to get power. Because that is all you care about."

Kane began to approach his son, his eyes filled with determination, convinced that his son didn't have the courage to pull the trigger.

"Boy, the way you are talking. It will get you killed. Now put that gun down, you won't shoot your own..." BANG!

Falling to his knees, the big man was overcome by the sensation of blood pouring out of the wound, before he even had a chance to locate where the bullet had struck. The sharp pain shot through his left shoulder, leaving him wincing in agony. Pulling the trigger was a moment Evan never thought he would experience, and the shock of it reverberated through his entire body. His hand trembled as he dropped the weapon, the weight of what he had done sinking in.

As Logan rose to his feet, he couldn't ignore the excruciating pain shooting through his wrist, nose, and face. Lincoln climbed up off the floor too. With the flames threatening to consume them all, they realised it was imperative to bring this to an end. As he stood back up, Kane's gaze fell upon the open wound his son had left on him, and a surge of anger coursed through his veins.

"You are no son of mine!"

The sight of Kane charging towards him sent a chilling

wave of fear through Evan's body, rendering him motionless. As he pondered, he couldn't help but wonder if his mother, who had always detested the way Kane treated him, would have felt a sense of pride. Turning towards Marcus, he flashed a smile that seemed perfectly orchestrated, as if he had anticipated this very moment. He mouthed the words 'I love you, brother'. Standing there, Evan braced himself for the inevitable, his heart pounding in his chest.

In an unexpected turn of events, Kane found himself being tackled by Lincoln, sending the big man tumbling into the blazing fire. He glanced at Evan and gave him a brief grin.

"You aren't dying today." Lincoln uttered.

In shock, Marcus witnessed his father's readiness to kill his own brother. It sparked a flame inside him; despite their disagreements, he and Evan were still brothers. Although he may have wanted to kill him earlier, he knew he lacked the will power to carry it out. His father would have been successful if Lincoln hadn't intervened.

As his lower body burned and his arms caught fire, Kane catapulted himself out of the flames, desperately rolling on the floor to put out the spreading blaze. Despite managing to extinguish the flames that had consumed his body, he could still feel the lingering pain as he rose up from the floor. His eyes drawn to Evan.

"Remi, activate the fire suppression system." Logan said.

"Activating now." Remi replied through the earpiece.

The fire was rapidly extinguished by the sprinklers spraying water. Standing next to Lincoln, he moved over and they both faced Kane. Ready to finish the fight. Evan joined the brothers, moving to their side.

Despite the excruciating pain in his arm, Marcus climbed up off the floor and made his way over to join Logan, Lincoln, and Evan. Casting a sideways glance at the man he had long viewed as his foe, he recognised the urgency of joining forces instead of remaining in opposition. Logan acknowledged him with a nod, and he reciprocated with a nod of his own. The sight of the four of them, standing united, was enough to startle Kane. He never expected his own family to turn against him.

"What are you doing?" Kane mumbled, his breathing laboured.

"You were going to kill Evan. We don't kill family, even after what he did. He is still a Hunt."

*I didn't see that coming. I suppose the enemy of my enemy. No wait… The son's of my enemy can be a friend, well ally. I'm confused. Fuck it, let's finish this bastard.*

Logan stepped forward. Despite the burns that had marred his body, the broken man ahead of him still held a determined look in his eyes. In an effort to appear strong and unwavering, he stood tall, his chest puffed out and his gaze steady as he faced his sons.

"You've lost Kane." He uttered and feeling grateful being able to say those words after so long.

His heart sank as he surveyed the four figures standing before him. He quickly realised that taking on all of them at once would be a futile battle. As he approached them slowly, the searing pain coursing through his body made his movements sluggish, but he refused to give up like most people would. The frightening thing was, he was laughing. Marcus had never seen his father laugh, so the sound of his laughter sent a shiver down his spine.

"You really think that you've won, don't you?"

With a sudden burst of adrenaline, Kane lunged at them, his heart pounding in his chest as he zeroed in on his intended victim. In a split second, Logan and his brother reacted and threw themselves aside, escaping any potential harm. Surprisingly, Evan swiftly darted out of reach.

Immovable, Marcus observed his colossal father advancing towards him, the world around him decelerating in response. Using his remaining arm, he launched a punch, the impact intended to land squarely on Kane. The missed strike provoked an immediate reaction from his father, who swiftly pinned him down and mercilessly battered his face with his fists.

"You side with them, you die!"

With a leap, Logan and Lincoln tackled the big man, sending him crashing to the ground and freeing his son. Their fists flew through the air, striking his face and body with a relentless force, bringing his attack to a sudden halt. Despite having only one good hand to punch with, Logan fought on, determined to overcome his limitations. Kane's determination was unwavering as he effortlessly tossed both men aside, swiftly returning to Marcus.

Just as he was about to launch his attack, his attention was drawn to the lasers trained directly at his chest. With a sudden force, several armed police officers stormed through the door, their presence unmistakable.

"Get down on the ground now!" The leader of the team demanded.

Kane shifted his gaze towards them, his presence towering over Marcus who remained weak and barely conscious on the floor. As he turned away, he stole one last glance at his son, etching the image of his battered face into his mind.

"I'll see you in hell son."

He wasted no time as he brought his foot down on Marcus' head, the force of his weight causing the skull to break with a sickening crunch. His son's eye bulged out of his head, as it crumbled inward. The scene escalated as two officers unleashed their weapons, the sound of gunshots filling the air. One of them targeted Kane's shoulder with a bullet from his MP5. His left leg was struck by yet another bullet, missing any bones by a mere six inches below the knee. As the big man dropped to the ground, the sound of his heavy thud echoed through the air, catching the attention of nearby officers, who swiftly surrounded him. As the handcuffs were placed on him, he winced at the tightness around his muscular arms.

"Noooo!!" Evan yelled.

With a quick burst of adrenaline, he charged at his father, causing the officers to draw their weapons in response.

"Do not move any further!" One police officer demanded.

To Logan's shock, Kane committed the unthinkable act of killing his own son, Marcus, a scenario he never could have imagined. For years, the man had been Kane's trusted right-hand person, always by his side. Lincoln got onto his knees, putting his hands behind his head. As Logan fell to his knees, the searing pain in his wrist made it a struggle for him to position his hands behind his head.

*He killed his own son. Now that is fucked up and that's coming from me.*

"My wrist is broken." Logan said, as the officers walked towards them.

As the officers closed in, Lincoln could hear the metallic click of handcuffs being placed around his wrists. Wanting to be sure about his brother's injury, one of them inspected his wrist to check for any signs of a break. Confirming it was broken, he gestured for Logan to follow him.

Evan's body turned stiff and unyielding, a physical manifestation of the shock coursing through him. His fear intensified as he saw the barrels of guns aimed directly at him. With a sense of urgency, the two officers advanced towards him, their swift movements resulting in him being quickly brought down to the ground and restrained with handcuffs.

Kane redirected his attention to Logan and his brother, his eyes lingering on them for a moment.

"You will pay. This is not the end." He uttered, his voice filled with rage.

# 48

As they sat in the police car, Madison and Bethany could feel the tension in the air, their anticipation growing with each passing second. The option of going to a safe house had been extended to them, but they both chose to refuse. Instead of leaving, they decided to wait, holding onto hope that he would make it. Time dragged on, surpassing the thirty-minute mark, and restlessness started to creep into their game of waiting.

"He should have killed them by now." Bethany said.

"Beth. Don't say that."

"What? I'm saying what we are both thinking." Her daughter moaned.

As the police outside the vehicle stirred, the sound of their radio transmissions filled the air, though Madison struggled to decipher any of the words. At that moment, she heard an officer announce their plan to bring them down. Who? She wondered. Had Logan survived? Questions flooded her mind, racing like wild horses.

The metallic click of the door latch echoed as it swung open, revealing a familiar face framed by the flashing red and blue lights of the police car. The scent of leather upholstery mingled with the faint aroma of coffee, wafting from the nearby convenience store. Francis greeted them with a beaming smile, his heart warming with a sense of comfort and relief.

"They are coming down now." He said.

"Is Logan okay?" She asked, her mind was consumed by worry, making it difficult to focus on anything else.

He was at a loss for an answer to that question because he didn't have sufficient knowledge on the subject. The officers had recounted the incident, describing the apprehension of four men and, sadly, one of them did not survive. He decided against mentioning it to her, aware that it would only amplify her worries. Without a doubt, he believed that the deceased individual could not be Logan. However, they couldn't confirm that until they stepped outside.

"I'm unsure. I think he will be fine. We will know for sure when they get outside."

Madison climbed out of the car, eager to escape the confined space, and her daughter quickly followed suit. With each passing second, her anticipation intensified, her eagerness to see him growing stronger than ever. The wait felt interminable, with every passing minute seeming to drag on like an hour, until a sudden movement by the entrance broke their focus.

Kane was the first to be brought out, and the police officer outside was taken aback by the extent of his injuries. His legs and arms were severely burnt, and he had bullet wounds, yet he continued to persevere. Madison gasped as she saw Evan emerge with his hands cuffed, a sight that shook her to the core. The man who had bravely saved them from Damien looked equally terrified and completely defeated.

Exiting the building, Lincoln felt a gust of wind from the open door, and behind him, Logan followed, taking in the scenery as he walked out. Her heart skipped a beat at the sight of him, and a radiant smile illuminated her face. She was perplexed as to why the man, whom she assumed was his brother, was being led out in handcuffs while Logan remained free. It was unfair that they were detained since they were the ones on the right side. She then noticed the reason why Logan had not been handcuffed - he held his arm up, wincing in pain, unable to conceal it from her.

"Why have they been detained? And Evan, that man saved us."

In that room, the officers regarded every man as a potential danger, treating them all as threats. In order to protect everyone, it was necessary to restrain each man.

"They won't be for long." Francis uttered.

As he approached the police officers, he could hear the faint sound of their footsteps crunching on the pavement beside Logan and his brother.

"That man is no threat, trust me. Nor is his brother. You

can release them."

With a perplexed expression, the officer contemplated whether he should heed the words of the man who was no longer part of the police force. With a nod, Detective Pilton approached Francis from behind, his presence only becoming known when he was right beside him.

"Release them."

The officer finally released Logan, and both men breathed a sigh of relief as Lincoln's cuffs were taken off. With a burst of energy, Madison sprinted towards him and tightly wrapped her arms around him, locking lips in a passionate kiss. A cry of agony escaped him, his battered and bruised body unable to bear the intensity. In an effort to spare him further anguish, she began to withdraw, but he tugged her back into his embrace and captured her lips in another kiss.

*Go on Logy! That is a bloody, well deserved kiss.*

Amazement filled Lincoln as he contemplated the underlying purpose driving Logan's determination to rescue this woman and her daughter. Lincoln was aware that once Logan grows attached to someone, he becomes fiercely protective of them.

"I'm so glad you are safe." She said.

When she turned to Lincoln, she couldn't help but notice the striking resemblance between them, from their shared demeanour to their physical features. While she admitted Lincoln had a better beard, she admired how it made him look elegant and sophisticated. She was judging from when she met Logan and saw his dishevelled appearance, particularly his big, scruffy beard, that reminded her of a homeless person.

"Madison, this is Lincoln. My brother."

Despite Lincoln's attempt to offer a handshake, she opted for a more intimate greeting and wrapped her arms around him.

"Thank you for helping him." Madison said

"We take care of family. It's nice to meet you Madison." Lincoln said.

In a spontaneous gesture, Bethany embraced Logan, holding him close for a heartfelt hug. Being cautious about his injuries, she held him gently, making sure not to apply too much pressure.

"I'm glad you are okay." Beth said warmly.

In that moment, Logan held her tightly, his arms wrapped around her like she was his own kin.

"I'm just happy that you and your mum are safe. I'm sorry about your dad." He said with a bittersweet tenderness in his voice.

As Bethany looked up at him, he could sense a bittersweet expression on her face, a combination of sorrow and a glimmer of liberation. The thought of his daughter witnessing such a thing weighed heavily on his mind. No daughter should witness the agonising death of a parent.

"This sounds bad. But I'm kind of glad he's gone. I'm sad that he is, but he wasn't a nice person. I prefer knowing that my mum is gonna be safe from him now. He did what he thought was right in the end, I guess."

He held her close, his embrace growing tighter with each passing moment.

"Well, he was still your father. So if you need to be sad about it, you are allowed to be. If you need anything, I'll be around. If you guys would be okay with that?" Logan said, looking up at Madison.

Madison turned towards him, her face lighting up with the biggest smile she had ever mustered. She looked at her daughter, searching for any signs of approval or hesitation about the idea of seeing him more. Bethany's face lit up with joy as she nodded enthusiastically and broke into a wide grin.

"We'd love that. Even with all this chaos. It has been nice having you around. I do have a question, though."

"I'm happy to provide the answer." He said with smile.

Her concern for his mental health made her ponder about his well-being. What if that other personality reappeared?

"When we was up there. A different version of you made an appearance, frankly it was quite terrifying. I just need to know that you will seek help for it. Will that other personality reappear?"

Logan's desire for openness led him to disclose his mental struggle to her, convinced that her support would be invaluable.

"It's always been a part of me, I just wasn't aware of how long until recently. At the current time, he is being nice. You could say we came to an agreement, work together to stop Kane. But yes, I will seek help for it. I attempted to ignore it for so many years and look where it got me."

*Can I not be referred to as it. I promise not to make such an entrance again. I mean I wouldn't wanna scare them off. They are good people, could even say I have started to like them. But let's not tell them I've got all soppy.*

Lincoln glanced at his brother, his face contorted in a mixture of surprise and bewilderment.

"Oh, I forgot to say. Yeah, I may have gone a little crazy over the years." Logan laughed.

"You don't say. I was stood here wondering what you was talking about. So my brother finally broke huh?" Lincoln chuckled.

"You could say that. He calls himself Magnus. I suppose nine years alone, you search for company. Even if it's in your head. Turns out, he has been there all along. Helping me during missions, doing the bad things, so in a weird way, I didn't have to. Even though technically it was still me. It's a little confusing. I will fill you all in soon. Let's get out of here."

With cautious tenderness, Madison and Bethany enveloped Logan in a heartfelt embrace, mindful not to cause him any discomfort. They were both committed to being there for him, fully aware that he would reciprocate with the same level of support. Despite their concerns, they couldn't help but wonder what would happen to Evan.

"What about Evan? Can he not be released? Kane is the bad one." Madison said.

"I don't think they will let him go, not yet. Because of his name and how he worked for the company, he will need to be questioned and could be charged, depending how cooperative he is." Francis replied.

"Could I speak to him before they take him away?" Logan asked.

With a nod, Francis motioned for the officers accompanying Evan to halt in their tracks. With a pause in their journey, Logan made his way towards the younger Hunt family member. With a swift motion, he retrieved a card from his back pocket and deftly tucked it into Evan's jacket pocket.

"If you need my help, call the number on that card. I'm sorry about how everything went down. I'll admit, I came here ready to kill your father and brother, but settled on seeing them spend the rest of their days in prison. What your father done to Marcus..." the image of Marcus' crushed head flashing in his mind like a light that needed to be turned off.

"Marcus wasn't always a good brother, hell, the amount of times I wanted him dead. But he was my brother and my fath... Kane just killed him like that. I will never forgive him for that." Evan uttered.

Marcus' death was a tragedy that Logan couldn't bear, as he had resisted the urge to take his enemy's life. Just for his enemy's father to eliminate him. The thought crossed his mind - was there a deeper, underlying reason for him to take Marcus's life?

"Kane will rot away, having to live with what he has done." Logan said, in an attempt to give some comfort to Evan.

Evan gave him a nod before the officers began to put him in the police car. Kane, with his hands cuffed behind his back, was led towards a police van, causing the suspension to sag as he stepped inside. Two policemen climbing in with him. With their new prisoners secured, the car and van swiftly disappeared from sight, blending seamlessly into the bustling city streets. Logan hoped he'd never have to see Kane's piercing gaze again.

Detective Pilton approached.

"You guys might want to clear out of here. We've gotta wrap this up. My boys are heading in to gather more evidence. Kane is going down for a long time, that big man will most likely die in prison."

Logan, Lincoln, Madison, Bethany, and Francis wasted no time in heeding the message, and they set off. With a nod filled with gratitude, Francis turned to the detective, silently thanking him for his help.

# 49

The prison officers led him down what seemed like an endless corridor, which was riddled with prison cells. In each cell, there was either a lone prisoner or sometimes two would be cramped together. Evan carefully glanced through the narrow windows on the cold blue metal cell doors, revealing the compact nature of the rooms. Each room had a single bed or bunk-bed, a toilet, and a small table. Surprisingly, one of the inmates even had a television in his room.

At the arrival of a newbie, the sound of inmates banging on their doors echoed through the prison. Gripped tightly by fear, he wondered if he would make it through his time in jail, the uncertainty weighing heavily on his mind. The thought of being locked up in that place filled him with a deep sense of injustice; he couldn't shake the feeling that he didn't belong there. Deep down, he understood that he was being held accountable for the actions of his family and the resulting loss of life.

The absence of Marcus made him acutely aware of the vulnerability he felt, as he wished for his brother's brutal, yet reassuring companionship. The officer in front of him was built like a tank, his bulging muscles giving off an intimidating aura that made him want to stay on the officer's good side. The prison officer following behind him was a stark contrast - shorter in stature and smaller in build, but exuding an undeniable air of authority. With determination, Evan aimed to stay low key and quietly serve his time.

Outside a dimly lit cell, Evan stood still, patiently waiting as the heavy door creaked open. With the hope of finding an unoccupied cell, he was adamant about not wanting to share it with anyone. Despite his preparedness for disappointment, he couldn't help but feel a pang of hope. When he looked inside, he was taken aback to find someone already seated on the bed, eagerly awaiting his arrival. He couldn't believe his eyes when he saw who was occupying the seat in his cell, completely catching him off guard.

"What are you doing here?" He asked.

Standing up from the bed, Logan motioned for Evan to sit down, his posture commanding and authoritative. The prison officer carefully removed the handcuffs from his wrists and gently ushered him into the dimly lit prison cell. With a gentle push, he closed the door and stepped away, leaving the two men alone in the room. Feeling the thinness of the mattress beneath him, Evan settled on the edge of the bed and became acutely aware of the sturdy bed frame supporting it. The bed in the prison left much to be desired in terms of comfort, but he had no illusions of finding luxury there.

"I promised to tell you what I could. I keep my promises." Logan said.

"Why were there things that my mum didn't want me to know about?"

"Your mother had planned to help me in taking your father down. She knew that if he controlled the country, it would be bad for everyone. She discovered some of his plans and was not willing to let him follow through with them. Kane is a dangerous man and Maggie had assembled a vast array of evidence to use against him. Only she vanished. We'd arranged to meet, but she never showed. I didn't hear from her again." Logan revealed.

Trying to process everything, Evan pressed his hands against his face, feeling the weight of the information sinking in. It was clear to him that his father's priority was safeguarding his business rather than taking care of his family.

"Wait… So my father killed my mum?" He questioned, his mind racing.

"That's the thing. I don't think he would. He must have told Marcus that I killed her to fuel his rage against me more. He needed her, which makes me wonder if she is still alive and being held somewhere."

Evan's brain kicked into high gear, piecing together the puzzle as he recalled the black sites he'd overheard his father discuss with Marcus. He considered the possibility that she might be held captive in one of those places, but then he realised that his father would likely want to ensure she stayed nearby. While his mind was busy processing the information, a thought sparked in his consciousness.

"I thought you were on the island for nine years and only ventured off it for supplies?"

Logan's eyes held a glimmer of curiosity as he observed him, acknowledging that the younger man had successfully figured him out.

"I made it seem that way. But no. I took on several of my own missions. I searched for Maggie for several months, but could not locate where she was being held."

*Killed some bastards along the way to get information that turned out to be useless.*

In his memories, Evan could still hear his father's stern voice cautioning him to never lay a finger on anything on the bookcase in his office. It sparked his curiosity, making him question if there was something more to it.

"If you can get me out of here, I may have an idea of where to look. But I need to get out of this place."

Logan studied him intently, questioning whether he possessed the skills to successfully extract the man from a heavily guarded prison. The mission to break him out would be perilous, necessitating meticulous planning.

"I will do what I can to get you out. We will find your mother."

# 50

In the navy inn, a lively pub in Penzance, Cornwall, the sound of laughter and conversation filled the air as Logan, Madison, and Lincoln sat together. The dimly lit room was adorned with rustic wooden furniture and colourful beer signs. Their hands wrapped around the chilled glasses, condensation forming on the surface, as they enjoyed the refreshing sensation of the cold beer. Bethany sat comfortably beside her mother, enjoying the fizzy sensation of Pepsi as she sipped it through a straw. As they looked at each other, happiness danced in their eyes, a testament to the seven days that had elapsed since the events at Catalyst Collective.

Madison had made jokes about how meeting Logan turned out to be the second dangerous thing she did, playfully reminding everyone that the first was meeting Damien. They attempted to find humour in what had transpired a week earlier.

The pub door swung open, and Stephanie, Alex, and Thomas made their way inside. With smiles on their faces, both kids eagerly rushed over to their father, their little feet pitter-pattering on the floor. With a sudden burst of energy, he stood up and scooped up both boys, holding them tightly. His face lit up with a huge, beaming smile.

"What happened to your face dad?" Alex asked.

"I fell down some stairs."

As he turned to see Logan's face, the young boy couldn't help but notice the bruises and swelling that made his face look worse.

"Did he fall down the same ones?" He questioned.

As Logan stood up, a hearty laugh escaped from his lips.

"You know what? I fell down more of them. There were so many. Next time we will both take the lift. I think it's safer."

Stephanie's laughter filled the air as she flashed a wide grin, overjoyed by the reunion of the brothers.

"Definitely take the lift next time."

Rising to their feet, Madison and Bethany exchanged a friendly handshake with Steph.

"Hi, I'm Madison, this is my daughter Beth."

"Lovely to meet you. I'm Stephanie, Lincolns wife. These two are our boys, Alex and Thomas."

As they mingled, exchanging introductions, the sound of their laughter echoed joyfully throughout the room, filling it with a vibrant energy. The air was filled with the sweet aroma of their shared excitement, and a warm, welcoming feeling enveloped them all.

The sight of everyone getting along seamlessly brought a smile to Logan's face, as he basked in the comforting ambience of familial unity. As he looked around, the absence of his wife and children slowly sank in, causing his smile to fade. A wave of sadness washed over him, as if a heavy cloud had settled upon his heart.

Suddenly, he felt a distinct presence lingering nearby, causing his hairs to stand on end. As he turned, he found himself captivated by the deep and emotional stare that Lilly fixed upon him. As soon as her smile, the one that always made his heart skip a beat, returned, he felt a wave of happiness wash over him.

"Hey brother, you okay?" Lincoln asked.

One moment she was there, and in the next, she had vanished into thin air. The person in her place was now Madison, who enthusiastically joined the kids in a game of hide and seek. Her constant giggling made it easy for the children to find her.

"You know she would have wanted you to move on. It's hard, but they will always be with you. The three of them would want you to be happy. You know Lilly. She'd have told you."

"Never dwell in sadness. Even in darkness, the light can prevail." Logan said, before his brother could finish his sentence.

"She was a smart woman." Lincoln smiled.

"The smartest."

"They will always be with you. It's what powers you to get

through everything you have. They live through you."

His brother's words resonated deeply, providing much-needed solace. Lilly's voice echoed in his mind, urging him to carry on with his life, just as she had told him countless times in case something happened to her. She wouldn't want him to spiral into a bottomless pit of sadness, forever trapped in its depths. He'd told her the same, always believing that he'd be the one to pass away before her. As Logan hugged his brother, he could feel the strength and love in their bond.

"Thank you. I miss them."

"Me too." Lincoln replied.

Francis pushed open the creaky entrance of the pub, and a girl in her early thirties quietly slipped in behind him. As soon as he saw Logan, a grin spread across his face and he made his way towards him.

"Mr Winters. Nice to see you and not be getting shot at." He laughed.

They greeted each other with a friendly handshake, Lincoln extending his hand in the same manner. Appreciative of the older gentleman's assistance, he suspected he was the one responsible for organising the presence of the police force that night.

"Good to see you. This must be Remi?" Logan asked.

As she approached Logan, he went to shake her hand, but she bypassed the gesture and went straight for a heartfelt hug.

"I'm a hugger. Also, thank you for not letting my father get himself killed."

"I mean, it was because of me that he ended up in danger.

After getting him involved, I was afraid that he may get hurt or worse. But I have to say, your father is good at what he does. I couldn't have done it without him."

"With help from me." She laughed.

"Exactly! Your assistance was vital in us actually managing to pull off what we did. I will never be able to thank you enough." Logan said.

"A drink or two will do." Remi grinned.

"I better get to getting them then."

Making his way to the bar, Logan was ready to order the drinks, but then he realised he hadn't even inquired about their beverage preferences.

*Idiot. Who doesn't ask what they drink?*

Turning around to ask them, their attention was immediately captured by the blaring news report on the television in the corner of the pub. Displayed on the screen was a haunting image of Kane, accompanied by a shocking caption detailing the tragic events that unfolded during his transportation to the courthouse. The vehicle had been targeted and violently exploded, tragically claiming the lives of all occupants.

Lincoln exchanged a worried glance with his brother, silently acknowledging the foreboding atmosphere. Despite their efforts, the report demonstrated that what they had done had not fully resolved what Kane had initiated, highlighting the absence of any guarantee for safety. If Kane met his demise, then the one responsible would surely set their sights on them next.

"This isn't over is it?" Lincoln asked.

*If more people had solved the clues in your puzzle ridden novels, we would have more help.*

'Francis was the only one who I could put any trust into.' Logan answered in his head.

*What about Dave, he was nice. I liked Dave. Although he was a bit odd. Breaking into song in the middle of the conversation, he was lucky it was you he was talking too. I'd have shot him. You have to admit though, we are going to need more help. Maybe the novel approach was not the way to go. Maybe it's time to try a different method of recruitment. We could use Anthony, Mr Draiden has a lot of money and resources. I mean, he has managed to stay under the radar over the years. We could use him.*

Magnus was right; they would definitely require assistance. Despite recognising the potential usefulness of the man he had saved, Logan felt hesitant about approaching him, considering their shared enemy. Without a trace, he slipped away into Mexico, a clever choice given that his reserved nature made him an unlikely candidate for such a perilous destination. He could be a useful ally, someone whose vast network of connections could provide valuable resources. On the other hand, making contact with him could inadvertently reveal his whereabouts to the enemy. Putting him right back in the line of fire. Logan didn't want to put anyone else in danger.

Although the brothers were a formidable force, if there was a threat bigger than Kane, then they would need all the assistance they could get. Even though he didn't want to accept it, Logan had to face the reality that it was a time that demanded seriousness rather than celebration. They believed they were safe, only to realise they had misjudged the situation.

"We better start preparing." Logan uttered.

*It seems we underestimated our enemy.*

# Epilogue

The interplay between light and darkness is a constant battle, with each having the potential to overcome the other.

"Activate echo protocol."

As Gregory Marks spoke, his voice reverberated with a sense of authority, filling the entire room. The board members of Catalyst Collective, dressed in suits, occupied every seat around the table.

"It seems Kane has failed in his plan to remove Logan Winter's from the equation." Gregory said with a disappointed tone.

As he leaned forward, the light cast an illuminating glow on his face, revealing intriguing shadows that added depth to his features. His age was evident in the creases and folds that adorned his face, evidence of the wisdom and experience gained over sixty years. There was not a single strand of hair on his head, suggesting that either it had all fallen out or he maintained a deliberate bald and clean-shaven look.

His face bore the marks of countless battles, a testament to the war-ravaged life he had endured. Life in the army was simple enough for him, with its strict routines and disciplined atmosphere. His expulsion from the military under dishonourable conduct marked a significant turning point in his life. The aftermath revealed a chilling truth - he had been pushed to the brink, faced with the unimaginable choice of taking three lives or losing his own. He chose correctly.

Shortly after, he found himself in contact with a dubious organisation, led by none other than Maverick, Kane's father. He was a man who had carved out a reputation for himself in the dark underworld of murder and espionage. His intelligence rivalled that of the legendary Albert Einstein. His strength and merciless brutality made him a formidable adversary.

Each board member let out a groan or sigh of disappointment. They could not understand how one man caused so many issues for their business. Gregory gestured for one of the security personnel to approach.

"Inform him that it's time. I'll send over the details of his targets."

With a nod, the member of security rushed off out of the room, the automatic door opening and then closing on his exit.

Down a long corridor, which was blinding because the walls, ceilings and floor was white. The doors along it were a few shades darker, so it was easier to see them. Lucas had been working security here for six years now, unable to leave unless instructed to do so. His wife worked in the facility too, so it wasn't the worst life. They had a home on the grounds and were paid generously for their work. But he could sense that something bad was coming, the company had been preparing for something and he guessed that whatever it was. It was happening soon. Which would explain there anger towards Mr Winters.

Lucas had heard a lot about the man who on the database had the code name The Contingency Man. Many of the people who work for the company, pin Logan as this evil man. But there had been whispers that disproved such theories, the man only sought revenge on those who murdered his family.

What did a security man know though? Not much according to the big bosses, but he listened and observed diligently.

Reaching the end of the corridor, a big metal door was ahead of him. But the red flashing light at the top indicated that the training room was in use. So he turned to the right, entering the monitoring room. He liked to watch him in action. The skill was extraordinary.

The room was pitch black, flashes of light appeared every few seconds from the barrel of the gun. The other thing that was only just noticeable at certain angles, a green pair of lenses. A night vision equipped metallic full head mask, with two breathing apparatus on each side. The person firing the weapons at the dummies, was moving at a rapid speed.

Eliminating his targets in quick succession.

Lucas looked on the monitor to the right side of the room, the camera that had infrared sensors on it showcased the masked man's abilities more clearly. He was lunging around, ducking, diving and sliding along the floor to take out targets. He jumped onto and bounced off the walls several times, using his blade to behead many of the dummies on his way back to the ground.

Watching a person with such skill, frightened Lucas. Who was it that they was sending him to take down? He wouldn't want the masked killer after him. His mission success rate rivalled Logan's, only in at a faster rate. He did not waste time.

The lights illuminated the room, revealing the masked man, wearing Kevlar armoured combat gear. A red phoenix was painted above the eyes of the mask. He approached the exit of the training room, he was not a person for talking, no one in the facility had seen him without his mask on.

Lucas rushed out of the monitoring room to meet him. As the door opened, fear almost made him fall to the ground.

"Gregory said…it's time." He stuttered.

No reply, not even a nod. The masked man stared at him for several moments and it felt as though the devil was peering into his soul. Any masculinity he had, left him at the moment. As the mystery man walked off, Lucas collapsed to the floor.

"Fuck me, he is terrifying." He mumbled to himself.

Gregory stood to address the other board members, turning on the large screen behind him. Which brought up images of Logan, Madison, Francis, Bethany and Lincoln.

"These are now our primary targets. Logan is number one, without him the rest will fall easily."

"What about his brother? Lincoln proved that he could evade us, we believed he was dead for all of these years. When he has been living right under our noses." One of the woman said.

"He is formidable. I would never say he isn't. But if we take Logan down, Lincoln will not think clearly and that will lead to his downfall." Gregory replied.

All of them turned their attention, when the door slides open and Kane entered. His burns were covered with bandages, his bullet wounds had been cleaned and stitched, he should have been resting, but he was not willing to let them make plans without him. He was the boss and was going to be the one to bring down Logan Winters, with the help of their secret weapon.

"We thought you had been killed." Gregory mumbled, awestruck that his boss was somehow still alive.

"Surprised? Well, I'm a hard man to kill. I will not die until I've had made him suffer for what he did." Kane uttered. Sitting down in his seat, at the top end of the table.

"Do you think he is ready?" Gregory asked.

"He has been made into the most lethal, unstoppable killer on the planet. Arsenal is the one who can bring them down." Kane replied.

"What about the weapon, is that ready for testing?" Gregory questioned.

A smile came upon Kane's face, a very mischievous grin.

"Testing will commence in the coming weeks. They won't know what hit them."

"Good, we have our targets. This country isn't ready for what is about to happen." Gregory smirked.

The reaping's coming.

# Acknowledgements

I want to thank my amazing wife Abi, who puts up with me, even on my bad days. There are probably lots of times, when I do her head in, I mean I do my own head in, yet she still keeps me going. She is the best thing that ever happened to me and I will never be able to thank her enough for her love and support.

My mother and father, the people who helped make me the man I am today. You are the best parents, supporting me through hard times. Thank you so much for everything you have ever done for me. Both of you have been supportive through my writing career. I will forever cherish you both.

I'd also like to thank my mother and father in law, thank you for everything you have done for me. I am always even more grateful for meeting Abi, because it also meant I met you guys and we became family. I know I'm not always the most talkative person, but I thank you for putting up with me. As the saying goes, I guess you guys are stuck with me now.

Now onto the brothers and sisters. Philip, you have been amazing as a brother and a friend. I always know that if I need to talk, or even just need a good laugh. I can come to you. You can put a smile on anyone's face and I'm so glad that I get to call you my brother, never stop being you. My sister Jade, although slightly crazy and sometimes hard to shut up, has always been supportive of my writing. She isn't much of a reader, but is always the person telling friends and colleagues about her brother writing books. Usually they don't believe her, until she takes a book of mine in. Usually managing to ruin the pages in the process. Jamie my older brother, you are inspiring to me with how well you done with your business and always busy with either work or family, but you push through it all. You are kind and caring towards everyone, thank you for being you and for being an awesome older brother. Now to my youngest brother Andrew, basically a little me as many people say. Apart from the fact that he is sports mad. You are growing into an amazing young man. I'd never really had anyone look up to me, the way you have growing up and I hope that you know that I made a good impression. You are an awesome little brother. I can't forget the sister in law either, the second Jade in my life. I have to admit, you are pretty awesome too, although I think that's just my awesomeness rubbing off on you.

My best friend Rhys also deserves a mention, we have been friends for 20, almost 21 years now. You are usually the person who finds out stuff about my books before anyone else, especially when I've written an exciting scene and just have to tell somebody. Thank you for being such a good friend and all the laughs we have had along the way.

A special thank you goes to my work colleague Barrie, who while I have been writing my book, has been asking me daily how much I managed to write. If I finished the book. A vast array of questions, all of which helped encourage me to get my ass in gear and get the book finished. Cheers Barrie!

Printed in Great Britain
by Amazon

41377877R00283